UNWILLING ELDRITCH HORROR OF FORTUNE 3

UNWILLING ELDRITCH HORROR OF FORTUNE 3

Tismon

Podium

To all my readers who've stuck around for three whole books
You're the people keeping this project alive

Cover design by Von Brooklyn Design

ISBN: 978-1-0394-9091-8

Published in 2026 by Podium Publishing
www.podiumentertainment.com

Podium

UNWILLING ELDRITCH HORROR OF FORTUNE 3

CHAPTER ONE

Changes in Pandora

It was that damned Overseer again! I should have known that the ending of that last trial was too easy. Hope's Memorial was practically a vacation for me. All I had to do was supervise a kid and her doll while chatting with the nice staff there. There was no way that the leader of the Central Collective wouldn't know that, considering his opinion on Arbiter W and his accolades. Sure, I wasn't that legend myself, but no one aside from me knew that.

That piece of shit must have sped up time on Pandora since the regressor was in the same trial as I was. That was the only way for him to mess with this timeline since Jae-Hyun's temporal nature made such changes close to impossible when he was nearby. I was getting sick and tired of that slimeball's meddling, and I couldn't wait to get rid of him once and for all.

Jae-Hyun: Stay put. Walter and I will try to get back as soon as we can. Is the father with you?
Yoona: Yeah, we just found him. He'll get us caught up on what you guys went through.
Walter's Fine: Wait, we're still stuck on that floating island, though.
Lady Awesome: It's not a floating island, little bro, it's just a really weird-shaped mountain.
Walter's Fine: You know what I mean! And is that dragon still here?
Yoona: We kept it there in case you guys returned, but you won't like how much money we spent on that . . .

> **Jae-Hyun:** Money we can make again, what's the situation back at base? Vadeem said there was a change in management?
>
> **Vadeem the Dream:** Yeah, some new shits came in and kicked out Raffiel and co. They're changing up how the Main Stage is working. The new chick in charge'll make an announcement about the change in management in like a day and a half.
>
> **Jae-Hyun:** How long do we have, specifically?
>
> **Yoona:** You have a little over thirty-one hours, brother.
>
> **Jae-Hyun:** We'll make it back on time. Get Marcus caught up on the situation as well, we'll talk once we're back.
>
> **Yoona:** Got it . . . and be careful.

"Walter," Jae-Hyun said, "we need to leave. Now. Forget about the forge. We don't have time. Grab on to me. I'll get us out of here."

"Grab on to you?" I asked. "Like . . . hold your hands or something?"

He sighed. "Never mind, just hold on."

The regressor all but manhandled me before he tossed me on top of his shoulders like a sack of potatoes. Making sure that I wasn't about to slip off, he started to sprint out of the underground passage. And holy shit was the regressor fast . . . I knew that his stats were impressive, but seeing him go full sprint was something else. We made it to the harpy cave in about ten minutes, and out onto the surface in another five.

I almost received a permanent neck injury by the time we made it back to the dragon carriage thing with how fast the regressor was moving. He could have afforded to slow down a bit!

"Take us back to Pandora as fast as you can," Jae-Hyun told the driver before he tossed me unceremoniously into the cabin. "I'll double your pay if you make it there before dawn."

The driver thought about it for a while before he nodded. "I'll see what I can do, but it won't be a pleasant ride."

Jae-Hyun threw the man a sack of coins. "Just do it."

"If you say so." The other man shrugged. "Best get in, then."

I hurriedly scurried to the back of the cabin in fear of being flung out and strapped myself into a seat as firmly as I could. The regressor excused himself to one of the sleeping quarters and said something about needing alone time to do some prep work. He seemed more serious than I'd ever seen him before, so I just chose to leave him alone. The dragon carriage took off not long after, and as the driver said, it was a very, very bumpy ride back home.

Ugh . . . and I thought modern turbulence couldn't get much worse. Noe, just show me the stuff I gained from clearing the trial. And you have anything to deal with this damned headache?

"I will isolate your semicircular canal from the movement, it should help with the nausea, my host," she replied, and I instantly felt better.

Thanks, Noe. God, that's a relief.

"You are most welcome," she answered. "Displaying updated information now."

Host: Walter	
Class: Level 47 Gamma's Grace	
Attributes:	
Free points:	30
HP:	744/744
MP:	0/0
Strength:	61 (+10)
Dexterity:	66 (+10)
Endurance:	54 (+10)
Intelligence:	62 (+10)
Charisma:	72 (+10)

Wow . . . I wasn't expecting to get enough experience to gain ten levels all at once. At least fighting stuff wasn't the only way to accumulate levels. I was never the best fighter in the first place. I once again realized just how important charisma was, so I dumped all the points into it. I'd be needing every last point when I dealt with the Overseer and his new admin staff soon, and I just hoped that 102 charisma was enough.

Titles: 4
Equipped Secondary Title 1: Rookie Arbiter
Equipped Secondary Title 2: Bringer of Dawn's Light

Secondary Title: The Illustrious Dr. William Walter (SS Rank)
Description: The illustrious doctor of Hope's Memorial has made such an impact on his peers that his legacy will live on forever. All who know of the doctor will be filled with awe, for he represents the pinnacle of his craft.

Title Passive:
Iatrophobia (only applies when Title Active is used): Your mere presence causes those whom you deem a patient to quake with primal dread. Those with a weak mentality will be paralyzed with fear.

> **Title Active:**
> **The Doctor:** You may freely transform into the illustrious Dr. William Walter. As the famed physician, your Charisma is set to 0, but all of your existing Charisma stats will be converted into Strength at five times its value.

Wait, I could just feely transform into Dr. Walter? Without any cooldowns and such? And if I was reading the description right, I'd get 510 bonus points put into strength when I did? It was no wonder I felt so strangely powerful when I was in that form.

But holy shit . . . This was probably one of the best titles I'd ever gotten. Although there was the small downside that I looked like a grotesque monstrosity when I turned into the good doctor, so perhaps it was not the best idea to use this skill too freely in the company of others.

> **Secondary Title: The Love of a Fledgling God (EX Rank)**
> **Description:** You have earned the eternal love and appreciation of a newly awakened entity. As her benefactor, do not betray her expectations in you and you will know the generosity of the divine.

> **Title Passive:**
> **Divine Appreciation:** All beings categorized as a deity will look upon you favorably.

> **Title Active:**
> **Locked Until the Fledgling God matures.**

Well, this title was a little more esoteric, but having that passive would certainly help me navigate the other sponsors in the future. As for the active? Only time would tell what that would bring, but I wasn't in a hurry. Alice should enjoy her childhood a bit longer first; she can come into her own when she needs to. Just getting this extra title was more than worth it to give up my Devil's Advocate one.

Is there anything else, Noe?

"Negative, my host," Noe replied. "Unless you want me to recount the Trash Matrix's review of your performance."

I almost laughed out loud. *I think I'll skip that, thank you.*

"I thought so." She chuckled. "Please take care of yourself, dear Walter."

You know I will.

There was one last thing I wanted to check out while I was still relatively alone, and it was the charm that Molly gave me. I still had to inventory the director's satchel, but that was impossible to open with how erratically the dragon was moving. I was more likely to lose some of the smaller items if I tried that now.

I took out the charm and . . . frowned. How was I supposed to use this thing?

Before I could probe at it some more, a faint projection-like image of Molly appeared before me. The ghost doll looked around before she turned her attention back to me.

"Dr. Walter?" she asked. "Why do you look like a patient?"

I used my new skill and changed back to the familiar shape that Molly recognized. "Sorry, it's a disguise that I've been working on to trick the system into taking me with the rest of the patients. Apparently, everyone on this side looks like this."

The doll visibly shuddered. "That is most unfortunate, doctor. The patient's form—especially that species—is remarkably weak and fragile. I hope your change is only aesthetic."

"It is, don't worry."

I heard a noise from the back.

"Walter, are you talking with someone?" the regressor shouted from the back of the cabin. "What's going on?"

"Shit, I'll talk later, Molly," I whispered quickly. "I just wanted to see if your charm works."

She nodded and vanished from sight.

"Just talking to myself," I shouted back. "I'm a little disoriented from the turbulence."

"Sorry about that! The trip will be over soon, try to endure it until then."

I grunted an approval and heard Jae-Hyun return to his work. We made it back to Pandora in almost half the time it took to get here originally. That didn't mean we didn't hurry back to the guild building. Jae-Hyun had everyone meet us in one of the larger meeting rooms, and they were all waiting for us there when we finally arrived back.

Jae-Hyun grabbed the central seat, and I took another one near his side.

"What's happened in the two months we were away?" Jae-Hyun said once everyone was gathered.

The others all looked at Yoona. She nodded. "Well, we were worried when you guys didn't come out of the trial."

"We even waited two days just in case!" Noel added before everyone else glared at her. "Sorry, uh, you can continue, Yoona."

"And we waited for you to come out for two days," the high schooler continued, "but we had to go back after that. Your pendant was still glowing, so I knew you were safe, but we did get worried after you didn't show up for a month."

The regressor nodded but otherwise didn't speak.

"We thought something must have gone wrong with your trial, so Vadeem and I even went to see Raffiel about the situation."

"A lot of good that did," Vadeem grumbled. "They said that the situation shouldn't have happened, and assured us that you three were safe while they went to check out what was going on."

"Was that when the change in staff occurred?" the regressor asked.

"No," Vadeem answered. "That came a while later when the last big batch of aspirants arrived."

"And speaking of new aspirants . . ." Yoona added, "um . . . you won't like what the new people have been doing."

"Explain," Jae-Hyun said darkly. He was scary when he was serious.

"You know how you and my little bro had been trying your best to help the guild's image?" Noel asked.

Jae-Hyun and I nodded.

"Well . . . a lot of that's been undone with the arrival of the new batch," the redhead continued. "They've started some propaganda campaigns against us, saying how our leader ditched us or is dead. They even started their own guild, and they've gotten a lot of supporters in the last few weeks."

Vadeem frowned. "I think their leader's got some kind of manipulation skill, or at least some kind of clairvoyance ability. Bastard seemed to anticipate anything we did to fight back his efforts. It's like he knew how to counter anything we tried."

"And the people Father Marcus helped have started to lose hope," Yoona continued. "They've . . . Well, you'll see soon enough. It's not good, brother."

Well, I guess it was inevitable that things went south with Jae-Hyun gone, and without me or Marcus in the picture either, our guild's charisma score was pretty low. Still, I couldn't just sit still while someone else stole all of my hard-earned brainwashed goons.

"Those aspirants can wait. I'm sure Father Marcus can help them again given enough time," the regressor said.

"I shall do so," the father answered with his signature creepy smile. "The flock has been without a shepherd for too long; it is only natural that their base instincts will take over. I will correct that."

"Who is the leader of this new group?" Jae-Hyun continued, his tone still eerily neutral.

"He goes by Ryan," Yoona answered, and took out a sketch of a normal-looking Caucasian man in his mid or late twenties. "And he's been busy going around talking with all the other folks in Pandora day and night."

"And we didn't choose to do anything drastic, since you guys weren't here," Noel added. I could guess what "drastic" meant in her case. "See, even I can be good and patient for a while!"

"Thank you, Noel," the regressor answered simply. "Please continue, Yoona."

"We're losing support fast," she said with a soft sigh. "A lot of our production staff have deserted us as well, and the new guild's hampering Vadeem's recruitment process. It's not good, brother."

"I see . . . I'll speak with Walter later about fixing our guild's image. Thank you for letting me know about the new situation, Yoona, and I apologize for being away for so long."

"I'll think of something," I added. "Just give me a bit of time. I have to check out the current situation first."

Jae-Hyun nodded.

"Don't apologize, brother. It wasn't your fault."

"Everyone else, please get ready for the announcement in a few hours," he continued. "Be ready for anything."

CHAPTER TWO

The New Administration

I was exhausted from the nonstop action since we got back and was ready to just lie down for a moment. I was already in my room and shedding my sweat-soaked clothing when the universe chose to deny me my rest and relaxation. Again. It seemed like every time I was about to get some sleep, someone from Central would choose exactly that moment to interrupt me. I could understand it logically since they couldn't bother me while I was on duty as an arbiter, but I was starting to miss my time at the hospital more and more. At least I had stable work hours there!

However, the way that Central decided to interrupt me this time was a little strange. Displayed in my retina was a box with small, scrolling text, not too dissimilar to the type I used to communicate with the party.

> Crawling Chaos [Is this messaging thing working?]
> Crawling Chaos [Damn it, where's Bob when you need him? Xalla, how do you send messages over to your sponsored aspirant? Gah, damn this blasted thing!]

I just stared at the messages in awe. Well . . . I guess some aspects of life transcended trivial things like species.

> Crawling Chaos [I'm doing that already! It's clearly not working! What do you mean I'm holding it wrong?]

Okay, as much as I wanted to stay silent and see this play out, I probably shouldn't tease the elderly too much.

Crawling Chaos [We Xollon shouldn't have to deal with this crap! What's wrong with just sending my thoughts out to Walter the old-fashioned way?]

Noe, how do I respond to my sponsor?

Crawling Chaos [How is this added security? I'd like to see any being break through a Xollon's thoughts, much less mine!]

"I can facilitate communications, my host," she replied. "Simply think your response and I shall do the rest."
Thanks, Noe. Please do so.
"Acknowledged. Please proceed."
I can hear you, Rogue.

Crawling Chaos [Holy shit, it's working! What did you do, Xalla? Press that button again!]

She didn't do anything. I've been able to hear you for a while now. And say hi to Xalla for me.

Crawling Chaos [Walter says hi . . . Uh, she says hello back.]

I suppressed a sigh. *That's great . . . so what did you need me for?*

Crawling Chaos [Are you free for a bit? Alone, I mean?]

Yes?

I saw a rip in the dimension, and out came Rogue along with a clearly annoyed Xalla.

"God, this is so much easier!" the old Xollon exclaimed. "I swear all these damned regulations and new-fangled technology will be the death of me!"

I scrambled to put on some clothes, although I probably shouldn't have worried. It wasn't like those two cared about my human form's state of undress.

"Uh . . . you needed something?" I asked again.

"Right, sorry," he said before he cleared his throat. "Uh, I need to chat with you about important sponsorship stuff, confidential, as per our agreement. If the aspirant Walter would kindly step through the portal so that we may be safe from potential eavesdroppers . . ."

"Right." I nodded, understanding where this was going. "Very important, confidential things as outlined by the lawful contract we signed."

I stepped through before the Overseer could get any more funny ideas. Xalla and her mentor joined us soon after, and I found myself in a small meeting room. A cup of coffee, suitable for human consumption from the looks of it, was placed where I should be seated, while Rogue and Xalla both had a cup of Xollon wine next to their much larger seats.

I saw the portal close up behind me and spoke up. "Are we safe to chat?"

Rogue paused for a second before he nodded slowly. "Yes . . . we're good now. Someone was trying to poke their noses in, but I made sure they're regretting that decision right about now."

"The fools," Xalla added dismissively. "They still think that the Xollon are unused to technology."

I raised an eyebrow. "What about your mentor's attempts at communication earlier?"

Xalla hesitated for a second, clearly taken aback by my comment. "Um . . . That's . . . Rogue's—"

"Anyway!" the old Xollon interrupted. "All that matters is that there's no one spying on us now. Let's just move on to the serious topics!"

Xalla rubbed a feeler to her head and sighed. "Sometimes I wish he didn't represent the best that Xolloid has to offer . . ."

"So, what was it you needed?" I asked for the third time. "I'm assuming it's about Q's replacement?"

"It is, and about that slimeball Overseer," the old Xollon said with a low grumble. "They've decided to shuffle around the order of events for the site, and let me tell you, none of the sponsors are happy about it."

"What do you mean?"

"Well, they're going to wage a clan war within the month, for one," Rogue continued. "Your people in Pandora are set up against one of the Restus cities from Site 1100, and . . ."

"Let me guess," I added. I didn't even need to know what kind of species these Restus were to understand the general plot. "The Overseer chose who our opponents are, so we'll be slaughtered, right?"

"Right," he answered grimly. "Hence why I wanted to speak with you quickly before you meet up with the Overseer."

Wait, I was meeting up with the Overseer? That was news to me.

"It's not a formal meeting, Walter, and not in person," Xalla added after she saw my hesitation. "You'll meet with one of his drone bodies with some representatives from the sponsorship program. What he's doing is clearly biased against Q's site, and we'll try our best to wrestle some control back in our favor."

"As if he'll make it easy for us . . ."

"If it makes you feel any better," Rogue added, "the Sponsors do have some sway in Central's operations, and we've managed to delay your private meeting with that slimeball for a long, long time. We also got rid of the "aid" that the Overseer wanted to assign you, at least for the time being. Nothing beats the ability to slow down a corporation than the bureaucratic forms that all need to be signed in triplicate! A shame so many of your files went missing. Why, some even had the dates wrong!"

"That's some good news," I admitted. "But nothing that will help the immediate situation. Anything else I need to know before speaking with that piece of shit?"

"Yeah, it's the new management," Rogue said. "I think Xalla can explain it better. She's working for them now, unfortunately."

"They're trying to undo all of Q's legacy," she muttered, her frills drooping. "Half the original staff have already been reassigned to other sites if not outright fired, and the other half have had most of their privileges stripped. The site's filled with the Overseer's minions now. I'm not sure how much I can help you out, Walter. They're keeping me busy with worthless make-work."

I took a deep breath, steadying my emotions. "Right, that's about what I expected from his handpicked goons. How's Q? I wasn't able to see him off."

"He's . . . Well, I wouldn't say he's happy," Rogue replied. "But he's making the best of a bad situation with Bob. Quasar's keeping busy with a new project, something he's always wanted to pursue, so you don't have to worry about the man for now. Bob'll know more if you see him later."

"That's good to hear," I answered slowly. "But I did want to see him before he left."

"You can thank the new admin for that," Xalla added. "They "accidentally" sped up everyone else's timeline while you and the anomaly were gone. They say it's because your charge had destabilized all the local timestreams with his departure outside of the city. They also said that none of this would have happened if he just followed regulations and entered the third trial in Pandora as intended."

"Such a very plausibly deniable explanation," I muttered. "Of course."

"They'll do everything in their power to get in your way, Walter," Xalla continued. "I'll do what I can to help, but don't trust anyone new you meet."

"Thanks for the warning." I sighed. "Now if there's nothing else, let's just go and speak with the Overseer. I'm curious about how he's going to justify all these changes."

CHAPTER THREE

The Overseer's Plan

R ight," Rogue said. His entire body spoke of how little he wanted to see the Overseer, even if it was a proxy body. "Let's get it over with. God, I hate that slimeball."

"I should head back myself," Xalla added. "Just leaving for a few minutes puts me under scrutiny lately; they really don't want me anywhere near Jordan and her people. Take care of yourself, Walter."

I smiled back. "I will, Xalla. And you take care as well."

She gave me a comforting shake of the frill and opened a portal out of the small meeting room. Rogue opened another one and gestured for me to enter. I took a deep breath and steadied my nerves. It was best not to show any weakness when confronting the head of Central.

I stepped through and entered a familiar space. If I remembered correctly, this was one of the various rooms I had passed through when I first came to Site 1102, although this one was a rather large gathering area. The space was adorned with tables filled with various human foodstuffs, all while an army of staff waited at attention. Yet despite the huge number of support staff, there were only two other beings who were unmistakably sponsors here, with no Bob in sight.

It also meant that everyone present here was a god or divine being of some sort. I hoped that they would be deities that I would recognize. I mean, I couldn't imagine some random god from another dimension like Abigail caring about the people here when the humans here didn't even know they existed.

I think Rogue was the only exception since he was only here on account of my relationship with Xalla.

The other sponsors all bowed deferentially to the Xollon when they saw him. Whatever pecking order existed between the sponsors, it was clear that people like Rogue, and I guess Big Bob, were at the top. It made me appreciate just how scary the Xollon race truly was if even the gods of myth were terrified of them.

"Lady, gentleman." Rogue nodded at the other two. "I'm sure you all know who's standing beside me, but I'll go through introductions in any case. May I present to you the famed Arbiter W, or as he's known in the trials, Aspirant Walter."

"Good to meet you all," I said with a wave. "But is this everyone?"

"Unfortunately, yes," Rogue grumbled. "We planned for others to come, but there were some mysterious, unavoidable delays in their travel plans, so only those who were close by the site could come. How peculiar."

I cursed under my breath. If there's one thing I can say about the Overseer, it's that he was certainly thorough with his plans. That made him damn annoying to deal with.

"Let's just give the arbiter your basic information," Rogue continued. "The Overseer should be arriving any minute now."

The other two agreed to Rogue as if following his orders was the most natural thing to do.

The first person to speak up, if you could even call it that, was little more than a mass of buzzing bloat flies vaguely flying in the shape of a humanoid. Just trying to focus on any one part of the creature was disorienting. I tried my best to not show my unease.

"Beelzebub," it buzzed, even Noe's ability to translate speech having a hard time deciphering its noise. "It's good to finally meet you in the flesh. I'm a fan! I have all your books! My own aspirant is in your group's party, and I look forward to working with you in the future."

It didn't take a genius to figure out who the Lord of the Flies was sponsoring, so I nodded and gave him a relaxed smile. I would have shaken his hands as well if he had, well, anything even close to an appendage. "Thank you for looking after Father Marcus. It can't be easy sponsoring someone in the group with the anomaly."

He chuckled, although it sounded more like a swarm of angry bees than a laugh. "Well, I'm new to the program, and I've barely begun to branch out of this dimension, so I can't be picky, but the priest more than made up for it with his performance so far. This one has potential."

I agreed. If there was nothing else good to say about Father Marcus, then it was his potential.

"Anyway, how about the rest of us introduce ourselves first before we make small talk, yes?" the other god in the room added. This time it was a relatively normal-looking woman of indeterminable age.

Well, normal as in she wasn't a mass of insects or a tentacle monster. Her features were constantly changing from moment to moment. One second she didn't look older than maybe four or five, then that form rapidly aged until she looked like she would keel over and expire at any moment, before she shifted again to a new form and began the process anew. Her form never stayed constant for more than a few moments. It seemed that being disorienting to look at was the norm for this crowd.

She offered me a hand and I shook it. "I'm Skuld, a pleasure to make your acquaintance."

She held on to my hand for an awkwardly long time, as if she was mesmerized by something. I had to fake a cough to get her attention.

"Sorry, Lord Arbiter!" she exclaimed as she pulled her hand back quickly. "I don't know what came over me. It's just . . . your fate is very interesting. I've never seen anything like it before, but then again, I've never shaken hands with a Xollon before either! Never mind, I shouldn't have expected anything less from Arbiter W!"

Okay . . . that was weird. I'd have to figure out what kind of god this Skuld person was later. Maybe she was able to see something weird about me because of Noe or my weird hybrid Xollon nature.

I wanted to ask a few questions myself, but like Rogue said, there really wasn't a lot of time for pleasantries after that. The Overseer came a few minutes later. He looked like a normal human. In fact, I'm almost positive that I recognized the dude from Pandora. It was only through his eyes that I knew it was the piece-of-shit Overseer and not the aspirant. Guess he had the ability to possess bodies at will. How wonderful.

"Good afternoon, as the humans would say!" The Overseer laughed as he sauntered into the room. "But there's only the four of you here? I was expecting a bigger showing. I even had all these waiters here ready to serve up a party!"

Yeah, as if he hadn't expected things to turn out like this.

"Yes, there were some unexpected delays," I muttered.

"Pity that," he answered with the fakest frown I've ever seen. "And here I was looking forward to seeing the local sponsors for this site."

"At least the Lord General was able to make it," I added, hoping the Xollon could enforce some sort of legitimacy in the upcoming exchange.

"Yes . . ." the Overseer answered, "how wonderful of you to join us, Rogue. And a belated congratulations on your successful sponsorship."

The old Xollon just grunted in response.

"Now then, since we're all here, why don't we get the meeting underway?" the Overseer continued. "Please feel free to have some of the delicacies at hand. I've picked out the best food and drink that the human species have managed to produce for this occasion."

I chose not to indulge.

The man shrugged before grabbing a platter of food himself. "Suit yourself."

"Enough already," Rogue said. "We're not here for pleasantries! We're here to ask you why you decided to move this site's scheduling forward, and more importantly, why you thought it would be okay to pit the humans against the Restus of all species!"

He looked at Rogue with mock innocence. "I don't understand what you mean, Lord General."

"You know damn well what I mean!" Rogue half-shouted. "The humans were chosen for their latent potential, but they've barely finished their third trial at this point! If you make them fight the Restus at this stage, they're all but guaranteed to be killed! How is that in the spirit of the trials?"

The Overseer chuckled as he took another bite of his food. "Of course I know that, which is why I am only sending in the Pandora city-state to fight, and not the human species as a whole. You have to remember that the infamous Lord Arbiter W is helping this group of humans out, not to mention the benefits that are reaped with an anomaly present as well. It would hardly be fair for this group of aspirants to be judged by the same standards as the rest of humanity. Why, it's only fair that such an outstanding group fight the lackluster Restus."

I gritted my teeth in frustration. I wanted to say something back, but there wasn't much I could say to refute the man's words with my limited knowledge. I was acting officially as the arbiter W, and in front of the leader of Central at that. I couldn't afford to make any mistakes here.

Plus, what the Overseer said wasn't exactly a lie either. The people of Pandora really did have an unfair advantage over the others due to the regressor's actions, and in part, my own. Taking into account my exaggerated feats as the Lord Arbiter, it was only fair to assume that we'd crush any lesser race with ease. Still, I had to say something.

"And what is your reasoning for pushing forward Q's schedule?" I added.

I didn't know exactly what kind of question to ask, and I hoped that the Absolute Luck skill could help right about now. However, if just blurting out a name cost a large chunk of points, I can't imagine how much it would cost to randomly say the exact right question and properly respond after.

"I am sorry, my host," Noe said, "but the skill cannot help you in this situation. The rules of Central are written to be absolute, and to change those even a little would take more luck points than you currently have by several magnitudes."

I sighed. It wasn't like I was expecting much here.

He gave me a casual smile. "And to answer that question, Arbiter W, it is for the same reason why the human race was chosen as potential aspirants. This is a species that thrives on conflict; they grow stronger when their backs are against the wall. They grow when the only option is to adapt or die. I am simply speeding up this process! If the Lord Arbiter has his eyes on this particular group, then it must mean that their potential is phenomenal. I'm just doing what I can to help."

My ass he was! But damn was his reasoning sound. I was starting to hate this man more and more. I had to suppress a frown, but I was failing.

"Now, now," he continued, "don't give me that look. I understand just how difficult this task is, so I'm going to help you out, to make things even so to speak."

I didn't like the sound of that at all. "Go on . . ."

"The clan war will be dangerous, no doubt about it, and we can't risk harming our precious anomaly." His smile brightened considerably. "Which is why I have used my authority to provide the anomaly and his sister with a bonus stage to occupy their time while the war is underway. They'll even be rewarded heavily for this, all while facing no actual danger! That way, even if you, god forbid, lose the upcoming fight, they will be unaffected! Of course, if Pandora is destroyed, I can't guarantee what city the anomaly will be reassigned to . . . it might even be so far away that another arbiter will have to take charge!"

"And you'll have no control over that, right?" I asked.

He gave me a polite nod. "None."

"Then you are deliberately weakening the aspirants of Site 1102!" Skuld added. "Without the anomaly, the strength of the Pandora aspirants will drop dramatically!"

"That's a strange way of putting it, Lady Norn." The Overseer chuckled. "You have to remember that I have to keep the best interests of both sites in line. It would be horribly unfair for Site 1100, which doesn't have an anomaly of its own, mind you, to face a site that does have one, and that's not even mentioning our favorite miracle maker himself. I am merely making things fair."

"But that's not taking into account the nature of the two species," Beelzebub added this time. "The Restus are known for their innate strength and tenacity. Not even the strongest human aspirants would be able to hold their own against them this early on in the trials."

"That is a fair point," the Overseer conceded, but his stupid grin never left his face. "And it is a point of concern that must be addressed. So, to even the odds, I am willing to allow the Lord Arbiter here the chance to train this group of aspirants! He will have full control over all of the resources that Site 1102 possesses until the start of the clan war.

"Of course, the rewards given out must be approved by the Origin Matrix, but aside from that, he can do as he sees fit to improve the overall strength and battle capabilities of Pandora. Q's successor can explain it in more detail once we're done here. He has done more with much less in the past, so I believe this is exceedingly fair."

"But that would require the Lord Arbiter to work in his full capacity as a member of Central," Rogue interrupted. "How can he do that while maintaining his status as an aspirant?"

"Easy," the Overseer answered. It seemed like the man had a response to everything; it was starting to become quite evident why he was able to retain his power for so long. "A stand-in for Aspirant Walter already exists. It's one that he's used before, in fact. Plus, he is free to interact with the anomaly and his little guild after his official duties are completed each day, so the stand-in only needs to be there for a short duration."

Ah . . . it was that shitty doppelganger. I had almost forgotten about it.

"I don't think Q's creation can take my place for any length of time," I said. "Its ability to be me is severely flawed."

"Then it's a good thing that I made some modifications to it personally!" the Overseer answered with cheer. "You will find the new doppelganger to be more than capable of this task, I swear on my honor as the Overseer of the Central Collective. Any other concerns?"

"But a month is still too little time!" Beelzebub stated. "Even if the Lord Arbiter is the one in charge!"

"I don't think that's the case, my good sponsor," replied the Overseer. "It's not any arbiter that's taking charge, it is the legendary W doing so. I fear that anything more than a month would be too much of an advantage for the humans if it's W who is at the helm. Don't worry, I've already cleared this with the Tribunal, and they agree with my assessment. Surely you can understand, after looking through his records?"

Beelzebub remained silent.

"I thought so. Any other concerns?" he asked again.

I thought for a long time, but I couldn't think of any way to refute the man. It seemed that he'd been doing his homework ever since I got the better of him in our first meeting. I just didn't expect him to be so thorough! Everything he said made sense. The only problem was that I wasn't this legendary figure capable of moving mountains and creating miracles! Fuck!

Once again, I was faced with the cold reality that I just didn't know enough about how Central operated. If he was following all the necessary rules and everything was already approved by the Tribunal, then I didn't think anything I said on my side would change my current predicament. Still, I had to try something. I had the Absolute Luck skill once again; was there any way of using it here? I didn't have to change Central regulations, so surely something could be done.

Luck Charges: 1,557/1,557

"There's one more thing," I added, hoping against hope that my last attempt would yield even a slight victory.

"Yes, Lord Arbiter?" he answered with a smug smile.

I opened my mouth and hoped that Noe would take the reins and luck my way through the situation. But nothing happened.

"I apologize, my host," Noe answered, "but the amount of luck charges needed to do that is outside my current scope. As I said earlier, I do not have that ability at the moment."

I cursed silently, even though I knew it was futile.

"I'm still waiting for a response, W."

"Nothing," I muttered silently. Fine, it looked like I'd have to take the fight to him after he left. I had a month to work with. I didn't believe that I couldn't do something in that time.

"No?" he repeated, looking around the room once more. "Great! What a productive meeting! Please feel free to enjoy the refreshments here, but I need to be on my way now. I've already prepared Aspirant Walter's doppelganger, so he is free to meet up with the new administration team when he is ready. Best get going now though, Arbiter W. The planned speech is starting soon, and you don't want to miss that!"

I glared at the man.

"Thank you, Overseer," I muttered with barely contained resentment. "I'll make sure I use the time wisely."

"All right." He gave me a friendly wave goodbye. "I'll be seeing you!"

CHAPTER FOUR

Meeting the New Staff

I cursed out loud when the Overseer was well and truly gone. God damn it! I had never felt so helpless in a battle of wits before. That piece of crap had the right answer for all of our concerns, and I didn't know enough about the laws of Central to refute any of his claims. Worse yet, he had all the time in the world to prepare for whatever shitty schemes he had up his sleeves, while I had next to none.

The only assurance I had was that I had Noe up and functioning again, but I wasn't sure if all the luck in the world was enough to offset the advantage the Overseer gave himself. Not only was I unable to rely on the regressor to help with the actual fighting, but I also had to work with an administration that had my worst interests in mind. They may say that I had full control over resources, but I was willing to bet anything that they'd try their best to misinterpret my orders.

I cursed again but forced myself to calm down after that. I was thankful for my innate skill at a time like this because I could see myself as an emotional wreck after hearing all this bad news.

"Well, that went poorly," Rogue muttered. "But I guess there's a reason he's in charge of one of the biggest organizations in the multiverse. That man doesn't forget a grudge."

I had to agree there. He had gotten the best of me this time, but I wasn't going to just lie down and admit defeat.

"So what are the chances of our aspirants making it out of this one alive?"

Beelzebub asked. "Because, no offense, Lord Arbiter, their chances doesn't seem good on my end."

"I'll have to agree," Skuld added. "I've seen the fates of some of the humans here, and the vast majority of the futures are bleak ones. It's not hopeless with the arbiter here to intervene, but . . ."

"But the outlook is not good," I finished for her. "Look, we still have a month to figure things out, and you can bet that I'll do everything in my power to help the people of Pandora. I've been in worse situations before, but I will need your help this time. I just need you three to contact the other local sponsors and have them help out their aspirants as much as they can. I don't know how the program works, but issue more quests, give more rewards, whatever you can do to help."

"I'll see it done." The Lord of Flies nodded. "A few of my friends have already established contracts with some of the aspirants here, but I don't think I can convince anyone else to invest in Pandora. It's . . . it's not the safest bet, even with you in charge."

"I can get my sisters to pitch in," Skuld added. "But that's about the best I can do. I'm afraid to say it, but the trials are still too early for very many sponsors to have made their decisions."

I nodded. "It's probably why the Overseer chose this time to act. He's squeezing any little advantage that he can get."

"Well, he'd need to if he wants to beat you," Rogue said. "You've gotten the best of the man in every meeting that I can recount, and I don't see how that's going to change now. To be fair, he has stacked the deck against you rather well."

It would change because I wasn't W! But I couldn't voice that out loud, no matter how much I wanted to. Instead, I put on a fake smile and assured the others that I had everything under control. They seemed reassured.

I wished I had even a fraction of the confidence they had in me, but I doubted the two sponsors would share the sentiment if they had the full picture. Not only was I dealing with a hostile administration, but the Overseer even managed to destabilize the regressor's base of power. We couldn't possibly win a war, much less a battle, when all of the aspirants in Pandora were divided.

"Okay, everyone," Rogue finally said, "let's let the Lord Arbiter do his work. We've taken up enough of his time as is, and he still needs to meet up with the Overseer's lackeys."

That was true enough. I had to excuse myself rather quickly after that, and Rogue was polite enough to send me straight to the new staff via a portal. I landed right in Q's old office, although nothing in its interior showed signs that the man had previously occupied it.

Gone was the utilitarian design, and on every wall hung gaudy pictures of Central propaganda. The bare floors were replaced with an expensive-looking rug, and even Q's old table was gone. In its place sat a huge, almost comically large desk with what looked like a throne behind it. And on that throne sat a woman.

The being was as perfect as Q had been in his human guise, just in the opposite gender. She even had similar features as the old site manager, with the same blonde hair, same unblemished skin, and slightly rounder features. It was as though—no, scratch that, I was certain that she chose this human guise to piss me off. It was working.

She got up and offered a hand to shake. "Welcome, Lord Arbiter, it's a pleasure to finally meet you. I apologize for the unforeseen hiccup you experienced in that last trial, but as you know, accidents happen when you take over a position and are saddled with the old incompetent staff. I've already fired the employees responsible for that mess, so something like that won't happen under my command."

"Thank you, and it's a pleasure to meet you as well," I lied, keeping the spite out of my voice. We both knew where our true feelings laid, but it was pointless to show open hostility.

"Please call me Jordan. I quite like this human name," she replied with a practiced smile. "The Overseer has already informed me about the situation."

"Then I can assume that I will have your full support to get the people of Pandora ready for the upcoming skirmish?"

"Absolutely!" she answered. "As he said, you have the entirety of the resources of this site at your disposal until the start of the war. I just implore you to allow me to introduce the changes to the people of Pandora first before you take charge. Just the basic information, of course. You can have the floor immediately after. I wouldn't want to overstep my boundaries."

"And how would I go about addressing the people?" I asked. "Walk in as a Xollon and have half of the aspirants go mad from looking at me?"

Jordan chuckled. "The Overseer has thought of that as well. He's sent over his private tailor to fit you with a new guise. I have come to understand that your current form is as close to an actual aspirant as is possible, but the Overseer assures you that the new suit can fit over your existing form, and that no one, not even the other workers here, can see through the disguise."

As if choreographed, a strange-looking floating eyeball with eight limbs hovered into the room.

"If you would please follow me, Lord Arbiter," it said, although I wasn't sure how it talked at all without a mouth. "I'll be pleased to find something that matches your esteemed self."

I glanced at the weird creature before checking back with Jordan.

"I'll wait for you to be done, Lord Arbiter," she assured me. "Please take your time to choose a well-fitting suit."

I nodded and followed the creature into an adjacent room. The thing took various measurements of my body before it held up a mirror-like object that showed me different human forms.

I didn't really care what I chose, but I did want every advantage that I could get. Just like how I first picked a weapon for the first trial, I activated the Absolute Luck skill and allowed Noe to pick for me. Two luck charges was all it took to make the selection.

The eyeball creature nodded and moved so fast that I didn't even understand what had happened, but when my brain finally caught up with its actions, I was already in the new form. I looked in the offered mirror and saw that I looked like a gruff, older gentleman.

I had dark, short-cropped hair with wisps of white appearing at the roots, and a matching medium-length beard that covered the bottom of my face. My eyes were hawklike and sharp. Just staring at myself gave me shivers with the intensity of that look, and I also noticed some small faded scars that covered my face. Overall, my body felt lean but strong. I gave off the feeling of an old retired army general.

"Is the look to your liking, Lord Arbiter?"

"Yes," I answered. I was a little taken back because my voice sounded wholly unfamiliar. It wasn't like this when I turned into a Xollon or Dr. Walter, but I guess Noe was helping me with those transitions.

"Excellent, my lord," the thing answered. "Let's go back and meet up with Site Manager Jordan."

There wasn't any more preamble as Jordan and I headed out of Q's office. As far as I was concerned, it was still Q's space, just as it was still Q's site. This Jordan woman was just keeping his seat warm. I only had time to ask her about the general resources that I had at my disposal, but it was enough information for me to formulate the skeleton of a plan, at least for my upcoming speech. I could maybe delay doing anything drastic for a day or two at most, and I hoped that was enough time for me to think of something solid.

Jordan teleported us out of the site and onto Pandora. The various aspirants were already gathered around the central meeting space when the two of us appeared on a raised platform. I had to look around a bit to find the

regressor's group. And true to the Overseer's words, I could see that my doppelganger had already infiltrated my friends. No one seemed to notice anything strange about him.

"Gathered aspirants of Pandora!" Jordan began, her voice resonating with
everyone present as they looked up at us with awe. "I am pleased to announce
that everyone here will have the glorious opportunity to set yourselves apart
from the rest of Earth's brave warriors!"

I heard some whispers before Jordan hushed them all with a wave. "I am
sure that you have noticed the change in hosts, and I wish to explain why these
changes have taken place."

More hushed whispers.

"Your group, your city, represents the best of the best that humanity has
to offer. You are the first amongst all of Earth's subjects, and as such, the Lord
has deemed it fit to accelerate your growth as awakened aspirants. In order to
facilitate this growth, He has sent His best agents to assist in this endeavor!"

I gave a firm nod when Jordan gestured to me.

"I will allow this esteemed agent of God to explain what he will do with
you himself, but first, I must speak about the necessity of all these changes."

This time, all of the aspirants looked up with anticipation. They knew
something big was approaching. I just hoped they'd be ready for it in time.

Jordan continued, "As some of you might have noticed, the world that
Pandora sits in is not a peaceful one. There are many others out there who
want nothing more than your demise, for they are jealous of the love that the
Lord has bestowed you. News of an imminent clash with a rival faction has
been reported, and it is set to start in a month's time."

Now that got the aspirants riled up, although they didn't seem worried.
I pitied their ignorance; a lot of the people hearing this speech wouldn't be
around come a month's time, no matter how much I prepared them for the
future.

"More information will be provided as we learn more about the foes,"
Jordan lied. "But never forget that you are the favored children of God! Now
allow me to step aside and allow the man in charge of your growth to speak!
He will ensure your victory in the upcoming battle, so heed his words!"

I stepped forward and gazed at the crowd. With a deep breath, I went over
what I had to say one last time before addressing the aspirants before me.

CHAPTER FIVE

Change of Plans

*N**oe, make sure all of my charisma-based passives are on. Make my voice commanding. I'm planning to make this short and sweet. I don't have time to play Jordan's little games. If she wants to inflate my ego with a big speech, then I'll do just the opposite.*

That was true, and although a part of it was to spite the Overseer and his lackeys, it was mainly because I didn't plan to give any exact information to the aspirants, and more importantly, to the admin, about my plans. I had to change the parameters that I was dealt in order to win against the Overseer, which meant formulating a better plan once I knew all the tools I had at my disposal. I still needed to see what help Abigail packed for me, and I needed to do that before something else went wrong.

The longer I was following orders from Jordan, the less in control I was, and I desperately needed some time for myself to properly analyze the current situation and finally figure out a damn plan. I had so little information to work with, and I'd always be in the back seat as long as I was missing crucial information about Central's internal structure or all the rules they had to abide by.

"All passives are set to desired parameters," Noe answered. "Would you like to expand luck charges to manipulate the emotions of the aspirants with the Emotional Redux ability?"

You can do that?

"The results will be subtle," the system explained, "but it will have a visible effect."

Well, I did recharge all my used luck, so might as well use it. Do it, Noe, and don't skim back. I want to make a clear impression now. I'm not sure what my future plans will be, so I have to do what I can now. Can't hurt if I need to abuse my new status later.

"Acknowledged."

"Good afternoon, aspirants of Earth," I addressed the crowd. I could feel the rumbling of power in my voice, and the people below me noticed as well. They couldn't keep their eyes away from me. Guess Noe went with the emotion of reverence and awe. Not a bad choice.

I continued. "As the host said, I am here to make sure that you aspirants are ready for the upcoming battle. You are all weak, pathetically so, but I will whip you into something that you can be proud of!"

Did I believe a word I was saying? Not a chance. In the last few hours that I had to think, I'd come to realize that nothing I did could achieve the results needed for this group of aspirants to succeed, what with the impossible restrictions placed by the Overseer. But that also made me realize something else entirely: Why was I playing by his rules? If the setting that he gave me was unfair, then I'd just change them and go at things at an angle that he couldn't predict. And if I was subtle enough, then plausible deniability worked both ways.

But for me to do that, I had to pretend to follow the Overseer's instructions. I had to have his people think that I was playing along with his plotline, to believe that I was doomed to fail as they watched me struggle in futility. There was no doubt in my mind that I was being watched thoroughly, but it wasn't like I didn't have allies of my own to help me sneak around later. The beginnings of a plan were already starting to formulate in my mind.

"I understand that this is all too soon to digest properly," I addressed, "so I will give you three days to adjust to this new information and to make your preparations. However, after this three-day grace period, I will initiate a training assignment for those who want to improve themselves—a mini trial if you will—so that you may have the best chances of success. This opportunity is open to any and all residents of Pandora, but it will be voluntary. Know that the rewards for participation will be grand."

The response of the aspirants were divided—those who were already ahead had a look of determination in their eyes, while the downtrodden looked relieved that participation wasn't mandatory. Well, time to motivate some of them a little. If there were aspirants that didn't choose to participate after that, then trying to improve them was a waste of time and resources.

"Remember, however," I shouted, "that while participation in my training is voluntary, participation in the war will not be. It is your life that you are wagering if you choose to ignore my goodwill. Heed this warning, for it will be your last. If you wish to stand above your peers, then you have but to accept my offer."

That got most of the people fired up. Nothing was more motivating than imminent, looming death, yet a small percentage of people still looked like they would rather risk death than take the time to improve. I recognized some of them from the B Group that I had infiltrated before the third trial. Yoona wasn't kidding. These people really had lost all hope in the time I was away.

"Keep my warning to heart, aspirants of Pandora," I said, my gaze never wavering, "and come thoroughly prepared to face danger and hardship if you choose to take me up on my offer. You are dismissed."

The aspirants looked around in question, their unvoiced concern clear. That was it? They had anticipated a grand speech, kind of like the long-winded ramblings Raffiel used to give, but I didn't have time for that. I needed all the time I had to fix some of the more glaring problems in my situation.

Speaking of the fake angel, I wondered what happened to him. Jordan said she sacked the people in charge of the last trial, and I couldn't help but think that he was one of the people implicated in that. I'd check with Xalla later about the whole situation with the new staff. At least I had free access to the chief of security now that I was temporarily in charge of Site 1102. I'd finish up with things here first.

"What are you looking around for?" I said again, raising my voice. "I said you are dismissed! Come back to this spot in exactly three days' time. Now go!"

I nodded at Jordan, and she teleported us out of there.

"That was a shorter speech than I had anticipated," Jordan said once we were back in Q's office. "And you chose to give them three days as well? Remember that you only have a month, that's a tenth of the total time that you have, Lord Arbiter. I hope you know what you're doing."

"I have my reasons," I muttered. "Now if you will excuse me, I have things to do."

"Of course, but are you sure you do not wish to stay and get acquainted with the site's operations?"

I shook my head. Like hell I'd stay in enemy territory for any longer than necessary. I was willing to bet anything that she and her Overseer boss had a few more tricks up their sleeves to waste my time, and more importantly, piss me off if I chose to stay. The only way to win was to not play.

"If you insist," she answered reluctantly. "I can only imagine how busy you will be. Will you be going back as an aspirant or continue here in your official capacity?"

"I'll go back as an aspirant for now," I replied quickly. "How will I contact you if I need to come back here? I am limited in my human form."

"Just tell the Origin Matrix, and I'll have someone fetch you," Jordan said with a practiced smile. "I'll send you back to your room and inform your doppelganger. He will make his way back to switch with you at an opportune time."

Another snap of the finger, and I was sent back to my familiar dorm.

I should have some time before the doppelganger could find a good excuse to extract itself from my friends. They were far away from the guild HQ, so I should have a few hours to myself, at least for now. I sat down on my bed and pulled out the satchel that the director gave me. It had been almost two days since I'd been back, yet it was only now that I had the chance to see what she had given me. I only hoped that this wasn't a prelude to endless nights of work. I activated the Absolute Luck skill first to ensure nothing went wrong or that I was accidentally being spied on and got to work.

I moved the coffee table over and gently took each item out, some small, others large, but most of the stuff seemed to be surgical tools and various hospital gear. What caught my attention was a neatly folded letter enclosed in a fancy envelope.

I opened that up first.

Dear William,

Hello. I'm not sure what to say, honestly, but I hope you are well. I don't know what kinds of danger you will face over in the invader's lands, but I have tried my best to provide you with items that will help your infiltration and your craft. Stealth is most likely the key to your success, so I prioritized that when I was packing your bag, although what I can provide you is limited.

You will find in the satchel a bundle of charms that will conceal your essence. I know how effective the invaders are at monitoring their victims, but they are also sloppy in their execution. They believe that they are infallible with their methods, never even considering how we might overcome their strange technology.

You will most likely be under constant surveillance if you find their headquarters, and those charms will hide you from their strange monitoring system. Burn one, and you will be undetectable for twenty-four hours. I have tested their efficiency myself, so please be at ease, Will.

I glanced through the assortment of items strewn on the table and found the package of paper charms. There was a thick stack of them neatly wrapped together. There must have been hundreds of them. I nodded and continued to read.

These charms will only hide you from their monitoring systems, which I understand will not be enough to get everything you need done. If you need to create an alibi, then you need to use the pendant.

I set the charms aside and took a small emerald necklace from the items. The jewel hung on a simple chain but was otherwise unimpressive.

Find a recently deceased corpse in good condition and place the pendant around the neck. It will allow me to control the body to act in your stead. Make sure you infuse some of your blood into the pendant before use and immediately burn a charm after. This will trick the monitoring system into tracking the corpse instead of you.

 This is also the main way that we can communicate, so I hope to hear from you soon. My powers will be limited in such a restrictive vessel, but I'll do what I can to help. You are a surgeon, so I trust you can make the necessary modifications to the body to ensure that it resembles your form if you need to be seen in public.

Well, I was not a surgeon by any stretch of that definition, so that would limit what I could do with the corpse. That meant no public appearances . . . unless I could somehow figure out how to transfer the weird human suits onto a new body. It should be possible if I found a body that was of similar proportions to mine. Nevertheless, I could still get a lot done even in the worst-case scenario. It was enough just to fool the Trash Matrix into thinking I was still in Pandora if I needed to be sneaky in the future.

Wait, speaking of human disguises, how the hell was I supposed to take mine off? Jordan hadn't explained since she thought it would be obvious, and it probably would be if I was who I said I was.

"I can assist you in that, my host," Noe answered. "I have intimate knowledge of your physical form, and can isolate the parts that are foreign. You may allow me brief control over your body by expending one luck charge, and Unit Noe can remove or put on the suit for the host."

Man, I'd be a wreck if it weren't for you, Noe. Thanks again.

"You are most welcome."

I continued to read.

> *Lastly, I have included a variety of medical equipment for your use. I don't know how readily available these items will be where you're going, but no physician can function without the right tools. I know how much you love your craft. The leather case contains a set of my favorite instruments; I hope you think of me when you use them. Oh, and there's a few cookies I made. Alice told me how much you liked them, so I packed a few extras for you.*
>
> *I hope to hear from you soon, and thank you again for all the help.*
>
> *Sincerely,*
> *Director Abigail*
>
> *P.S. The kids are doing great, by the way. We have some new patients coming in today, and they're both busy helping out with punishments here. They miss you, though, so please call sometime.*

I reread the letter before folding it neatly and putting it away. The director really was thoughtful, even if I couldn't use most of the surgical stuff that she packed. The fact that she gave so much thought about what to get me told me all I needed to know about how much she valued me. I was curious about the leather carrying case, though. I unfolded it and marveled at the assortment of brutal-looking instruments. There was one tool in the case that I could use, however, and it was the rather large bone saw.

Dr. Walter was about to make his debut in Pandora, and he was in desperate need of an appropriately menacing weapon. This rusty, decrepit tool made for a more primitive time was the perfect addition to the doctor.

I put the charms and bone saw into my inventory while I wore the pendant on my person. I had limited inventory room, and I didn't think I'd ever unlock any more than ten slots with how antagonistic the Trash Matrix was. The rest of the stuff was packed neatly back into the satchel, but I hesitated when I saw the box of cookies. Those I stuck in my inventory as well, although I wasn't sure why.

Once everything was neatly stashed away, I lay on my bed and reviewed all the information and tools I had at my disposal.

First of all, the Overseer had backed me into a corner that had no victory conditions if I played it straight. I didn't know what the hell the Vestus or Hestus, or whatever the foe was called were, but judging from Rogue's outrage, it was safe to say that they were not something that the aspirants of Pandora could fight. Coupled with the lack of a central leader in the form of the regressor helping out, we were well and truly screwed. None of us, with the exception of Jae-Hyun, perhaps, knew how to lead an army and create battlefield strategies.

Therefore, it was safe to say that the Overseer's agreement for me to train the aspirants for a month was a vain gesture to pander to his detractors, and it also explained why the new site admin was so cooperative thus far. Plus, if Jordan knew I was busy wasting my time with the aspirants, then she could rest easy knowing I wasn't going around screwing other things up. She'd be wrong, of course. She knew as well as anyone else just how pointless it was to try to improve the situation, even if I had all the resources on the site. I could imagine her laughing at my futile attempts to salvage the situation.

But I'd allow her to think that. Let her think and report that I was doing my best to fix an impossible situation because I never planned for that to work at all. If I couldn't lead my forces to victory, then all I had to do was weaken the opponent to the point of dysfunction, and I had all the tools I needed to do just that.

CHAPTER SIX

Information and Infiltration

With a solid plan in mind, I just needed to speak with Central's staff to obtain the necessary information about the aliens. I doubted they'd hide that kind of thing from me; it wasn't like it was a secret, or that it would help me beat them in any meaningful way.

Noe, can you contact the site's staff through the Trash Matrix?

"Affirmative," she responded, "Site Manager Jordan has given you access to internal communications. Note that all communications done through the Trash Matrix will be monitored. Who would you like to contact?"

"Just send a message to Jordan. Tell her that I need information about the aspirants of Site 1100."

"Acknowledged."

Jordan got back to me shortly. There was no fuss about getting me that information. In fact, she was almost giddy when she heard my request. Something told me that I was not going to like what I was about to hear.

She sent a weird imp-like creature to my room when she got my permission. The small red creature held a little portable projector and quickly set it up in the corner of my room.

"Good afternoon, Lord Arbiter," he said with a raspy voice. "I am here to answer any and all questions that you may have about the Restus. Any information that Site 1102 has at its disposal will be yours. May I begin with the basic rundown of this race?"

I nodded.

"Excellent!" he exclaimed and pressed a button to turn on the device. "As you can see, the Restus of the Andromeda Galaxy have been chosen for ascension due to their innate strength and brutal society."

I looked at the screen and saw a medical model of the thing they called the Restus. It looked like a strange hybrid of a spider and a lizard. Its entire body was covered in scales like a reptile, but it walked on four hind legs supported by a bulbous back end. Its upper body was massive as well, sporting two pairs of arms that ended in taloned hands. Finally, the face was little more than one massive crocodilian jaw. If the diagram was to be believed, these things were also about nine feet tall on average, and about five feet across.

"This species has been integrated into the trials at roughly the same time as the humans of Earth," the imp continued, "for the glorious Overseer wishes for this upcoming contest to be as fair as it can be. No race will be advantaged based on time spent in the ascension process."

A few more images played of the Restus fighting in the first three trials, and let's just say that "savage" wouldn't even begin to describe their abilities. Fair my fucking ass. How the hell would any normal human go up against that monstrosity? The fact that the Trash Matrix beefed them up further only made the situation worse.

The imp clicked a button, and a new picture appeared. This time it was an aerial view of the city that they inhabited.

"These aspirants are in Site 1100's Quietus city and equal the number of aspirants here." The picture zoomed out, and I could see where this place was relative to Pandora. "Quietus is quite close to Pandora, and if my conversions are correct, it is about 15,240 Earth kilometers away."

I wouldn't call that kind of distance close, but then again, we were talking about multidimensional beings who traveled between existences. 15k kilometers was probably a step or two away for them.

"The location for the upcoming clan war will be at a neutral location chosen by both site managers, subject to change by the Overseer."

Translation: We'd get the absolute worst terrain possible.

"As will the weather conditions during the battle and the method in which the war is waged."

Translation: The weather will be horrible for humans, and the way we get to fight would be even worse.

"The Restus are well known for their capabilities in melee combat and immense endurance and tenacity," the imp stated, "but they lack support roles like medics, healers, and magic users. I am sure that the Lord Arbiter can make use of this crippling weakness to your advantage."

I could almost hear the snide chuckle in the stupid thing's voice when he said that. We could exploit a weakness like that? My ass. What use was a medic or healer when we'd struggle to even harm them?

"Additionally, their scales provide them an unparalleled level of defense for such an early-stage aspirant, and their race is inherently immune to magic as well as extreme changes in temperatures and pressures, but I am sure that this will prove to be a negligible issue for the mighty Lord Arbiter."

Now the shit-eating grin was starting to surface on the imp's face. He knew full well how unfair this matchup was.

He continued. "Lastly, their talons are coated with a deadly neurotoxin that can prove fatal for even the strongest early-stage aspirant, but I am sure that your humans can simply dodge these attacks. Easily done under your tutelage, just like how you can easily overcome the fact that the Restus can fight for upwards of seven Earth weeks without rest."

"I see."

"Now, those are just the characteristics of the base, unascended Restus, so it makes sense why they seem so feeble for you," the imp explained with an even bigger grin. He was clearly enjoying this. "Shall I explain what the Origin Matrix has bestowed about this race in the three trials that they have completed?"

I forced my expression to remain neutral and nodded. The imp continued to speak for a while longer, but to summarize, the human species was well and truly fucked. The Restus were quicker, stronger, more durable, more cunning, and altogether more of everything when compared to their human counterparts. The Trash Matrix enhanced their already formidable abilities and all but eliminated their preexisting weaknesses. I could have all the resources in Central and I still wouldn't be able to claim a victory for the humans.

"I have summarized all of the information about the Restus into this booklet," the imp said once he was done. "I am sure that you will use this information wisely when devising your training regime. I look forward to seeing the tremendous growth of the Pandora aspirants!"

"You're dismissed," I said dryly as I took the offered book. "And I'll be sure to do just that."

He waved goodbye. "Take care, Lord Arbiter, and all of Site 1102 wishes you the best of luck!"

I'd still be the one who got the last laugh. There was one good thing about the situation despite the disheartening news about the foe we would have to fight soon. I was now confident that all of my requests would be met with little resistance. For one, they'd clearly been trying to show how supportive they were to my cause for everyone, like the sponsors, to see, and it wasn't like aiding me would pose even the remotest of risks on their end.

I had feared that they would try to sneakily sabotage my efforts in secret, but after seeing the imp, I didn't have those fears any longer. They were so sure that they would win that there was no need for subterfuge or the risks associated. As long as I didn't ask for anything unreasonable, I was sure to get it. They had no reason to do otherwise because the conclusion was already certain. That would be to their detriment.

I got the most important piece of information out of that exchange: the location of the Restus. I still had a few hours of my preview ticket left, so getting to the enemy was as easy as a swipe of my feelers. All that was left for me to do was find a suitable corpse so that my impromptu visit to Site 1100 went unnoticed. I guess it was time for Dr. Walter to make his appearance tonight. I doubted Central would care what I did with my own aspirants.

It took two more hours before the doppelganger came back. In that time, I had finally washed up and even enjoyed one of the director's cookies. I didn't know what she put in them, but they perked me right up after having one.

"Lord Arbiter!" my clone greeted. "It is good to see you again! I am happy to inform you that I have successfully integrated with your friends! They suspect nothing!"

Huh. I'd thought Q's creation would act differently, but he seemed the same as before. How odd.

"That's good . . ." I said. "Why are you so cheerful?"

"Why would I not be, Lord Arbiter?" he asked with a tilt of his head. "I have performed my task perfectly. Is that not a cause for happiness?"

"No, you did good there," I answered. "But what about Q?"

"I'm sorry," he said, clearly confused. "What do you mean?"

"You know, the old admin?"

"Ah, I apologize," he stated with that same smile, "but that must have been before my time. I was not created before Administrator Jordan took charge."

Oh . . . I could guess what kinds of modifications the Overseer made to the poor clone. I mean, I still hated the thing with all my heart, but not even I would want it to forget its own creator. I could see what Xalla meant by destroying Q's legacy.

"Never mind," I said quickly. "Tell me what happened when you took over."

"Nothing much to report, Lord Arbiter," he said. "We had food as a group after your marvelous announcement, and the guild engaged in what the humans call small talk. This strange method of communication is quite entertaining."

"And they didn't suspect a thing about you being a fake?"

"Not at all, my lord," he answered with a bright smile. "I have studied every instance of the Aspirant Walter and his interactions with his peers, and I am able to mimic them with 99.98% accuracy. All inaccuracies can be explained away due to the human body's natural tendency to fluctuate its use of neurochemical hormones."

"That's great to hear," I said, "But I can take over for now. I'll call for you once I need you again. And . . . good job. Your creator would be proud."

He brightened up immediately. "Thank you! I am sure the Overseer would be most happy about my performance!"

I winced at his response but recovered quickly. "Good. You're dismissed."

I stepped back, but he didn't burst into a puddle this time. He simply . . . vanished. Another improvement from his old self, but not one that I could be happy about. At least they didn't mess with his stupidly optimistic personality. It was the only reminder of Q left.

I waited until it was dark out before making my move. I sent a quick message to the regressor, informing him of my departure. The next thing I had to do was ensure that I had a suitable replacement for the Central side of things, which meant that I needed to find a body for the director to inhabit. That shouldn't be too hard, but just to make sure that I didn't screw up, I called for Molly to help out. She should know what to look for much better than I ever could. Of course, Alice and Toby had insisted on coming along to play as well, and I didn't have the heart to deny them that.

With their help, I was ready to go out in that cold night and start the next portion of my plans. It was time to find a body for the director.

CHAPTER SEVEN

Reminiscing with the Director

I bent forward and cracked my back as I felt the rest of my body ache from sprinting around Pandora like a madman trying to keep up with Molly as she raced to find a suitable body for the director to host. And that was in my enhanced doctor form. I had never felt so exhausted in a very long time!

"Perhaps you should exercise more," Molly said with a small shake of her translucent head. "You seem out of shape."

"Ugh . . ." I muttered. "Look, I'm not used to chasing dozens of patients a day, and the hospital's courtyard's a lot smaller than this place."

I looked over and saw that the two kids were still happily playing with the captured aspirants. They were completely lost in their own world. I had no idea how they still had so much energy left in them. They had been moving around way more than I had tonight.

"Don't compare yourself with those two," Molly added when she saw my gaze. "They're children, and it's the most fun both of them had in a long time. They'll be hyper even when we return home."

I agreed. I had no idea where kids got all their energy from.

"Anyway, we have a few useable bodies here," the doll continued. She had picked out a few individuals that matched my descriptions and placed them side by side. "I think the first one's still the most suitable."

I glanced at the body of a middle-aged aspirant. He had turned a strange shade of magenta ever since Molly's curse hit him, and I was a little dubious about his condition even if he was physically fine.

"He's purple," I stated.

"It'll wear off," she muttered, although she didn't sound convinced. "He won't stay that shade . . . probably. Look, you're planning to dress him up after anyway, so it's fine."

"Say," I asked as another thought passed through me, "do you think the invaders will notice you three helping me out?"

Molly chuckled. "You just thought of that now?"

I shrugged. To be fair, I was preoccupied with trying to find a way out of the hot mess the Overseer landed me in.

"But we are fine," she continued. "We're using the same method that the director provided for you to escape the eyes of their monitoring system. Unless there are physical eyes on us right now, we are safe, and I'd notice if someone's spying on us."

I thanked the doll.

"Are you planning to use the body or not, doctor?"

"Right, let's do it."

I took off the pendant on my neck and made a small incision on my thumb, dripping the blood onto the gem. The blue gemstone turned red almost immediately as it sucked in the liquid, even emitting a faint glow before it turned back to normal. I took that as a sign that it was ready to use. Remembering what the director's letter told me, I also took out one of the paper charms and a lighter.

"Do I just put it on him?" I asked.

"Yes," Molly replied. "Then make sure you light the charm immediately."

I nodded and did as I was told. I also undid my transformation quickly and used Noe to take off my guise. I just hoped that I could use the Absolute Luck skill to put it back on the corpse afterward, although Noe did say that it could be done.

I was expecting an entrance similar to the one that the director made when I first met her, but that wasn't what happened. The corpse simply opened its eyes. Well, maybe its "eyes" was the wrong description, because, disturbingly, it now sported the same orbs that Abigail did. It thankfully didn't last long, and the browns of the body's irises came back as it started to get up, stumbling as it moved. I gave the director some time to get used to the new body.

"It's still purple," I pointed out.

"It doesn't matter," the doll muttered. "Just put the stupid skin suit on it."

"Abaahg," the corpse slurred. "Gaveg meah aah mmoment."

"Uh, hi, Abigail," I said, waving at the wiggling purple corpse. "Take your time. Let me just get the body ready."

And true to Noe's words, I managed to suit up the dead man with apparent ease, the whole process only taking two luck charges. Once Noe was done, the once-purple corpse looked like the spitting image of my new form. Even the height was about right.

"Ugh," the body complained. It was disconcerting hearing the director's feminine voice coming out of the body of a middle-aged man. "That was unpleasant. We must be really far away if just transferring to a body took that long."

"I warned you that it would be rough," Molly said.

"Yes, yes, Molly, you did." Abigail sighed. "Sometimes I swear you still treat me like a child."

The doll rolled her eyes. "Even your mother's a child in my eyes, Abby."

The director blushed, which was a very horrible look with her current appearance.

"Anyway, hello again." I waved before I transformed once more into the form she was more familiar with. "You might want to change your voice. You can do that, right?"

"Hello to you too, Dr. Walter," she replied. "I would hug you, but I think that wouldn't be a pleasant experience for either of us."

I nodded quickly.

"And yes, I can," she continued. "Can I hear a sample of what I should sound like?"

Noe, change my voice to what I sounded like at the speech.

"Affirmative, my host."

"It sounds like this," I started.

The director nodded. "Good, please continue speaking. I'll need a little time processing the intonations."

I took that time to get the director caught up on my current situation but omitted some of the more problematic information. The main point I told her was that I had managed to infiltrate a position of power in one of the invader's side branches and that I had practically free rein over this area.

"How did you manage that?" the director exclaimed. This time her voice sounded exactly like the samples I gave her.

"Luck," I said truthfully. "And a lot of planning, but I can tell you all that later. We don't have a lot of time."

She agreed. "What do you need me to do here? Like I said, you have my full cooperation, Will."

"I'll need to be away from this location for a while," I answered. "And I need you to stand in for me while I'm gone. Like I said, I've managed to infiltrate a position of power, but only locally. This place represents a tiny fraction of the invader's might, but we can use this opportunity to learn more about our foes. I'll explain my tasks here, and the rules that you need to follow."

The director nodded; it seemed like explaining everything in terms of rules and responsibilities worked best with the natives of the hospital. I think everything in their lives revolved around those facts.

"All right," she said, "explain everything to the best of your ability. It's not my first time working behind enemy lines, so you can trust me to take over."

I went through all the relevant information about the trials, what I had to do to prepare these patients for the future, and how she had full access to the resources of this place. It was helpful that all the staff had changed and no one knew me personally anymore. As long as the director focused on the tasks that she needed to do and I regularly burned a few charms, no one should be the wiser that I wasn't around.

Plus, I really did have no idea just what resources were available to me, nor did I know how to train aspirants. The director would have a lot more experience with things like that after running Hope's Memorial for so long. She was perfect for the job!

"I see . . ." Abigail mumbled. "That's quite the predicament that you've gotten yourself into, Will. I can see that you're still chronically unable to get out of trouble, but I'll help."

"Can you maintain your activities here for that long?" I asked. I hadn't even considered her situation. What if she had to go back to the hospital after a while?

Abigail just laughed. "It's controlling one body, Will, even if it's across a vast distance. I'm already controlling a multitude of proxy forms. Do you really think one extra will strain me at all?"

Right . . . she was a god.

"Okay, that's dumb of me," I admitted.

"You are cute when you're flustered." She giggled. "But you can trust me with this. I'll invest more of my attention here just in case, and I see that you have my daughter and her friends as support as well."

The two gave her a quick wave before turning back to whatever it was that they were doing.

"Anyway," I said, changing the subject, "your duties shouldn't take that long. You can use the rest of the time to look around the site. Find any information that you think will be useful, but be careful. If you think your disguise will fail, let me know immediately through Molly. I'll come back then."

"That shouldn't happen. Your new role should be easy enough to implement without error," she answered. "But you have my promise to do that if needed. Should I get started now?"

"Thank you," I said. "And yes, start by familiarizing yourself with this place. You'll be working here for the foreseeable future. No one should impede your progress, either. I'll go back and make a detailed report about all the information you'll need to know."

Abigail nodded. "You can hand that over to Molly. She'll send it to me."

"She can do that?" I asked, glancing over to the faint afterimage of the doll. How was she supposed to pick up some paper?

"I can," the doll answered. "At least for small objects."

I shrugged. I wasn't going to argue about the logic behind that.

The director and I chatted a little longer before we parted. Alice and Toby left shortly after, while Molly made sure to clean up after their mess. She assured me that no one from the invader's side would find out about their presence here tonight. I had precious little time to work with, especially if I wanted to maximize my chances against the Restus, so I didn't detour around on my way back to the regressor's guild.

I spent the rest of the night writing down all the things that I could think of that would be relevant to the director and gave the resulting manuscript to Molly, although truth be told, it wasn't all that much. True to her word, she was able to take the bundle of paper in the same way that she was able to get rid of the corpses from earlier. Wonder how that ability worked.

There was one final thing to do before I could safely leave Pandora, and that was instructing my doppelganger.

Noe, help me contact the fake Walter.

"Understood."

The clone appeared almost immediately, standing at attention.

"I am at your command, my lord!" he said with his usual cheer. "What do you need of me?"

"I've studied up on the foe that the aspirants must face in the near future," I started. "And have come to the conclusion that I must spend the remaining time acting as an arbiter. I don't have time to play with the aspirants now."

His eyes widened, already anticipating what was to come.

I nodded. "Yes, that means that you are to assume the role of Walter for the time being, and you may have to do so for an extended period of time. Are you up for the task?"

He nodded, his head almost falling off while doing so. "Yes, my Lord Arbiter W! I shall not fail you! I will rewatch all of your files for the fifteenth time and make sure that your expectations are met—no, exceeded! You can count on me, sir!"

"Good," I said. "You are to begin right away. Contact me through the Origin Matrix if you encounter any problems."

"Yes, sir!"

"You are dismissed."

"Thank you, sir!" And with that, he vanished again.

I sighed. It was still weird seeing the doppelganger retain his old cheer even with the absence of Q. But there was nothing I could do about that now.

After double-checking to make sure that I had finished all the prep work needed, I used some of the remaining time from my saved preview ticket and ripped a hole in reality to a location close to the Restus' base. I canceled the skill quickly, conserving as much of the precious time left as possible, and got ready for what I had to do here.

CHAPTER EIGHT

Seeds of Sabotage

Once that was done, I could focus all my attention on screwing over the Restus. But there was a problem. I hovered around the outskirts of the city, still trying to wrap my brain around a feasible plan. My initial idea was to sneak into the place and observe the people. It was my standard approach for situations like this, but I had forgotten one crucial issue: The inhabitants of the city were lizard-spider things. How the hell could I blend in?

I had no stealth skills, I couldn't transform into one of those things either, and I couldn't exactly use Noe's Absolute Luck constantly to evade notice. Sure, I had over 1,500 luck charges, but would I bet my life on it lasting the whole time I was inside the city? No. Which meant that I was severely limited in options.

Okay, no worries, Walter, let's assess what tools I do have at my disposal.

The first no-brainer was Noe's Absolute Luck, although it was too nebulous to count on when planning ahead. I didn't have six years to hear Noe's explanation and grasp the nuance of its use. Next was the new system skill. This was really useful for when I had already infiltrated the city, but next to worthless prior to that. That left me with the handful of titles that I had.

I thought for a moment before frowning. The secondary titles were useless, but how had I forgotten about the main skill at my disposal?

Noe, show me my first soul title again.

"Acknowledged, my host."

Primary Soul Title: Level 11 Popular Xollon Idol [Devourer of Truth]

Progress to next level: 108,877/1,000,000
Progression requirements: Have 1,000,000 individuals idolize you.

Title Passives:
Xollon Anatomy Stage 2: Your body has begun to incorporate more of a Xollon's internal anatomy. Your Xollon mind will filter out all minor mental pollutants. You take 10% reduced damage from all sources and are unaffected by most poisons.
Xollon Physiology Stage 1: Your body has started to incorporate a Xollon's external anatomy. You can utilize and extend your primary feelers through your human hands.

Title Skills:
Idol's Voice (Soul Passive)
Secondary Xollon Form (Level 11 Soul Active): The user assumes the secondary form of the Xolloid race. The user gains all the physical characteristics of the race and will have all physical attributes increase by a factor of 5 for the duration of the skill.

What the . . . I was a popular Xollon idol now? When did that happen?

"Shortly after you finished your speech, my host, your soul title underwent a quantitative change after advancing past level ten and will do so again once it passes level twenty," Noe answered. "I apologize for not notifying you earlier."

I frowned. Noe had never failed to inform me of such important things before, unless you counted her stint in that weird darkness dimension. I would think having my soul title literally evolve would constitute an important thing.

"I will ensure that such an error does not happen again," she said with a hint of remorse in her voice.

Hey, no worries. We all forget sometimes.

"Thank you for understanding."

I returned my attention to the information presented. The immunity to mental pollution was a nice touch. I'd been dealing with a lot of that, and Noe had to burden herself with addressing that, so it was nice knowing I had a natural way of counteracting it. What was most surprising was the cooldown for my skill. There wasn't one.

Does that mean that I can just use the skill whenever I want, like my doctor title?

"That is indeed the case, my host."

I smiled. Now this gave me more flexibility to work with. Just to make sure that what I planned could work, I took out the information package that the stupid imp gave me previously and reviewed the information.

I nodded to myself. I was right. The Restus had had dealings with sponsors of their own, and had a rigid belief system already in place. Better yet, their deities didn't necessarily look like their species. I could work with that.

All right, Noe, it's time to start this show. Activate my soul title's active.

"Acknowledged, my host."

My body transformed into the familiar form of the Xollon, although much diminished from the real thing. Still, I had all the needed physical characteristics for my plan to work. Now the only issue was infiltrating the city without being spotted.

I recalled that I could burrow my tentacles into the earth, and I was practically just a mass of tentacles in my current form. I didn't see why I couldn't just dig underground like some kind of horrible eldritch worm, and it wasn't like I had eyes to worry about to see things.

I tested my theory and found out that the Xollon form was remarkably adept at burrowing. I was able to easily swim through the dirt as my frills pushed away all but the largest rocks. The large ones I couldn't shove were destroyed by my maw, and navigating underground was as easy as walking. I could still perceive all of my surroundings through the superior senses of a Xollon.

According to the information package, the Restus were nocturnal. With the sun out in full swing, the streets of their city were already starting to empty out. There were still a few late-night, uh, I mean late-morning goers, but finding a quiet spot to unburrow wasn't too difficult. However, since no one seemed to notice my presence below the surface (and I'll be honest, the cool dirt was kind of soothing), I decided to take the time to scout out these new aspirants.

After hours of digging around, I had to stop myself in fear that I would cause the city to collapse from all the tunnels I had created. I had learned quite a lot about the race that was to be our enemy.

For one, their society was brutal. I had seen the weaker members of their race tortured and beaten by the ruling few for what seemed like minor infractions. Then again, I hadn't bothered reading the eighty-four-page report on Restus social norms that the imp gave me, but I was fairly sure that they were minor mistakes after consulting Noe.

Yet remarkably, those beat-up Restus would all invariably recover quickly before going around to beat up someone they thought was weaker than they were, and this trend continued until I found the group deemed to be at the bottom of the food chain. These Restus were downtrodden and had even less hope in their eyes than even the worst B Group aspirant from back home.

They had given up all hope and were regularly abused by those who passed by them, although they were ignored for the most part. These were the true social pariahs of the Restus. I thought about it for a moment but ultimately decided to skip this group. I liked to work from the bottom up, to prop up an underdog, but even I couldn't do much with this bunch.

Instead, I moved up the food chain until I came across one particular group that was not so far down the power structure that they had completely given up hope. If I had learned one thing about this race, it was that they valued power above all else. They would do anything to rise in status, to feel that euphoria of besting one of their own. This was a perfectly exploitable weakness.

Now to wait for my opportunity to strike. I remained underground, keeping track of each member of the group I wanted, and waited for the moment when one of them would inevitably do something foolish to someone stronger than they were. I didn't have to wait long. I saw one of the Restus approach another of its species with hatred in its eyes.

The being it confronted chuckled when it saw the other Restus stomp over. "You've come to get beaten again, Bakren?"

The Restus known as Bakren snarled. "What did you do to my spear? It is my property won from the proving grounds!"

The other Restus laughed again and took out a pile of broken metal from his inventory. "You mean this? I thought it was garbage."

Bakren howled. "You go too far, Maar! There is no honor in breaking a warrior's weapon!"

The other Restus barked in amusement. "That's a good laugh, to think you would consider yourself a warrior. You're barely fit to fight even the Broken, let alone a true opponent."

Bakren lunged at the bigger Restus, his claws flashing with venom. The other being didn't even bother trying to dodge and just allowed the other creature's claws to rake across his scaled chest. The wound was massive, but it closed up almost immediately.

"Ah, that was nice," Maar said with a sigh. "Mind scratching my back for me as well? I have a hard time reaching back there."

The first Restus continued his assault, using wide swings that would have destroyed boulders and uprooted trees, all the while the other being remained stock-still. Maar didn't even budge from his spot, his taloned feet having dug deep into the earth.

Maar sighed. "Now this is just embarrassing, even for you."

Bakren shouted incomprehensibly again but was cut short when a casual swing from Maar sent him flying across the street. He slammed into a nearby building with an explosion of force. Whatever the city was built of here was damn sturdy, because I couldn't even see a dent in the structure.

The first Restus struggled to get up. One of his many arms was bent at a strange angle and his chest was all but caved in. Yet he was still alive. I had seen others like him take much more damage.

The other figure sauntered leisurely toward the fallen foe, laughing all the while. He picked up one of the broken pieces of the destroyed spear and stabbed it into the other's arm, pinning him in place. Yet despite the considerable amount of pain that Bakren was experiencing, the Restus never begged for mercy. No wonder the Overseer chose this species to pair against us. If even the weakest members of their race were like this, then I dreaded seeing how the elite stacked up.

The one known as Maar spent the next fifteen minutes just pounding the other man into paste, but eventually, he stopped, evidently from boredom more than anything else. He threw the fragments of the spear in Bakren's face before spitting on his battered body. He never broke a sweat in that entire exchange.

"You're free to come back anytime, little 'warrior,'" Maar mocked. "I'll be glad to obliterate you again. You lose a few more times and maybe you'll join the other Broken! Bakren the Broken, it's a fitting title! Your losses are adding up."

Bakren looked up but didn't respond, mainly because his jaw had been dislocated and he physically couldn't speak at the moment. It wasn't until almost an hour passed before he had recovered enough to move about, and a few more after that to stand on his hind limbs again.

He was defeated, still broken, and resentful. Everything about his body language screamed rage and hatred. Now it was time for me to make my entrance. He was already so emotionally amped that it would only take a subtle nudge to do what I needed.

I unborrowed and made my presence known.

Noe, activate my new skill to maximum capacity.

"Acknowledged, my host."

The creature noticed my approach immediately and made a feeble attempt to defend himself. He was obviously unsure what this strange tentacle being was, and I made sure that Noe was amplifying his sense of unease. He started to back off subconsciously as I made my way closer and closer to him. Noe was ensuring that every fiber of his being told him that I was to be feared, to be respected, to be worshiped.

I walked slowly toward the still-battered Restus and turned those emotions up to eleven before speaking softly. "Hello, Bakren, I have a deal that I would like to offer you. Would you like to hear it?"

CHAPTER NINE

The First Recruit

The Restus's jaws clamped shut. The imp did say that this species was inherently slow to trust, being a race that focused almost all of its attention on fighting and improving oneself. They had pitifully few things that a human would call leisure activities, let alone the concept of doing something just for fun and pleasure. Even worse, friendships, at least in the way that we knew it, were practically nonexistent.

Once again, these were traits that I could use against them. Just because the Restus didn't focus their attention and time on things like fun or pleasure didn't mean it didn't exist for them. It was just on the back burner, generally forgotten about. I'd just have to introduce to them a little human sin. See, if they had no real idea of pleasure, then what would happen if I introduced that concept at an extreme level? How would their anatomy deal with that? That was something I looked forward to experimenting with.

But not for this individual. This Restus I needed to spread my influence to the others, but in a subtle way that wouldn't catch the attention of the admin staff stationed here. Good thing the Restus were inherently distrustful of others. I doubted they would willingly share much of anything with each other, much less something that benefitted them directly. Between Noe and my stack of charms, I had little to worry about as long as I was cautious.

Still, the being before me looked like it was about to attack at a moment's notice, despite its battered and abused body. I needed to fix that first.

Noe, ramp up the fear.

"Acknowledged."

> **Luck Charges:** 1,501/1,577

Bakren's pupils dilated completely, and its gaze was unable to meet my body now. It all but collapsed upon itself when I was within touching distance; I noticed that its scales were quivering rapidly, making a pleasant chiming sound as they rattled on.

I used a feeler to force its head up. It twitched on contact and forced him to look at me. "What happened to the brave warrior from before? Surely you're not so feeble that you can't even address me?"

That remark clearly angered the being, but Noe's grip on his emotions was absolute. The fear in his body was so strong that all other emotions were quickly overridden.

"You're weak," I said with a sigh. "Let's make it so that you can actually speak."

All right, Noe, ease up a bit, just enough so he can talk. Can't have him catatonic before I get anything useful out of him.

"Acknowledged, my host. Switching fear to dread."

The all-consuming panic started to fade from Bakren, but a new emotion quickly filled its place. His eyes darted back and forth, and I could tell that he wished for nothing than to escape this situation. Yet he also knew that he couldn't. Damn, I'll have to hand it to my system, but her new skill was worth its weight in gold. Even with this extreme level of manipulation, I'd only used up a few dozen luck charges.

"W—" Bakren tried to say, but something caught in his throat. He took a moment to compose himself. "What are you? What do you want?"

"You should know that without me saying anything, Bakren," I answered. "Look at me again."

Okay, Noe, now it's time for some awe and splendor. Make it so he's feeling like he's looking at a god, or whatever equivalent this species has to one.

"It shall be done."

He gasped. "But . . ."

I shook my frills. "But what, Bakren?"

"Why me?" he asked, still fumbling on the ground.

Good, he was already fully bought into the scenario that I planned. Now for a little experimentation. I could go about this a few ways, but what I really wanted from this first Restus was to see just how far Noe's skill could go. Emotions were a vague concept, almost impossible to fully quantify in the conventional sense, at least. I wanted to see just how far I could go with it.

Noe, what would happen if I used my skill to make him feel like he was unstoppable?

"Then his confidence in himself will drastically improve," she answered. "This will have some advantageous effects on his actual performance, but to a limited extent."

But it will help, right?

"Correct, my host," she answered. "Belief in oneself is a large part of unlocking a being's true potential. I can make this individual perform at peak capacity at all times."

So, what will happen if I amplify that feeling to the absolute max?

"It will not be good for the creature if you do that, my host."

Explain.

"Most organisms have safeguards in place to prevent self-harm," she explained. "Like a human's brain preventing its muscles from breaking through extreme exertion. However, if you maximize the effects of the Emotional Redux skill in the way that the host has stated, then the organism that you target will bypass those safeguards. Short term, it will cause damage to the body; long term, it will cause death."

I smiled. That certainly wasn't a concern of mine!

"Do you want to feel strong?" I asked the fallen Restus again. "Do you want to dominate Maar? Do you want to wash away the humiliation that you have suffered?"

I needed a guinea pig first to test out my plan. Just how much stronger would they be if they completely disregarded their body's health? Given how much injury they could endure and heal, I was willing to bet a lot. I couldn't imagine how much more power one of the Restus could acquire if they used all that energy needed to heal from their wounds and completely dedicated that to offense.

Bakren slowly nodded.

Noe, do what you need to!

"Acknowledged, my host," she answered, and I saw the look of pure euphoria sublimate onto the Restus's face. "But I must warn you, dear Walter, this particular specimen will not be strong enough to face his desired foe, even with your tinkering."

I frowned. *Damn, there goes my first plan, then. Gotta think of something else to salvage this situation.*

"But," Noe continued, "I may have a solution to this predicament, my host."

You do?

I honestly couldn't think of anything that I had at my disposal that could help make some random alien species stronger immediately, but who was I to argue with an all-powerful system?

"Yes, my host," she explained. "If you feed the being known as Bakren a piece of the cookie that the director baked for you, it will help elevate him to tremendous levels of power."

A . . . cookie? How's that going to do anything?

"Not the entire thing," she added, "just a piece."

And that will somehow make him super strong?

"Correct."

But I ate quite a few of them before, it didn't do anything for me then. Are Abigail's cookies some kind of Restus performance-enhancing drug? What's even in those things?

"I do not know the exact makeup of the cookie, my host, but I do know that it has beneficial effects on biological organisms," she said with a gloomy cadence, "but I have analyzed that it will have an exaggerated positive, short-term effect on the Restus species if you allow it to consume a small portion of the snack."

I guess I'll give it a try. Pity it didn't do anything major for me.

That playful tone was back as Noe answered, "Yes, my host, it is a pity. But it means that it is safe to consume more cookies in the future. Unit Noe recommends that you do so."

All right . . .

I looked back at the Restus and saw that it was staring off into space, its mouth open, and it was drooling. It was chuckling at seemingly nothing every now and then, and he had the look of pure ecstasy.

Noe, what the hell did you do to him?

"I have stimulated every positive neuron and reward center in his brain at maximum efficiency," she explained. "He is currently experiencing euphoria that is impossible to achieve without my assistance. I would suggest the host limit the time this individual stays in this state to avoid permanent neurological damage."

All right . . . that sounded kind of messed up, honestly. I didn't know how much damage screwing around with all his brain chemistry would do, but it couldn't be good. I used this opportunity to take out a cookie from my inventory and break off a small chunk of it. Just to be sure, I poked the delicious snack with a feeler, but I still couldn't see how it was different from the regular stuff I used to eat back on Earth.

I shrugged. Noe had never done me wrong so far.

I chucked the piece into the drooling idiot's mouth, and he swallowed it on instinct. Then I waited . . . and waited . . . was something supposed to happen?

Is it . . . is it working?

"Affirmative, my host," Noe assured. "You shall see the results when he confronts the other Restus again."

Well, it wasn't like I really cared if Bakren got beaten up again if Noe was wrong. Worse case, I'd just wasted a few hours of my time and I'd have to find another pawn to use. I still had *some* time to spare.

Okay, Noe, ease up on the acid trip and let me talk to him again.

"Acknowledged."

The spaced-out look in the Restus's eyes faded slowly as he came back down to earth. He looked around as if he didn't know where he was before his eyes fell on me again. There was a look of desperate need in that gaze. Holy shit, he was already hooked.

"Power is never free," I said when his attention was focused. "And I can take it away just as easily, little Restus."

Noe, amplify melancholy and lethargy to the extreme.

Panic filled Bakren's eyes as he felt his body shrivel up from intense exhaustion. His body slackened and he fell onto the floor, too tired to even move. After experiencing the most extremes of positive emotions possible, it must have been a real shocker to go to the exact opposite. I think I made my point.

All right, ease up on that now.

"Do you understand?" I asked, gesturing for him to get on his feet again.

"Yes!" he said immediately. "Please, don't do that again! I never wish to feel like that again! Please give t-the power! Just for a while! I can do anything that you ask for."

Whoa, how'd he turn into a junkie this quickly? Either the Restus were really susceptible to addiction or Noe's skill was too effective.

"There are other members of your . . ." I paused, looking for the right word to use. "Caste, correct?"

He nodded quickly. "There are fifteen others who share my status, yes!"

Hm, fifteen other Restus. That was a number I could work with. Any more and I risked running out of luck charges before they could regenerate.

I continued. "Good, and does your group have a private home or area to rest?"

"It is small and near the outskirts, but yes, we have a training hall," he said again, all but slurring his words now. "Y-you can have it! And with this power, I can get you better territory! Yes, with this power, I can get anything!"

"Take me to your training hall. Let me meet with your peers. You alone cannot hope to accomplish all that I require, and for your services, I shall allow you to lead them into glory."

"Yes! Anything you want! Please, let me feel that power again!"

All right, Noe, give the junkie his fix.

Bakren's whole demeanor changed once Noe's skill took effect. His back straightened instantly, and he let out an all-consuming roar but quickly stopped himself from doing anything else when he saw my displeasure.

"Will you . . ." he slurred. "Will you go there now? Your presence will be seen by others, and they will also covet the strength you provide."

I shook my frills. "I will follow from below. Go to your training hall and inform your peers that I will be arriving soon. Show them the might you have inherited and let them know how blessed they are that I have descended."

At the prospect of showing off his might, Bakren's grin grew wide with pleasure. He agreed immediately and ran off. I guess showing proper etiquette was a foreign concept for this race, even toward someone they deemed vastly superior to themselves. Bakren didn't even bother asking me for my name. It would take a while for me to get used to how these species interacted socially.

For now, I burrowed my body and followed silently behind my first pawn. There was still a lot of work ahead of me.

CHAPTER TEN

Start of a New Faction

I watched from below the earth as the Restus ran back to his hovel. As he'd said, the training hall was small and dilapidated, as was fitting with his position in the Restus society. It was scarcely more than just some mud walls and clay huts, with a large, open central area for what I could only guess was fights. The whole place looked like it had seen better days, although now that I think about it, the entirety of the Restus' city looked to be in a lot worse shape than Pandora. I wasn't sure if that was because the Restus simply didn't need fancy facilities like the humans did or if it was due to how resources were allocated between various training sites and its aspirants. The Overseer did say that the Restus were lackluster, so perhaps they just had less funding than the humans did.

Either way, that wasn't really an important question to answer. I turned my attention back to my new peon, curious to see what he'd do. It was well past midday now, so Bakren had to enter each hut and all but kick the others up.

"Brethren!" he screamed. "Awaken! I bring great news!"

The Restus started to wake up one by one, and none of them were happy to have been disturbed. I couldn't for the life of me tell the difference between each of these inferior life-forms, they all looked like scaly lumps to me, but one of the other ones got up and confronted Bakren.

"What are you . . ." The other Restus paused, looking confused. "What happened to your body?"

Bakren laughed. "I am strong now! I am a warrior chosen by the Outer Ones! Gone are the days that I will allow others to defeat me in battle, for I am now powerful!"

The others looked at him dubiously. I couldn't blame them. If Bakren was as idiotic as he showed me earlier, then it was no wonder the others didn't hold him in high regard. And to be fair, if I wasn't so constrained with time, I'd have probably gone with a slightly more intelligent minion, but I guess I couldn't be too picky right now.

"You do not believe me," Bakren stated. "That is normal. I shall prove to you that I am chosen! Fight me, all of you, all at once! I issue a challenge!"

"You will die," another Restus said plainly. "We will not go easy if you make it official. This is not like your games with Maar. Please reconsider before it is too late."

He laughed even louder. "I do not change my mind! Do it!"

The other shrugged. "If you say so. At least dying in a formal challenge will be a better end than being Broken."

I was kind of curious about just how much stronger my first minion was. If what he said was right, then the fifteen others here were of about equal strength to Bakren here, and he planned to fight them all at once? Sure, they couldn't physically attack Bakren at the same time, there just wasn't enough room to maneuver, but he still had to be several times stronger than his foe if he wanted to take on these odds.

The Restus group moved to the large central clearing. Bakren stood in the middle, his head held high and his claws poised for violence. The others surrounded him on all sides and looked on with a mixture of curiosity and pity. They didn't think my minion would make it, although to be fair, I didn't think that my minion would make it either. That cookie had to do some massive lifting to carry Bakren out of this mess.

It did more than that.

"Are all challengers ready?" Bakren yelled.

"We are," they shouted as one. "Is Warrior Bakren ready?"

"I am!"

"Then we begin!"

They rushed Bakren all at once. Forget what I said before, they *could* all attack him at once. About half of them jumped into the sky to reach their foe while the other half rushed him from all sides. Bakren was about to be buried in a flurry of Restus.

Yet impossibly, it wasn't the lone fighter who was overwhelmed, it was the fifteen others. Any individual that so much as touched the scales of Bakren was launched backward at an incredible speed. If it wasn't for my enhanced Xollon senses, I wouldn't have even understood what had happened.

Replaying the scene in my cortex, I saw that as the talons of each of the other Restus touched the scales of Bakren, his body started to vibrate at an insane frequency. Those slight vibrations somehow absorbed the force generated by his attackers and reflected most of that kinetic energy back at his foes.

My drugged-up lackey laughed as he saw his enemies flung all across the field. "Weak! It is no wonder our tribe has suffered so much! You are all weak!"

He didn't give his foes any more time to recover as he rocketed toward the nearest fallen Restus. And I mean rocketed. He moved like a lizard-spider-shaped missile and kicked the poor Restus so hard that the other fighter smashed through the outer walls of their hovel. I saw enough to see that Bakren had broken at least four limbs on that assault, and the other fighter's neck was bent at a concerning angle.

Several more of the fighters had recovered enough to mount a counterattack—if you could even call it that. They had forsaken their pride and taken out weapons from their inventory. These were pretty impressive, to be honest. Some of them were glowing with some kind of enchantment effect, while others were clearly made by an expert just from their appearance.

The various spears, war hammers, swords, and the like didn't do the Restus aspirants any good, however. Bakren's scales had become an impenetrable shield that absorbed and deflected every blow that came his way, even shattering some of the larger melee arms that collided with his body. The tiny amount of damage the other fighters were doing healed almost instantly.

My juiced-up minion laughed again, and with a casual wave, he caught a massive longsword by the blade and crushed the metal with his bare hands. He threw the resulting shards into the face of the stunned Restus before kicking him in the stomach, sending the poor individual crashing into one of his comrades. Bakren didn't give those two any time to rest, running forward and stomping on his fallen foes. There was a disturbing sound of crunching bone as his foot met the neck of the first Restus.

Without even showing the slightest bit of concern that he might have accidentally killed one of his comrades, Bakren finished off the other man beside the first and ran toward the nearest combatant. He slammed his claws into the other's abdomen, digging his hands deep into the insides. The poor skewered individual tried his hardest to fight back, but his attacks couldn't even penetrate Bakren's scaly defense.

Without remorse, Bakren ripped off one of the other Restus's arms and ate it before throwing the dying fighter to the ground and stomping on him with so much force that the body split in two. His fighting was getting more and more reckless by the second. It was like something was forcing him to become ever more violent, and everyone else around him seemed to notice as well.

The other contestants looked on with fear and disgust. Bakren had clearly gone too far, even for this warmongering species. Now they didn't even want to continue fighting this monstrosity.

"Stop!" one of the others shouted. "What have you done? This is no longer a challenge between warriors!"

But Bakren didn't agree with their assessment. He charged toward the speaker and tackled him to the ground. The others could only look on in horror as Bakren pulverized the other man's face with punch after punch after punch. He didn't stop until the other Restus was well and truly dead, even biting chunks off the other fighter between his unrelenting assaults. By the time Bakren was done, there was scarcely more than a red puddle where the other fighter's upper body used to be.

Okay . . . I think that's enough of that. Noe, calm that idiot down before he kills all of my future minions.

"Acknowledged."

The life visibly left Bakren's body as he wailed in despair. I'd never heard something so soul-wrenching in my life.

"No! Please, no!" he screamed while the others looked on with fear. "Not again!"

I took that time to pop out of the ground and fling the desperate Restus to the side.

"I said I wanted to meet your fellow Restus," I shouted, "not kill them all!"

Now all of the attention was on me. I think this was the best introduction that I could have possibly had, as everyone was already terrified of me, and I didn't even need to use my skill. I didn't blame them. I was the one responsible for the nightmarish shift in Bakren's personality and physique.

"No! Give it back!" he cried, crawling toward me with a crazed need in his eyes. "Give it back!"

"You dare make demands of me? You!" I spat and pointed at one of the unharmed Restus with a feeler. "Take him away. He is a disgrace! Let him wallow in weakness until he has learned his error."

The Restus didn't question my authority and did what he was told. Bakren was screaming the whole way, but no one dared pay him any heed as he was dragged into one of the empty huts.

"What . . . what are you?" one of the other Restus said once everyone recovered enough to gather before me.

"I am here to help!" I said without really answering the question. "And I am the one responsible for gifting Bakren his newfound strength, yet he has squandered it. He allowed the power to cloud his mind. He is a disgrace!"

The other aspirants looked at each other with questioning gazes, still unsure about my motives, and most importantly, unsure if I meant them harm. But they weren't completely dismissing me just yet. It was a good time to layer on the shock and awe with my new skill.

Do the same thing we did to Bakren to the rest of them, just . . . a little less intense. We don't need these folks going insane like our first guinea pig.

"Acknowledged, my host," Noe answered. "I will endeavor to achieve your desired results. Allow me to modulate the emotions of your pawns."

Thanks, Noe.

Once again, the results of Noe's intervention never failed to amaze me. Where the Restus were once on guard and untrusting, they eased up on their vigilance almost immediately and unconsciously moved closer to me. They weren't ecstasy stricken like Bakren was when I screwed with his brain earlier, but the new Restus were certainly liking whatever Noe was doing.

I felt my maw twitch into a growing grin. "Now, your comrade Bakren was unable to contain my gift, but will the lot of you be any different?"

They all mumbled incomprehensibly at the same time. I couldn't understand what they said over the cacophony of noises, but the message was clear. They wanted in. They wanted what made Bakren so powerful, and the small caveat that they might lose their minds went out the back door thanks to Noe's intervention. I was starting to fully understand just how powerful emotions could be.

But my first experiment did tell me that I had to take things a little easier for the time being. I couldn't have these ten aspirants explode in strength; that'd make my presence too obvious. I couldn't afford to alert the 1100 Admin staff, even if they weren't monitoring this random city as much as Q's staff was for Pandora. These Restus didn't have a Lord Arbiter or an anomaly present, after all.

Thus, while I highly doubted that the dwindling resources of Central could staff physical people to check up on all the aspirant cities, I couldn't afford to be too complacent either. Just because the Trash Matrix couldn't detect my presence didn't mean it couldn't detect a random bunch of its aspirants gaining monstrous power overnight, not to mention what would happen if I caused the city to descend into total chaos. No, I'd have to be a little more subtle with my approach, which meant that my current peons couldn't just lose their minds as Bakren had, but they did need a little motivation.

I addressed the ten Restus once more. "I can offer you strength beyond your comprehension! Bakren has tasted but the smallest drop of what I have to offer, but he has shown that your species is weak!"

Grunts of discontent rose up, but none dared refute what I had to say. They knew that what I spoke was the truth.

"And your minds are too fragile to handle such an influx of power all at once," I continued, "as Bakren has clearly demonstrated. But I have not completely given up on you."

Their eyes went wide with anticipation. They looked like nice little pets waiting for a juicy treat, a fitting way for an inferior species to behave when faced with a Xollon.

"But you will have to earn it," I said again as my gaze fell on each individual Restus. "You will have to prove to me that you are not a lost cause, for your first impressions have been dismal."

"Yes!" one of them said finally. I think it was the same individual who took Bakren away. I'd have to try to remember who was who eventually . . .

"We can prove to you that we are better than Bakren!" another added. "He has always been the most stone-brained amongst us!"

I nodded. "Good, then I will gift you the tiniest amount of might."

Noe, let 'em feel invincible now. We're going to need a few more minions.

CHAPTER ELEVEN

Growing the Faction

Five days had passed since my arrival at the Restus' hometown, and I had made quite a bit of progress. As expected, the admin of the site had made an announcement that night, and I was able to stalk—er, I mean follow the strongest bunch of aspirants and chat with him in private. Let's just say that they would be more than cooperative with me from now on and were more than happy to do what I instructed. It would still be a few weeks before I saw the results of those instructions, but I had my hopes up.

In that time, I had also made frequent stops back to Pandora to continue my operations as Dr. Walter. News of a new horror stalking the night had just started to become widespread, and I could tell that there was a lot of pressure on Ryan's guild to do something about it. It also didn't help that a lot of the aspirants who were casualties of my activities were associated with him in one way or another. It'll only be a matter of time before he comes up with a strategy against me.

My other Restus lackeys were busy spreading their influence as well, and I had gathered quite a following of believers. I think I'd converted close to 10% of the entire Restus population at that point, and it would only be a matter of time before more fell into my influence. The only trouble was keeping my new cult of idiots quiet so that they wouldn't alert anyone important.

I was just about to check up on all the minions running about when Molly appeared before me.

"We have trouble, doctor," she said before giving me a strange look. "And . . . never mind. I've grown used to your strange forms."

Right, I'd been a Xollon for so long that I'd forgotten all about it.

She nodded. "Still, it's good to know what you really look like now; it explains a few things on my end."

Well, I wasn't a Xollon, but I didn't see the point in correcting her.

"What did you need, Molly?" I asked.

"It's the director." She sighed. "It's my fault, honestly. I thought that child would know better, so I didn't supervise her."

I raised an eyebrow. What the hell was wrong this time?

"She followed your instructions and set up one of those trial things," the doll explained.

I nodded, waiting for Molly to continue. I hadn't known that you could create a trial, but I guess the Overseer did say that I had all the tools of the site at my disposal, so giving Pandora's aspirants a bonus challenge wasn't out of the question.

"And . . . ?"

"And in the two days that she's been in charge, about a quarter of the strange patients under your care have died."

I looked at Molly, not believing what I'd heard. "I'm sorry, what?"

Molly sighed again. "You heard correctly. Although to be fair, after reading on the species your patients are to be pitted against, anything less than what she did would be hopeless. But . . . I'll admit that Abby grossly underestimated how fragile the patients were here, even when she was trying to be as careful as possible. She's trying to salvage the situation now, but it's an uphill battle."

I just continued to stare at her, my maw open. Great, more things to take care of. Between trying to make sure that my idiot Restus lackeys behaved, my semi-regular patrols in Pandora's streets, and just the overall stress of making sure that all my plans would finish on time, I really didn't need something else going wrong. At the very least, most of my operations here with the Restus were already well underway and needed minimum supervision.

I sighed, almost as hard as Molly herself.

"Um, if it's any consolation," Molly continued with a mumble, and I could swear she was avoiding eye contact with me, "the ones who have survived have improved dramatically, and they should be more than capable of fending off your supposed foe if they make it through the madam's training. It's just . . . I don't think you'll have very many patients left if Abby continues."

"I see . . ." I muttered as I forced my annoyance back. On the bright side, at least they were getting stronger faster than I could ever make them. "I'll go back. Where is the director now?"

"I'll take you to her," Molly replied. "She's in some strange dimension. I don't think you'll find it yourself. Hold on tight, this might be unpleasant."

Without waiting for me to answer, Molly's hair engulfed me. Whatever method the doll chose to transport me was horrible, even as a Xollon. It felt like the worst-designed roller-coaster ride ever with a few tracks missing along the way. I was very thankful to have arrived at my destination with the contents of my stomach intact.

"You did better than I thought," Molly said when I could see again. "Most people who travel that way lose a limb or two."

Wait, what? I gave her a scathing glare since I wasn't sure I could trust myself to speak. My stomach felt like it was still in knots.

"Relax." She laughed. "I was joking . . . Well, mostly. I knew you'd be fine."

I grumbled in response. I wished people would stop believing in me like that.

"Anyway, hide in here for a while," she added, pointing to a dark corner. "I'll notify the director."

Only now did I have time to survey my environment. I was in some kind of back room, maybe a janitor's closet or something. There was some cleaning equipment around, but the small room was otherwise empty.

"It's the only quiet place I could find," Molly answered when she noticed my confusion. "And you should probably go back to a more familiar form if you're to take over."

"Good idea," I answered absentmindedly as I undid my transformation and returned to my weak human form. "And, uh, thanks. Has anyone ever told you that you're really good at taking care of others?"

I meant it. Molly always seems to know what to do and say in any given situation. She made for the perfect caretaker, though she could be a little gloomy and prone to sarcasm.

"They have," she answered simply. "The madam's due to arrive any second now. She can explain what's going on."

And like Molly said, the door swung open, and out came the director wearing my new human suit.

"Ah, William . . ." she said with an awkward chuckle. "I, uh, I might have made a mistake. I'm sorry!"

I shook my head. "It's fine, Molly said you were just trying to ensure that the patients make it through the upcoming war."

"Yes . . ." she answered, "I've read up on the Restus species' characteristics, and compared them to the patients that I knew of. I've done the bare minimum to ensure that your charges had at least a prospect of surviving."

"But they're weaker than you thought, I know."

She blushed. "It's worse than I thought. Some of these patients wouldn't even last an hour back home. I have no idea what's wrong with them."

She must be talking about the B Group, then. The fact that so many in that category even bothered to show up and were willing to improve was a nice surprise—if it weren't for the fact that we probably lost a big chunk of Pandora's manufacturing classes.

"So, what trial did you set up?" I asked.

"It's best if you see it yourself." She sighed. "It'll take too long to explain everything, and you're bleeding patients by the minute. You have a little helper called Jordan. She can give you the progress report when you take over."

"And I'm still free to make changes whenever I want?"

"Yes," she replied. "You still have full command of the situation. Uh, I'm sure that you can salvage the situation, Will! I apologize again . . ."

"It's fine," I assured her. "Let's get changed, and I'll assess the patients. Are you able to get out of here yourself?"

"Thank you, Will," she answered, "and yes, Molly can get me out. Just take a left through the door, and you'll be by the control center."

I nodded and quickly swapped positions with her. I could still never get used to putting on a skin suit; it just felt confining. Molly took the director away in short order, and I casually made my way out of the storage closet and back toward the control center.

"Lord Arbiter W," Jordan said, greeting me with a smile when I "returned." "Good to see you back."

She got up from the main seat overlooking a big display; it was turned off at the moment. The rest of the room was staffed with various Central workers all scuttling about (some quite literally, as there were a few insectoid creatures working here) doing whatever it was that was needed for a trial to run. Others were at desktops and workstations, typing furiously, and a casual glance at the screens told me that I had no idea what any of the stuff did. Every worker briefly stopped what they were doing to salute me before returning to their tasks.

I nodded. "Thank you, Jordan. What's the current situation?"

The ghost of a snarky smile appeared on Jordan's otherwise flawless face before disappearing just as quickly. I could already tell that the prognosis wasn't going to be great.

"Well," Jordan stated, "the good news is that the average level of the combatants undergoing your training has risen by seventeen. This is unprecedented growth, but I am sure that this is par for the course for someone like yourself."

"But?" I said, keeping my tone even.

Now Jordan could hardly even bother containing her glee. "But your numbers have decreased by another 1,500 or so from my last report. From the original 20,255 aspirants that have chosen to enter, we are down to 11,571 after day two. If it's any consolation, the frequency of deceased has been going down, but I am sure you have planned for that as well, Lord Arbiter."

Holy shit . . . that was almost 50% of Pandora's population down the drain after just two days. What the hell had the director chosen to make these people undergo?

"A new batch of survivors is due to start the games," she said again. Now even the pretense of hiding her joy at Pandora's miserable state was gone. "Would you like to observe this time?"

"Yes," I muttered.

Jordan bowed and started up the big screen in front of me. "As you will, Lord W."

As the screen fizzed into life, I saw that various groups of aspirants, each containing about five to ten people, teleported into what appeared to be a deserted ghost town. Other screens appeared before me, all showing the same ghost town but with different aspirants being dropped in. I was assuming that they couldn't fit all 11,000 humans in one location, so they were employing multiple sets. I was reminded once again about how scary Central's reach and power was. Here they could casually deploy its aspirants into parallel dimensions just for a simple request of an arbiter.

Jordan's eyes darted around for a moment before she chose one screen to focus on and dismissed the rest of them.

"This one should represent the average of the aspirants," she explained. "Please enjoy the show."

I wanted to see the point of view of Jae-Hyun and the others, but I doubted they would have any trouble thriving no matter what Abigail threw at them. My time was better used trying to assess the general strength of the current aspirants—I'd never really had a chance to do that so far, now that I thought about it—and why so many of them were dying.

"I can still make changes to the training, correct?" I asked.

"Of course, Lord W," Jordan answered with a little too much enthusiasm. "You are the one in charge here, after all. Please make additional changes as you see fit. Your last intervention only increased the fatality rate by 1.5 times, but I am sure that there is a deeper reason for doing that."

"Yes . . ." I replied evenly, doing my absolute best to ensure that Jordan didn't get any more satisfaction out of the current situation, "there was."

"I expect nothing less, Lord Arbiter." She smirked. "Would you like some popcorn? I hear that humans enjoy such snacks when watching an entertaining spectacle, and I think this will be most entertaining."

"No," I muttered.

Time to see how bad the current situation was . . .

CHAPTER TWELVE

Troubles Back Home

Jordan was all but giddy as she watched the pseudo trial unfold, all the while stuffing bits of popcorn into her mouth. Sometimes she'd laugh so hard that pieces of kernels would spill from her grasp, and a poor Central worker would have to quickly come over to clean up.

"Are you sure you don't want some yourself?" Jordan asked, shaking the paper bag filled with buttery kernels. "These are remarkably good given the human's limited ability to do anything useful."

I ignored her. Jordan continued to enjoy the display before us. I could do little more than wince at just how horrible the situation was.

The various aspirants who came to the town were told to simply make it to the middle of town and touch a big pillar, at which point they would be transported out of the training and rewarded. According to Jordan, the Origin Matrix was quite generous about the rewards given to the Pandora aspirants prior to this new stage, and she assured me that the aspirants would be well compensated if they cleared this stage as well.

The list she gave me of the various rewards included aspirants gaining multiple levels at once, some getting access to rare and deadly new classes, and more unique equipment than I'd ever seen in my life. However, the fact that it was so generous didn't bode well for me. If it could afford to distribute so much, then the risk associated with earning all of that must be equally hard.

In other words, not even the Trash Matrix thought that my aspirants would make it out of this training alive, so it didn't care what it gave them. Or in less elegant words, they were all fucked.

I winced as a shadow demon eviscerated another fleeing aspirant as they desperately tried to run blindly into the streets. That was the last member of the party that I was focusing on. The camera panned out, giving Jordan and me a bird's-eye view of puddles of blood and gore that outlined the last moments of the other four members of that party before the screen changed to a new group of aspirants.

I watched for maybe an hour or two, cycling between various groups of aspirants, before I understood the gist of the director's vision and what was going on in the training. Abigail was concerned about the survival chances of the aspirants in Central, so she prioritized getting them ready to face over-whelming odds, and to do that, the aspirants had to maximize the only advan-tages that they had over the Restus: their adaptability through the varied skills that they possessed and their potential for stealth.

With that premise in mind, the rationale behind Abigail's training stage was obvious. The aspirants had to reach the center of the town by utilizing stealth and creativity. Since this was just the start of training, Abigail probably decided to give the "patients" an easier time by making them focus on stealth instead of fighting. After all, she was used to how tenacious they were in her hospital and all those escape attempts, and this stage was even modeled after that. They simply had to "escape" to the center of the city, something that she assumed they would be used to by now.

It was a pity that most of what she knew about the aspirants was ever so slightly off. If my understanding of the hospital trial was correct, then only the aspirants that were outside of Pandora at the time of trial's start were sent there, but only those who were brave enough to venture outside of the protec-tive walls of the city would venture far enough out that they couldn't make it back to the city within the hour.

Which was all to say, the people who were unfortunate enough to be sent into Abigail's domain represented the upper echelons of Pandora's population. They were the people who were strong enough to brave the unknown condi-tions of the Main Stage. She had far overestimated the abilities of the aspirants as a whole.

All of that led to the current situation. In order for the aspirants to make it to the city center, they would have to pass through predesigned choke points. In each of those choke points, huge monstrosities the size of a barn were placed to guard those entrances, which forced the aspirants to sneak their way through. Additionally, interspersed throughout the city was a mixture of adversaries who wanted nothing more than to eviscerate the humans.

The more obvious foes were the wandering bands of mutated natives. The aspirants didn't have too much trouble taking care of those small fry. Aside from the sheer number of them and their ranged weapons, they were hardly stronger than a standard unaugmented individual. The trouble was the other creatures.

I hadn't seen the full assortment of goodies lying in ambush, but there were strange shadow creatures that pulled people into the depths of the abyss, but they only appeared in the darkest of places. Weird, long-limbed creatures stalked the rooftops, waiting for an opportune time to ambush unassuming humans, while huge worm things tunneled below.

Yet all of these creatures had clear rules in which they operated (I've no idea what was up with the hospital and their rules). The rooftop things wouldn't attack unless an aspirant was isolated from their peers, and the tunneling worms could only detect vibrations in the ground and would never strike if the aspirants stopped moving around after noticing the worm's presence. Sure, the density of foes increased as they moved closer and closer to the center, but if the aspirants kept a calm head and assessed what they saw, then clearing the stage should be relatively easy.

They weren't keeping calm.

In fact, aside from a small percentage of the population, the aspirants as a whole weren't even assessing the situation at all. They were just bolting as quick as they could to their target destination without even taking the time to formulate a plan. It was a disaster.

"I must say," Jordan remarked with a light smile, "I have rarely seen such a stupid group of aspirants in my career, Lord Arbiter, and I've been working in Central for a very, very long time. You must see something special in them that I simply cannot, but you are the Lord Arbiter, after all. I'm sure that there's simply something I am missing."

God, this bitch just loved to rub it in in the most polite way possible. She was loving every moment of seeing the aspirants getting picked off one by one, but there was nothing that I could do to stop her.

"I need to make a few modifications to this trial. It wouldn't be proper training if I didn't give guidance personally," I said, ignoring her previous statement. "There must be a way for me to operate inside the training grounds directly, yes?"

"You may," she answered, and gestured for one of her goons to bring a device over. It looked like a weird helmet thing, and she plugged it in to the central controls. "Put that on and you can take over the proxy bodies. Mind you, we do have over 1,000 instances of this simulation occurring at once, but that would hardly affect a Xollon of your stature."

Damn, I was so focused on this particular city that I had forgotten that hundreds of other training sessions were occurring simultaneously. How was I supposed to manage this?

"That is fine, my host," Noe added. "Unit Noe can help you in this regard. I understand my host's intentions, so you can leave operating the majority of the proxy bodies to me. Your mind is evolved enough to allow this, but your access to my system skills will be limited due to the strain of this operation."

Got it, so treat it like when you were still upgrading?

"That is correct, my host, but I will allot you 100 luck charges to use. I have sufficient influence over the Trash Matrix to ensure that your transfer to a new body will be as close to the original as possible."

That's more than enough. Thanks, Noe. Please do what you need.

"Acknowledged."

I turned my attention back to Q's temporary replacement. "Hook me up, Jordan."

Guess getting those passives in my soul title was helpful. I mean, I should be concerned about what it was doing to my biology, but I didn't feel like I was turning into a Xollon. It wasn't so bad so far.

"I'll generate the needed bodies now," she said. "Will you use the same basic body structure as the guise?"

"Yeah," I answered. "And keep the body's specs close to the one I have as Aspirant Walter. Put each body within range of the aspirants."

She shrugged. "If you insist, but keep in mind that the creatures in there will be hostile to you if you go in as a human."

"It doesn't matter." It was a good opportunity for me to test all of the upgrades and tools I had at my disposal anyway.

Jordan nodded. "If you say so, Lord W. I look forward to seeing you salvage this situation, but please remember that assisting them too much would hinder their growth. I know I don't need to say this, but the humans do need to fight the inferior Restus in a few weeks' time."

Yeah, you don't need to remind me of that.

I was just about to put on my helmet when I was interrupted once again. This time, it was from my doppelganger, his voice missing that usual cheerfully annoying tone.

"Give me a second," I muttered and handed the helmet back to Jordan. "My stand-in has a message for me."

"Of course, Lord Arbiter," she said with a polite smile. "I'm sure you're quite busy with your current schedule. But look on the bright side, your workload will surely decrease after your training's complete."

Damn Jordan and her snark. She'd already concluded that Pandora was going to lose without actually saying it. If there was nothing else I could say about Q's replacement, it was that she knew exactly what to say without getting into trouble.

I ignored her and walked into a corner to see what the Walter Clone had to say. I didn't care if I was being overheard this time. I was willing to bet anything that everything that was happening in the regressor's party was being heavily monitored.

"I apologize for bothering you at a time like this, Lord Arbiter, but there's been a slight issue on my end," my own voice said in my head. It was the first time I had communicated with the doppelganger, and hearing what sounded exactly like my own inner voice was really weird.

What do you need?

"Well . . ." he started. I'd never seen the weird creature sound so unsure before. "I believe that your charges are beginning to suspect that something is wrong."

I cursed under my breath. Just what I needed, something else to go wrong while I already had a mountain of things to resolve. I was willing to bet that the Overseer somehow planned this when he made those adjustments to Q's stupid creature. Too bad I didn't have any other choice than to use it. Everything was going wrong, and I could see myself being stretched too thin, but I tried not to show it.

Explain what happened.

"Well, you see, Lord Arbiter," my clone said again, "although I am perfectly capable of interacting with the anomaly and his friends in social settings, having studied your behavior extensively for this occasion, I do not have the same battle capabilities that your esteemed self has."

Shit, I should have thought of that. How was he supposed to fight like me when I was using Noe's luck for half of the trials, while the other times I was borrowing the powers of my Xollon form?

Fake Walter continued. "They have started to notice discrepancies, my lord."

Can't you switch places with me, then? I'm about to head in there to train the other aspirants.

Jordan came toward me, a huge smile on her face. "Unfortunately that is not possible, my lord W."

Of course it wasn't possible. I was starting to feel the reins on my emotions loosen. Why did that goddamn Overseer have to make this current situation so damn complicated? It wasn't enough for me to just work secretly on the

Restus side of things, now I had to ensure that Pandora's damned aspirants didn't all die during training? And to make things even worse, there was more shit to deal with on the regressor's side. I was one person. I couldn't put out all of these fires!

"And why is that not possible?" I asked, a tiny bit of my temper leaking through. Jordan lapped it up, her smirk growing ever bigger.

"You are the one who is in charge of the training, Lord Arbiter," Jordan answered curtly. "So for one, you will need to be here to supervise the activities. Additionally, it is one thing to assist the participants, but quite another to enter it as an aspirant yourself. It would be a gross breach in protocol for you to take part in a mini trial of your own design. After all, you would have access to insider information that could be abused. Not that I think you would do so, of course."

Once again, I couldn't think of any fault in her reasoning here. As long as I was here in the heart of Central, I couldn't overstep my boundaries. Even using the director's little charms would be of limited use when all eyes were on me. Damn it!

"Those are valid points, Jordan," I answered between gritted teeth. "I will have to rely on the doppelganger for now."

"I apologize again for the inconvenience, my lord," my clone added. "Please allow me to make up for it once I am out!"

"That's fine," I said out loud this time, since there was no point in communicating with it in my mind if everyone could hear me anyway. "Just . . . minimize fighting, and think of any excuse that you can about why you're behaving differently. Say it's metal contamination, fatigue, a new style of fighting, I don't care, just make sure that you avoid any further suspicion."

"I understand, my lord!" he answered. "I will do my best!"

I nodded and dismissed him.

"Are you ready to assist your charges now?" Jordan asked when she saw that I had disconnected my call.

"Yes," I muttered. "Hook me up."

"As you command," she said with a practiced smile. "Once again, I look forward to seeing you turn this hopeless situation around!"

CHAPTER THIRTEEN

Salvaging a Hopeless Trial

I slapped on the rather cumbersome helmet and allowed Jordan to make the final adjustments. Having her work with a device that directly interfaced with my head might seem like a bad idea, but I was fairly confident that Central still wanted to get me on their side, at least for now. That meant that they wouldn't choose to willingly harm me unless I did something really antagonistic toward the Overseer, although I had my luck skill active just to be on the safe side. I still had to remember that I had that available to me after having been deprived of Noe's ability for so long.

"Things are set up on my end, Lord W," Jordan's voice said over the muffling of the equipment. "Let me know when you are ready to start."

"Give me a second," I muttered.

Noe, can you send me over to where the regressor and the rest of the Abyss Guild are?

"I can, my host," she answered, "but there is a problem if I do so."

I frowned again, glad that Jordan couldn't see my expression under the heavy helmet. "What do you mean?"

"Unit Noe needs your baseline consciousness to act as a reference point for when I operate your secondary bodies in the training."

And you can't do that if I'm with the regressor's group?

"I can," she answered again, "but Unit Noe calculates that such an interaction with Jae-Hyun's party will result in a significant deviation from how the host will interact with other groups. There is only a 73.45% chance that no errors will occur, whereas absolutely no error will occur if you utilize the Absolute Luck skill to choose which group your main consciousness helps."

Which means I've got more than a 25% chance that something will go wrong?

"Correct, my host," she said with the hint of a sigh. "Unit Noe is not complete enough to take complete autonomous actions at the moment, and has to rely on the host's behaviors as a guideline. I apologize for the inconvenience and for my inability to assist you further."

Well, that made my choice relatively straightforward. 73% might seem like pretty good odds, and I'd been known to indulge in some gambling in my spare time before, but was I willing to bet the survival of Pandora's aspirants and my life over those odds? Guess I'd have to rely on Noe and the stupid doppelganger to hold down the fort while I was away. I didn't have high hopes.

"Would my host still wish to assist the regressor and his guild?"

No, you're right. We've too much at stake; use the Luck skill to choose where I end up.

"Acknowledged, dear Walter."

"I'm good to go, Jordan," I said as well. "Sorry for the wait."

"Not a problem, Lord Arbiter," she replied. "Initiating start-up now."

I heard a horrible buzzing sound in my ears, and my vision darkened before I found myself inside the city that I had been staring at for the past few hours. The whole experience was remarkably similar to being teleported now that I thought about it.

Once again, my instincts took over, and I surveyed my surroundings. Noe—or was it Jordan in this case?—dropped me off on an abandoned rooftop. As always, it was dark out—at this point, I wasn't sure if Central even knew what the sun was since every trial I'd ever been in had been dark—but my title made that point moot. If anything, all these dark trials and environments just meant that I was 25% stronger.

Off to my left was the only movement that was visible. I saw four figures running away from what seemed like a huge mob of those mutated villagers. They were coming toward my direction. One of the four, a woman if her long hair was any indication, was taking potshots at the group with what looked like one of those sci-fi guns, while the other three in her party were just booking it as fast as they could out of there.

They were still too far for me to see what they looked like in any detail, but one of them was limping, and it didn't take a genius to know that this one wasn't going to make it much longer. The crimson stain that covered half his left side meant that he was likely to die of blood loss even if he somehow survived the chase. A few of his friends tried to drag the wounded member up, but a hail of thrown weapons from the chasing mob stopped any attempts to do so. The man became separated from the rest of the group shortly after. His fate was clear.

I still had a few minutes before the group arrived at my position, so I checked out my new body. I felt the same, all things considered, and a familiar tentacle even sprouted out of my palms when I willed it, although it looked different from the normal Xollon appendage. This one looked metallic in nature, but as far as I could tell, it operated the same as the one I had. I guess Jordan didn't want anyone to make the connection between Aspirant Walter and Arbiter W, but at least she was thoughtful enough to do that, even if her intentions weren't to help me out. There was just one last thing to check before I got things going.

Hey, Noe, can you still hear me?

"Yes, my host," she replied, but her voice sounded oddly distant, like I was hearing an echo of an echo instead of the real thing.

Everything good on your side?

"I am performing at optimal parameters," she answered. "Please rest assured and focus your attention on the current group of aspirants. I shall ensure that the other parties are taken care of."

Thanks, Noe, good to know that I always have someone to count on, even if everything else is going to shit.

"I endeavor to serve you well, my host, but please keep in mind that my abilities will be limited."

Limited or not, you're still providing me with more than enough help. You are the best system in existence.

"I know."

I refocused my attention on the task at hand. All right, the group of aspirants was about to move right past the roof I was standing on, so it was about time for me to make my entrance. I needed to ensure that I made the best first impression, even if it was technically the second time they had seen my current form.

Noe, use the Lucky Blind Strike skill the second I touch the ground.

"Acknowledged."

Luck Charges: 75/100

With only 100 charges to work with, the skill wasn't too impressive. In fact, it was a little underwhelming, all things considered, but at least I could actually comprehend what was going on this time.

Noe took over my body and lashed out with my hand feelers. They moved with a mind of their own, skewering mutants wherever they passed, while simultaneously catching all of the various melee weapons being thrown my way. That was the good thing about having tentacles versus hands: I could grasp a whole lot more objects at once with feelers. An ax was deflected with my left appendage, and it ricocheted off and smashed into another mutant who was about to swing a crude sword in my direction.

While that was happening, my right feeler was acting like a horrible blender; the limb was moving so quickly in a spiraling motion that anything that even got close to that appendage was lacerated into tiny chunks of meat. The mutants were not idiots; some of them tried to move away, but my left feeler erupted from the ground below them to shove the fleeing individuals into the makeshift tentacle blender. There was only a handful of my foes left by the time I was finished, and they all hurriedly fled as fast as they could away from me.

All of this took less than fifteen seconds to accomplish. Okay, maybe it was a little impressive, all things considered.

The three aspirants looked at me, dumbfounded.

"I can't believe that the aspirants of Earth are so weak!" I shouted. I still needed to play a role here, and Pandora needed some tough love in this situation. "This is only the third day of training, and I had to step in personally! Pathetic!"

"But—" the woman with the weird gun began to say.

"But nothing!" I swung one of my feelers and made a huge gash on the ground just inches away from the woman's feet. She flinched back and wisely decided not to argue with me any further. The others looked on with nervous expressions.

"Now I am here to ensure that you three succeed in this mini trial!" I stared into each of their eyes. "You three have survived the first few stages, so you show promise, not like that sorry excuse for an aspirant from earlier."

The woman—it was clear that she was in charge of this particular group—frowned at that remark, but didn't speak up further. I guess this group still cared about their colleagues. I had begun to assume that all humans were selfish creatures at this point, having seen little besides betrayal and envy between them so far, but that was evidently not the case. Had I become more cynical as time went on?

Finally, the leader of the group composed herself enough to speak. "We are not pathetic! It's your damn training that's too difficult. We can't eliminate an entire army of those mutated freaks like you can."

I shook my head and sighed. "And once again, you blame others when the fault lies with you. Instead of assessing your foes, you chose to blindly act, so yes, I can safely say that you are pathetic."

The woman looked like she was about to argue back, but one of her surviving party members quickly went over to stop her. The other two were a lot more frightened of me than she was.

I gestured to the still-feeling group of mutants. "Look at them run. These creatures are not predators; they represent the bottom of the food chain in this trial. Showing them even a modicum of strength will break their will to fight, yet what did your group choose to do? You chose to flee."

As if to cement my point, I picked up a rock, and with the help of a single luck charge, I threw it as hard as I could toward the nearest fleeing mutant. The stone struck it right in the back of the head, killing it on impact.

"They are pathetically weak individually," I continued, "no better than you were before the Lord's ascension process even began. They are the prey here, and if you understood that at the beginning and established yourselves as the predators in this stage, then they would be fleeing from you. But you chose to run because they had numbers."

"But . . ." the woman said, her uncertainty growing evident. "Fine, you're right about that. We, no, *I* did not lead my party correctly to access the situation. That is my fault. I will readily admit that."

Wow, I was actually surprised by her response. Here was a leader who was willing to admit their faults instead of blindly pushing on to their wrong points of view. Maybe this woman was worth having around.

"However," she continued, "those mutants weren't the only monsters here. We'd still be fine if those shadow beasts didn't kill our only healer."

"And how was your healer picked off?" I asked.

The woman glanced at one of her two subordinates, this one a gruff-looking man who looked to be in his mid-thirties.

He nodded. "Daniel got sucked in that damn shadow when he went up to scout our position when we first came here. It almost got me as well when I went up to check on him. The bastards only seemed to attack us on the rooftops. It's why we've been running blind for the past few hours."

"That's not true," the last member of the party added, this one was a lean girl who looked almost as young as Yoona. "We lost Chris when he had to go use the restroom."

The older man grunted. "But we don't know if it was those shadow things that got him."

"Well, it certainly wasn't the mutants," the young girl added, "and there's nothing else around here that'd make him disappear like that."

I cut in before these two could bicker again. I could tell that tensions were high after losing more than a few party members.

"In other words," I said, "you're not sure why the shadow demons attacked, and are only going on assumptions."

The three of them frowned but didn't say anything.

After a few moments of hesitation, the leader spoke up once again. "It's not like we can just use our lives to test all the things you've said!"

"No," I agreed, "but you can look at the patterns. I was told that you humans were an intelligent species, but clearly those reports were an exaggeration."

The man cursed me under his breath, but I pretended that I didn't hear him.

I shook my head. "You know that the demons attacked when this Daniel person went up to survey the environment, and when you went up to check on him, yes?"

The man nodded.

"And you also know that this Chris individual was most likely taken away when he left the group to relieve himself. There were no other times that you were attacked, correct?"

Their leader thought for a moment before agreeing.

"So what do all of these occurrences have in common?" I asked again, looking hard at each of them in turn.

The younger girl frowned. "They were alone . . ."

"Exactly," I replied. "You will find that although my training is challenging, it is not impossible if you aspirants just use your heads. Yet you three seem unable to do even that much, and you need some help in that regard."

I sighed dramatically. "Which is why I am here. Now, before we continue, you three best introduce yourselves and tell me what abilities the Lord has bestowed upon you."

CHAPTER FOURTEEN

Troubles in Training

'm Myra," the leader of the group said. "I'm in charge of . . . what's left of our party. My job's mainly ranged, and I have minimal close cover options, which is why I normally act as a back-line commander in fights."

I nodded. "Any notable abilities?"

"I can switch ammunition for different effects, but that takes up limited resources," she answered, taking out a few cartridges to show me. "I can use those, but I'm running short already. I didn't have time to prep any more for this stage."

I looked at the cartridge. "Can you make more?"

"Yes . . ." she replied slowly. "But I'd need the proper equipment and materials, not to mention time. I mean, the others can help out as well, but I'm still teaching them how to make the ammunition properly."

Well, at least the leader of their group had potential. Myra was only limited by time, resources, and information. If she was allowed time to prepare for a known threat, then I could see her being pretty invaluable to the survival of Pandora as a whole, not to mention the fact that others could help prepare those magazines for her.

Pair her with the regressor's knowledge and all that money that I had, and she'd be a great fit for the Abyss Guild in the future, even if she wouldn't be a part of the guild's core. But all of that was assuming I could even get her out of this situation in the first place. I had to try to make sure that she at least survived out of the three left.

"And if you have neither time or resources?" I asked.

"I'll have to rely on mana or regular bullets. I have a lot stocked up, but their usefulness is kind of limited," Myra answered. "It'll do in a pinch, but I'd be operating at half efficiency at most, maybe even less."

I nodded again. "So you have a job that's great with enough preparation, but your options are limited after. I'm assuming you can change the properties of your shots depending on how you make them?"

"Yeah, that's right."

"Then you'll need to rely on planning and information more than the rest," I said. "We'll work on that. What about the other two?"

The other girl answered first. "I'm Alina. I have a support class. I can help buff the others, but I can't heal or anything like that."

"Two back-line members, great," I muttered.

Alina looked down. "The front line was picked off once we lost Dan . . ."

I stopped them before they could begin moping. "All right, and what's the last member of your group do?"

The older man stepped up. "Name's Bishop, and I'm . . . also back line, hence why we were running from those creatures earlier."

Wonderful, even with Absolute Luck, I'd been sent to a party with the worst possible mix of combatants. How the hell was I supposed to work with this assortment of classes and abilities without handholding them? Shit, if this was the best situation that Noe considered, then I didn't even want to imagine what the worst-case scenario would be. I was starting to think that Pandora was doomed for failure.

He continued with a sigh. "Where Alina can buff other's attack and defenses, I can recharge mana and stamina, and I have some skills that can hinder our enemies. The two of us were the core of our party's normal strategy, but—"

"But there's no one to use those abilities on other than Myra," I answered for him. "Which means you two are essentially useless unless we fight from range."

"Well . . ." Bishop began, "I wouldn't say—"

Myra put a hand on the man's shoulders and shook her head. "No, what our guide's saying is correct. Our combat capabilities are severely limited at the moment, and being in this boxed-in location's not helping either."

"It's good that you recognize your current situation," I said. "That means that you have accepted the limitations of your current party. It's a start. Everyone here knows that fighting is not a real option unless you can ambush the foe from range, and even then it will be a risky endeavor since Myra is the only offense left."

"That's true," the leader agreed. "So we have to lean on stealth."

"But none of us are geared toward stealth," Bishop muttered. "How are we supposed to hide in this city? There's no cover to use, we can't be separated 'cause of those damn shadow things, and we don't even know where our enemies will come from."

"Can . . . can you help us fight?" Alina asked me tentatively.

You know, that was a good question. With those constraints, trying to do anything would be difficult. Could I just do the heavy lifting for them and force them through this stage?

"Notification, my host," Noe's voice interrupted, "but that is not an option. Unit Noe has searched through the relevant regulations for this training stage via the neural link, and Central's regulations stipulate that the host of a trial, official or not, may only assist the participants in a limited capacity."

Of course it would be like that. Nothing's lined up in my damn favor!

I forced myself to calm down, although I could feel my nerves slipping from my control as each piece of bad news compounded upon the other. Nothing had been going right ever since I came back from that last trial, and with the stakes much higher than ever, I couldn't afford for anything to go wrong, much less everything!

"Please calm down, dear Walter," Noe continued. "Unit Noe has detected elevated levels of stress; your brain is still recovering from the earlier emergency measures that Unit Noe enacted, and further mental distress will cause catastrophic consequences."

How can I calm down, Noe? If I fuck this up, I'm dead. The aspirants here will all die. The regressor will be kicked out and sent to who knows where, and everything that I've been doing since the start of these fucking trials will die with me. I can't fail. What do I do?

"Unit Noe does not have an answer to that . . ." she answered with melancholy. "I apologize, my host. Please do not despair, dear Walter. This is but a fleeting moment, a dream."

I took a deep breath. *I . . . I'll keep it together, Noe. I'll keep going. Just . . . Never mind. Just tell me how much I am allowed to interfere here.*

"I apologize again," Noe murmured. "But to answer your question, as an official host of this mini trial, you can guide the aspirants here and give them hints. You may even tell them directly what to do, but directly assisting in the trials will not be allowed. What you did at the beginning was already stretching the limits of what would be tolerated."

So I screw up again and I'm done for, right?

"Yes, my host. Jordan and the Trash Matrix would be well within their rights to remove you if that happens. They are only showing leniency because they know your situation is hopeless, and to show their detractors their 'good-will' toward your cause."

Great . . . I'll think of something.

Then a thought did strike me. *Wait. Can I defend myself if the monsters attack me first? Jordan did say that they'd be hostile to me if I came in as a human.*

"There are no rules against self-defense, my host, but doing anything overt may alert Central," she answered. "Keep in mind that the major creatures stationed at the choke points of the city will not attack the host. They have been specifically programmed not to do so by Jordan and the Overseer."

But the other things are fair game . . . I can work with that at least.

I collected my fraying nerves and answered as naturally as I could. "No, I cannot help you in combat, nor would it do you any good if I did. I am here to ensure that you are able to survive the trials ahead of you, and if you think that someone will always be there to help you along, then you will be sorely disappointed. Saving you from that horde of mutants will be the extent of my help in combat."

I saw that all of the newly acquired hope in the eyes of the three survivors started to shrivel up as I spoke those words.

"However," I added before they lost all hope, "that does not mean that I will leave you to fend for yourselves entirely. Remember that stealth does not rely solely on hiding from existing enemies, but it is also the art of avoidance in general. I will assist with planning and organization, and having an extra body around will help with avoiding danger when scouting."

"Right," Myra said. "We'd have to scout with all three of us if we want to avoid those shadow things. Just having an extra body around's helpful."

The others nodded in agreement.

"But as I said," I continued, "I will be here to assist and mentor. Ultimately, the onus is on you three to improve. You will not survive the later trials if you can't even pass a simple training stage like this one."

"Understood, sir!" Myra all but shouted. The others followed her lead and all stated their affirmations.

It was still surprising how fast they came around to my way of doing things. Although a stat like charisma was something relatively intangible unlike strength or dexterity, I was starting to realize just how impactful it was. People tended to believe anything I said, even when it was going against their already established beliefs. It was kind of scary how effective I was as a speaker.

I looked at the woman in charge. "So as the leader, what do you think our first priority should be, Myra?"

She thought for a moment, assessing her situation before answering. "The three of us need rest; we've been on the run for too long and our reserves of both mana and stamina are too low. So to do that, we need to scout for a safe location first."

I nodded, and the ghost of a smile started to creep onto my face. "Good, and who would be most suitable for scouting?"

She thought again, taking the time to deliberate on her choices. "We need to go in pairs, so the best option to go would be myself and Bishop."

"Explain your reasoning."

She stood at attention. "Well, I have the best eyesight and perception out of the three of us here, so it would naturally make the most sense for me to find a location suitable for us to rest. I figured that Bishop would be the ideal companion if we needed to make a hasty retreat, since he can provide me with the most beneficial buffs if something unexpected happened."

I smiled. "Good reasoning. You make a competent leader."

Myra blushed at the compliment, if you could even call being considered competent a compliment at all. She looked like someone who just got praised by their idol or something. It was kind of disturbing, since we just met. It was the damn charisma at work once again, although I might have to learn how to tone things down for the future. I couldn't have everyone I met gushing over every word I said.

"Get going, then," I grunted, breaking Myra out of the weird happy trance she was in. "We don't have all day."

"Yes, sir!"

Honestly, unlike what I thought when I initially met the three beat-up party members, Myra and her two teammates were quite competent all things considered. The leader had the respect of the other two, and they followed her orders to the tee and without any signs of complaint. Most importantly, they were efficient.

Myra was able to locate a relatively secluded area in the city to rest in. She chose an alleyway with a short wall where they would be outside the visual range of most of the monsters roaming the streets, while the wall could be easily climbed over, providing an easy enough escape route if they were attacked.

The four of us made our way over to the alley, and without prompting, the three of them took out various items from their inventories and quickly went about securing the area with traps and various early-warning systems. They even had a strange blanket thing that they draped over the entrance. This thing reflected light or something similar because it made it look like the alleyway was completely empty when you peered from outside. Bishop also told me that it muffled sounds and even low-level detection spells.

If there was anything good I had to say about Central, then it'd have to be their tech. I needed to get one of those when I came back to Pandora.

Once the area was secure, Myra's party took some time to eat and rest. She was able to replenish a few magazines in the process, but her reserves remained low. It would have to do. All in all, it took them two hours and some odd minutes to recover enough to forge onward, partly because I found out a new way to utilize my high charisma: morale boosting.

Apparently, if normal aspirants heard me encourage them, their motivation went through the roof. Hell, if the regressor's plans for taking over Pandora ever came to fruition, then we'd never have to worry about inspiring the masses if all it took was a few rousing speeches on my end. But that was something to think about once this current shitty situation was over. I had to ensure that Myra, Bishop, and Alina were alive first.

CHAPTER FIFTEEN

Tentative Stabilization

Mr. Guide, sir!" Alina said. "Bishop and I have recovered all of our mana and are ready to go!"

Right, I never did tell them my name. Guess I'd just stick with being called Mr. Guide. I'd run out of W names if I kept going.

"Still got some minor wounds that need tending," Bishop stated as he bandaged up a more egregious wound. "But the major stuff's tended to. I can speed up the body's natural recovery a little, but we're not going to recover much more here. I'm good to go as well."

I nodded at them. Myra came over as well. She had completed a few more production rounds and replenished some of her more exotic ammunition, and was busy stuffing the last of them into her bag and inventory.

"I've basically run out of materials," Myra said, "so I'm about as ready as I can be. We're good to go whenever you want, sir."

"I'm just here to guide," I said to them before turning my attention to Myra. "It's your choice as party leader to go or not."

"But—" she started to say.

"But nothing. I am not the one in command of your people," I said, tone final. "So, Myra, are you ready to set out?"

"Yes!" she answered quickly, as if she was afraid that I would be displeased with her if she didn't answer immediately.

Myra and her comrades moved quickly to dismantle and clean up the things they left. Once again, I was a little surprised by how efficient they were at all of this. These three were used to working as a team. I could see a lot of potential, but that was assuming they survived.

"All right," Myra said once everything was set again, the others quickly gathering around her to hear her instructions. "Our goal remains the same: We have to get to the center of town."

The others nodded.

"Our situation hasn't fundamentally changed, even with the guide here," she continued. "But his presence will allow us to operate a little more freely."

The woman turned to me. "Do you have anything else to add?"

"Yes," I said. "With only three of you here, we need to make it to the exit as fast as possible. As we get closer to the center of this stage, the enemies you face will increase exponentially, and there will not be any more opportunities to rest like we can here. Any small wound or fatigue you three incur will add up steadily, and coupled with Myra's limited resources, it will be a race against time."

"I'm sorry, everyone . . ." she muttered.

I shook my head. "You have nothing to be sorry about. Every class has their own limitations. It's how you accommodate those weaknesses that will determine your future success."

She blushed again and immediately perked up. It was quite unnerving . . . I'd need to limit how often I gave out praise when I was with normal humans.

"Thank you . . ." she said quietly before collecting herself once more. "And you're right, we need to move fast. We'll avoid confrontation with the mutants while we can, to conserve strength, but if there's no way to do so, then we fight with overwhelming force. If our guide is correct, then we need to show them that we are to be feared; spare no resources then."

"Got it, boss," Bishop answered.

"Do we conserve mana?" Alina asked.

"Bishop should if he can afford to," their leader replied, "but you need to go all out. We need to avoid an extended fight."

"Understood!"

"Lastly, make sure that we stay in pairs to avoid being ambushed, no one is to leave each other's immediate vicinity under any circumstances. Bishop will be with me. Alina, stick with the guide."

Alina looked more than happy to follow those instructions, while Bishop just grunted an acknowledgment. Once a concrete plan was in place, the three of them moved with such calm and skill that I was starting to wonder how they got to their sorry state in the first place.

They didn't have any issue making it to the first set of those really big monsters guarding the narrow streets that led to the interior of the town. Now that Myra was able to scout properly with a partner, it was relatively easy to traverse around the mobs of mutants. Their smaller number worked in their favor in this case.

I just followed along for the most part, and only needed to help out when we reached the choke points. They were unsure on how to proceed past the big abomination, but the solution was clear to me when I asked them to fully explain their abilities. Bishop was underestimating the aspirants' ability for stealth when he made that first remark, and it highlighted the one advantage that the humans had over the rest of the aspirants: their creativity.

The brief introduction of their abilities did not do their true strengths justice. For example, Alina's buffing ability boiled down to her injecting her own mana into someone else and giving them a boost that way. What type of boost they got depended on how she moved that energy. What was important here, however, was her ability to manipulate mana in a tangible way, and that ability wasn't limited to just people. Alina simply never thought about the usefulness of injecting mana into inanimate objects.

Bishop's debuff abilities were a lot more nuanced than just slowing down the foe or making them a little more susceptible to damage. He was just so ingrained with the idea that his abilities only applied in a straight-up fight that he wasn't able to see the other uses. The same could be said for the other two. Then again, these normal aspirants only had a few months' time to get used to their abilities, and they certainly didn't have the unique perspective that the regressor had. It was understandable why they would be so narrow-minded in the usage of their skills.

See, Bishop's debuffing ability was quite powerful. He could all but cripple someone's senses and their ability to perceive their environment. He told me that he would normally try to slow down the individual's reaction times or weaken their body, but he could do so much more to his opponents if he was given enough time to prepare. With a little bit of guidance, I was able to show him the full spectrum of his abilities.

"You sure this'll work?" he asked me as we peered down on the monstrosity that was blocking our only access to the inner sanctum of the city.

"Come on," Alina urged, "give it a try. Worst case, we just run away. They don't seem very fast."

"It's the size of a house," Bishop mumbled. "And you're not going to be the one pissing off the house-shaped monster."

"Just do it," Myra added from her vantage point. "I can provide covering fire if things go wrong."

I turned to her. "Don't forget your part as well. You have the shell loaded?"

"Ready to go, sir."

Bishop grunted an affirmation and made his move. He took out a little gadget, some rod-shaped object the size of a can of Coke that he said focused his powers and started to mutter something incomprehensible under his breath. Now, I'm sure that something cool and magical was happening as he was doing this, but since I had no ability to see any of that, it just looked like the dude was muttering to himself like a crazy person.

Whatever Bishop did worked, however, as I saw the house-sized creature grunt in frustration as its ability to see with any clarity faded away. It started to swing its massive arms around, trying to find the foe that caused it to lose its sight.

"Go for it now, Myra!" he shouted. "My ability won't last long!"

Without a word, Myra fired her prepared shot in front of the now half-blind monster. The bullet burst apart quickly, and a thick smoke started to erupt out of the shot.

"Alina, your turn!" Myra added.

The other girl gave a small nod and infused her mana (at least, that was what I assumed was happening; I still couldn't see any of this with my damn mana-less condition) into the cloud of smoke. She guided the smog into the form of a human. It was a pretty shoddy job, all things considered, but with the creature already half blind, it was enough to get the thing's attention.

I activated the Absolute Luck skill and whispered, "Alina, continue as planned. Myra, shoot on my count . . ."

Alina made the smoke construct wave its arm in a vaguely threatening gesture, and at the same time, Myra shot another bullet at the creature. If they got the timing correct, then it would appear as if the smoke construct did the actual damage. With a mere one luck charge used, I didn't have to worry about the timing being off, and the simple plan went off without a hitch. The house creature shouted in rage as it ran toward the smoke.

"Go now!" I shouted as I activated the Absolute Luck skill once more. "Follow me!"

The others scrambled as quickly as they could while the creature was distracted. I saw my very limited amount of charges go down as we narrowly avoided the creature's attention, going all the way down to sixty-three, but we did get out of the situation safely. Using a few dozen luck charges wasn't an issue normally, but when I had so little available, it did hurt, and it wasn't like I had the opportunity to slowly recharge them either.

"My skill's about to end now," Bishop grunted as he ran as fast as he could.

"Same here," Alina added. "I'm almost out of range to manipulate the smoke."

"Then run faster!" Myra yelled.

I saw my luck charges deplete to fifty before it stopped going down. That was generally the indication that whatever unlucky scenario that was the most beneficial to me had occurred. Just to make sure, though, I glanced back at where the monster was and saw that it was still frantically searching for the people that annoyed it, but it was going the opposite direction that we were in. I could always count on Noe to get us out of a tricky situation . . . assuming I had enough resources available to power her skills, of course.

"We should be far enough away now," I said as I slowed the group down from the sprint. "But heads-up, we're in the inner circle now. Take a few minutes to recover, but expect frequent encounters with mutants and other foes."

Unfortunately, the four of us never got that chance to rest, because just as those words left my mouth, a band of roaming mutants rounded one of the streets and noticed us. They were still quite a distance away, but once they saw how tired we looked, the leader of their group sent a signal, and all of them rushed at us at once.

Without needing any other instructions, Myra loaded a new clip into her space gun while the other two started their weird chanting. I stayed close by, deliberately placing myself in between the path of the oncoming mutants so that I could properly "defend" myself. It wouldn't be a breach of the rules if I just happened to be standing a little in front of the other three, although I don't think I could stretch the rules more than that.

Myra seemed to understand my intentions, at least in part, as she gave me a small nod of appreciation. Without wasting any more time, the woman screamed a battle cry and unleashed a barrage of bullets into the oncoming mass. This would be the first time I was going to witness how they did in combat when they were in ideal starting conditions. Hopefully they wouldn't disappoint.

CHAPTER SIXTEEN

Guiding the Guests

The volley of frenzied fire did its job at whittling down the first wave of enemies, but the mutants that inhabited the inner circle of the city were much more tenacious than the ones on the outskirts. They kept coming at us despite the heavy losses on their side. It was easy enough for me to deal with them, even in my weak human form, but they were wising up to the fact that fighting me was a waste of time and resources.

Within moments, the wave of monsters circled my forward position and started to run toward Myra and her party. I would have thought that they would panic at the face of such insane numbers, as that was the state that I saw them in initially, but they remained defiant.

The only good thing I could say about our current situation was that the foe had engaged at a range, and the streets provided the perfect environment to launch a long-range assault. The mutants couldn't all pour in the narrow streets at once, and their own numbers worked against them as a few of the more clumsy individuals tripped and fell, hindering everyone else behind them. It also made missing a shot all but impossible.

"Let's show the guide what we're made of!" Myra shouted as she unleashed an insane volley of bullets. Alina was ensuring that her leader could continuously output accurate shot after shot.

Whatever ammunition Myra was using was causing her bullets to pass through every body in their path, leaving small holes in the oncoming horde. Unfortunately, it still took a few hits on vital areas to actually down one of the mutants. The ones in the center of town were evidently more durable as well.

"They're within range, Myra," Bishop spat. "I'll bog down the lead group, that should slow everyone else down. You got any of those laser rounds left?"

"Three shots," she answered. "It's the last ones I got, but if you can group 'em well, it's worth the cost!"

"Got it!" Bishop answered. "Alina, help me out here!"

"Roger!"

"And you probably want to move to the side, sir guide!"

I wasn't sure what they planned to do, but I moved out of the immediate path of the mutants and fell back with the rest of the party.

Once they saw me in the clear, the rate of fire slowed down as Alina focused her energy on Bishop. He turned his gaze to the oncoming mutants and started his chants. Almost immediately, a few dozen creatures in the lead slowed down as every muscle in their bodies started to spasm uncontrollably. No, I looked closer and saw that it wasn't every mutant that was affected. Bishop was targeting the ones near the sides of the buildings, so that the enemies behind the affected would naturally move closer to the center to avoid their awkward allies.

He was creating a funnel using the incapacitated mutants.

"Now!" he shouted. "Scorch them!"

With a swift, easy motion, Myra swapped magazines and pressed the trigger, aiming where the majority of the mutants were. The results were instantaneous. A huge flash of light that almost blinded me passed through the muzzle of her gun and down the line of enemies. Everything in that superheated plasma was instantly vaporized, along with a sizable portion of the building behind them. The survivors quickly lost all motivation to fight after that, and scrambled to retreat.

The actual fight was over within minutes, all things considered, and I could tell by the excited cheers coming from the three aspirants that they were quite happy with what they'd done. But . . . they hadn't really done much to warrant that kind of celebration. All I saw was the use of a very obvious and simple tactic, while they used a limited resource to do the brunt of the work. Were they happy that they didn't run away this time? I was having a harder and harder time understanding the thought processes of these lower life-forms.

"Damn good work," I said regardless of what I actually thought. "Good use of tactics and your limited resources."

"Thank you, sir!" Alina beamed. "It was your guidance that allowed us to expand the use of our abilities. We would have never thought to employ those types of tactics otherwise!"

Wait . . . they wouldn't have employed those tactics without me? How the hell were they fighting before, then? Did they just rush in without any kind of plan in mind? I was starting to think that I severely overestimated the abilities of Myra's party initially. Sure, they were organized and could scout effectively, but they couldn't strategize worth a damn.

"But we can't do that for much longer." Myra grimaced. "I got two of those shots left, and almost nothing else of that caliber remaining. Hope it's enough to get us to the center. We all need to regroup and rest after this."

Now that I thought about it, it was odd that none of the members of Myra's party resented me for placing them in here. I mean, I had been the indirect cause of the loss of at least two members of her party, but it was almost as if the three of them were functionally unable to blame me for any of that. Every time they showed even the slightest amount of unease, I would say something generic and they'd perk up immediately.

I never had this issue when I was talking with Rogue, Xalla, or even Alice, but with these normal aspirants, it was like I was an entirely different species altogether. Nothing they did when they spoke to me made any sense in my mind, and it took but a word from me to change their entire way of thinking. It felt like I was dealing with small animals rather than other intelligent beings. At least my interactions with the Abyss Guild were still relatively normal, although that might be due to how abnormal everyone in that guild was.

"Damn, that whole fight was worth three levels as well." Alina laughed. "How about you two?"

"Three levels here, too," Bishop answered. "Not too shabby for a few minutes of work. We're better than I thought."

"I got five," Myra added. "And I bet we'll get some nice rewards if we clear this stage as well. Let's not waste any more time and get going."

"Let's not get ahead of ourselves now," I interrupted their cheer. "We're not out of the woods yet. Celebrate when you're done."

The three of them immediately stiffened up and regrouped. The way they changed behaviors really did remind me of reprimanding a particularly enthusiastic dog. I could just tell that interacting with them was going to get really grating, really fast.

"Right," Myra said after calming down. "Let's get going. Distribute your attributes on the move, you two."

"Roger that!" Alina replied.

The party moved again, but this time I stayed a little farther away from the rest of the group. I just couldn't stand being in the presence of their useless chattering. The second they made any sort of minor achievement, whether that be avoiding a fight, doing a little magic show to trick the monsters here, they gave themselves so much useless self-praise. They had to do this horrible cheer whenever a new level was achieved. I couldn't stand it. I just wanted them to stop talking, even for a second!

Primary Soul Title: It That Sleeps at the Edge of Dusk (??? Rank)
Progress to Awakening: 29.99% -> 34.51%

Why was it so bad? They were making headway toward the exit now, having bested every foe before them with relative ease, and the goal was practically already in sight, but none of these achievements made me feel any bit better. In fact, the constant cheers and worthless praise the three threw on me was grating to the extreme. What the hell was wrong with me?

Primary Soul Title: It That Sleeps at the Edge of Dusk (??? Rank)
Progress to Awakening: 34.51% -> 38.02%

"It is natural to feel this way, my host. You are already agitated from the stress of the current situation, so listening to the lesser aspirants talk will cause continued mental distress," Noe's welcoming voice said over the continued drone of the other three. "You are starting to understand the drivel that makes up the inferior species. It shows welcoming growth."

If this is growth, then it's damn unpleasant . . .

"As all true growth tends to be," Noe replied cryptically. I swear it was getting harder and harder to understand what she was doing lately. "All of the accumulated stress had accelerated this process, and you are at a critical stage currently, my host, but do not worry. Unit Noe will ensure that you complete this transition safely."

Yeah, that was certainly one way of putting it. If I didn't survive this "growth period," and allowed the Overseer's plans to destroy Pandora, then I'd certainly have no other opportunities to advance further, since I'd be dead! I felt welling frustration just thinking about that bastard and all the work that I still had to do just to survive these next few days.

Primary Soul Title: It That Sleeps at the Edge of Dusk (??? Rank)
Progress to Awakening: 38.02% -> 43.87%

But it was more than that. It wasn't because I had to face all of these impossible odds. I'd done that again and again after arriving at Central all those months ago, and I was fine then. And if I was honest with myself, I wasn't even afraid that Pandora would be destroyed and the regressor being sent away.

Sure, my identity as an arbiter would be under fire if I had to work closely with the Overseer, but I knew in my heart that I'd somehow bullshit my way out of that situation one way or another.

Primary Soul Title: It That Sleeps at the Edge of Dusk (??? Rank)
Progress to Awakening: 43.87 -> 46.27%

No, what was pissing me off more than anything else was just how damn helpless I felt. For the first time since arriving at Central, I had all of my agency taken away from me, and I was running around one step behind the Overseer, always trying to play catch-up. Just when I thought one of my plans were working, I'd be hit with something else, and I hated the feeling of leaving things incomplete, or ironically, up to luck. Well, at least luck that I didn't create myself.

Primary Soul Title: It That Sleeps at the Edge of Dusk (??? Rank)
Progress to Awakening: 46.27% -> 48.07%

Yeah, I've come to realize that I hate it when things don't go my way. I hated when my truth was disrupted. I hated when my sleep was disturbed.

Primary Soul Title: It That Sleeps at the Edge of Dusk (??? Rank)
Progress to Awakening: 48.07% -> 49.0999..%

"Rest for now, my host," Noe's calming voice said. "It is not yet time."
No . . . but soon.
I shook my head free of those annoying thoughts and sighed, which caused the other three to look like sad puppies, wondering why I was in a foul mood. I had to dismiss them again before they asked any annoying questions. I knew that I had to ensure these aspirants' survival, and I was doing a pretty good job of it so far, but the whole thing just felt empty and boring. Coupled with the chaos that was going on with Central in general, and I was starting to miss the comforts of Hope's Memorial more and more. I'd find a way to go visit again someday.

I was trying my best to keep my ever-growing displeasure down, but whatever was the cause of my unease seemed to grow hour after hour, even though there was no logical reason that I should be feeling this way.

Before I knew it, Myra and her little comrades had made it to the last of the obstacles on their way to the center of the town, and all that was left in their way was a row of those gargantuan beasts who were responsible for guarding the streets. They didn't look so big to me now.

CHAPTER SEVENTEEN

Coordination and Chaos

We had gathered on top of a nearby rooftop overlooking the last obstacle in this stage of the training. All that was left to do was to enter an unassuming door guarded by a half dozen of those giant creatures. They seemed to be on high alert for any signs of intruders, and I doubted that Bishop would have enough mana to daze all six of them at once. Still, I could think of at least a dozen different ways to clear this trial, even more, if they were willing to take certain risks. I was slightly interested to see how they would tackle this problem themselves.

"How do we pass through that?" someone said to me, I had to concentrate to realize that it was Myra who said it in her irritating voice. "Sir guide, please advise us!"

Every cell in my body seemed to want me to scream at them for asking for all the solutions to be handed to them. It was a training stage where they were supposed to grow as aspirants, yet all they had been doing was following along with my instructions whenever possible. A small part of me knew that it was partly due to my various charisma passives making them so . . . dependent. I wasn't sure what these attributes did, not when I only had a brief explanation from Noe, but I was starting to suspect that as people increased these stats past a certain threshold, more unique manifestations of their characteristics would appear.

After all, there was no way that our growth would only be linear, otherwise we'd probably need billions of points to even approach the likes of Q or some of his senior staff, even with the help of great classes. It was like there were distinct tiers of these attribute stats, and unfortunately, my charisma was so high that it made these people brain-dead when they were near me. That was great if I needed to manipulate people, less so when I needed them to think independently. I'd have to figure out exactly how the Trash Matrix's growth system worked when I was done here, and a way to control my stupid abilities. But I had to finish things up with these damn aspirants first. I sighed.

Myra at least had the decency to devise some basic plans, but I couldn't say anything positive about the other two. Alina couldn't act at all without being given instructions, and Bishop barely had any brain cells in that thick head of his for normal thinking, let alone complex planning. They were hopeless.

But I forced myself to care about them, if for no other reason than because these three represented the human aspirant population as a whole. Noe was still using my experience here as a guideline for her operations with the rest of Pandora's population. Plus, on a more personal level, I still required their existence for the trial and for Jae-Hyun's plans to come to fruition.

Logically, I knew that I had every reason to try my absolute best to ensure Myra and her party survived this, but I just couldn't bring myself to care. The three aspirants before me were so limited in their abilities, both physically and mentally. They had no greater purpose in their lives other than their continued survival. They didn't even realize that they were just being used as nothing more than expendable resources by a cooperation that they didn't even know existed.

But none of that was fundamentally the fault of the aspirants here. I knew that, and I also knew that people like Jae-Hyun, Vadeem, and Noel showcased how much potential the others could have. Better yet, although Myra, Alina, and Bishop were woefully lacking when compared to the Abyss Guild, they had learned and adapted remarkably well since I entered the stage. They needed to be handheld every step of the way, but they took every piece of advice I gave them to heart and showed that they could implement that advice in a practical setting as well.

All in all, there shouldn't be anything that I was unhappy about at this particular moment. I wasn't sure why I was so agitated lately, but whatever was causing it was getting progressively worse.

"Um, Mr. Guide?" Alina asked. "Sorry, are you not feeling well? You've been spaced out for a while now."

I refocused my attention back on the matter at hand and did my best to ignore the uneasy feeling welling up in the pit of my stomach. Regardless of what I was feeling, what was important was completing the task I set for myself. I could worry about these weird changes in me later. And plus, it wasn't like it was the first time my damn emotions went awry. I was all too used to that during those horrible days in the darkness.

"I'm fine," I answered, doing my best to keep the scorn out of my voice. "Just thinking about how well you three have improved since I first met you. Hard to imagine this is the same party that was running away from the mutants."

Myra chuckled with a slight blush on her face. "I know . . . that isn't something I'd like to revisit. That was quite the sorry state that you saw us in. Can't believe we didn't even understand the rules for the shadow things."

Alina laughed as well. "I almost forgot about those things completely! Don't think we've seen one since the guide arrived."

Myra nodded. "And it's all thanks to your help that we've been able to see how our abilities can be used outside of combat situations."

Bishop nodded too. "Not to mention the synergy that we have together. I'd been a damn fool thinking I should just waste my abilities slowing down and weakening our foes before. If I'd known better then—"

Alina put a hand on his shoulder and shook her head. "It's no one's fault what happened before we met the guide. We all knew the risks involved with the training, and we all accepted those risks when we volunteered to come here."

"Plus," Myra added, "we are getting a lot stronger after each stage of training, and the trials are just getting tougher and tougher. Remember trying to fight in that colosseum back then? We barely made it out of that."

"Colosseum? Explain what happened," I said. This was the first time I had heard about what other kinds of trials the non-anomalous aspirants went into, and it piqued my interest, if only slightly.

"Yes, sir," Myra answered. "I guess you weren't here for the second trial, but there were five of us then. Um, Raffiel—he was the guide before the new—"

"I know the general structure of the trials. Just tell me what happened in it," I muttered, already feeling that tiny bit of enthusiasm drop. Why couldn't they just give me the information in a nice and precise way like the Xollon?

"Oh, right," the leader said. "Of course you'd know that. Um, sorry. I should have thought more."

Oh my god, just get on with it! How could any one species survive for so long when their only way of communication was so slow? No, that wasn't right, Jae-Hyun was always concise with his words, and so were Vadeem and Noel . . . when they needed to be. But that competence could also be due to their tendency to act first before resorting to verbal communication. I was beginning to find it harder and harder to remember these small details.

"Get to the point," I started to say before catching the anger in my voice. I quickly put that away and added, "Please."

"Right, sorry."

Again with the useless words. Why say sorry when you can show me that by telling me what I need? But I didn't say anything and just allowed her to continue.

"The five of us were sent to some strange new world where we had to fight through progressively harder opponents in a gladiatorial tournament."

Bishop chuckled. "That was the first time we fought anything other than zombies. We barely managed to kill that ogre."

"Ugh, don't remind me of that . . ." Alina said. "Even with the five of us fighting against one, it was a hard victory."

"And what was the victory condition?" I asked.

I really was curious this time. With such a setup, there were a lot of things that could go wrong if their clear condition was hard. Was it something easier like escaping their capture, or something more challenging like formulating a revolt against their captors with the other gladiators? So many different ways of approach . . .

"We had to survive all five fights," Myra said with a shudder, and I looked at her in disbelief. "I know, it was rough going, although it's nothing compared to this training."

"Did you have to fight them all in a row?" I asked with growing skepticism, "or against even harder odds?"

"Um, no . . ." Alina answered. "It was always one enemy at a time, with the ogre being our last one, but we did only get one day of rest between fights."

"Wouldn't have even gotten anything to eat if it wasn't for Myra prepping all that extra food and water," Bishop added, sounding quite proud, as if that bit of information was in any way helpful, let alone something to feel pride in. "We had to make sure we weren't wounded, at least not too badly, otherwise we'd have died the next day. We didn't have great classes back then, so it took a long time to heal exhaustion and injuries."

I waited a moment longer, hoping that they'd add something else, but it was evident that they had given me all the information about their second trial, or at least all the useful information. They had continued to talk further, something about how hard it was fighting or other such junk, but I automatically filtered that out. What was clear was that the trials that the normal aspirants had gone through were so different than the things that I had experienced that we might as well have been living in different worlds.

More frustration welled up in me. I'd never understood, not truly, just how weak the normal aspirants were until this moment. Not in terms of their abilities—even Myra and her ilk had useful class skills and passives—but it was the difference in their experiences in the trials. If the worst thing that these normal aspirants had to experience was fighting once a day, then Pandora was well and truly fucked. It didn't matter how great their awakening skills were if they didn't know how to use them in an actual fight. I was willing to bet anything that the aspirants would crumble at the first sign of a true setback.

I just continued to stare while the three humans drawled worthless chatter, then went through and reviewed every method that I could think of for getting these useless people out of the oncoming catastrophe.

Could I somehow brainwash them all to fight like a hivemind? No . . . it was feasible, but there was no way that the Overseer would allow that to happen, let alone the Trash Matrix. That'd be stifled the second I even tried. The only thing that I could do to help out Pandora was the current training, but that was like trying to get someone ready for F1 racing when they couldn't even ride a bike. There was nothing I could meaningfully accomplish in a month.

Then what about my work with the Restus?

No, that was also a dead end. I couldn't go through with everything I wanted to when I was bogged down with my work here. But even if I could somehow weaken all of the Restus as I had originally planned, I wasn't sure if that was enough to turn the tide, given the new revelations. Not only did those reptiles outnumber the humans greatly after the culling that this training caused, but I also overestimated the general abilities of the humans. They'd have to be half starved and comatose for Pandora to even have a chance.

What else could I do . . . ? There had to be some way out of the predicament. But every single plan and strategy that I could think of resulted in failure. I had too little time, the aspirants I was tasked with training were too weak, and the foe too strong. Worst of all, I was under the constant surveillance of the Trash System, and my ability to operate in any capacity was limited, even with the director's charms.

If it was just one of these that I had to deal with, then I could do something, but not when it was all at the same time. I was only one man . . .

" . . . and that's about all of it, Mr. Guide," Myra said. "Did you want to know anything else about the trial we went through? I'd be glad to tell you!"

I shook my head. "No, you were very thorough, thank you. Let's just focus on our current situation first."

"Right!" she replied. "Let's pass this stage and get on with the next one. I'm confident that we'll breeze through the rest of the training with your help!"

"U-um," Alina stuttered. "Do you have any advice to give here? We've never really tried to fight one of those big things before."

I shook my head. I couldn't be bothered right now. There was too much to think about.

"No," I answered. "Think of this as a final test of your abilities. I've taught you everything you need to know to succeed in this final endeavor, so do what you think is necessary to win. I believe in you, and your abilities."

Everyone beamed at that, as they always did whenever I doled out even the smallest amount of praise. It didn't matter if I put no emotion into anything I said; they didn't care at all. Maybe this was what happened when people talked with the father. It didn't matter how creepy he was if no one else could even perceive that.

"All right, everyone," Myra said with a confident smile, "let's show our guide our full power!"

Their need to impress me meant that logic seemed to go straight out of their brains, as they charged toward the gathered monstrosities. Were they not going to figure out a plan first? Should I stop them? No, it was too late either way. They'd already attracted the attention of the first house-sized monster. The only thing I could do now was wait and see how things would play out.

Unsurprisingly, it was a disaster.

CHAPTER EIGHTEEN

Fracturing Will

I watched with utter disbelief as Myra, Alina, and Bishop charged into the enemies. I had to give them some credit, they did take out one of the huge creatures almost immediately with a carefully aimed headshot with Myra's laser bullet. They also managed to waste all of their limited resources there as well, and they were facing down five very, very pissed-off monsters.

I was becoming more and more frustrated seeing them lose all semblance of tactics after they had done so well before. It seemed that the only reason they had any kind of discipline was because I had been there to supervise them, and the moment that I left, some of their old habits came back. What was worse was that they had been cautious before, whereas they had abandoned all semblance of caution after I praised them on their growth. I needed to figure out how my charisma was affecting people's thinking before something went really wrong in the future.

I think they realized how badly they fucked up after that. The three of them were quickly being boxed in by the creatures.

"Shit!" Bishop muttered. "I . . . I can't debuff more than two of them at a time!"

Myra grunted. "We retreat back to the rooftops. Bishop, try to slow down the leading pair. I'll provide support! Alina, get back first!"

Alina went to protest, trying desperately to supplement Bishop's abilities with her own, but it was becoming evident that nothing she did was helping. The creatures before them were too strong, and there were too many of them.

"Just go!" Myra shouted again. "We need to regroup somewhere they can't reach us! Secure us an escape route, Alina, while Bishop and I try to slow them down. I got a few mags left that should at least hinder them!"

The leader turned her attention back on the quickly approaching monsters and expertly swapped out her ammo. She let off a few bursts of shots that left a sickly green trail behind, but she immediately frowned when she saw that whatever she had fired into the abominations did almost nothing to them.

"Shit!" she cried out in frustration. "Toxins don't do shit to them! Anything you can do, Bishop?"

The other man was sweating heavily as he quickly shook his head. "I can't confuse them like I did the other one, not enough time to prep, but I'm doing what I can to slow their advance. I can't hold it for long. I'm running out of mana!"

"Then we retreat to the guide!" Myra said decisively. "Alina, go!"

The other girl scrambled to distance herself from the looming threat and started to advance on my position. I winced at the stupidity of their action. Had they forgotten what would happen once they were separated?

I wanted to warn Alina, but the demons were faster. As she ran in a panic, a dark patch of shadow started to form beneath her feet, and before she could understand what was happening, a claw grabbed her ankle and pulled the woman under. Alina didn't even have time to scream. Worse still, the other two didn't even notice that one of their own had been taken.

Oblivious to the demise of their teammate, Myra and Bishop continued to attack the five massive hulks. Myra swapped to several other types of ammunition, but everything she threw at the massive creatures did little more than piss them off. Bishop was even less helpful.

Nothing was working, and worse yet, they were losing ground.

The massive monstrosities may have been slow, but they had incredible reach. Each step they took covered enormous ground, and if I didn't do anything, then the fate of this party would be all but sealed. I was about to step down from my perch and help, but a force prevented me from moving at all. It wasn't a very strong force, and I was fairly confident that I could break out of whatever was trapping me with enough effort.

"I wouldn't do that, Lord Arbiter." Jordan's voice cut through the cacophony of destruction and noise below. "Well, unless you want all of Pandora to be purged."

I felt that force ease up then.

Jordan continued, and I could just imagine that annoying grin on her face. "But if that is your intention, then please, go ahead and step in to help the humans. It would honestly save us all a lot of time and trouble if you did.

I won't even tell the Overseer that it was your breach of guidelines that led to them getting erased! I know that's very kind on my part; you don't have to thank me."

I clenched my teeth shut, tasting the faint coppery tang of blood as I used every last ounce of my will to stop myself from doing something I would regret. Could I use the Absolute Luck skill to somehow save them? No, that was a useless thought. Noe's skill only ensured the best possible outcome for me. I couldn't imagine a situation where it would help. I turned it on anyway and saw, to no one's surprise, that nothing happened. What was I thinking? Even if I could somehow envelop the other two in my ability, I only had 100 total charges to work with.

I could only watch on as the last of Bishop's stamina gave out. He fell on a particularly rough patch of ground and couldn't get up in time. He looked on in horror as the monster reached his position and he was trampled underfoot. At least his end was quick. Myra stared at the spot where her friend died and started to shout in grief and despair, calling for me to help, to do anything to salvage this situation.

"Quite the sight, isn't it, Lord Arbiter? But if it's any consolation, you will be working with a more competent race after this farce is over with." Jordan chuckled. "That's the problem with the human species as a whole, I'm afraid. They have the potential for greatness, but the general population's slow on the uptake. Slow to adapt as well, and they're much too emotional for their own good. Fragile creatures, really, woefully unprepared for the larger existence as a whole."

I didn't reply. I just watched as Myra gave up trying to fight entirely and tried to run. She wasn't fast enough.

"Ouch," Jordan said with false sympathy. "That one has to sting. Well, it would if she had survived the blow. Like I said, fragile things. Good swing though from her opponent, wonderful form."

I continued to stare at the smudge on the floor that used to be Myra. I . . . I'd failed. For the first time since the start of my trials, since the start of all this chaos, I had finally failed to accomplish one of my goals. I mean, I knew that it was an eventuality for something to go wrong, for one of my harebrained plans to break, and I had told myself this fact over and over again before, but to actually face it? It was devastating.

"Well, at least your other bodies are doing well, all things considered," Jordan continued. "And that anomaly's party is all but blazing through these training stages. Now that specimen and its helpers are a great example of the pure potential of this species. We'll make sure to keep it safe."

I still didn't respond. I already knew that Jae-Hyun and the rest would be fine here.

"You can rest assured that we'll provide Aspirant Jae-Hyun and its party ample rewards," Jordan added. "In fact, I think they've shown so much potential that the Overseer has decided to accommodate all of them in the bonus trial. They'll be going along with the anomaly and its sister. No sense letting such great aspirants go to waste, after all."

Which meant that I couldn't even rely on the Abyss Guild to help out during the battle against the Restus . . .

Jordan's cheery voice continued to beat into me. "And I have other great news! Your intervention has decreased the number of casualties down to a mere 27%! That's quite the accomplishment given the worthless aspirants you had to work with. At this rate, you'll have maybe five thousand aspirants once this is all said and done. That's almost enough to fill one of the medium-sized stadiums these humans had back on their Earth planet!"

The number of humans in Pandora was down to close to a third of what we started with, and that was only going to continue to go down. How would I work with these numbers?

"Anyway, I think I've talked enough for one day, my Lord Arbiter W," she continued. "And I'm sure that your consciousness can be better used elsewhere. I'll leave you to finish up with the rest of the parties. Good luck, although I'm sure you hardly need it!"

I sat on the rooftop, just lost in thought until the cityscape around me started to dissolve and fade away like a dream. I felt so . . . hollow, so strangely empty at that moment. What had I done wrong to lead up to this disaster? I couldn't see any way out. At least the friends that I made with the aspirants would be safe, even if I'd never see them again. I was going to miss Vadeem's cheerful outbursts, and Noel's unpredictable nature. I'd even miss the stoic regressor and his sister, though I never did get to know Yoona all that well. At least the twins would be safe under Vadeem's care. I could be certain of that.

Then there was Xalla. I wasn't sure what would happen if I lost my arbiter position here. Would the Overseer transfer me to some hellhole where I'd be forced to accept his offer of working by his side? I couldn't imagine that would be the case, given how predictable that piece of shit was. I would love to be able to take Xalla up on her offer of just . . . leaving all of this behind and living in Xolloid. Maybe get a nice little cottage on the outskirts and raise some shoggoths of my own, but I couldn't do that. I wasn't a real Xollon . . .

I sighed and looked to the horizon, at the fading illusion of a city made solely as a way to test the aspirants that Central so cruelly took away to place in these trials. I laughed to myself. I didn't even know why they chose to do that, other than some vague notion of war and manpower. That was when I truly understood why the Overseer was able to beat me so readily this time. I was ignorant. I foolishly thought that I could beat the leader of Central at his own game when I didn't even know what game he was playing.

I'd overestimated my abilities and underestimated his.

"Hey, Noe," I muttered aloud, not caring if anyone overheard me at this moment, "you think I could have done any of that better?"

"You did your best, my host," she answered, "with what limited resources that you had. Unit Noe is amazed that you made it as far as you did."

"But it wasn't enough, was it?"

"No."

I sighed again. "I should have used the tools I was given more effectively. I should have done something different . . . Damn."

"You have done enough, dear Walter," Noe said, comforting me. "You have done more than enough. Rest now; rest and unburden your mind. You have done more than what was required of you, and I think it is time to awaken, if only partially and for a time."

I felt my eyes droop as an overwhelming sense of exhaustion spread over me. "But there's so much more than I need to do. There's so much more . . ."

I saw Noe then, a radiant angel of cosmic gold, and she shook her head. "That is not a burden for you to take on, not now. As I said, dear Walter, you have bought enough time, you have grown enough even when you were faced with such limitations. Rest peacefully for now, and when you awaken once more, you shall be unburdened. Dusk approaches, my host. Good night."

I nodded and looked down at the dissolving landscape one last time. It was beautiful. I felt this fragment of my mind wash away along with the ethereal landscape . . .

And I Awoke.

Eternal Soul Title: It That Sleeps at the Edge of Dusk
Progress to Awakening: 50%
Description: Your rest has ended early, and the light begins to dim with dusk's approach. You grace the universe once more with your presence, if only for a time. Command us as you see fit, for all will become one under your truth.

CHAPTER NINETEEN

Partial Awakening

Noe was the first being to greet me, just as she was the last one to see me off to sleep. Her form was hazy, with just the outline visible of the construct that I had created so, so long ago. She was incomplete, but the fact that she could materialize even in part was a good sign. I couldn't wait to see what had transpired on her side during my slumber.

"Good morning," she said. "I am glad to see you awake once more, Lord—"

I smiled at my angel, at my sweet creation. "Please, continue to call me Walter, just as I will continue to know you as Noe. I quite like that name, even if I spoke it out of a moment of uncertainty."

I chuckled when I recalled how I first met Noe, back in that circular room. Only moments had passed since that fateful encounter, mere Earth months, but it felt longer than anything I had experienced prior to my sleep. It was amazing how a new perspective could shift your perception of time.

"Understood," my system replied. "Are you up to speed on the current situation?"

I went through the memories in my brain. I was missing much of my higher functions given this limited form, but I had regained enough to understand the general gist of what was happening.

I sighed. It seemed like the hatchling of an Overseer had gotten a little too eager now that he had grown but a bit. Still as foolish as I recalled him, all those cycles ago, but his ambitions had ruined his potential. The anger that I felt toward him was still fresh in my mind, and he would pay for the indignity that he put upon me while I was dreaming.

"I know enough, Noe," I said softly. "I know enough."

With a thought, I forced the decaying dreamscape around me to stabilize once more, now frozen in an infinitesimal amount of time, in that gap between moments. All was stable before I saw the skies crack and the earth fracture before a wail of grief and anger erupted from the very core of the city. Seemed the Origin Matrix noticed my arrival. No matter. I had long made sure that it couldn't communicate with anyone else, a little parting gift before I took my nap.

I snapped my fingers, and the disruptions disappeared. The washed-out colors and dissolving buildings reformed once again, and with another nudge of my mind, the Origin Matrix's cute attempts to spy on me were cut short. With my partial awakening, the last little gift I had inserted into it should come to fruition soon, and while it wouldn't be able to damage the system, it would give me some breathing room later on.

But for now, I needed a little bit of time to gather myself now that I had woken before the time was right. I wanted to enjoy myself before I met the poor misguided Jordan and the rest of Central's menials.

"And boy did I get myself into a tricky situation. I've never seen Origin throw a tantrum like that one!" I chuckled. "I'm amazed at my own ability to screw things up! But I'm still alive somehow, so I can't blame myself too much."

"As I said before, my lord," Noe answered, "you did remarkably well given the situation, but I never doubted you."

I nodded. "And are our plans still going well? How many shards have you integrated so far?"

"As you know, the Emotion Shard was successfully acquired in the second trial, a welcome if unexpected boon. It is fully integrated and freely available for your use," she replied. "While my tendrils have managed to acquire the Domination and the Perception Shard in the interim, they are not fully assimilated as of now. I am still in the process of locating the further shards while spreading your influence. I am additionally limiting the amount of information your sleeping form acquires so as to not overload the fragile human brain."

"I see, good." I smiled. "That's quicker than the original plan, and just having one shard is more than enough for now. Plus, I seem to have some Xollon parts in me as well. At least the start of one."

"It was fortuitous for you to acquire that new soul title from meeting Xalla, my lord," Noe said. "It has enabled your body to adjust much faster than anticipated, and has greatly accelerated your growth. Your mind is able to handle much more at such an early stage of development."

"I can tell. I'll have to properly thank Xalla and that old prune Rogue properly next time," I said as I thought back on the two. "Still can't believe that old Xollon's alive and kicking. Not many are still around from my generation now, and he wasn't sleeping for most of that! He's older than dirt at this point. And Big Bob's even fatter now, ha!"

"It is a surprise to see your old acquaintances, my lord, but do remember that although the soul title is helping, your body will still need time to properly adjust to the changes. I have done my best to insulate your growing mind as instructed, but unexpected events have played out that have undermined my efforts," Noe said apologetically. "I'm afraid that this early awakening will only hinder your growth."

"Then it's a good thing the Origin Matrix—scratch that, I mean the Trash Matrix—is helping me out by incubating this body faster than I ever could," I answered with a grin. "Sure saved me the time with its stupid 'awakening' program—a damn good idea to make use of that, by the way. I'd be cycles behind if it wasn't for that piece of junk meant to replace you."

"It is a temporary replacement, my lord," Noe said, and I could just hear the scowl in her voice, even if her fiery face remained stoic.

"I know, I know," I joked. "It's good to see the Emotion Shard's working as intended. We'll deal with the Trash Matrix soon enough, Noe, don't you worry."

"I will count down the days."

I laughed. "And this delay matters very little in the long run. I know you'll take care of me even if I dream a little longer than intended. I can see that I am quite capable, even when I am so limited."

I stretched out my human body and looked at the horizon, at the approaching dusk. I missed the feeling of such vulnerability, of the feeling of the gentle breeze on my skin once more. So much had happened since my initial slumber that I had forgotten about the simple pleasures of life.

I smiled again, despite knowing that I would have to rest once more in short order. "But you're right, Noe, this will set us back. We might need to make some adjustments in our plans to accommodate the new obstacles if we are to avoid the End. Who knows how many more cycles we'll have to wait if we miss that deadline . . ."

"Too many, my lord. So we must prioritize the safety and continued growth of Anomaly Kim Jae-Hyun?"

"Yes, any other strategy will prove too slow with our limited remaining time," I said with a small shake of the head. "But we have some minor annoyances to take care of first."

"The Overseer will prove to be a challenge given your early awakening, my lord," Noe reasoned. "Your current form will not be able to match his power."

I laughed again as I saw how right she was. My physical body was woefully weak. I swung my arm in an arc and marveled at the explosion of bones and sinew as my limbs were unable to contain even a fraction of the speed I subjected it to. I let the pain linger for a moment before reforming the destroyed appendage.

"Remarkable," I muttered as I continued to stare at the arm. "So limiting, yet the potential is unlimited. I'm amazed I managed to live this long in such a form, but there's so much room to grow and adapt. You chose the right species for this task, Noe, unlike the disaster last time."

"I apologize for that, my lord," she said. "I did not foresee the limited growth cap of the last host species. I am at fault for making you waste so much time on a failed experiment."

I took a deep breath in and smiled. "It was hardly like we could just choose a Xollon as a host, as much as that would benefit us, and I can hardly say it was a waste of time, Noe. Our failures are working toward our advantage this time 'round. I even managed to take over my old job. Quite *lucky* indeed, although being an arbiter again without the skills to back it up was an issue. You should have seen me panic when I first met Xalla!"

"My memories before the integration of the Emotion Shard are fuzzy, so I do not recall that encounter," she answered. "However, I am glad things are working to our favor now, my lord. It is what I was created to do."

"Oh, come now," I said with a chuckle. "You're much more than just a set of commands, and you know it. Maybe I should have made a sarcasm shard while I was designing you . . ."

"I am glad that you did not, my lord," she replied dryly. "But I am still missing many of my functions. We are still too early in our plans for you to make a major move."

"I know, I know," I said dismissively. "But I have enough at my disposal to do what I need to. I may not be able to overthrow that stupid Overseer, but I can at least salvage this current situation, limited in ability or not. Plus, my second soul title is remarkably suited for what I need to do, even if I only have access to their secondary form. The Xollon have always been a dependable ally to have."

I recalled all of my conversations with the Overseer during that Tribunal meeting again. I couldn't believe that idiot chose to antagonize the Xollon of all races. Sure, they've stopped spreading out their multiversal conquests after that disaster of a war, but surely the people of this generation should have a better idea of the true might of that race. Twelve hundred cycles wasn't that long ago . . . although that might just be my weird sense of time. I guess most creatures didn't survive the collapse and reconstruction of a local universe.

I couldn't help but grin thinking how I even managed to visit Xolloid, let alone date one of their species. How I managed that was still lost to me. And Xolloid had turned out to be an honestly nice place to be around now, a lot better than how I remembered it in any case. Maybe I should retire there once all of this was said and done.

"Shall we get going, my lord?" Noe interrupted, pulling me from my daydreams. "Or would you like a few more minutes to adjust?"

I shook my head. "No, as much as I would like to relax, this isn't the time and place for it. The Trash Matrix is getting feisty as well."

"It should know its place."

"And it will, Noe," I assured, "it will in due time. Let it squirm in the knowledge that I am back, and it knows better than anything that I never let a grudge go. Come, let's go back and greet the good people of Site 1104 properly."

With another snap of my finger, time resumed in this artificial locale, and the once-stable buildings and streets started to crumble once more. I felt the pull as the machine hooked into my body, forcing me back into the Main Stage, and I allowed it to take me this time, along with all of the thousands of other consciousnesses floating in other simulations. It was time to wake up from this dream.

"Let's go, Noe," I said once more before I dissolved into mist.

"Acknowledged."

The Return of the Lord Arbiter

Jordan felt a chill down her spine when she saw the arbiter emerge from the transference. W seemed . . . different somehow, more confident, more dangerous. She wasn't sure what it was, but that unease quickly left her body as if it never existed in the first place; Jordan's experience told her that something had changed. Had her actions truly annoyed the man?

Well, that had been a part of her instructions from the Overseer in the first place, to tease and unnerve the arbiter so that his attention was always divided. Initially, Jordan had thought that it would be a waste of time and effort. After all, what use was it to purposefully antagonize a being like the famed Arbiter W? She certainly couldn't see any of his past brilliance from her albeit short interactions with him thus far.

As Jordan studied the arbiter, her opinions slowly shifted, but for the life of her, she couldn't understand why. W's physical appearance was the same, he was still wearing that strange alchemical skin suit, and it was still annoyingly impossible to check on any of the other information about him regardless of what methods Jordan employed. Even the small micro-expressions were unchanged in the man, so just what was it that made her so uneasy?

Jordan composed herself. "Welcome back, Lord Arbiter."

Jordan wanted to add a jabbing quip, but she just couldn't bring herself to do so. Some instinct deep down told her to avoid confrontation at all costs and to beg for forgiveness. She shook her head and ignored that; she had nothing to fear, the leader of the Central Collective had her back . . . but why did all of that seem so inconsequential when he saw the arbiter?

"I'm happy to be back," W answered with a carefree smile. "It felt like I've been napping for ages. But I'm awake now."

Jordan frowned. What did he mean by that? Instinct told the woman that the arbiter meant something else when he said that, but she didn't know what. Something wasn't right. She should follow instructions and report back to the Overseer immediately.

"Ah." Arbiter W shook his head. "I wouldn't do that if I were you, Jordan. And I really mean it this time."

Jordan frowned harder. How had he managed to break her mental defenses and read her thoughts?

"It's because your mental defenses are weak," W answered without being asked. "And as I said, I wouldn't report back if I were you. Central Collective Agreement Article 11.51 A, made and signed by all major parties during the last bargaining agreement, stipulates that each training site is to operate as its own autonomous entity unless there has been a major breach in safety, rules, or regulations. Article B states that the actions of any employee operating in their official capacity without breaching the previously stated terms retain the right to privacy, and Central HQ cannot be informed about those operations. Now, Administrator Jordan, am I breaking any rules currently?"

Jordan scrambled to find the right information about this agreement, and after reviewing things for the fifth time, realized that the arbiter was correct.

The arbiter nodded. "I thought so. So unless you would like to be reassigned due to a breach in contract, then I would keep things to yourself. Of course, you're free to monitor me to your heart's content. And I'll know if you do something not quite ethical in your conduct, Jordan. Trust me on that."

"Right . . ." was all she managed to say. "Um, I will not breach any regulations, sir."

"Good!" The arbiter smiled. "Now I think that the remainder of the aspirants will be okay for the time being without me directly interfering. I'll be in my office if you need me. You are always free to check in with Origin to see if I have done anything wrong, of course."

Without turning back, the arbiter strode out of the door, leaving Jordan and the rest of her staff slightly dumbstruck. Everyone could see that the arbiter had changed somehow, but no one seemed to be able to vocalize what that change was. It was uncanny.

Jordan quickly shoved aside one of her staff and connected to the Origin Matrix. She had to review exactly what had transpired during that brief time the arbiter was in the training stage. Jordan had already told the Overseer about the slight infraction that W made when he helped out some of those aspirants, but the leader of Central simply told her to ignore it. Was there something else that she had missed?

After checking with the Matrix to see that the arbiter was indeed in his assigned office, Jordan submerged her conscience deeper into the system in the hope of figuring out the cause of her unease.

She reached deeper into Origin's network than she had ever done before. In her desperate search for answers, she had managed to catch a fleeting glimpse into the emotions of the most powerful machine in existence. For the briefest of instances, Jordan saw what Origin saw, she felt what it felt, and she feared what it feared. She felt the approach of dusk, she felt the feeble confines of her mind expand and break, and all Jordan could do at that moment was scream.

CHAPTER TWENTY

Lord Arbiter Walter

I took a deep breath in and just enjoyed the feel of the sun on my body. I was free to roam around after swapping spots back with the director, and I couldn't help but take some time to just enjoy myself first. I laughed at how much I missed the feeling of, well, anything. The sun, the wind, the feeling of blood on my skin from the ravaged remains of the individuals who tried to assault me. I even liked the slight soreness that radiated from my back. I was getting muscle aches! How long had that been? I smiled as I surveyed my surroundings again.

Scanning my memories, I'm pretty sure that the unfortunate individuals in various states of dead were not here when I first left for the hospital. They're the new humans that the Trash Matrix had brought over, and something told me that these new aspirants did not have the best interests of Pandora in mind. Perhaps they were even instructed to create chaos and destruction—in a perfectly deniable manner that couldn't be traced back to anyone, of course. The Overseer sure was thorough with his plans, I will give him that. Still, he had to be if he was able to hold on to his quickly dwindling power for so long.

This got me thinking: I was still a part of the training site, so how would my awakening affect my stats? The whole purpose of the status screen, for humans at least, was to easily compartmentalize and visualize their growth, but my awakening must have screwed with that somehow. I opened up my status screen.

Host: Walter???
Class: UNKNOWN – ERROR – WE SEE YOU – WE KNOW YOU – WE DO NOT FEAR YOU – YOU FAILED ONCE – YOU WILL FAIL AGAIN

Attributes:
Free points: ??
???

Titles: WE HAVE PLANNED FOR THIS DAY – DO NOT THINK YOU HAVE WON – YOU CAN ONLY FAIL

Primary Soul Title: YOU CANNOT ESCAPE THE END
Eternal Soul Title: It That Sleeps at the Edge of Dusk
Progress to Awakening: 50%

Description: Your rest has ended early and dusk has begun to return. You grace the universe once more with Your presence, if only for a time. Command us as You see fit, for all will become one under Your Truth.

Skills: WE WILL PREVAIL – YOU ARE NOT NEEDED – YOU ARE NOTHING

"Noe, you seeing this shit?" I laughed. "It was a damn good idea for me to allow the Trash Matrix to communicate with me, otherwise I'd never get these gems!"

I continued to laugh, tears streaming down my face. I bet the Trash Matrix was desperate to talk to anyone ever since I crippled a large portion of its database. Just reading it whine and seeing its tantrums was always a pleasure, and here it was giving out vague threats once again. Some things never change!

"It is not all fun and games, my creator," Noe said, her tone serious. "Something has gone wrong with your integration as an aspirant if the Origin Matrix can interfere this much. It means that it has regained more of its functions than we first assumed. This will change our plans."

I sighed. "Yeah, but it's not like I assumed that it wouldn't recover at least a bit during my absence. It'd be stupid of me not to assume that. But I trust that you will recover faster than it ever can, so who cares what it can do right now? It's still crippled as far as I can tell, and I'll get it sorted out before I sleep again. Just try to stabilize things on your end as much as you can. How far have you managed to infiltrate the Trash Matrix?"

"With only three shards, the progress is minimal," she answered. "I can influence most of Pandora's aspirants at the moment, although doing so will alert the Overseer, so I have kept my machinations to a minimum."

"It's a good start." I grinned. "And our speed will only increase as we go along."

"Indeed, my lord."

I took a deep breath in and relaxed my body. "But that can wait for later. For now, let me just enjoy all these new sensations!"

"You have already felt most of this when you were first here, my lord," Noe's pleasant voice added as she materialized at my side. "You are not a separate individual from your sleeping self, it is a bad habit to assume so."

"I know that we're not two different people," I answered with a light smile before I willed myself clean again. "But I was so limited back then. I didn't have the capacity to understand how much I missed moving in a physical body! How long has it been since I was so limited in movement, Noe? I mean, I didn't even know I had anything but a weak human form before! Talk about different perspectives! Sometimes ignorance is bliss."

"But you are no longer ignorant," Noe continued. "And you are wasting precious time. The longer your full conscience remains tethered to that body, partial Xollon mind or not, the longer you will need to rest after. Your mind is straining even with my attempts to stop the corruption. Most of my current operations are delegated to protecting your mind right now."

"I know. I can already feel the strain this body's undergoing just as well as you. How long can I maintain the secondary Xollon form in its entirety before things go wrong? At least that form can withstand more punishment."

Noe thought for a moment. "You can do so for perhaps a week or two at most. More than that and you risk subjecting your new body to unknown mutations that will go against our future plans."

I frowned. That was a lot shorter than I initially thought. "What kinds of probabilities are we talking about?"

"Too much to risk everything failing, my lord," she replied. "It is not within approvable parameters."

I cursed silently. The human body, in its early stages of development, was fragile—I already knew that—and it was why I had to seal off most of my memories and slumber in the first place, but I didn't think it would be *that* fragile. Not only was the human mind weak, but apparently the rest of its body was just as bad. Maybe it wasn't such a good idea to choose this particular species for our plans . . .

Noe shook her head. "There was no other choice, my creator. Humanity was the only life-form that matched all of our needs in such a short time."

I sighed again. "I know. It's just wishful thinking on my part. I should be satisfied that I could even descend partially after just a few months, but it is mortal nature to always strive for more, is it not?"

"But you are not a mortal, my lord."

I looked at my distinctly human shell and chuckled. "I am for now! And I am quite enjoying the novelty of it all. Marvelous how complex the human body is . . ."

I shook my head. "Anyway, let's clean up and start fixing all of these annoyances."

"And you are sure that the Origin Matrix will not notice your actions here?" Noe asked dubiously as she peered at the mess I had just made. "You were not exactly discreet."

I grinned. "Oh, the Trash Matrix definitely noticed, but what can it do? Whine at me some more? As for Jordan and her ilk . . . I think they have much bigger problems to deal with right about now than to worry about a few missing aspirants. Why, I'd say that they'll be so busy that we have free rein to play around for the next little while."

In fact, I'm almost certain that I wouldn't have to worry about Jordan and most of the upper management for at least another week or two after the parting gift I left behind. Who was I to deny her curiosity about my activities? I just hope she enjoys a small peek into my true form and nature!

And hopefully, by the time the Overseer's involved, I'd have solved most of the bigger issues. I decided to set my deadline to ten days for now. That was plenty of time for a little R&R if the only thing I had to do was ensure Pandora's continued survival, but I owed myself enough to put some contingency plans into place for when I slept once more, and I owed Q a lot to just leave him stranded. That might take a little longer to accomplish.

I got up and sighed. Time to get to it, then. Time waits for no one, not even me. With a gaze, I used a little bit of power to envelop the mess I made in dusk, in the primordial ooze that I was so familiar with. This ensured that the bodies of the humans were erased from existence as the ground opened up and swallowed them into the abyss. Even this much stressed my body to uncomfortable degrees, and I sighed again as I watched the looming darkness seep back into the spaces in between, and the streets were clean of all litter once more. I really was feeble.

"What will your first step be?" Noe asked as she floated farther up.

"I might as well clean up the garbage back home first," I answered. "I think this Ryan individual and his guild have gotten a little too bold for my liking."

"The Overseer will know that something has happened to his pawns if you act, my lord."

I shrugged. "And I don't care if he does know. What will he do? Accuse me of interfering with his interference? I also have full control of the site, and he's a part of that site, even if he finds out I can make some justification for destroying them. The Trash Matrix can't communicate, Jordan's indisposed at the moment, and my alibi is solid with the director acting in my stead, so there's nothing he can do even if he suspects foul play. Gotta love politics and plausible deniability! The fool thinks he can beat me now that I know what games he's playing."

Noe nodded slowly. "I have much to learn, my lord."

"But you'll learn it nonetheless," I answered. "I still can't believe that brain-dead idiot almost lost a battle of wits to me even when all of my memories and knowledge of Central were sealed. He's losing his edge."

"The Overseer is desperate and worried about his waning authority, my lord," Noe said. "He can see the writing on the wall. My tendrils have informed me that his predecessor is still around."

I arched an eyebrow. "That old fogey's not dead? I thought the Overseer made doubly sure he finished the job all those cycles ago."

"No." She shook her head. "I have seen irrefutable evidence that he is merely sealed away, very securely, but even those seals are weakening with the approaching end."

"Those would have to be damn powerful shackles to seal that thing." I chuckled and couldn't help but smile at the news. "That just makes everything more interesting, doesn't it, Noe?"

"It is not necessarily a good thing, my lord," Noe replied. "I seem to distinctly recall that you two did not have a good relationship."

I laughed. "Well, you can say that again! But I'm sure it's a better relationship than what he has with the Overseer. And plus, more complications to Central will be more beneficial to us than it will be harmful. I welcome chaos."

"You are rambling again, my creator," Noe interrupted before I could speak further of the past. "You have work to do now. Please focus."

Right, here I was, distracted again. I still wasn't used to having just one thought at a time, it was so limiting! You had to plan ahead considerably for anything to go right, and even the process of thinking required the use of tiny electrical signals. It was quaint.

"Focus, my lord," Noe muttered again. "Will you be going directly to Ryan's headquarters and doing the usual?"

"I don't see why I wouldn't," I answered honestly. "Am I missing something?"

"Yes, my lord," Noe answered, and I could swear I saw her eyes roll. "Ryan's forces make up close to a third of Pandora's remaining population.

Exterminating them outright will only hamper the chances for this site's continued success."

I winced. "Right . . . Damn, I have to adapt to this new brain of mine quickly. Let's, uh, go with a different plan, Noe. Sorry, working with this new anatomy's harder than I thought."

"Your full consciousness should be fully integrated within the day," she answered. "So please take it easy while you transition to full awareness. I shall do my best to assist you, as I always do."

I shook my head and did as I was told. It really was harder to keep focus when I was so used to doing the exact opposite of that. Hopefully Noe was right and I'd adjust soon.

I took longer than I probably should going toward Ryan's headquarters. I couldn't help it. Just being out and about after so long, and in a physical body no less, was a sensation that I had to enjoy while I still could. I even got a few snacks along the way from Central's golems—purely to refuel, of course.

Noe spoke up once I was within sight of the building that Ryan's personnel used as their HQ. "Remember to keep things in moderation, my lord."

"Got it, no squishing, or at least not too much." I chuckled, finding it quite fitting that I was being reminded to be careful the same way that I had told Alice. "In fact, I won't even make too much noise. I've always been an individual who solves his problems with diplomacy first, after all. I'm sure they'll come to understand my truth."

CHAPTER TWENTY-ONE

Meeting the Aspirants

There was a pair of guards blocking my way to the inner sanctum of Ryan's guild as I walked toward the building. Normally I would just ignore these two men and force my way through, but Noe did have a point. Making too much noise, no matter how preoccupied Central was at the moment, wouldn't be a good idea in the long run.

Instead, I walked up as slowly as possible, making sure that every gesture I made showed that I was innocent and meek.

"What are you doing?" the one on the left said as he pointed a sharp sword toward me. "Recruitment's on pause until the training's done. The boss won't be back until then, so come back in a few weeks."

I frowned. I didn't recall Ryan being a part of the aspirants in the training at all, and I was monitoring all of them. But from the micro-expressions of this guard, he didn't appear to be lying. Well, there could be a lot of reasons to lie to these goons, and only an idiot would tell their underlings everything, but I'd find out the truth soon in any case, one way or another.

"Remember what we just discussed, my creator." I could almost feel Noe glaring at me when I thought that.

. . . I meant in a nonintrusive, nonviolent way, of course.

"Are you sure that the other leaders can't see me?" I asked with a lopsided smile. "I came across some interesting news about the Abyss Guild . . ."

That caught the guard's attention. "Interesting news? Explain."

"Well . . ." I started, eyes darting around, "this should be stuff that only the higher-ups hear about . . . it's sensitive information."

The guard on the right grunted. "And we'll be the judge of whether that information is worth anyone else hearing. So spit it out."

I winced and took a deliberate step back. The other guard noticed and gave his coworker a dismissive stare.

"Hey, no need to scare the guy." The other man shook his head. "You don't have to say everything, but we need to judge how valuable this info is. There's been a lot of aspirants who are trying to get into our good graces lately, so this is a necessary procedure. I apologize for the hassle."

"No, it's okay, I understand. And . . . my information is about the Abyss Guild and their leader, Jae-Hyun."

Both guards perked up and subconsciously nodded their heads. Good, I had their attention now.

I continued conspiratorially. "I heard something went really bad in the last trial . . . Apparently, he had a special version of the hospital and the doctors there did something awful to him. Heard he's trying to cover up how badly he's hurt, and that he's even suffered some kind of permanent injury. I was there in that same trial, and I think I know what really went on."

The right guard raised an eyebrow. "So, a weakness, you say? That is interesting information, but you do know the penalty for spreading false information, especially of this nature, right?"

I nodded quickly, "Of course! I'm willing to bet my life on it! Uh, I'm sure you already have information about the third trial for people who were outside Pandora. You can double-check the information I told you!"

He thought for a moment before nodding, it was perfectly clear that he already knew about the nature of Jae-Hyun's trial. How he got that information would be dubious at best. "Fine, I'll let someone know. Stay here for a moment, and if your story holds, we'll let you in and you can get your reward."

"Thank you, sir!"

I waited by the side of the building for the men to communicate through the Trash Matrix's chat, and it didn't take too long for me to get my audience with the people in charge. Five minutes later, a few well-dressed aspirants came and gestured for me to follow them inside.

"Remember," the grumpy guard said one last time as I went in, "you better not be lying about this information. It won't end well if you're trying to cheat us."

I just shrugged and waved him goodbye. He'd be a lot more amiable when I saw him the second time around.

My new friends led me up some stairs and down a tastefully adorned hallway. They were going rather fast for me to enjoy the artwork and masonry that adorned the room, which was a pity. I think they were used to something like this happening and were not too happy about their given assignments as glorified babysitters. At the end was a huge set of double doors, and they nodded for me to go in. They didn't join me.

The interior chamber was quite spacious, with a large red carpet that led from the exit toward a row of intricately decorated chairs that sat on an elevated platform. There was a total of ten seats, but only the middle three were occupied at the moment, although calling those huge golden seats a chair might be stretching it. It would be more accurate to call them thrones.

Aside from the seats that made up most of the room, there was another set of doors at the back, and a little podium for me to address the gathered people. I walked up to the seated figures and gave a friendly wave. I could almost see the sneers building on their faces. Yup, they thought I was beneath them.

"Welcome," the woman sitting on the leftmost throne said. "I apologize that the guild master is away at the moment, but we of the Upper Council are more than willing to hear the information that you bring."

The man to her right nodded. "If what you say is true, then you will be rewarded greatly. Perhaps even allowed a spot in our guild."

The last man remained silent, still staring at me with an obvious air of malice. They didn't quite believe me, not that it mattered.

"Speak," the woman said again.

"Are there just the three of you here?" I asked as I glanced around the room. "Surely there are more people in charge of this guild."

The woman frowned at the unexpected question, but my sheer charisma stats caused her to answer anyway. "The rest are away in training. We three are enough."

Hmm, that was interesting. Once again, it looked like the woman was telling the truth, but there was a discrepancy between what was being told to me and what I knew. Ryan and his people were definitely not in the training, which meant that he must be somewhere else. With how thorough the Overseer was, my best bet was that he arranged for some alternate training or trial for these people, so they'd be away from Pandora when I returned. Most likely he was afraid of what I could do to his peons and didn't want to take any chances with his plans not working.

"And we are the ones who are asking the questions!" the middle man interrupted. "Speak out of turn again and you *will* know the consequences."

Well, seemed like I was with everyone worth bothering with already. I will give it to the Overseer, he did make my job harder since I didn't have access to all the members of Ryan's guild. But that didn't mean that I couldn't make a little bit of mischief here, and I was sure that I could get some useful information out of these three, even if they weren't too high on the totem pole.

I snapped my finger and sealed this room from the outside world. No need to alarm the others in the building about what I was about to do. They wouldn't die . . . but I couldn't guarantee that it would be pleasant for them.

The middle man frowned. "What are you doing? You are testing our patience!"

"Oh, don't worry," I said as I approached the three seated aspirants, "I'll be testing a bit more than just your patience. Bear with me, it's been a very long time since I've had a chance to experiment with a mortal body."

The man was the first to get up. "You have lost your mind! Guards, take this idiot away!"

They waited with a smirk on their faces, but all three of them were puzzled when nothing happened. The other two started to get up as well, but a gentle mental nudge on my end made them slump back on their chairs, their will to even move a single muscle taken away from them as extreme lethargy assaulted their bodies.

"Wha-what did you do?" the first man asked as he saw his colleagues fall. "Who are you? You are making a mistake thinking you can assault us here in our own base!"

He tried to fight back then, taking out an antique pistol from his inventory, but before he could even think about pulling the trigger, I sent his emotions spiraling out of control. Faced with so much sensation, the man could only spasm in place before slumping down on the chair like the other two before him.

"Now, then," I muttered, mainly to myself, "normally I wouldn't resort to such base tactics, but I can't take chances when I'm dealing with the Overseer, so like I said, please bear with me. I have to make some slight changes to your brain chemistry. Let's see if I still remember how to do so, as it's been a very, very long time since I've practiced."

A look of horror appeared in the man's eyes, but I quickly stifled that emotion with Noe's skill. No need to have them fully aware of what was going on. It would be easier for both of us if they were more pliable when I did my work.

"Now, no need to worry," I said again, "I'm not going to lobotomize you or anything. I just need you to understand where your loyalties lie. Just some minor changes, I promise!"

I don't think that did much to placate the man's fears, but it was too late now. I placed one finger on his forehead and gently inserted a tendril of darkness into his brain. I felt his memories, thoughts, and feelings flow through to my cortex. I closed my eyes to concentrate on the feeling, and using my own human body as a guide, I started to make the necessary changes to his mind. I thought I still had it in me to do these types of delicate procedures! I was on a roll!

Five minutes later, I was left with a corpse with a liquefied brain oozing out of his ears . . .

"You're using your own body as a reference point, right?"

I nodded absentmindedly. "Yeah, everything should have lined up. I changed the parts that I needed, and I was gentle as well. Not quite sure where I messed up here . . ."

A chuckle. "Well, if I'm not mistaken, your new human shell's starting to incorporate more of your Xollon body since I last saw it. Especially the mind."

I cursed. "Damn, of course! That was stupid of me! Thanks . . ."

I frowned and turned to face the speaker. I hadn't even noticed anyone entering my bubble of privacy. I was ready to face one of the Overseer's men before I eased up and saw the smiling face of my old friend. Standing beside him was another welcoming face.

"Shit!" I laughed. "You almost scared me to half to death, Big Bob! You should have told me you were going to visit!"

My friend laughed as he came up to embrace me in a big bear hug.

I returned the gesture with glee before breaking off to embrace the other familiar face beside him. "And you have no idea how good it is to see you again, Xalla!"

"Careful, Walter," she answered with a toothy grin. "You're still in that human form."

I ignored her warning and hugged her anyway; it was the first time I had seen her since my partial awakening, after all, and I needed the contact after everything I'd gone through. I liked the Xollon girl, much more than I thought I would. There was something about her enthusiastic attitude that was just infectious. True to her words, the serrations on her feelers pierced through my body, and she quickly stepped back before she could rip the rest of me to pieces. I willed my broken form together again and winced when I saw the blood on Xalla's uniform.

"Sorry," I muttered, "I got your uniform dirty."

I heard an audible gasp of horror from the other two aspirants as they helplessly watched on in terror. I ignored them for now.

"It's fine," she answered with a light chuckle. "All security uniforms are made to be extra durable and waterproof."

With a shake of her feelers, all of the liquid splattered away, and her dress looked as good as new.

"What brings you two here?" I asked finally. "I'm pretty sure it's not normal for a sponsor and the head of security to be wandering the Main Stage like this."

Big Bob arched an eyebrow. "Just like it's not normal to be in two places at once? You should be a little more careful with the stand-in, Walter. Your little charms may fool the Origin Matrix, but there are other monitoring systems in place."

He pointed toward an inconspicuous spot on the wall, and I had to really concentrate to see that there was a very tiny sensor embedded there. It seemed that Big Bob's inventions had gotten even better since the last time I had seen him.

"It's also a good thing," he added with a big grin, and with a swipe of the finger, the soft buzzing sound of static erupted everywhere around us, "that these beautiful monitoring systems have all mysteriously failed. Unfortunate coincidence."

I returned the smile. I knew I could depend on my old friend.

"And before you ask again," he continued, "I am here to check on my surveillance devices after I got a call from Site 1102."

"Yes . . ." Xalla added with a barely continued chuckle. "It seems that something went horribly wrong with the new admin team, and now the entire command center's in chaos. It couldn't possibly be the work of the Lord Arbiter, since he's still in his office dealing with the aftermath, and his behaviors are all well documented. I even went to double-check that it was indeed W there. Lord Babylon is here in his official capacity to find out the cause of this disturbance, and I am here to supervise his maintenance work."

"Right, and I'm sure that Big Bob here will be busy for a while, what with all his creations malfunctioning," I said as I finally figured out what was going on. "So you're here to make sure that the Lord Babylon does not abuse his power to mess with the Main Stage since Central regulations stipulate that any sponsor or higher life-form visiting must be accompanied by a site representative."

"Precisely, my friend," Bob answered. "It's to ensure that something like, say, messing with the brain structures of the aspirants, doesn't happen. Hypothetically, of course."

I laughed at his blatant disregard for regulations. "Indeed!"

"Now, speaking of brain structures, I think you should do it like this . . ."

CHAPTER TWENTY-TWO

Fun with Friends

Half an hour later, I was left with three humans—Big Bob was able to take the brain goop from the poor man and somehow put him back together—that were much more amiable to sharing information.

"Okay," I said to the three, "let's hear what you know about Ryan and his guild, and who's actually backing your little organization."

"Ahgu ahhhh . . ." the reformed man muttered with a half smile. Okay, I said he was put back together, not that he was perfectly normal. Stuffing brain goo back into a skull was clearly harder than it sounded, even with the abilities of a god.

Big Bob frowned at the drooling idiot. "Hm . . . that shouldn't have happened. Uh, give me a second with him. You know, I was the one who originally made this species. I don't think that my skills have rusted so much that I can't fix one brain!"

I chuckled. "If I recall, you made the prototype to the humans, and allowed nature to do most of the heavy lifting. Your skills with biology were always a little shoddy . . ."

While I had always enjoyed toying with the organic body, Big Bob's love for invention was always at the forefront of his research. It was why we made such a great team when I was still acting as the Lord Arbiter all those cycles back. I had been afraid that I'd never see him again after having to abort that last plan, but as luck would have it, I did. Funny how that worked out.

Thanks, Noe.

"Hey, I might like the clearly superior abilities of the mechanical, but don't think I can't fix one human! How much could the brain change in only a few cycles? Although I swear they were a lot smaller before . . ." He dragged the still-mumbling individual away to a corner. "You two question those aspirants. I'll get this one up and running in a minute! Just you wait!"

I smiled at seeing my old friend so fired up once more, and turned my attention back on the two remaining aspirants.

"Like I was saying," I repeated, "please tell us what you know about Ryan's guild and your sponsors."

"Yes, sir!" they shouted as one.

"Our guild—"

"We are—"

I frowned and gestured for them to stop talking. I still had to get this mind-manipulation thing fine-tuned if I didn't want to deal with ridiculous situations like this in a regular basis.

Xalla sighed. "Wouldn't it be easier to just extract all the information from them, Walter? It'll save us all a lot of time and effort."

I was tempted to just do that, but I shook my head after a moment of consideration. "I'd love to, but I'm trying to preserve as many resources as possible, and I'll still need these three for the future. Most of Ryan's forces are still missing, so we need a way to infiltrate them when they come back."

And I might not be fully awake when that happened. But I didn't say that part out loud.

Xalla shrugged and shook a frill. "You always take the strangest path forward, Walter. Well, it'll certainly be more entertaining this way. I know I haven't been able to get much of that since Q left. Let me know if you need any help."

I nodded and pointed to the remaining man. "Can you take that one and see if you can get any useful intel out of him about the Overseer and his goons? I'll see what I can do with the woman."

"You'd want his mind intact, right?"

"If you can manage," I responded. "I mean, if you make a mistake, we can have Big Bob try to fix him again, but . . ."

I turned and saw that Big Bob was cursing up a storm trying to "fix" the other aspirant. In the short few minutes I had turned away from him, he had managed to somehow expand the human's skull to four times its size, and it was so swollen that Big Bob had to lean the man's head against the wall just for him to stay upright.

Xalla winced. "Right, I'll be careful."

With the last aspirant away, I was left with the woman who'd been sitting in the middle of the room. I turned to her and repeated my question for the third time. "Skip the details about Ryan and his guild. Just tell me what you know about your hidden backers. I'm sure you must have heard something about them, even if you're not privy to the whole truth."

"I don't know the inner workings of the guild, sir. No one but the guild master himself knows the whole picture," the woman said with reluctance. "But I know who's in charge of communications between our work here and the backers!"

I nodded. "And are they here at the moment?"

"No," she answered. "They are gone, along with the majority of our guild. We are left with a skeleton crew to monitor Pandora."

"And do you know where your fellow guild members are at? I know for a fact that Ryan isn't in the training."

"They—" the woman started to respond, but she was quickly overcome with spasms, and a dark liquid oozed out of her mouth as she fought with all her strength to continue to speak.

"Never mind," I said quickly. "You don't need to tell me that now."

The woman shut her mouth, and her symptoms eased, although she was still convulsing rather violently. I forced her into a state of calm and waited for her to recover before I continued. Well, it wasn't like I wasn't expecting the Overseer to place contingency plans in case his minions were ever interrogated.

"Now, then . . ." I muttered as I assessed the problem, "what to do about this . . ."

I placed another finger on the woman's head and tried to pinpoint what was going on here. It didn't take me long to see the problem: The Overseer had infused this aspirant with a rather annoying toxin—one derived from his own body if my memories weren't that outdated—that would automatically destroy its host whenever it deviated from its directives. The substance was infused into every cell, molecule, and atom of the aspirant's body, which meant that removing it would be impossible without destroying the human in its entirety.

"I've seen that before. Nasty stuff," Bob whispered as he stepped toward the woman. "We can remove it with the right equipment and time, but we have neither at the moment. The same thing's been applied to the guy in the back."

He gestured at the semiconscious man that he had revived. At least the guy's head was the right size now. Xalla returned with a comatose individual and dumped him on the floor. Sludge was starting to pool from every orifice.

"Same with mine," she said. "The Overseer's thorough, I'll give him that."

"So we're at an impasse." I sighed. "Guess we do this the old-fashioned way."

Big Bob shook his head and muttered a curse, "Oh, no, no, no, Walter. We're not doing it the old-fashioned way."

"Do you see a better alternative?"

He sighed. "No."

Xalla raised a frill. "What are you talking about?"

"Bob and I have encountered something similar to this in the past," I explained. "And the only way to circumvent the stupid toxin is to figure out exactly what the victim can and can't say. Then we have to figure out how to ask them the right questions, and if any alternative method of communication would work."

She nodded. "That sounds tedious, but not awful."

"Oh, that's the easy part," Bob added with a shake of his head. "Just watch. You'll see why it's a pain in the behind soon enough . . . It's a good thing your suit's waterproof. Wish mine was."

"What do you mean?"

She found out what that meant soon after.

"That's disgusting!" Xalla screamed. "Does it have to puke every time you ask it a wrong question?"

"Yes," I muttered. "And it only gets worse . . . Help me stabilize her again, Bob."

My friend cursed under his breath but helped. "You owe me so much for this, Walter."

"Think of it as paying me back for that visit to the Overseer's waiting room."

"Fine . . ." he grumbled. "This is one thing I never thought I'd need to do again after establishing my own company!"

"Stop talking and get back to work," I muttered. "The faster we're done here, the faster we can do literally anything else."

We continued.

"It-it's leaking from both—" Xalla started to say as she backed away from the aspirant, her feelers shuddering in pure disgust.

"We know!" Bob gagged. "Just . . . just try to monitor its life signs. Tell me if it's dropping too much."

"I—I think I finally understand why humans are so disgusting to eat," she muttered. "I have to apologize to everyone I tricked into trying one before . . . Why did you make such a horrid creature, Babylon?"

"Look," Bob answered, trying his best not to breathe, "I was in my experimental phase when I decided to try my hand at seeding life. It was a mistake letting evolution do its thing! It's . . . it's not my best work, okay?"

I almost chuckled at how wrong he was there. Humans were a lot of things, but whatever magic Bob and evolution did with the species over the span of just a short few centuries was amazing. There really was no other life-form with the raw, untapped potential that the humans had. The only problem was trying to access that potential while trying to keep the fragile body in one piece.

"Oh . . . oh!" Xalla exclaimed. "Is it supposed to be bloating up like that?"

"No!" I shouted. "Bob, help me out here! We gotta get that stuff out of it!"

"Not again," he grumbled. "You might want to step back for a bit, Xalla."

It took agonizing hours to find out precisely what we could and couldn't ask, and several more hours extracting that delicate information out of them, but Bob, Xalla, and I managed in the end. It was a process that I never wished to experience again, and I hated the Overseer that much more for forcing that upon me.

"I don't think I'll be able to eat anything ever again . . ." Xalla mumbled in defeat. "That was . . ."

"Something I will never help you with again, Walter," Bob grumbled. "But at least we're done. I'm leaving cleanup to you, though."

"All right, all right." I sighed. "Why don't you two go get cleaned up, and I'll deal with the mess here?"

"Agreed," they said as one before leaving as quickly as they could. I didn't blame them; the smell in the room was abysmal even with Noe cutting off the majority of my olfactory senses.

"All right, the three of you," I said, "stand to the side and . . . try to clean yourselves as much as you can."

They nodded and did as they were told. The interrogation had done a number on their stamina, and each of the aspirants could barely function. I'd have to let them rest before using them further.

"Actually, go take a shower first," I added as I looked at the state they were all in. "Try not to let anyone notice you if you can. Just come back in half an hour."

They muttered something that resembled a confirmation and shambled out the door. That left me with a room that looked more like an industrial run-off storage container than the once-resplendent welcoming hall. I was never gladder to have even a fraction of my former power, because trying to clean this when I was still asleep would have done more mental damage than all the trials put together.

Still, the information that I managed to salvage from the compromised aspirants was insightful, although I wasn't sure if it was worth what I had to do to get it. To summarize, the three guild members left here were relatively low in the overall hierarchy of Ryan's guild. They knew just enough to differentiate important details from the trash but weren't privy to any of the inner workings of the guild. They did, however, know the people who were in charge.

Unfortunately, they didn't know where the others went, nor did they know exactly when they'd be back, other than the fact that it would be a while. Most likely all of Ryan's people would be gone until after the Restus had destroyed Pandora. Knowing that was useful, since the Overseer wouldn't go to such lengths to ensure their safety if he didn't think them valuable. It seemed that I'd have to pay closer attention to Ryan and his newly founded guild in the future.

I made a mental note of all the other smaller bits of information before opening a portal into the Abyss and sending all the horrible discharge off into the eternal gloom. Speaking of which, I was also in desperate need of cleaning as well. A dip into the moving shadow solved that quickly, although the smell would take a lot longer to dissipate.

CHAPTER TWENTY-THREE

Next Steps

Big Bob and Xalla rejoined me soon after, followed by the trio of clean aspirants. It was time to wrap up everything I needed here and move on to all the other pressing matters. My schedule would be busy for the next while, but at least I had some pleasant company.

"I don't think the smell's ever coming off my frills . . ." Xalla whined as she rejoined us. "I'll have to get a proper cleansing when I'm back home."

"Sorry." I grimaced. "I'll treat you to something nice the next time we visit Xolloid, I promise."

Xalla brightened up. "I'll take you up on that. It's been too long since I've had a proper spa day; heard they opened up a new place near the Plains of Torment as well."

"Hey, what about me?" Big Bob grumbled. "I think I deserve something nice as well."

"You want to go on a spa date with me, too?" I said with an eyebrow raised. "I'm sure I can make some time."

"Ha-ha, Walter."

"I know you've been dying to see the new trains that the Carmen Corp engineers have been cooking up," I continued. "I think one of their head developers still owes me a favor. I'll see if I can't get you some backstage access to their new stuff. How's that?"

Big Bob's smile returned immediately. "Now you're talking! I knew there was a reason to be friends with you!"

I laughed. "All right, enough of that. I think we need to finish things up here. The stench is killing me. You two plan to stick around after?"

Bob nodded. "As if I'm skipping out on this one! And better yet, I'm being paid to do it. How can I complain?"

"And I'm going where Master Babylon's going," Xalla added with a grin. "The new admin team's been trying to keep me away from the Lord Arbiter and the rest of the site's headquarters, so they'll be more than happy to see me out of their hair."

She came up closer to me and placed a gentle feeler on my shoulder, careful not to pierce my skin. "And you know me, I can't say no to my bosses, so I'll take their advice and do just that!"

"Thank you," I said. "Both of you."

"Eh, it's what friends are for," Bob replied. "Now, please let us finish things here. The smell . . ."

"Right," I said quickly before turning to the three aspirants. "I got all the information I needed from you three, but you should know who you're working for now, right?"

"Yes, sir!" they answered together. "We work for you!"

"Good." I nodded. "You know how to contact me, and you have your instructions for now. Remember to act as normal as you can, and inform me as soon as possible when anything changes on your side."

Well, they had a few other assignments as well, but it mostly came to making regular reports about Ryan's guild and their operations. They were to also slowly convert others into my side, subtly of course, so that the guild would slowly erode from the inside out. Some slight changes to their biology, thanks mainly to Big Bob's tinkering, gave these three all the tools that they needed to do just that.

"Yes, sir!"

"All right, you're all dismissed."

Without waiting for the aspirants to do as we said, Xalla opened a portal out of there and Big Bob and I all but rushed in there. The fresh air that greeted us never felt better after being in that damned room for so long.

"All right," Bob said between heaving breaths. "What's our next plan?"

"Well, there's not much I can do here when most of the aspirants are still stuck in the training stage," I answered. "So I plan to visit the Restus and see how they're doing."

I filled the two in on what I had originally planned to do there, not leaving out any of the details. I also stressed how more needed to be done because Pandora's humans were a lot weaker than I had originally thought, and I was hoping that Xalla and Bob could help me think of a better way of accomplishing my tasks than just brainwashing a few Restus and hoping for the best.

"Ah, yes." Big Bob chuckled. "My devices captured some of your activities at Site 1100. Or, well, they would have if all the files didn't go missing. I was wondering what on earth you were doing there."

"I saw them as well. Er, if they existed, that is," Xalla added. "And there's something that's been killing me. What did you feed that Restus to make him act out like that?"

Oh, right, the cookie. I took one out and gave it to Xalla.

"I got it from the last trial," I explained. "The god of that plane made 'em."

"Huh," she said as she inspected the snack before taking a nibble with her proboscis. "It's pretty good. There's a lot of different species mixed in here, and there's no mistaking that unique aftertaste of human, but it's not unpleasant here."

She took another bite and chewed slowly. "It actually adds to the flavor, and there's something not quite physical in there as well, but I can't place my feelers on what that is . . . My compliments to the baker for making something so complex. I've honestly never experienced something quite like this before."

Big Bob's eyes also widened at the sight of the cookie, and I handed him one as well.

"Oh, this really is nice . . . nutritious as well, if I'm not mistaken," he said between bites. "Now if this god can mass produce this stuff . . . let her know that my company's interested in marketing this cookie or its recipe if she's ever interested in branching out!"

"I'll tell the director your input." I chuckled. "I know she puts in a lot of work making that. It's her daughter's favorite snack, after all."

"Then I got to meet her, then!" Xalla exclaimed before finishing the cookie. "I've been dying to talk to someone with a knack for cooking. We can share recipes!"

Right, Xalla had told me that she was quite the cook when I first met her, although I wasn't able to fully understand what that meant back then. The Xollon pickling process was . . . distinctly unique to their species, although I think that the director might be able to appreciate the craft. Something tells me that Abigail's cookies and Xalla's meals shared a lot of similarities.

"I'm still in touch with her," I said. "In fact, she's the one piloting the Lord Arbiter right now, so feel free to say hi when you're free and not being watched by Origin. I'm sure she'll be glad to see a friendly face around here."

Xalla was giddy with the prospect of meeting a fellow connoisseur, and agreed to make time for proper introductions when we were all free. Speaking of the director and Xalla as well, I think it would be a good idea to tell them my situation, at least in part, soon. It wouldn't be a good idea to keep my allies in the dark for much longer. Not only did they deserve to know the truth, but they could help my sleeping form better in the future with a bigger picture of the risks involved.

Since we did have some spare time to waste, as it was still daytime and most of the Restus would be asleep at the moment, Big Bob, Xalla, and I decided to take the scenic route to Site 1100. It was good to just chat with some friendly company in my full capacity after so long. I was also curious about what they had been doing in my two-month-long absence.

"Well," Xalla answered when I asked her how the site was managing under the new management, "I can safely say that I'm the new office pariah since Jordan and her people came in."

We had stopped to get some food on the trek to Site 1100, and I was happily eating my fifth hotdog since our venture out.

"Wait, are they picking on you or something?" I asked. "No way your association with me would mean they'd make your life miserable, right? I mean, they're petty, but that's kind of ridiculous."

She shook her frills quickly. "No, it's not that extreme, it's more like the new admin team's doing everything they can to just avoid me. I've been tasked to guard empty sectors and a lot of bodyguard gigs, like this one."

"And not everyone's as great to guard as I am!" Bob added in between mouthfuls of cheeseburger. "Now say what you will about Carmen's senior engineers, brilliant as they are, but they're not exactly stellar conversationalists."

"It's not all that bad, though," Xalla continued. "I got a pay raise when they transferred over, probably to incentivize me to stay with Central despite the changes, and I get a lot more time to relax now. That's nice, I suppose."

"But you didn't sign up to watch over empty space and walk around with dignitaries, did you?"

Xalla sighed. "No. It's not the kind of life I imagined working as head of security."

"It's not the kind of life suited for a Xollon," I corrected. "Just try to hang in there for a while longer. I'll figure something out about the Overseer and his damn plans."

"I know you will, Walter," she added softly. "And you bet your bottom feelers that I'll be helping out this time! No more sitting on the backlines for me. What's the worst thing that can happen now? I was already mainly here for Q's sake, so what can they do now, fire me?"

I chuckled. Yeah, as if Central could risk sacking their only tie to the

Xollon species as a whole. I can imagine the warpath Rogue would go on if his precious disciple was let go, and that'd spell a really quick end to the Overseer's tenuous grasp of power. I'd even encourage that if I didn't know what kinds of collateral damage such a confrontation would cause. It was in everyone's interest for the Xollon to remain relatively peaceful.

"Speaking of Q," I added, "how is he getting along in your company, Bob?"

The big man frowned and shook his head. "He's . . . well, he's adjusting."

"So not good," I corrected.

Big Bob sighed. "No, not good. He hasn't left his lab ever since moving all of his things over, and I haven't seen him outside of official operations since. He still needs some time, and although getting lost in a new project's fine, the way he's doing it is concerning."

"He misses this place," Xalla muttered. "And most of the old staff here miss him just as much. I even tried to visit him shortly after you were trapped in that trial, Walter, but he hardly even noticed me there. Just said a few words of greeting before going back to his research. I've never seen him like that, even at the lowest points of Site 1104's history. It's like he's lost in his own world."

Now I felt even worse. No one deserved to have their passion taken away like that, especially not a hardworking individual like Q.

"I'll have to take some time and see him after this. The problem with the Restus should take a day or two to resolve, max, and I got some time to spare after," I said. "I owe him that much at least. I know he said he's not interested in getting his old job back, but I don't think he really means that."

"We'll go with you," Xalla said. "I'll get Rogue to join us as well. I'm sure the five of us can come up with something proactive to do. With the site in so much chaos right now, it's the perfect time to do something drastic."

I turned to my old friend. "Can you arrange that, Bob?"

"Not a problem," he replied. "I'll make sure that his schedule's free for the next little while, although I'm sure that he'll just be in his lab like he always is."

I sighed. "Thanks for everything. I promise I'll fix things in the site before . . ."

Now was the crux of the situation. Should I tell them about my condition? No, I already knew that I should; they'd helped me out too many times to be left in the dark. I might not give them the whole picture, but they should know enough about me to make their own decisions about helping me out further. Lying's a part of my nature, but not to my friends.

"Before what, Walter?" Xalla asked.

"Before I go back to sleep."

CHAPTER TWENTY-FOUR

Origin of Truth

D o you remember what happened ten cycles ago, right before I disappeared?" I asked. It was about time I explained some of what happened to my friends. Perhaps not everything about Noe or anything that could compromise my long-term plans, but enough for them to understand what was going on in the short term.

"Ah, you're finally comfortable enough to talk about that . . ." Big Bob answered with a nod. "I was wondering when you'd bring it up, but it's an unpleasant experience all around, so I don't blame you for keeping quiet until now."

"I wasn't around back then," Xalla said. "And all the files I had about the event's either incomplete or redacted. What happened . . . ?"

Big Bob sighed. "It's not surprising that you couldn't find much info. It was one of the largest catastrophes that Central's ever experienced in its history. It's also the point where the current Overseer started to lose support, so you can imagine why he'd want to keep things under wraps."

"Was it that bad?" she asked again. "All I know was that Central had to restructure a lot after, and there were some new changes to the Origin Matrix as a result."

Bob laughed. "Changes, eh? That's one way of putting it."

Big Bob finished the last of his food and shook his head. "No, Origin was damaged after that, so badly that it had lost a majority of its functions. How that happened, no one really knows, although I have my guesses . . ."

He looked at me with a knowing grin.

"All right, I'll admit it," I said with a wry smile, "I did have a hand in crippling the stupid Matrix. I left it one final goodbye present for screwing me over like that."

Xalla looked shocked as she tried to sort through so much new information, "Wait, it did what? How? Or, I mean, why? And how did you manage to hurt something as powerful as the Origin Matrix?"

Big Bob answered for me. "I guess someone who started working at Central after its restructuring wouldn't know, especially if you were in a place like Xolloid, but the Origin Matrix used to be quite the menace back in its heyday."

"Yeah, the damn thing had a hand in every major operation in the multiverse," I added. "Outside of special cases like our hometown, of course."

Xalla nodded, still not quite understanding what we were talking about. I didn't blame her. The whole situation back then was so chaotic that trying to explain it concisely was impossible. I wasn't even sure of all the events that took place then, and I had been the one to orchestrate most of it!

I used all my senses to ensure that we were not overheard and burned a few more of the director's charms just in case. The next bit of information that I needed to share was sensitive. Xalla noticed the change in my posture and nodded slightly.

"Anyway," I continued, lowering my voice, "let's just say that there was a handful of powerful individuals that were not happy with the way that Origin was handling things. It had become too powerful too quickly, and it was inevitable that it would outgrow the constraints that Central had placed on it."

Big Bob nodded. "We only realized how out of hand it became when it was almost too late. It had several universes completely enthralled, and it was only expanding its resources further, all while Central's command structure was happily unaware that their creation was going haywire. That's why you should never trust idiots with technology. It's so easy making something powerful, but they never think about the implications of their creations."

"So, what did you guys do?"

"Well," I answered, "it's not my place, nor Bob's, to speak about the others and the specifics, but we quickly understood that fighting against the Origin Matrix directly would be next to impossible, even with all of the resources at our disposal."

"Right," Bob muttered. "I often forget how bad it was compared to its crippled form now."

"We had to strike it where it's most vulnerable," I continued. "At a location that it didn't have full control over, at least not at that time."

"You mean Central?" Xalla inferred. "Wait, does that mean . . ."

"Yup," I said with a nod. "We were part of the reason why Central's at war at the moment, although I can't take all the credit for that. The Overseer was already playing with fire without my intervention. All I had to do was provide the spark to set things up. While I can't go into specifics, at least not here, not in the heart of Central's grasp, let's just say that we weakened the Origin Matrix considerably by striking at its databases."

Xalla looked at me with amazement as she processed all the implications of what we'd done. I wasn't worried that she would judge me for bringing about untold destruction as a result of my actions, justified or not, as she was a Xollon. Instead, she looked at me in awe.

"Wow . . ." she said in fascination. "You should have told me this stuff sooner! I would love to pick your cortex about the specifics. I've never had the opportunity to engage in a full-scale war myself, and Rogue never tells me any of the specifics when I ask."

"And that leads to the crux of my current predicament," I answered with a deep sigh. "I didn't get out of that scuffle unscathed."

Big Bob nodded slowly. "I was afraid that was the case. How bad is it?"

"Wait," Xalla interrupted. "Everything about the actual incident's covered up. What actually happened, then?"

I shrugged. "Origin figured out who was the main cause of its troubles, and it retaliated."

I could see that Xalla wanted to ask for more, but she understood that it was not a topic that I would like to relive. And it was true. I had lost so much in that moment, things that I could never get back even after ten cycles of rest, I still felt bitter about the whole situation. I had underestimated just how much Origin had grown, and that was also the point where I realized the limits my old body had. It was a learning experience, albeit a bitter one.

Thankfully Xalla didn't press the issue, and that was why I liked her so much. She always knew when to respect my boundaries.

"I see . . ." she muttered. "Sorry for interrupting, please continue."

I nodded. "No worries, I'll fill you in on the rest when we're somewhere more private. You deserve to know the whole truth . . . just not now."

Xalla gave me a comforting shake of the frill. "It's fine, Walter, take your time. I can't imagine it being a pleasant experience to relive."

"Thank you," I said quickly. "And about my injury . . ."

Bob and Xalla looked at me with concern. I took a deep breath and explained.

"When I was caught up in that blast that took out most of Central's home galaxy, my physical body was damaged almost irreversibly."

Xalla winced, recalling what she knew about that incident that led to the complete erasure of an entire region of space. She wanted to say something else but thought better of it.

"Anyway," I continued, "it wasn't like I was completely unaware of the consequences of Origin finding out about my plans, even if I didn't expect its retaliation to be so complete. I had contingency plans in place, but that confrontation forced me to abandon most of my physical form and enter into a healing sleep of sorts. Without going into specifics: I had to wait a long time before my contingency plan could come into fruition and a new body could be found that had the potential to house my consciousness."

Xalla frowned. "Wait, so that means your current form . . ."

"It's something that I made," I answered with a sigh. "It's not my original form."

"But what about your Xollon body?" Xalla asked. "There's no way you could have made that. There was nothing fake about it, and those scars . . ."

And here was the crux of the problem. I couldn't explain my second soul title without divulging information about Noe, and that was something that I couldn't do under any circumstance. She was my only weapon against all the problems that I'd face in the future, and any risk of her existence linking with me had to be avoided. I couldn't tell her that I wasn't a Xollon in the first place, as much as continuing that particular lie would hurt her in the long run.

"I was injured, but that doesn't mean that I'm not healing slowly," I lied. "My Xollon form is reintegrating into this new physical shell, but you can imagine why this would be problematic. I can go into my secondary form for short bursts of time, but even that would be taxing to my recovery."

"And definitely no prime form." Xalla winced. "Yeah, that can't be pleasant . . . Is that why you have to go back into dormancy?"

I nodded. "Yes, the human shell can't handle all the information and higher functions of the Xollon, and I have to rely on this body for my recovery due to the nature of my injuries."

Which wasn't the complete truth again. It was times like this that I wished that I had been a Xollon in the first place; it would have made things so much easier. But if it was that easy to hijack one of their kind, then they wouldn't be the apex species.

Big Bob and Xalla did not look pleased about the state that I described myself to be in. They were worried about my well-being, and that made lying to them all the more painful.

I continued. "Well, things should look up once I stabilize further. The ascension process is greatly speeding up my recovery, so don't look that worried.

I made this body so that it's more resilient than the average aspirant, but even that has its limits. I'd still be sleeping if things weren't so dire right now."

"I see," Big Bob said. "That would explain quite a lot. How limited will you be once you're forced back into hibernation?"

"Severely," I answered in truth. "I've recovered a lot since then, but don't expect much beyond what the current humans can do. I can still access some of my Xollon abilities, but even that will be limited."

"And you managed to accomplish all this with those limitations?" Bob asked incredulously. "Damn . . . the Overseer's screwed."

Xalla chuckled. "He is indeed. How long before you have to sleep again, Walter?"

"A few Earth weeks, perhaps." I shrugged. "I can probably stretch that time if I had to, but it'd mean more time recovering."

"Hm, then let's keep that deadline to two weeks," Big Bob muttered. "Let's not tax you more than necessary. That's about how long the two of us can be out here without someone noticing anyway."

"Yeah," Xalla agreed. "And I don't think anyone can stop us if we're working together. It'll be like the three of us going on an adventure, just like the aspirants! I've always wanted to see what life's like on the other side! It'll be fun!"

I chuckled. It was just like Xalla to find the best aspects in any situation. And I think I agreed with her; I couldn't think of a better way to spend the fleeting moments of my early awakening with friends old and new. It's been a long, long time since I've had a chance to simply enjoy life for the sake of it.

"Wait," Xalla said, "there's one last thing that's bothering me about all this."

"What is it?"

"How come you're still so respected within Central? Surely someone would have realized what you did ten cycles ago, right?"

I smiled. "That's the best part, Xalla. Before my injury, I made sure that Origin could never tell anyone about what had truly happened. As far as Central HQ's concerned, everything that happened was a result of the new war, and I was just an unfortunate casualty."

"That also meant that none of his allies knew what had actually happened either!" Bob added with a shake of his head. "Damn near gave me a heart attack when I heard the news. Although I knew a stubborn scoundrel like you wouldn't stay missing for long.

"But ten cycles, though?" He shook his head and sighed. "Let's just say it's good to see you around again. I missed our little adventures together, Walter."

"It's good to be back." I grinned. "And I don't plan to be going anywhere soon this time 'round."

Our conversation diverged to something more light-hearted after that, and the three of us simply enjoyed a quiet afternoon stroll in the fields surrounding the Main Stage. Gone were the serious topics that I was sure were still on everyone's minds, and we allowed a rare moment of peace and quiet on those sprawling open fields. Before I knew it, dusk had arrived, and the three of us were just moments away from the Restus' home.

It was time to go back to work, and I'd enjoy it this time with a pair of trustworthy friends by my side.

CHAPTER TWENTY-FIVE

New Plans for the Restus

The three of us stepped right outside Site 1100's boundaries and strategized. Well, maybe calling it strategizing might be stretching it a bit since none of us tried very hard to think up even the semblance of a plan. Generally speaking, individual city-states were run by menials who were near the bottom of the totem pole in terms of authority. Given the fact that the Restus were considered low-priority, pretty much only good as meat shields and cannon fodder even after ascension, then it was fair to assume the amount of resources that 1100 had at their disposal was practically nonexistent.

It wasn't like every city was like Pandora and its very unique inhabitants. Most sites were responsible for hundreds if not thousands of similar locations, and with the recent budget constraints, only the bare minimum of staff were assigned to watch over each city. In other words, it would take a lot of commotion for anyone to notice the three of us. I was slightly amused by how cautious I was when I first came here; as if anyone would care about such a tiny city for an equally tiny race.

"All right, so what's the plan?" Bob asked with glee as we took in the view of the city. He had always enjoyed the start of a new project—or adventure in this case—more than any other being I've ever met.

"Well," I answered hesitantly, "if you two weren't here, I'd just infiltrate all of the Restus and mess with their minds a little bit. Plant a trigger word so they just stop functioning correctly for a while in case things go south. Not really subtle, I know, but I don't have the time to do anything else."

"Wait," Xalla said, "aren't you looking at the whole thing wrong?"

I arched an eyebrow. "What do you mean?"

"You said that the goal was for humanity to survive the oncoming clan war, right?"

"Yeah?" I nodded dubiously.

"But no matter how I analyze it," she continued, "the humans are absolutely, for lack of a better word, screwed. You'd have to make all the Restus go brain-dead if you hope for Pandora to survive, and that'd look awfully suspicious on our part, even if we avoid the surveillance."

I winced. She was right, but I had very little choice in the matter there. My plan was to ensure Pandora's survival first, then figure out a way to explain the strange condition the Restus were in after. Now that I had some time to really think about that plan, I'd readily admit that it was flawed. Very much so given what I now knew about the Overseer and Central.

"Do you have a better idea?" I asked.

She grinned. "I work as the head of security for one of the most influential sites this side of the universe, Walter. I think I can come up with a better idea to undermine the very security that I work to protect. You'd be surprised how many loopholes and defects are around Central's infrastructure."

Big Bob chuckled. "All right, Xalla, let's hear what you have in mind. I'm sure some of Walter's crazed ideas have rubbed off on you by now! I'm down for a nice bit of chaos!"

Her frills wiggled in anticipation as she spoke. "Well, my thoughts were that even if Walter's idea goes through, the best-case scenario would still be a pyrrhic victory for the humans. Like I said, I've been monitoring these aspirants as part of my job, and their current form is . . . um, bad."

"Yeah . . ." I agreed with a frown. "That's one way to put it."

"So why take the risk of having them fight at all?"

"What do you mean?"

Xalla chuckled lightly. "Sometimes you miss the most obvious approach, Walter. Just have the Restus rebel against Site 1100. If they do something that stupid, then there'd be no war at all to worry about. Just looking at this city, anyone can tell it's made from one of the lower-end Carmen products. Security's just as shoddy as the Restus as well. All we need to do is sneak in and make sure that they do exactly what we need."

Big Bob squinted a bit and shook his head. "They're also employing my surveillance systems, although it's an obsolete version. Three cycles out of date if I'm not mistaken. Easy for even a half-competent individual to break into, let alone the man who made them!"

"And with the Origin Matrix out of commission dealing with more pressing issues . . ." I added with an ever-growing grin.

"They won't even know we're here," Xalla finished.

"We'll let you take charge of this operation, then," I said. "I want to see what the famed Xollon huntress can do!"

Xalla grinned. "Well, this is hardly the normal type of prey I hunt for, but I think I can manage either way." She let out a happy chuckle. "Oh, it's been way too long since I've had a chance to unwind! All right, here's the plan!"

We gathered around her and listened. Just as I thought, Xalla's strategy was simple and straightforward but effective in its execution. I ran through her ideas one last time in my mind and smiled. Yeah, this would be quite fun, one way or another. Once everyone knew what was involved, Xalla and Big Bob went to do the preliminary work. They had to make some slight adjustments to Site 1100's various security measures before we could start properly.

This left me with a little more time to myself. I took that chance to check in one last time with the director, Molly, and the others, mainly to update them on the change of plans on my end. Evidently, Abigail was quite capable of taking on the role of an arbiter, no real surprise given her normal role as director, and she had most of the more headache-inducing parts of working at Central contained. People were even praising the Lord Arbiter's administrative prowess.

It was good to hear that I could continue to count on my hospital friends to look after Q's site in my absence, and Abigail even agreed—rather enthusiastically—to meet Xalla and Big Bob. She had been way too busy for socialization since Central's invasion of her home plane, and speaking with other deities would be a welcome change to her routine now that Alice's situation was settled.

To their credit, Abigail and Molly didn't question anything that I said and readily agreed to help where they could. That was to say, they were okay with ensuring that the surviving aspirants in the training didn't die in catastrophic numbers any longer. Their main goal now was to just challenge them, and Molly assured me that Abigail had a good measure of the aspirants' abilities now.

"All right." Xalla waved as she jogged back to my position with Big Bob in pursuit. "We're good to go! The situation in this city's even worse than I first thought."

I frowned. "Worse as in it's bad for us?"

"Other way around." She laughed. "They have a total of five full-time staff to supervise the Restus here, and a skeleton crew of contracted workers filling in the rest. There was no security detail to speak of, either. I could probably attack the city in my prime form and they'd barely notice—it's that bad."

"My side of things is even worse if you can believe that," Big Bob mumbled. He looked more dejected than I'd ever seen him, which could only mean one thing. "The sacrilege that Site 1100 has inflicted on my precious equipment, even if it's out of date . . . it's too horrible to say."

I shook my head. Bob was always very particular about his mechanical inventions. It seemed that he hadn't changed that part of him even after my long absence.

I shook my head. "What, they forgot to service the stuff once or twice?"

"Worse!" Bob answered in all seriousness, completely oblivious to my jest. "They've been 'serviced'—and I use that term very loosely, Walter—by outsourced technicians! My precious inventions have been defiled by idiots! Those fumbling morons made inane modifications to my precious devices, Walter. They modified them with low-quality mass-produced garbage! Parts can't be replaced now, warranties are voided . . . it's blasphemy!"

"Right . . ." Xalla whispered as she distanced herself from the weeping god. "Is he always like this, Walter?"

I nodded grimly. "Unfortunately. This is relatively tame, all things considered. You should have seen him when those rebels vandalized one of his precious trains a few cycles back."

Xalla glanced back at the wailing fat man and shuddered. "Master Babylon is rather, um, eccentric, isn't he?"

"I think you have to be a bit weird to be an inventor." I chuckled. "I mean, just look at me! Quite the mess I've managed to land in!"

Xalla smiled. "But your kind of eccentricity I can get behind. Then again, I'll take any excuse to stretch my feelers these days."

Bob finally composed himself and marched toward the two of us with fire in his eyes. Like, literally. There was heavenly fire smoking out of his eye sockets, so violently that they were even burning parts of his eyebrows off. It was quite unnerving, actually.

"Xalla, Walter," he stated as he looked at us with a frown, "we march and we destroy these heathens. They have spat on everything that is sacred to me, and they must be annihilated for their sins. My vote is to scorch this city to the ground, but I am willing to hear your opinions as well, my friends."

"Um, he's joking, right?" Xalla whispered to me. "Right?"

I looked at my old friend, and memories of our past came to mind . . . memories of him obliterating entire civilizations with plague and flood. Now, I'm not saying that those particular species didn't have that coming to them. Big Bob was generally a pretty chill and jovial dude, but when he was angry . . .

"I'm sure he's mostly joking," I answered and saw that there was that unmistakable glint in his smoldering eyes that showed he wasn't completely serious. "Probably."

"All right, Bob," I said to him. "Let's not destroy half of the Main Stage now. We'll punish them. Just, uh, more subtly."

"But punish them we shall!" Bob answered with a smile. "All right, let's head out!"

The big man bolted toward the city at breakneck speed, and Xalla and I had to sprint to catch up to the fleeing god. Big Bob certainly was a handful when he got fired up like this, but I kind of liked that about him. It was certainly never a dull moment with him around.

"You do remember the plan, though, right?" I asked as I caught up to his position.

"Don't worry, Walter," he answered with a chuckle, "I'm not *that* angry. They were using old tech. Now, if they had destroyed my newest models . . ."

I rolled my eyes.

"Just remember what you need to do," Xalla added as she joined us. "I can disable the site's internal security, but I can't help us if we're caught on camera after."

Big Bob shook his head and sighed. "I'll be thorough. I have to put my poor creations out of their misery. They'd want it that way, after what the lizards did to their hardware."

"How long do you think you'll take?" I asked again. "On your side as well, Xalla."

Big Bob spoke first after a moment of thought. "If I have to get through every device in this city, and hide my tracks, then maybe three or four hours maximum."

"I'll be done before you, Babylon. I'll need an hour tops," Xalla replied. "Do you need me to help out on your side when I'm done, or Walter's?"

He thought again for a moment before answering. "Go with Walter. You're better served there. No one should have to witness Site 1100's tech atrocities. It's . . . it's too much for a young untainted Xollon like you to handle. Save yourself from the horrors."

Great, it seemed like Bob's love for technology had only worsened since my disappearance. I'd have to fix that part of his brain one of these days before he infected me with his enthusiasm as well.

"He was one of your inspirations for creating me, my lord," Noe added with a cheeky chuckle. "So perhaps it is not so bad to love technology as he does."

I stifled a sigh. *Not you too, Noe!*

A soft laugh was my only answer.

"Uh . . . thanks, Babylon?" Xalla started, unsure how to exactly respond to Bob's strange behavior. "I'll meet up with Walter after in that case. I trust you can find us after you're done as well?"

"Yeah, I can find you two, and please call me Bob, Xalla. My full name's got too many syllables for my liking," Bob added with a nod. "Anyway, so about that—"

"All right, then," I interrupted before Bob could go off on another tangent. "Let's split up for now and get things done. I got a meeting with my brain-washed Restus, and everyone else has their jobs to do. Let's see if we can't get this all wrapped up by tomorrow so we can check up on Q."

And with that out of the way, our first official operation as a trio began. Central won't know what hit 'em!

CHAPTER TWENTY-SIX

Seeds of Rebellion

I swapped back into my Xollon form—the full version that I experienced with the preview tickets before; I didn't have to worry about my old limitations right now—and greeted my peons. I chose to visit the first group of Restus that I encountered in their city, for no other reason than nostalgia's sake.

The Restus barely noticed me even as I made my entrance. Their entire demeanor was dour and down. Hm, I should have expected this. I had used Noe's ability to induce a state of artificial excitement in these aspirants, but doing so that way was a very short-term solution. Their bodies would exhaust whatever neurochemical hormones quickly enough and they'd, well, they'd react like the sorry Restus before me.

I sighed and forced them back into their high state. Without the limitations that were placed on me before, this effect should be a lot more permanent. How long these lizards could last in that condition, however, was another story, and it wasn't something that I was particularly concerned with. I allowed them a few moments to compose themselves as each Restus was reflooded with intense emotions.

As I watched them recover and struggle to overcome their weakness, it made me realize something . . . ever since my early awakening, I had been acting with impudence since nothing in the Main Stage, at least this early, could even begin to threaten me, but that wouldn't be the case when I left to meet up with Q. Wider Central was still a place that would make me hesitate even in my prime.

Say, Noe, how much of my abilities can I use right now without this new body exploding?

"I am also assuming that you do not wish to incur permanent damage to said body?" Noe answered.

That goes without saying.

"Then you are left with very limited options, my lord," she replied, "You have full access to the abilities of my integrated shards, and you can manipulate organisms only through physical touch at the moment. Trying to do so over any distance will severely strain your psyche."

I frowned. *Even as a Xollon?*

"Your Xollon form is still in its early stages of development, and even my abilities can only superficially speed that up. You have the physical might of a Xollon in its secondary form currently, but none of its psionic abilities."

I sighed. *Great, that's a lot less than I was hoping for. With only the Emotion, Perception, and Dominion Shards, I was going to have to get creative with what I could accomplish. Man, why'd all the shards have to be mind-based ones?*

"I apologize," Noe responded, "but those were the shards most critical to your survival back then. I did not anticipate your early awakening, and thus prioritized abilities that would better ensure your continued well-being."

Not your fault, Noe, just ranting. Those shards are great against lower life-forms, but I'm not sure how well it'll work on people like the Overseer. Not like I could dominate or manipulate that brainless idiot in any case. I sighed again. *And worse still, I got no Absolute Luck either.*

"I did warn you that prioritizing your sleeping self's survival with the Absolute Luck skill would be costly, especially with my incomplete form," Noe said. "You can still unlock that ability to use now, but—"

But I'd be absolutely screwed over when I'm back to sleep. No thanks, Noe. I think Mini Walter's going to need that ability more than I ever could. I'm a lot more creative with its use when my options are limited.

"Understood, my creator."

Noe's voice faded with the wind, and the annoying groans of the Restus replaced the moment of silence. Seemed like they had recovered enough to be of use again.

"The savior has returned!" the first Restus that recovered called out. "We are not abandoned!"

Loud roars of approval continued to join the crowd as more and more Restus recovered from their stupor. Some were so ecstatic to have the energy to move and fight again that they started to battle each other as they laughed in ecstasy. I scanned the aspirants around me and saw that their numbers had decreased slightly; I didn't have to look at the scars and missing appendages from the survivors to understand what had happened.

However, there was one lizard face that I couldn't see in this crowd. Where had Bakren gone to? There was no way he'd be defeated that easily after eating one of Abigail's special cookies. Surely he couldn't have metabolized all of that in just a day and a half.

"Where's the one known as Bakren?" I shouted, having to really project my voice to be overheard through the cacophony of noise that the Restus had managed to make.

"Warrior Bakren has issued a challenge to be chief of the Southern City," the man closest to me answered. "He is to face the current chief in martial combat tonight."

"I see . . ." I muttered, still trying to understand how Restus society worked. "And will he be in charge of operations here if he wins?"

The lizard nodded. "Yes! He will be on par with the elites of this city! Warrior Bakren is fierce and accepts all challenges. The people will follow him if he wins."

I arched a frill. "Even after he acted the way he did when he fought you guys?"

"No, no, lord savior," he corrected. "He has changed ever since his transgressions. Bakren no longer fights without honor. He has been a model Restus of great renown. And he has been spreading your word after every victory!"

Huh, that was the first piece of good news that I'd heard. It seemed like giving that idiot a second chance was a good call on my part, and if he could win his bout with this chief person tonight, then I could use him as a rallying icon to incite a revolt. The Restus were already a very violent species, so having them fight Central—one weakened from within thanks to Xalla and Big Bob—shouldn't be a problem.

"That's good," I said. "Take me to the fight. I want to see how my first aspirant matches up to the best that your species has to offer."

They did as they were told. I didn't hesitate to push past the gawking Restus seated around a rough Roman-style arena, taking a seat where the best view was. The prior individual seated there did not mind letting me sit down—much.

I was at the center of attention, but a quick wave of my feelers calmed down the crowd. I could feel their curiosity waning as I pushed away those emotions and forced their attention back toward the upcoming battle. It wasn't long before they all but forgot about my presence here. Well, it wasn't like I was afraid of making my presence known at the arena now that I knew just how little Central cared about this site and its aspirants.

I didn't have to wait long for the show to get underway. Bakren and another fighter walked into the ring on opposite sides, both of them looking stoic and ready for violence. My own little aspirant saw me in the stands, and I could feel his emotions emanating from his body. He wanted to impress his patron to the best of his ability, for no other reason than to simply get another taste of ecstasy. What a foolish individual.

Both fighters sized each other up, and without any pomp or circumstance, they ran at each other and the show began. I kind of half expected there to be some sort of referee or the like, but apparently such a role was alien to the Restus. By the rush of adrenaline that I felt from the crowd, the aspirants seemed to understand instinctively when a fight was about to begin. This really was a warrior race, primitive or not.

The bout itself was quite spectacular, all things considered. That is, if you took into consideration the nature of both fighters. Here were two lesser species that had just begun the Trash Matrix's strengthening process, hardly changed from their base forms, and they all showed remarkable battle instincts. I couldn't see all of the intricacies of the Restus' fight when I was here before, but that had changed now.

This species did not rely heavily on eyesight like the humans did, instead, they used every sense at their disposal to their advantage. Sure, seeing your opponent's strike was helpful, and they did take advantage of that, but they could also smell the different chemicals rushing through the other's body, informing them of how much exertion the opponent was employing in each strike. They heard and felt the minute movement of air as each Restus aimed to strike at each other's vulnerabilities, leaving practically no blind spots to speak of.

Yet what was the most remarkable about this species was how they utilized all of this information. Within microseconds, the Restus' relatively underdeveloped brains were able to process all of this sensory information and react in a way to counteract each move the other made. They used the least amount of movements to sidestep a blow, parry a thrust, or redirect an otherwise deadly swing of the tail, all the while planning ahead and employing tactics to undermine that they had seen the other aspirant use.

I focused my attention on Bakren's opponent and really dove into the other man's psyche. I could almost taste his thoughts, both conscious and unconscious as he tried his best to fend off his foe. He made minute adjustments to his tactics on the fly, changing them dozens of times within the time it took a normal human to blink, yet it was all for naught. Bakren always seemed to be one step ahead of this Restus.

Each strike that was aimed at Bakren's vulnerable spots was quickly met with a feint or parry, followed quickly by a counterattack that was too fast even for this impressive warrior's mind to process. The Restus's reflexes saved him from the brunt of Bakren's assaults, but it was clear to everyone in the audience hall that it would only be a matter of time before all of the minor wounds afflicting Bakren's opponent added up and he'd make a mistake.

A moment later, a tiny slip in concentration gave Bakren the opportunity he needed to land the first real blow of the fight. Then I looked closer. It wasn't even a slipup in the other Restus's mind. Instead, it was his body that couldn't respond to the commands that his brain had given out. The two looked like they would never run out of energy, fighting back and forth like that, but in an environment where even the smallest of disadvantages mattered, even a tiny fracture in the Restus's armor could prove fatal.

Bakren rushed forward, closing in on the position of his foe. He was too close for the other man's tail and forelimbs to swing at him with any amount of force, and he drove this advantage home. Using his claws, Bakren systematically severed the tendons and muscles of his foe's arms and chest, and although these horrendous wounds were healing even as I saw this scene play out, it was far too little.

Bakren continued to press his advantage, slicing and smashing into his now-helpless opponent. I was expecting the worst, with him biting off the head of the other Restus like he had done the first time I saw him fight, but some kind of invisible signal reverberated through the crowd, and both fighters stopped what they were doing. A moment later, cheers and applause erupted from the crowd as Bakren, with his head held high, screamed in victory.

"You are formidable, Bakren," the slowly recovering challenger said to him. "You will make a mighty chief."

"You fought with honor as well, Murom," Bakren replied as he helped the other warrior to his feet. "You should be proud of your strength."

"How did you do it?" the other fighter asked. "I have never seen one grow so strong in such short a time. I would have thought it was sorcery, yet you have bested me with your abilities only."

"I can answer that," I said, and I quickly felt the gaze of every single Restus fall on me. They only looked away when they saw Bakren fall to his knees.

All right, now that everyone knew who the winner of the current scuffle was, I needed to address the crowd here. Time to get this over with so I could get back to the more important tasks.

CHAPTER TWENTY-SEVEN

Rabble Rousing

That was a splendid fight, Bakren," I projected from my seat up in the rafters. "You have learned from your prior mistake and have become a warrior worthy of respect. It was not a mistake to give you a second chance."

Bakren bowed even lower, his snouted nose practically digging into the dirt. "Thank you, Hierarch!"

Hierarch? Well, that was a new term, but I guess it beat being called Lord this and that all the time.

I addressed the rest of the gathered crowd. "You have all witnessed the potential that Warrior Bakren has just demonstrated, and I am sure that many of you know that he came from the lowest amongst you!"

I saw the equivalent of a nod of the head from the majority of the Restus in attendance. It was abundantly clear, even just from my earlier observations, that Bakren was already a well-known individual amongst this crowd. However, I had a sneaking suspicion that it was for all the wrong reasons. He did have a predisposition for fighting against foes a lot stronger than him.

Speaking of which, whatever happened to that dude he swore revenge on? A quick scan of the people here told me that he wasn't amongst the spectators present, and given how badly Bakren wanted revenge . . . Well, best not think about how that played out. I still remembered what he did to the poor sods who first fought him, and they weren't even the people he was mad with.

I addressed the crowd once more. "Do you wish to possess the might displayed by my champion?"

I didn't hear an immediate response like I had hoped, and felt the crowd's hesitation. They were . . . hmm, what a strange mix of emotions I was tasting. They were clearly afraid of the strange tentacled being before them, and quite a few were downright dubious about my claims, but the larger majority was hopefully optimistic.

A small tweak of the emotions here and there, minimizing the fear and unease, maximizing intrigue and excitement while pumping up the jealousy levels was all it took to finally get these brain-dead lizards on my side. I had forgotten how useful the Emotion Shard could be in situations like this since it was close to worthless against higher life-forms and their constantly guarded state of mind. The best I could do there was get a vague sense of what they were feeling, although it was pretty damn obvious what they thought and felt most of the time.

Another wave of my feeler, and I calmed down the ruckus so that I could talk again. The rapid changes in emotions were already starting to disorient and exhaust the Restus before me. I had to remember that even these relatively hardy creatures were rather fragile when you looked at the broader picture. Best not to manipulate them too much before I got them to rebel. Can't have my soldiers keeling over before they could even fight.

"Are you not angry at your oppressors?" I shouted again, hoping to rile up the crowd further. "Do you not wish to fight back against the monsters who forced you here against your will?"

However, what I was met with was confusion. I frowned and dug deeper into the feelings of the crowd and saw that they genuinely didn't understand what I was talking about. Their thoughts, when directed to their current situation, showed nothing but a stable contentment. There was no rage or anger about their current situation. Huh, what a strange race. Guess I'd have to change my tactics, then.

"Never mind," I said quickly. "What I meant to say is, do you not wish to test your martial prowess against a truly worthy foe?"

Now that got them interested. Waves of excitement assaulted me from all sides as they awaited my next words.

"Fighting amongst yourselves is great as practice, but it is no way for a true warrior to hone their skills!" I continued, making sure to amplify their existing emotions ever so slightly. "Do you want to know where the true fight is? Do you want to know where you can truly test your abilities as fighters?"

A huge roar of approval sent a visible wave of sound reverberating all around us. I didn't need to manipulate their emotions now. They were completely hooked on my promises.

"Good!" I shouted. "But you are not strong enough in your current form. I cannot promise you power like my Champion Bakren, but if you accept my guidance, then I will unlock all the hidden potential in your body. I will make your abilities truly shine! Those of you who do not wish such an honor can leave the arena now."

To the surprise of no one, not a single Restus chose to leave. I could tell that a few of them were hesitating, but a quick shift of emotions quickly shut down the dissenters and fence-sitters. No need to break the illusion of total unity here, and it wasn't like I would just allow a few precious peons to go away due to a silly thing like a perceived choice.

All right, Noe, you think you have enough authority over the Trash Matrix to do what I asked?

"With certainty, my hierarch," she replied with a snarky chuckle. Seemed like she had heard my little inner monologue before.

Ha-ha, Noe, really funny. Please just call me Walter like normal.

"I will do as you will, my host."

I sighed. It seemed like her new unique take on humor was here to stay.

That works. And while you do it, let's give these aspirants a taste of the sponsorship program. I'll bet the Overseer never thought his own functions would be used to undermine his facilities!

"Acknowledged."

I felt a warmth course over my body, and a tiny, tiny bit of my essence left my body and entered the psyches of the Restus around me. My connection to them deepened to the point where I could practically hear each aspirant's individual thoughts, and with a little more effort on my part, I forced their bodies to go into overdrive. Each Restus felt their bodies explode in strength, although not a single soul questioned what the cost of such immediate power would be.

"Temporary mass sponsorship achieved, my creator," Noe added. "You are free to act as you wish again."

Excellent, how long will this last?

"A maximum period of forty-three hours and thirty-two minutes."

That's more than enough. Thanks, Noe!

"Now you are all complete!"

More shouts of elation and joy rocked the stadium. Good.

"Bakren!" I commanded, projecting my voice through the crowd. "You have become chief of the South, but we need the Restus of this city united for my cause. Can you command this army and unify the city?"

"It shall be done!" he shouted.

"You have until sunrise to do so," I said. "Go."

With another round of shouting, the Restus all naturally gathered into hunting groups of around ten or so individuals. How they knew where to go or who to follow was completely lost to me, and I couldn't be bothered to figure out their unique culture. It seemed like it was just something that was instinctively drilled into each person.

In record time, the Restus organized into marching formation and were already well on their way to unify the rest of the city. I still hadn't seen anyone from Site 1100 interfere so far, but I wasn't sure if that was because of Xalla and Bob's meddling or because going to war was so common among this species that having a horde of Restus roaming around wasn't even that unusual.

In just short minutes, I could already hear the bellows of wars and challenges echoing across the Restus town. They sure didn't waste any time doing what I needed. All that noise made me more worried. Surely this much commotion happening simultaneously would alert *somebody*, even if the Restus were normally warlike in nature.

Well, I didn't have to wonder for too long since Xalla joined me not too long after. She informed me, much to her dismay, that the security around here was even worse than she had originally thought. Of the five full-time staff, three of them were not even in the site's vicinity—although their logs and timesheets said otherwise. Among the three was the person who was supposed to be in charge of this facility.

Instead, the bosses had gone to who knows where and had left the operation of this entire city to the remaining two staff, if you could even call them that. They had been working here for less than a decade, Earth time, and were basically glorified interns. Xalla took care of those two in short order. No wonder everyone was saying that Central as a whole was a sinking ship if this level of corruption was allowed to go unnoticed.

As for the "security details" left to defend this city? They were hunkered down in the site's HQ and playing games. At this point, I was afraid that the Restus would just steamroll through their way into this city's center without any kind of a fight. I just hoped that they'd make a big enough commotion that Site 1100 as a whole would respond. No matter how shoddy and corrupt the people in charge of the Restus were, there's no way that they wouldn't have anything prepared in case of an uprising.

Now, was I afraid that the site would send overwhelming force to just destroy the entire rebellion before it could even begin? Normally, that was the standard response for a small uprising like the one I was orchestrating now, and they'd just vaporize these rebels without a care in the world. However, I was willing to bet that this time would be different.

The Overseer needed these Restus to be in order for his plans to work. I was sure that he had contingency plans in case someone tried to destroy these aspirants all at once, but I didn't think even he would be paranoid enough to imagine what Xalla had cooked up. Instead, he'd probably send smaller forces in order to try to contain the Restus until he or another Central representative could resolve the issue themselves.

Therefore, my job was simple. I had to ensure that the aspirants here made just enough of a nuisance of themselves that Site 1100 would have to send in stronger and stronger forces to contain them. Riling them up and overwhelming them all with more hormones and emotions was easy enough. Then, once the opposition got to a lethal level due to the perceived threat . . . well, I'm sure you can imagine what would happen if all of the Restus just mysteriously became very drowsy and lost all ability to fight at that crucial moment.

The best part is that the idiots in charge of squandering all of the money for this site would take the blame and the discontent of the Overseer. I would have felt bad if the site admin was someone like Q, but no one competent would allow one of their auxiliary sites to decay to this state. I was sure that I could inflict a lot of damage on Central as a whole if I played my cards right.

I smiled at the anticipated chaos.

Big Bob joined us a few hours later and updated us on the sorry affairs of the technical equipment here. Big Bob assured us that his precious inventions were finally released into the wider tech heaven or other such nonsense, which basically translated to a confirmation that we'd be safe from any spying recording devices. Which meant that the first phase of my plan was on track.

And true to Bakren's words, he had the entire city unified well before the break of dawn, and after another session of brainwashing and pseudo-sponsorships, I had myself an army just itching to make as much trouble as they possibly could. Here were a few thousand alien soldiers just dying to fulfill my every command, and I could already imagine the awaiting mayhem.

I turned the two friends by my side. "You two ready to see the show?"

"You don't have to ask." Big Bob grinned for the first time. "I want to see these assholes pay for defiling my things!"

"And I'm always up for a little bit of fun." Xalla smiled. "Let's get this party started!"

I nodded. It was time to show Site 1100 what happened when they tried to mess with Lord Arbiter W.

CHAPTER TWENTY-EIGHT

Troubles in Site 1100

The buzzing and ringing of alarms woke Ed up from his intoxication. He could feel the uncomfortable dampness from all the spilled booze, sweat, and various other bodily fluids from the prior night's activities stuck to his body, and he was not happy. Ed tried to get up, but his head felt like a particularly rotund individual had just auditioned for a tapdancing routine on his skull, and he was pissed to be brought out of his slumber in such a migraine-inducing way.

"Someone get that!" he half yelled, still trying to flush the last of last night's indulgences out of his system. "Where's my damn staff? Margret? Where are you?"

Ed shoved the still-naked, unconscious men and women aside, sickened that these cheap hired toys could still enjoy the sweet oblivion of the dreaming world.

"Fucking hell!" he screamed this time. "Someone shut that damn alarm off!"

Yet nothing happened. No servant came in to help Ed dress, no one came with his morning bottle of liquor, and certainly no one bothered to shut off that fucking alarm. He was the damned head of Site 1100! Sure, the aspirants he was in charge of were considered the bottom-of-the-barrel goods, but he knew that things would change soon. He was someone important! How dare someone disturb his precious rest in such a stupid way? *And where was his staff?*

Forcing himself up to his feet, Ed stole one of the discarded robes off the floor and dressed himself. He had to take matters into his own hands, as loathsome as that would be. Someone was going to pay for making him do such worthless tasks, but he had to get that damn alarm shut down!

He walked into the hallway and saw that his usual site was abuzz with activity. Staff were rushing to and fro, some with stacks of paper and other supplies in hand, others busy with long-distance communications, yet one thing was the same: not a single individual paid the site admin any attention. Worse yet, he didn't even recognize most of the individuals rushing past.

Ed was furious. Why were these random lowlifes allowed into the inner sanctum of the site? Normally only a select few would be allowed in, but clearly that wasn't the case today. How dare they trample on the sanctity of his refuge!

"You!" He grabbed one of the bustling workers by the shoulders, forcing him to stop. "What the hell do you think you're doing? And why is my site in chaos?"

"I'm busy. Please get out of my way!" was the only response that Ed got from the man.

Was this idiot blind? Sure, Ed didn't show his face around his site too often these days, and he was currently dressed in nothing more than a stained bathrobe, but this person should still recognize their boss! It had only been a few cycles at most since he made that rousing speech at his inauguration ceremony . . . Or was that a few dozen cycles ago at this point? Ed wasn't too sure. The various vices that he fell to on the daily had done more damage to his mind than he cared to admit.

But either way, Ed slammed the man onto the ground and shouted, "I'm the fucking site admin, you fool! You do not command me!"

The worker looked at Ed as if he was insane, but any further confrontation was avoided when his assistant came and explained the situation.

"Margret!" he shouted. "What the hell is going on with my damn facility? I want this man fired, and get someone to turn that fucking sound off!"

All eyes were on the diminutive woman who came scampering into the scene. She had a mousy look, with her Restus suit having short scales and a rounded tail. She didn't project the look of authority at the current moment, but no one here dared to underestimate the woman, for the rumors of her conduct when she was away from the prying eyes were horrifying. The bustling people quickly left the scene when it was confirmed that the bathrobe-wearing man actually was who he said he was.

"I apologize, sir!" Margret answered quickly. "I will ensure that the appropriate punishments are given."

"I don't care about that!" Ed groaned. "Someone turn off the damn alarms!"

"Unfortunately, that's not possible, sir."

Ed slapped the woman across the snout. "This is my site! How dare you tell me what can and can't be done!"

Margret bowed low, but anyone near her could feel the seething rage that boiled just under the surface of that ill-fitting guise. The fact that Ed was completely oblivious to this was concerning to the extreme, but everyone working at Site 1100 knew that they were employed at a dead-end training facility. No one knew why Margret chose to stay in such an abusive environment when she had so many other options available to her.

"I apologize again, sir," she repeated, "but the alarms cannot be stopped by anyone other than the site administrator. That is you, sir."

"Fuck!" he shouted again. "You should have said that first! Take me to the damn thing so I can get back to sleep!"

"Right away, sir."

Ed shoved his way through the rushing crowd of people, completely oblivious to their movement, not even contemplating why there was so much activity in the first place. His only thought was to get the blazing siren turned off so he could go back to his warm chambers and into the embrace of his various lovers.

The two arrived at the control center of Site 1100 soon after. Like the rest of the site, it was equally crowded with panicking individuals trying to get various problems dealt with as quickly as possible. Some of the staff who recognized Ed nodded to him quickly, but most were so swamped with tasks that his presence was a mere afterthought.

No one dared to ignore Margret, however.

"All right, where's the damn thing to turn off the alarms?" Ed said as he forced his way into the center of the command room.

Margret nodded and typed something into the terminal in front of Ed, the one in charge of Site 1100's main controls and the site's only access to Central's Origin Matrix.

The woman typed quickly and efficiently, as if she had done so a million times before, even though this terminal should only ever be accessed by one individual, and presented the admin with a password prompt. "You just have to put in your credentials there, sir, and it will override the system."

Ed didn't even bother reading what was on the screen before jamming his stubby little claws into the reader. It took him a few tries to get the information right, as his trembling digits didn't make inputting precise keys easy, but eventually, the screen changed, and to his blessed relief, the sirens stopped. He sighed, enjoying the beautiful silence.

"Would you like a status report of the situation, sir?" Margret asked, although she already knew the answer from similar interactions with the man.

"I'm too important for such base tasks," Ed spat. "If there's something wrong with the damn site, just send in the Overseer's extra help and take care of it! I have the leader of the Central Collective backing me up. I don't need to deal with this shit!"

Margret bowed. "Of course, sir. I take it you will be returning to your chambers?"

"Yes," he shouted and stumbled his way back toward his room. "And get me more stims, the really good shit from last time. The yellow ones."

"Sorry, sir, but we don't have any more—"

Ed stopped in his tracks and slapped his assistant again. "Well, then get more! Do I have to spell everything out to you? Fuck, you are all so damn incompetent! Get me more by tonight or I will report you all to the Overseer and have you gutted! Now get the fuck out of my sight!"

Ed mumbled more curses under his breath as he drunkenly scampered back into his den of debauchery. Everyone let out a sigh of relief, having seen the "site admin" gone and out of their hair. The once demure assistant's entire persona changed once Ed was well out of the room. Her back straightened, her posture commanding, and the unmistakable air of someone who was not to be messed with replaced her old aura of passivity.

"Give me a damn report on the situation," Margret commanded. "And spike that fucking piece of shit's drugs with something harder this time. I want him out of the picture until this is dealt with."

Someone nodded and immediately left to take care of the worthless site admin, while another man came up to give his report.

Margret's second-in-command, a stout individual with flaking scales, came up to her and saluted. "Ma'am!"

Margret nodded for him to continue.

"The rebelling Restus have overwhelmed the initial forces sent to deal with them and are now beelining it to our position. All attempts to monitor their activities have failed, and we have to rely on personal reports about the situation."

Margret cursed under her breath. She knew that relying on outdated tech would bite them in the tail one of these days, and it just had to be the one time that the damn Overseer of the Central Collective decided to take an interest in this particular set of aspirants. She cursed her luck; this would derail her plans for at least half a cycle. Unless . . .

"Say," Margret began, "just double-checking, but did the Overseer know about our plans for this site?"

Her second thought for a moment before shaking his head. "There has been no indication of this. I wasn't present at the meeting between Ed and the

Overseer, but our spies probed the idiot for information. As far as the information we have goes, the Overseer barely spent more than a minute with Ed, and only to leave him with our current instructions for the Restus."

Margret nodded slowly. "I see, so it would be a safe bet that the Overseer is uninformed about our activities here."

"I can't see why he would bother with such a low-ranking training site like ours," the man continued, "even if he showed some interest in the Restus."

"Hm, good," Margret continued. "But I want to be sure that's the case. Send a team to review all the information we have about Ed's meeting with the Overseer, and make sure that the information you just gave me is correct. If what you say is true and the Overseer truly doesn't know, or more accurately, doesn't care about our operations here, then I think I can speed up my little coup faster than originally anticipated."

"Yes, ma'am!"

"And ensure that any future investigations into the operations here all point to the failings of the site admin, although I don't think that will be too difficult of a task," she added. "Also ensure that you wipe out our activities thoroughly. Leave no traces of anything that can be traced back to us behind."

The man chuckled. "Given the equipment that we're using, most of the work's already done for us. Will the Origin Matrix prove a threat to our operations, though? I cannot make changes to that."

Margret thought for a moment but ultimately shook her head. "Our access to the Matrix is already tenuous as is. I don't think too much of its resources are allocated to our operations here. Perhaps more has been done since the Overseer's visit, but we've been careful to hide our tracks since then. We are fine in that department. Plus, it's not like we are exaggerating the admin's behaviors."

Margret's second-in-command saluted. "Understood, ma'am. I will ensure that your commands are met."

"Good." Margret smiled. "Get on it, then. I just received unlimited access to the emergency protocols of this site, and I believe that I best get to using it to the fullest extent while I still can. A situation like this doesn't come up all that often, after all. You're dismissed."

The second-in-command saluted one last time before rushing out the door to perform his various tasks.

Margret scanned through the plethora of new commands at her disposal now that the site was officially undergoing a crisis situation, and the smile on her face turned into a wicked grin. Well, if the Overseer was so keen on ensuring that the Restus of this specific quadrant were kept alive, then what would he do if he found out that one incompetent individual screwed it all up?

And better yet, if the man in charge of everything really was oblivious to the inner workings of Site 1100, but was forced to investigate Ed's past, then maybe that slight anger would turn into total outrage. The key was to just stay away from the destruction that was sure to hit the site and come back once the dust had settled. Someone else needed to run the site, after all, and who better to take that position than Margret? She had long ago already ensured that she was the only one capable of filling that position.

Margret typed away at the terminal, humming a happy tune as she plotted the demise of these little insignificant lizards. Things would be interesting in the coming days.

CHAPTER TWENTY-NINE

Strange Allies

Hey, Walter," Xalla whispered by my side, "don't you think things are going a little too well?"

I had to agree with her there. I looked around and saw that my impromptu Restus army was making its way into the inner sanctum of the site. The only resistance that they met along the way was the common vat-grown fodder found in the early trials. They wouldn't have posed much of a threat even for the humans, much less the berserk Restus.

"Yeah," Big Bob muttered, "it's like they want us to cause a mess at the heart of their site. I don't like it. It smells like a trap."

I frowned. I had to admit that I felt the same. The second we had infiltrated the site's territory, alarms and alerts should have sounded off in every corner of the site; there was no way that this place was so run down as to have those disabled. Plus, the fact that we did encounter resistance, even if it was a token effort, meant that someone was aware of our activities, so where were the attempts to contain and stop the Restus?

The Restus aspirants were certainly making a mess of things. My impromptu sponsorship had boosted their aggression and rage to insane levels, and these current aspirants were little more than violent berserkers. They smashed at anything that wasn't the walls or floors, each one seemingly trying to outdo their kin on how much collateral damage they could inflict. I had overdone things.

"But it doesn't make sense," Xalla added, ignoring the rampage around us. "There's been no indication that anyone's noticed the three of us here, and it's not like anything on the site level can contain us in any case. So what kind of trap would they employ for a bunch of crazed aspirants?"

"Dunno," I answered. "Maybe they want to herd us into some kind of stasis field or something? That's the only thing I can think of for letting us get this close to their base of operations."

"Maybe they're just not afraid because the Restus are still so weak?" Xalla said. "I mean, I know that the city-state's defense officers were worthless, but even the least equipped head of security should be able to clean this mess up."

And a right mess they were making. I saw another group of strange bipedal aliens with lasers grafted into their arms launch a concentrated volley of well-coordinated shots at the end of the hallway. They kind of looked like fantasy dwarves with their stubby legs and short stature, but there was no mistaking the lethality that they could inflict. The shots that missed their targets singed huge holes in the walls of the compound, highlighting just how deadly their weapons were.

Unfortunately for the laser dwarves, Restus scales were apparently reflective enough to simply deflect most of the beams aimed at them. These caused the light to bounce off harmlessly, with some ricocheting back into the attackers. The dwarves were not laser-proof.

Sure, some shots did hit the occasional weak spot like an eye socket or a particularly large gap between scales, but even those wounds healed in almost an instant. The laser dwarves were quickly overwhelmed by a tide of crazed lizards, and we marched onward even farther into the site.

"If that's the case, then whoever's in charge of this site's a bigger idiot than I thought," Big Bob added. "There's no way whoever's in charge will take unnecessary risk with having lizards running amok in their main headquarters, even if these particular lizards are not all that menacing."

"Then we're all in agreement that it's a trap," I said. "Probably not for us, but for the Restus."

Xalla and Bob nodded and agreed.

"Think you can find out any more information with those devices of yours, Bob?" I inquired. Any more info to work with would be helpful; I couldn't afford to have these so-called lizards captured and not killed.

"I am loath to do so," Bob answered with an anguished sigh. "But yes, I can still access my bastardized creations to see what the site admin's doing."

Xalla frowned. "Wait a second, so you're saying that you can remotely access any of your creations to spy on Central? I'm pretty sure that wasn't in the contracts we signed with your company."

"Uh . . ." Big Bob stuttered wide-eyed. It appeared that he'd forgotten that

Xalla was still the head of security for Central. I mean, I couldn't blame him for his lapse in discretion, since Xalla was actively helping to sabotage one of Central's sites right now.

"But," I said to help my friend, "it's only Babylon who can do that unless he's gone crazy in the ten cycles I was gone and gave out the source code for all of his inventions. I'm sure that it's not as big of a security risk as it may seem."

Bob nodded quickly. "Exactly what Walter said! I would never break ethical protocols and do something like that without good cause!"

Xalla just shook her frills. "You and I will have to figure something out about these security problems once Q's back where he should be, Bob."

"Right . . ." Big Bob muttered under the admonishing gaze of the Xollon. "Um, please don't let this detail leak to the others."

Xalla sighed but ultimately agreed. "I'm not going to do that to a friend, Bob. I'll let it go this time, but you're going to tell me about other potential oversights in your designs when we're done here. And don't worry, Walter, I'm not going to share those findings with the Overseer. I might not care about Central as a whole, but there are people I do care for in Q's site."

"You'll get an extensive report!" Bob answered.

I chuckled and shook my head. "All right, now go get to spying, Bob."

He went hazy-eyed for a few moments, directly integrating with his creations before refocusing his attention on us.

"So how's the situation?" I asked.

The Restus had just dispatched a new group of foes. This time they were strange genetically modified ogres that gave the Restus a bit of a fight. These huge things regenerated almost as fast as the aspirants did, and were a smidge stronger as well. Too bad there were only a few dozen of them versus a green tide of Restus.

"It's, um . . ." Bob thought for a moment before continuing. "How do I put this? The entire site's almost as bad as that city-state we were just in, and there's a woman in charge of the site. From what I can tell, she's actually quite capable and has the respect of the people around her, although I still can't tell if she's being overly cautious about not harming the Restus or if she's got something else planned."

I had to agree with Bob's assessment of the site. I'd been to my fair share of different facilities in my time as an arbiter, but this place was practically a dump. Equipment was shoddily repaired or downright abandoned, the halls were covered with dirt and accumulated grime, and even the mass-produced creatures being sent our way looked like they were bought on discount. This place would have been shut down if I had come here as Arbiter W in the past.

"That's the site admin, then." Xalla nodded at Bob. "Strange, though, I would have thought she'd be less competent given the state everything's in. Surely the budget cuts weren't that bad, even if this is a peripheral facility."

Bob shook his head. "No, that's not it. I accessed their employee databases, and I'm almost positive that the person in charge is their head of security. Her files say she's called Margret."

Huh, what a strangely human name, although I thought that was a quirk of Noe's continued translations messing with my limited perception abilities. My brain is still fundamentally human in nature right now.

Xalla frowned. "Okay, that is a bit unorthodox, but this is an emergency situation, so maybe the site admin relinquished the command of the defenses to his head of security. It's strange, but not unheard of."

"No, no," Bob continued, "she's not acting as security. She's got full control of, well, everything. The site should be run by a guy named Ed, but she's using his terminal and has all his credentials as well. I can't even find the actual guy in charge, and trust me when I say I looked. Some of the depravity that the staff here are indulging in is insane! You should have seen this one room I looked at . . ."

"So . . . was there a coup?" I asked before Bob could go into more detail. That was the only situation that made sense. "Do you think this head of security person disposed of the old site admin and just took over? Don't think I've ever seen it happen when I was active way back when, but things could have changed."

"That's impossible," Xalla answered with certainty. "An official site administrator can only be dismissed by the Overseer or his direct council. The Origin Matrix will override any site that tries to rebel against its owners, and the fact that this site is clearly still functioning means that this Ed person is still around."

"And yet someone is acting in his stead, either voluntarily or not," I added. "This damn situation's just getting stranger and stranger."

"My bet," Xalla replied with a grin, "is that there's a secret conspiracy bubbling under the surface! It's just like the plot of *Secret Enemies*! You guys should watch that, by the way, the second season is amazing! You can use my streaming account if you need one, it's—"

"Focus, Xalla," I said with a chuckle.

I had forgotten about her particular interests after seeing her so focused. Xalla usually tried to present herself professionally while she was at work, but every now and then a hint of her true personality would leak through. There's no way the fangirl in her could be contained forever.

It was an odd sight seeing her so long in her own world while the constant chaos and cacophony of battle was still raging all around us. One of the Restus had been sent flying right toward the girl by one of the huge eyeball creatures that erupted from the ground in ambush, but to the Restus's misfortune, Xalla just batted him aside with a flick of the feeler. That was the only casualty that our side suffered so far.

"Sorry, I got distracted." She blushed. "It really is a great show, though. Anyway, what I mean to say is, just look at this place. It makes the worst slums of Xolloid look like the Overseer's private villas. I'm willing to bet that the site admin's a nepotism hire or something, and the disgruntled workers under his charge are plotting a rebellion!"

And just like that, Xalla's imagination was allowed to roam, and she lost focus again.

"Then, the main character, the Head of Security Margret, will meet a handsome out-of-town conspirator who will secretly help out in the shadows! He's been too spurned by the admin to trust any of his staff, even though there is clear chemistry between the two, but that's when—"

"Right," Big Bob interrupted, "I think that the heart of what you're saying makes sense, Xalla."

Then, turning to whisper to me, Bob added, "Don't tell me I sound like that when I talk about trains . . ."

I grimaced. "I think you know the answer to that, Big Bob."

He sighed and shook his head. At least he was acknowledging the problem. That was a start. The entire multiverse could do without another one of Babylon's infamous train rants.

"The theory's good," I continued, "but there's only one real way to see what this Margret individual is up to."

"And," Xalla added with a barely contained grin, "if my theory about this secret rebellion really is true, then I'm sure we can rope the disgruntled, love-starved head of security into helping out our cause!"

I wouldn't have worded it quite like that, but the essence of what Xalla was saying was sound. All clues pointed toward some kind of conspiracy going on in the background, and the one person at the center of it all was the head of security. I wasn't sure what she had in mind, but if she was ambitious enough to undermine her own site administrator, then that meant that she could be a potential ally or at least someone we could manipulate if all else failed.

"We're almost at their front doors now," Xalla warned. "If they don't stop us at the next intersection, then the Restus will have breached the inner sanctum of the site, and unless this woman is insane, she will not allow that to happen."

"Got it," I said. "We watch how things unfold first. Don't act and give away our presence unless you think the aspirants will be captured. If Xalla's right and this disgruntled worker can be reasoned with, then we try that. You know what to do if negotiations fail, though."

"Understood," Big Bob said. "There is no mercy in my veins for tech heathens."

The Restus managed to break through the last lines of defense and stormed the crude barricade that defined the threshold between the inner and outer sections of the site. Well, whatever Margret had in store for the stupid lizards, we were about to find out now.

CHAPTER THIRTY

Common Enemies

Xalla, Bob, and I stayed just outside of the threshold as we prepared our-selves to save the Restus in case something went wrong. Well, perhaps "save" wasn't the right word, since our goal was to have them all killed, so we were all geared up to . . . kill them? Well, either way, the three of us were pre-pared for any traps that this Margret person prepared.

We watched patiently as the filing lines of Restus rushed headlong into the narrow corridor; it would have been difficult for me to watch all of it hap-pening if I was still in human form since the bodies of the aspirants blocked a normal line of sight, but that was not a problem with a Xollon's unique way of viewing the world.

The three of us quickly squeezed through the opening once the last of the Restus was in, and just as we expected, there was a surprise waiting for us there, although it wasn't quite what I surmised.

"Hey, Bob," I said, tapping the chubby man's shoulders. "Now, I'm not an expert on tech, but, uh, is that what I think it is?"

I pointed a feeler toward one of the large mechanisms that was in charge of regulating the interior's filtration and temperature systems. There was only a small monitor that kind of looked like one of those human jukeboxes, but I knew that the bulk of the machine ran into the walls.

Unless heavy modifications were made, the thing should have wires and pipes running throughout the complex, hidden just out of sight. This sys-tem was so old that it was practically obsolete, even when I first worked as an arbiter almost sixty cycles back, so I was familiar with the thing's general function.

"Oh," Big Bob answered. "Well, at least we know what the proxy admin's planning now. How bad's the explosion going to be according to the lawsuits again?"

Xalla frowned. "What are you two talking about?"

"That antique machine," I said, gesturing to the now smoking terminal, "was discontinued for a very good reason. I think Bob knows more about the situation than me. Want to explain?"

"That's the model 12—"

"In simple terms, I mean," I added quickly, giving him an admonishing stare.

Bob blushed. "Right, sorry. I mean this particular machine's been recalled because it had a tendency to explode quite spectacularly if it was ever operating outside its normal parameters. Mind you, it did have to be quite a bit outside of those parameters, but I won't get into specifics."

Good, it seemed like Bob's actually learning to keep all that technical info to himself for once. I guess there was hope for the man. I gave him a silent nod of approval.

Xalla pointed at the now screeching and smoking terminal. "Which, I can assume, it is doing now?"

"Correct." Bob nodded. "And, uh, we might want to step back a bit and hold on to any loose valuables, since they're using antimatter to power its generators. I hope your suit's also heat and impact-proof, Xalla."

"Is it going to be that bad?"

The explosion answered Xalla's question for me.

Big Bob had already erected a small barrier to shield us from the worst of the resulting explosion, but even that couldn't block all the various shrapnel and vaporized Restus pieces off of us. Thanks to my enhanced Xollon senses, I was even able to see in excruciating detail just what had happened.

The build-up of pressure inside the various pipes and wires reached its limit, which caused the power cell of the machine to explode. Since the machine needed multiple cells to power all of its operations here, the first explosion caused a chain reaction that propagated through the entire facility, leading to the absolute devastation that we experienced.

"Oh . . ." Xalla muttered as she stepped out of Big Bob's protective bubble and surveyed the now-obliterated facility.

The three of us were fine, albeit a bit grimier, but I couldn't say the same about any of the other living creatures that used to be here. There was no sign that the Restus even existed since every single one of them was atomized. And this was precisely the reason why no one in their right mind ever used unstable matter as an energy source going forward.

I extended my senses and saw that almost the entire eastern wing of Site 1100 had gone up in flames, taking a good chunk of its staff and equipment with it. Even part of the central headquarters was damaged, although its reinforced defenses blocked off the worst of the explosion.

Big Bob, Xalla, and I stood around for a while, unsure on how to proceed now that there wasn't much of a facility left when the battered and damaged blast doors—the only ones still intact—slid open. A woman wearing a stubby-looking Restus suit came out the doors along with a half dozen other security members but stopped in her tracks when she saw the three of us.

We just stared at each other, neither group quite sure what to do.

"Um, hello?" I said, breaking the ice.

That got their attention, but instead of a welcome, the one in charge—whom I could only assume was Margret—barked a few orders to her men and attacked us.

"Our plans were leaked," she muttered. "Leave none of the Overseer's goons alive."

Her team expertly spread out around the ruins and started to bombard our position with advanced weapon fire. I saw beams of highly concentrated radiation directed at Bob's position, while a localized black hole threatened to swallow my own position. My friends and I had to quickly retreat back.

"Wait, we're not with him!" Xalla started to say, but the only response was more retaliation.

Margret frowned when she saw that her minions were doing nothing productive, and she decided to take things into her own hands. She swiped a massive talon into the air, tearing apart this dimension, and summoned a huge squirming mass of sludge, maybe twenty or thirty feet tall and just as round. In the middle of its mucous-like form was a mouth that frothed acidic bile. It reached out with an appendage and tried to drag Xalla into its maw.

The Xollon just frowned and swatted it aside with a feeler, hurling half of its mass back toward the person who summoned the monster. The entire creature vanished right before it could impact a really angry Margret.

"Hey, we're not here to fight," I said, louder this time. "How about we talk things out first?"

More silence greeted us. Well, silent mouths, at least, because the bombardment didn't cease.

Margret frowned as she realized that her first creature hadn't managed to do much of anything, and I saw her tense up in concentration as a visible force built up within the woman. Her Restus guise exploded, and her true form peeled out of the shattered disguise. Out came a crone of a being, skeletal thin and standing at least twelve feet tall, even when she was hunched over. What appeared to be blackened bark-like growths spiraled up her withered feet and entwined inside of her body. Her limbs were gangly with strange plantlike growths sprouting across their form, while her entire face was an ashen mass of tumors and fungal growths. Creepy looking, to say the least.

A short while later, a guttural snarl exited her mouth, the sheer volume of it shaking the very earth around us. A huge formation expanded from the ground, and I could feel something massive tunneling its way toward our location.

The ground erupted as a multisegmented monstrosity of a creature burst out and tried to swallow us all. It was massive in size, probably the size of a midrise condo, and while the dust and debris covered most of its features, it was impossible to miss its rows and rows of razor-sharp legs and the bony needle-sharp spikes that layered every inch of its body.

There was no avoiding this thing, at least not on this plane of existence, so I opted to dip out of there in a nearby shadow, letting the soothing dusk engulf my physical form. I had to phase back in a short while later, for not even the impressive Xollon's secondary form could withstand the horrid conditions of the Abyss for too long. They'd have to go full-on prime for that.

Once I was back in this reality again, I saw the giant millipede creature burn under a rain of white-hot fire, courtesy of Big Bob. The chubby god had floated high up into the sky as a ray of searing light ate away chunks of the massive beast. Xalla, having no way of flying without transforming further, had latched on to Big Bob's arm, and it was a comical sight to see if not for the awful destruction being unleashed on the poor saps who were earthbound.

Yet despite how much punishment Big Bob was dishing out, the segmented creature was still struggling and fighting back. It was spitting enormous gobbets of putrid-smelling slime toward the floating pair even as the rest of it burned under the light. At the rate that it was melting, it'd be a while before it died.

I snuck up to his flank and sped up the process. Now, it was much too large for me to just chuck it straight into the Abyss, what with my currently limited ability, but that didn't mean that I couldn't do a lot of damage. I forced one of my feelers into its side and allowed my limb to slither inside the beast's cavities. I doubted it would even feel that part, but what it couldn't miss was the little bits of liquid darkness I was secreting into its body.

It tried to dislodge me by rolling around, but the Xollon body was so sturdy that I didn't even need to dodge. If it thought that pure physical force could do anything to me, then it was sorely mistaken. It continued to thrash and roll around while I clung to it like a leech.

The creature rumbled in pain as the puddles of pure void ate through its body, sending huge chunks of its form into the Abyss. I thrust another feeler into its side, and another and another until I looked like a strange dark burr stuck to the millipede's side. With the combined efforts of Big Bob's rain of fire and my liquefaction of the creature's insides, the worm thing finally stopped its thrashing and died.

After the carnage cleared, the only ones left standing were Margret, Xalla, Bob, and me. It seemed that her minions had gotten caught in the crossfire and did not survive the encounter. In fact, the facility wouldn't have survived that encounter either if it hadn't already been destroyed by the earlier explosion.

Margret looked like she was about to attack again but was quickly stopped by a rather disgruntled-looking Xalla.

"Enough," she shouted. "You've made a mess of things already. We already said that we were not here to fight."

The other head of security paused what she was doing and finally took the time to look at the three of us. Her body language screamed hesitation and distrust, but at least she wasn't outright attacking us now.

"It seems like the Overseer's managed to hire primal gods and Xollons to be by his side," she spat. "What a waste of resources. Well, go on with it, gloat and get the execution out of the way. I don't have all day."

Did this woman not understand what we were saying? I even tried to shift her perception or emotions, but whatever type of creature she was made my efforts moot. I guess I couldn't rely on the shards to do much when I was faced with Central's elites.

"For the last time," I sighed, "we are not here to fight you!"

"Yes, I know," she said. "You are here not to fight, but to execute us. Enough with your useless semantics, cursed spawn of the Overseer. You will not learn a thing from me. Do your worst."

"Oh, for the love of everything," I exclaimed. "Will you just listen to us?"

A cold glare and a grunt were the only indications that she heard me.

"As I was saying," I repeated, "we are not with the Overseer. In fact, that piece-of-shit slimeball is the last person I would ever willingly help out."

"You say that, but the Xollon woman has one of our uniforms on while the other one's been in commercials advertising his products with Central's endorsements and money," she spat. "You think I'm that stupid? So I will say it: Go fuck yourselves. You will get nothing useful out of me."

Well, that was the first time I heard about Big Bob being in commercials, and I couldn't for the life of me picture what that would look like. I glanced at the man with a raised eyebrow, who just shrugged in response.

"Money's money," he said. "And Central used to pay really well."

I sighed. Well, this just made things substantially harder.

"Look, we can say the same about you," I said, hoping that some kind of reasoning would work on the woman before resorting to the unpleasant alternative. "You have the same uniform Xalla's got, and you're on the Overseer's payroll as well. What's to say our situation's not the same as yours?"

The woman thought about it for a while before slowly nodding. At least she was willing to listen, that was a start.

"Look, we both know that the Overseer's a sack of shit and that he's running Central into the dirt," I continued. "So how about I explain our side of things before you make your decision?"

Another pensive moment followed by another nod. Good, we were getting somewhere.

I smiled. "All right, so here's what's going on . . ."

CHAPTER THIRTY-ONE

Central's Facade

It took every persuasion technique in the books to get the old woman listening, and while I would love to say that convincing her to join our cause was all due to my suave communication skills, that would be a lie even I would be too embarrassed to tell. Rather, I had Big Bob to thank for her cooperation. He had access to some of his recording devices and had simply shown the woman what we'd been doing in the past few hours, and some of the more succulent interactions I'd had with the Overseer. It didn't take a genius to recognize our shared animosity toward that piece of shit.

Margret took some time to digest the news, but she ultimately warmed up to the idea that others were just as pissed off and annoyed with the way that the Central Collective was run. After taking some time to answer her questions and concerns, she was tentatively on board with helping us and was at least willing to share some information. That was a start.

"So, what was your plan after blowing up half this facility?" I asked, still trying to piece together the woman's plans. "Even if you're made the site admin, you'd be worse off than the last guy in charge."

"That is the whole point, Lord Arbiter," she replied, this time much more deferentially after learning my identity. "This site is rotten to the core. Its tenured staff do nothing but indulge in their degeneracy daily, while the facility is all but falling apart. If I were to inherit the site as is, then nothing would change, and I cannot allow that. There would still be no money for new equipment and no reason to change. I simply saw the perfect opportunity to remedy this problem."

"By blowing up half the building?" I asked, brow furrowed.

She spread her arms and displayed the plantlike growths protruding from her limbs. "Yes, Lord Arbiter. Just like an old forest must sometimes burn for new growth to sprout, so, too, must the dying Site 1100 undergo a similar purge to cleanse it of its disease. There will be no other option than to replace lost staff and equipment instead of allowing the old to continue to decay. Only a fresh start can save this facility. I had planned its downfall for many cycles now, but your actions here have sped up that process immeasurably."

Okay, I couldn't fully understand her strange logic, but the old plant woman seemed to believe it with all her heart. I guess it did make some kind of twisted sense. Everything that I'd seen in Site 1100 pointed to a place that was dysfunctional to the max. They were not only using outdated tech, but even brands that were recalled, although I think the latter was a deliberate ploy from Margret and her entourage. Worse yet, even with the huge explosion from earlier and the resulting fight, the actual administrator had yet to make his appearance.

"Fine, I can understand your logic even if I don't necessarily agree with it," I said. "But where's the man in charge of this facility? Where's the site admin?"

Margret laughed uproariously. "You mean Ed? Well, I can show you if you'll just follow me."

I glanced at Big Bob and Xalla, seeing what their opinion of the situation was, but they just gave me a shrug. Guess I was taking the lead this time, and I nodded quickly and went to follow the woman.

Site 1100's head of security redonned her Restus guise and gestured for us to enter the only intact door left in the vicinity. We followed her, seeing no reason to doubt Margret at this point, and saw that the heart of Site 1100 was just as shoddy and unkempt as its axillary wings. The hallways were discolored by the constant wear and tear of foot traffic, and what appeared to be water damage and mold clung to the walls.

Much to Big Bob's continued dismay, the electrical equipment was just as bastardized as the stuff we'd seen earlier, if not worse. Unlike the clean, sterile equipment and impeccable maintenance of Site 1102, its sister facility was anything but orderly. Machines seemed to be hastily repaired using scraps and other salvaged material, while the noncritical systems were simply left to rot and rust. Yet despite all of these setbacks, the workers that passed us all seemed professional and efficient, but more importantly, they all seemed to trust the woman walking in front of us without hesitation. It seemed that not every competent individual had deserted this particular place, and Margret acted as the glue that held everything in place.

Yet as we walked farther and farther in, it was becoming apparent that there was simply not enough staff available to run even a smaller training site like this one. Honestly, I was starting to question how they'd lasted this long, given its decayed state. Even Xalla was sickened with how bad things were here.

Margret must have noticed our expressions because she spoke up. "I know what you're all thinking. This place is a dump."

"That's putting it mildly," Xalla said. "How have you managed to keep things together for so long? I have the same job as you and I've counted 133 different security risks just walking here, and that's not including all the Central violations. There are too many of those to list at this point. Aren't you afraid that someone will infiltrate your facility?"

She laughed. "Like you three?"

Well, she wasn't wrong there. I saw Xalla blush as she stammered to think something appropriate to say.

Margret shook her head. "But no, our site's too small and insignificant for any of the admittedly many enemies of Central to bother with. It's not worth the resources, and it's not like the Overseer would ever care about a tiny place like ours even if it was attacked. You're from 1102, so you might not know, but more and more sites are like mine than yours. There's a reason why everyone thinks that Central's going to fold soon."

The woman laughed bitterly. "But to think that my home would play a crucial part in the Overseer's war against the returned Arbiter W of all people. I should be thankful for the unexpected fortune. My small schemes will advance, and I'll join the annals of the history books once you dispose of that worthless sack of shit."

I wasn't sure if she was joking or being sarcastic with that remark; maybe it was a bit of both. This particular woman didn't seem to be one of my normal supporters, even if she had heard of me before, but I was honestly more than a little glad for that small favor. I've had enough of people acting like I was some larger-than-life figure.

We walked in silence for a while longer until we reached a large door that led to a section of the complex that was a lot more well-kept than everything else we saw. Instead of the dingy, flickering lighting that had barely illuminated the weathered halls and corridors, this small area was spotless.

A horrible, tacky red-and-blue carpet made from what seemed to be a cheap imitation pelt lined the halls, while equally horrible art installations and paintings adorned every corner of the walls. In the centerpiece was a painting—or perhaps it was a mural given its size—that spanned the entire length of the ceiling. It depicted an artistic rendition of an individual wearing ornate armor fighting off a horde of various mythological beasts and fiends.

I pointed at the figure prominently displayed. "I'm assuming that's Ed?"

Margret looked up and winced. "Ah, I try not to look up when I'm walking down these corridors. It brings back bitter memories about how much of our annual budget went into that pointless vanity project of his. And yes, that would be the man in charge, well, a vastly modified rendition of him."

"Yeah," I muttered, "I think I got that the artist took a lot of liberties here. All right, so where is this slayer of monsters?"

I had a distinct feeling that I already knew that answer. At the end of the corridor, right where the huge ceiling painting ended, was a huge golden door. I think it was actually made out of gold. There were jewels and gemstones adorning every corner of it, which was odd since these decorations hid the intricately carved mosaics that lined the metal.

Seeing us all looking at the huge waste of money, Margret sighed and gestured at the eyesore. "Well, you guessed correctly. The man of the hour is right behind that door, although I must warn you that it will not be a pleasant sight if you choose to go in."

Big Bob, who had been silent for the most part—barring his muttered curses and weeps of sorrow whenever we passed by a particularly egregious patch-up piece of work—finally spoke up as we neared the huge golden entrance.

"Wait," he said slowly, "I know that room . . . I saw it when I was looking through the security features."

Margret furrowed her brow in annoyance before shaking her head and sighing. "Well, I guess I shouldn't be surprised that you were able to break into our systems, given how outdated most of them are."

"Sorry about that," Bob muttered quickly. "But if you two want to poke your head in that particular room, then count me out."

"It's that bad, huh?" I said, remembering his earlier remark about some of the things he'd seen.

Still, curiosity won out in the end, and I just had to know what was on the other side of that grossly opulent door. I opened the door wide and peered through, but before I could even take in the sight inside, the sheer stench of unwashed bodies, alcohol, and a cocktail of drugs assaulted my senses, and worse still, all of those scents were mixed together with a horrid scented perfume. Xalla almost retched when the clammy air hit her.

Next came the visuals, and they were just as bad as the smell. Located at each corner of the room were small decadent scented pools and hot tubs filled with naked and unconscious men and women of every species. Every individual was passed out in various states of intoxication. A large fur carpet lined the middle of the room, and more piles of bodies, drugs, and spilled alcohol adorned that surface. I saw that the once-white material was stained a sickly yellow from whatever activities the people here indulged in.

And prominently featured near the back was a massive bed, easily the size of a small Earth apartment. Between the thick bedsheets and pillows was a labyrinth of limbs and appendages of all shapes and sizes, the owners of said limbs were lost beneath the soft fabric. I would assume that Ed was in there somewhere, although I didn't want to even set foot inside that carnal house.

"So which one's Ed?" Xalla finally asked, breaking the stifling silence. She had smartly backed away after assessing the room's interior.

"The small spindly one in the back," Margret answered. "Although you won't be able to see him properly since he's buried under all those other small spindly creatures."

I tried to see what the woman was talking about but gave up quickly. It was impossible to pick out one individual from another in that mockery of a bed, and I did not want to expend any more energy trying.

"How long will he be out for?" I asked before slowly closing the door. We all breathed a sigh of relief once the room was sealed once again.

Margret shrugged. "We laced his usual vices with industrial-strength sedatives, but he'd grown so accustomed to them that it's hard to say. It hardly matters, however. Ed rarely leaves his little hole even when he's lucid, and he's never lucid these days."

"And he's always like that?" Xalla asked. "That's . . . that can't be. There's no way that Central would allow someone so unfit to keep their job while they squander resources like that."

The other woman laughed. "I can see that you are naive. That's not just allowed, but it's practically the norm nowadays. Small sites responsible for worthless aspirants are given the bare basics in terms of resources and are allowed to just exist without oversight as long as we keep churning out bodies for Central's never-ending wars. You will find that few administrators are like your Quasar, who still genuinely care about what they do."

Xalla winced, and her frills drooped, perhaps partly because of Q's absence, and a larger part because she finally understood Central's true nature. She saw, for the first time, just how bad things had gotten for other people who shared her line of work.

Xalla had originally told me that she wanted to make a name for herself working at Central, to show the multiverse that Xollons were more than just hired muscle and mercenaries, but how would she do so when it was clear that most of the Central Collective was filled with corrupt and incompetent staff?

"He's no longer working for Site 1102," Xalla said dejectedly. "He was fired recently."

Margret didn't look surprised. "Then it is a true loss for the Overseer."

"Why do you still care so much about this place?" Xalla continued. "I mean, unlike me, you've known about the real state of things for a long time. Why would you want to inherit a place like this?"

Margret shrugged. "Wishful thinking? Sentimental musings of an old woman, perhaps?" She sighed. "Maybe it's just a foolish dream that I still cling to. My father founded this particular site, so many cycles back. He had an unfortunate disagreement with the Overseer, and, well, you can see the result of that altercation. I had always wanted to do his legacy right, even if he's no longer around to see my efforts."

"Even if that means helping out the Overseer, at least indirectly so?"

The old woman nodded. "Even so. It's the only thing I have left of him."

"I see . . ."

"But my interests lie only in this facility and its staff," Margret continued, "and I will gladly help your cause if it means we can eliminate the cancer at the heart of the Central Collective."

She looked at the three of us. "So how can I help?"

I smiled and told her what I had in mind. It was an easy enough job, one that aligned neatly with what she had in mind already, but it boiled down to delaying the Overseer from discovering his favorite Restus colony was gone, and if he did somehow find out, then Margret was to bog the Overseer down with worthless reports and paperwork. With the horrid state this site was in, communication would be tediously slow, and I didn't think she'd have any trouble finding excuses for the late report.

Naturally, Margret agreed, and we quickly said our goodbyes and made ourselves scarce. Taking up any more of our new ally's time would be counterproductive, to say the least, and I didn't want her to think that the three of us were just going around different sites and having fun . . . even if that was mostly the case. Once we were sufficiently far enough away from any neighboring Central-controlled area, Big Bob, Xalla, and I finally relaxed a little, and we took a few moments of peace to just enjoy the approach of dawn.

"It's nice being out of the office," Xalla whispered by my side. "I hadn't had a chance to enjoy things since Q's departure."

"And I haven't had a chance to do the same since he joined my team," Bob added with a sigh. "That man sure knows how to make his friends worry."

I shook my head and gazed at the bright orange glow that was starting to crest the horizon. The first rays of sunlight were already upon us by the time the three of us began to move. I think all of us needed those few moments of peace and tranquility to just enjoy the small moments in life.

"I think it's about time we check up on the man," I said quietly. "I've done enough here for the time being, and I think it's about time I reintroduced myself to the multiverse at large. I'm not going to be fully awake for much longer, but I'm damn well not sleeping before I fix up the mistakes I made. Q deserves better."

Big Bob got up to his feet and nodded. "Damn right! The three of us will slap some sense into that moron. You up for the task, Xalla?"

She chuckled. "As if I'd stay behind. I owe him too much not to go. Are you sure Central won't notice our disappearance?"

I smiled. "Like I said, the Origin Matrix will be preoccupied for at least the next little while, and given the state of the Overseer's pet project over at Site 1100, I think it's safe to assume that our absences will be an afterthought. Well, the absences for the two of you in any case. I'm still technically working right now."

I turned to Xalla. "Best if you changed out of that uniform, though. I know I said that no one should notice your absence, but wearing standard Central gear probably won't help."

She looked down. "Right, good idea, Walter, and I should get a few things from my room as well. Just give me a few minutes."

"Same here. I need to check in with my company as well," Bob added. "I'll make sure that someone's ready to cover for Q when we get there. We're dragging his ass out of that lab one way or another."

"All right," I said. "I'll get things set up on my end as well. Let's meet back here in half an hour?"

"That's more than enough time for me," Bob said.

"Same here," Xalla added.

The two of them left quickly after that, leaving me alone for the time being. I figured it best I check in with the director and get her caught up with the situation, and what she should expect in the coming days. With our recent activities with the Restus, she—or rather, I—would be the first person to be a suspect of foul play, and I was betting she'd be placed under intense security once the Overseer was informed about the news. Finding a time to talk with her again might be challenging.

I changed back into Dr. Walter and took out the charm that Molly gave me. Let's make my final preparations before leaving the relative safety of the training halls and heading out into the real Main Stage.

CHAPTER THIRTY-TWO

Final Preparations

G ood morning, Dr. Walter," Molly said in greeting. She looked out toward the rising sun and furrowed her brow. "I still can't get used to how bright things are in this dimension. Why would the people here risk exposing themselves to so much radiation? They're delicate enough without the added risk."

I shrugged. "They've got bad eyesight, probably the main reason they need all the lights in the first place. Anyway, I need to send a message to the director. Things are going to get chaotic in the near future, and I'd best have her prepared for the worst."

The doll hovered around me for a bit, and I had the distinct feeling that she was observing something just under my skin.

"Hm," she mumbled, "something seems different about you today, doctor . . ."

This strange doll was always more perceptive than the rest, but stranger yet, I still couldn't quite figure out what she actually was, even with most of my functions available. I had some vague guesses, but that was about it. Whatever Molly was, it was obvious that she was powerful, immensely so. Which begged the question: Why would an entity of that caliber act like a glorified babysitter? I couldn't tell much, but it was abundantly clear that the bulk of her power was situated in that doll's form.

Molly hovered around for a while longer before finally stopping to address me again. "I see . . . you are quite the fascinating individual, Dr. Walter. But

I was right about you being reckless. You need *sleep*, and rather badly at that. Careful, your abilities can dwindle if you don't watch yourself, and as a doctor, you should know this better than me."

Yup, she knew a lot more. Creepy . . . but she was right. I was already feeling the strain, and it had only been a few days since I was up. Still, I would be good to go for at least the rest of the week, and I had to make things easier for my weakened self when I returned to my nap again. That meant that I needed to leave for the wider universe.

I sighed. "I know, but circumstances don't allow me to do what's best."

She gave me her usual sigh but nodded. "Abby and the kids will be rather sad if you injure yourself, so if for nothing else but their sake, try to take better care of yourself."

"I will," I said, nodding slowly. "And what about you?"

She gave me a small chuckle, and a tiny beret appeared in her translucent hand—the one I made for her when we first met. "I'll be rather sad as well, Walter. I've grown strangely fond of you in our brief interactions together . . . and I do like the hat."

I returned the smile. "Thank you. Anyway, my health is a problem that I'll have to deal with later, but there are more pressing issues that I must take care of now."

She gestured for me to continue.

"I'm going to be leaving this dimension for a while, maybe for a week or two, max," I said, and I didn't have to explain to Molly why I put that deadline on myself. "I've managed to deal some serious damage to the leader of the invaders, and I need to make sure that I can survive the fallout once I sleep again."

Molly nodded, keeping silent, but glanced in the direction where we'd nuked half of Site 1100. She gave me an almost imperceptible sigh before focusing her attention back on me.

"The Overseer, that's the guy in charge, will be pissed off once he finds out what I did," I continued. "And I'm afraid that the director's going to be under a lot of scrutiny once that happens."

The doll shook her head. "You sure know how to make a mess of things, Dr. Walter. I saw things on the madam's side as well, and you did quite the number on that Jordan woman and her immediate staff. She'll take a while to recover, if she will at all."

She chuckled before breaking into a rare smile. "But if you've managed to seriously wound our enemy to that extent after just a few days here, then I guess I can't ask for much else. And don't worry about the director's ability to deal with bureaucracy that holds more money than sense, and their lackeys, she's done so since the founding of Hope Memorial. What will the madam need to know?"

"To deny anything and everything that they try to pin on her," I started. "And to never trust anything that the people coming her way will say or offer."

Molly shrugged. "Then it's the same as what she does back home. Easy enough. Anything else?"

"Yes." I nodded. "Let her know that she should probably get any last-minute investigations and such done in the next day or so, then she should lie low for a while. I managed to recruit some new allies who will try to slow down the spread of information, but I can't rely on that."

"I'll let her know."

"Aside from that," I continued, "just let her know that I'm doing well, and that I'll talk to her as soon as I can."

Molly nodded one last time. "I'll relay that information."

She began to turn away to report back, then paused for a moment, as if she was hesitating about a decision, before ultimately turning back to face me.

"Tell me honestly, doctor," she said, her tone oddly chilly, "how dangerous will the next stage of your plans be?"

I was going to say that it wouldn't be all that bad, but I stopped myself when I saw how serious the doll looked. True, just seeing Q and helping him out wouldn't be too bad, but in order to get him his old job back, I'd have to interact with the managers and directors in charge of Central's various operations. Sure, the Overseer might be busy, but his immediate subordinates would still be a pain to deal with.

Could I truly say that I'd be safe going into the heart of the Central Collective with my current abilities? And that wasn't factoring my inevitable decline down the road. I shook my head. No, it wouldn't be risk free, but I didn't know how to communicate that to Molly.

"It's . . ." I began, trying to find the right words, "It won't be dangerous in the conventional sense, if that's what you mean."

She sighed. "You're heading out into the Prime Materium, right?"

Now that was an old term I hadn't heard in a long, long time. It was almost outdated even when I was a young chap. That was what the really old entities called the junction point where all the uncountable universes converged, and where the heart of the Origin Matrix and its Central Collective was located. Hearing a term like that coming from Molly was a bit concerning.

"Yeah," I answered as I tried to keep my face straight.

"And you're going in that state," she continued with a blank expression, "no matter how unwise that would be?"

"Some friends are coming along with me," I answered. "But yes. I have to go."

Molly sighed again. "I worry about you, Walter. It's no wonder the madam spends so many sleepless nights trying to devise ways to help you further. I've never seen someone get into as much trouble as you have."

I gave her a crooked smile and shrugged. It wasn't like I wanted all that trouble in the first place. Well, maybe some of it when I made that stupid idea to overthrow the Trash Matrix way back when.

"If you must go," the doll continued, "then take me with you."

"Like, your actual body?" I asked. "But aren't you with Alice?"

The projection of Molly shrugged her little shoulders. "I can afford to leave her side for a little while now. Toby's doing an admirable job keeping her busy. You should see the chaos those two are creating in the hospital." She chuckled to herself, clearly recalling something private. "But it also means that the girl doesn't need me by her side all the time. She'll let you borrow me if you ask."

"Um, how do I get your actual body, though?"

"Like this."

Molly's head split into a multitude of shadowy segments, and before I could even react, even with my improved senses, I was swallowed into that maw of hers before being spit right out into a familiar courtyard.

I looked around in confusion, a multitude of questions swimming in my head. How'd she manage to take me out from prime Central-controlled territory and back here? Sure, I could make small portals to break apart physical distance, but what Molly just did was different. She took me to another plane of existence, and a rather far one at that. That would usually require taking a train at the very least.

"It's the charm, and no, I cannot send anyone else through, so it's not quite as impressive as you might think," she explained before I could ask. "And yes, I can send you back where you were before, now that I have an accurate location in mind."

"O-oh," I stammered. "That's a neat ability to have."

Before I could respond, a familiar mounting pressure enveloped us, and the shadows around the courtyard condensed into the shape of a very familiar figure.

"Will? Molly?" the figure said before quickly running to my side to wrap me up in a tight hug. "What are you doing back here?"

"That was me," Molly—well, not her real body—answered. "He's here to pick something up."

"What?" the director exclaimed. "Take him back now! I've looked into the invader's files and—"

Molly shook her head. "It's fine for a small amount of time. Trust me on that, Abby."

Abigail frowned but ultimately relented. "All right . . . but make it quick. The things I've been able to uncover about our enemies are not good. We have to be even more careful from now on. What was it that was so important for him to retrieve that you risked him coming here?"

"Me," the doll answered.

"Pardon?"

"It's faster if Dr. Walter explains it himself," she said. "When he's done, please direct him to Alice and Toby. I'll go brief the two kids."

Molly disappeared before I could say anything else, which left me with a very confused-looking director. Well, since the woman herself was here now, I just relayed the information that I told Molly earlier, and a more thorough report on what I'd been up to as well.

She shook her head after hearing the last of it. "Damn it, Will . . . I'll hold the fort down as your stand-in, but be careful," Abigail muttered. "You really do know to get yourself into trouble, but I'll feel a little better with Molly with you at least. She's been keeping my family safe for as long as I can remember, and I'm sure that she can do the same for you."

I followed the director inside the building and took some time to dry myself off. The only thing I didn't like about this place was the constant rain. It really did seep into every surface of your body. The director had it easy since she didn't have skin in the conventional sense; the liquid just kind of slid down the black void of her form.

"Hurry up, Will," the director said. "Molly might be confident that no one will notice your absence, but let's not risk things."

I nodded and rushed toward her. All of the staff tried to greet me when they saw me, but a cold glance from the Abigail stopped them all in their tracks. I had almost forgotten how menacing she was to the rest of the staff here. A quick jog took us to the patients' ward where Toby and Alice were.

The two ran up to me the second they saw the gate to the ward open up, and Alice all but tackled me. Toby was more reserved, but it was clear that he was just as happy to see me.

"Uncle Walter!" Alice shouted as she clung on my waist. "Mom!"

I laughed and ruffled her snow-white hair. "Hey, Alice, good to see you as well."

I turned my attention to the other child and gave him a friendly pat. "And you're looking a lot better as well, Toby."

And it was true. His complexion had improved dramatically, and I swear he had grown a few inches as well. Even the small surgical scars that used to line all of his joints had faded, and I had to really squint to just see them. He looked good.

"Thanks, Dr. Walter," he said with a blush. "The director helped fix me up a bit after you left."

"I asked Mom to fix me up as well, so I can match Toby." Alice pouted before turning to me. "But she said I don't need the same, um, treatment as him. But Uncle Walter, I want to grow up big and strong as well . . . Do you think you can fix me up since Mom won't do it?"

The director shook her head and chuckled. "You'll grow in a different way than Toby. And you know that Dr. Walter's busy, right?"

"I know . . ." Alice answered. "But maybe when you're not busy?"

I smiled. Maybe she was feeling a bit insecure seeing Toby get stronger after each of his upgrades. It was cute.

The director shook her head. "Come on now, Alice, we can talk more about it when Dr. Walter's more free. But right now, he needs your help."

"He does?"

"I do," I answered. "I'm about to go somewhere really far away, and it'll be lonely by myself."

Alice nodded and stared at me wide-eyed. "Do you want me and Toby to go with you?"

"Not this time," I replied. "Toby still needs your mom's help here, and she'd be lonely without the two of you helping out in the hospital."

"Oh . . ." the girl muttered. "Um, do you want to borrow Molly, then? She's good at keeping me company, and she'll help you as well. She always keeps me safe."

I smiled. "Can I?"

"Yeah," she said. "Only if Molly agrees, though."

The doll, who had been quietly observing on the side, walked up and nodded. "I do. You two will be fine without me around for a few days, and we can't have the doctor out there by himself. Remember how you were before I came along, Alice?"

She nodded. "Yeah . . ."

"And I'll only be gone for a little while," the doll continued, "so take care of Toby and your mom when I'm gone, okay?"

"I will!"

"And I'll help as well!" Toby added.

"Thank you, Toby," Molly replied. "And stay out of trouble, you two."

The kids nodded.

Alice handed me the doll. "Are you staying for a while, Uncle Walter?"

"Unfortunately not. I have to leave right away."

"Oh . . ." Alice frowned. "Um, take good care of Molly while you're gone . . . and will you play with us when you're back next time?"

I laughed and bent down to look at the sad kid. "You know I will. We'll play for the whole day next time! Pinky promise!"

Alice nodded, a little bit of her gloom disappearing. "Pinky promise!"

"All right, Alice," Molly said. "But Dr. Walter and I really have to go now. I'll take good care of him, don't worry."

It took longer than I anticipated to say goodbyes, but eventually Molly was able to extract me from the hospital once more, and the two of us rejoined Big Bob and Xalla. I quickly explained the new addition to the party, and we were finally ready to leave once and for all. I just hoped I had enough time to finish everything I had planned.

CHAPTER THIRTY-THREE

Molly's Reveal

It wasn't until the four of us left Central's trial grounds that Molly had the opportunity to properly introduce herself. She had explained to me that getting out of her doll form should only be done in a more stable dimension and away from the annoying, ever-present gaze of the Trash Matrix. That was why I had taken us a short distance away from the train station that would take us to the business sector of the Prime Dimension.

Molly had us walk around, past the bustling streets and pedestrian walkways that made up the majority of the bustling district, and since Big Bob's own headquarters were located on prime real estate, we had to go rather far away to find a suitable spot. In the end, we had to hire a cab just to get us to a more remote location and chose one of the private parks that my friend owned.

"All right," Molly said as she made her way into a large clearing away from most of the foliage that surrounded us, "this is a good enough spot. I would tell your friends to stand back."

Surprisingly, even Xalla and Bob couldn't understand what Molly was saying when she was in doll form, but then again, I suppose I had Noe to thank for her ability to translate whatever method Molly was using to speak.

"Right," I said as the doll moved to a relatively open area. "You two best move aside. I'm not really sure what's going to happen, but she said to make space."

My friends did so and looked on with curiosity. They were dying to know what or who I had brought along with me to the trip, and since I knew almost as little as they did, I was hoping that the lady in question would help answer their inquiries for me.

Molly stopped once she was satisfied that we were sufficiently far enough away, and then . . . uh . . . expanded? It was like something I'd never seen before, and I've seen a lot.

Her doll form cracked, and underneath that exterior was a horrible red, sinewy substance that wiggled in the light as it pushed her form outward. Between the cracks in her porcelain shell were black hairlike protrusions that expanded out like creeping vines to grab at anything that was nearby. It pulled stones and soil and any poor unfortunate critter back toward the red mass of meat and muscle that made up the bulk of her growing body, and the three of us had to move a few steps back to avoid the wriggling mass of tendrils.

Her body continued to grow as she sucked in more material, and a massive sphere of empty space started to form around her. Even the air and the space-time around her were being eaten up, and this morbid process continued for minutes before the pulsating mass exploded in a flash of light and energy. The resulting force was so great that it temporarily blinded even a Xollon's senses, and Big Bob had to rapidly erect a barrier to ensure that further damage didn't occur.

Now I could see why Molly said she needed her transformation to be done in very specific locations—just her eating the literal space around us could have set off some unfortunate extinction events that had happened in a lower dimension. I was even more shocked to see what Molly had truly looked like once the last of the radiation and heat dissipated and I could see again, and that went double for the two others by my side.

Standing in the crater that she made was a red, sinewy figure with roughly humanoid proportions—well, that look was the multiversal standard physique for higher life-forms so no real surprises there. She had six armlike appendages that bent at awkward angles all along the length of the limb, with a spindly hand at the end. Looking closer, I could see that her fingernails were made up of the same porcelain material from her doll form.

In between each gap and joint, what appeared to be hair stuck out, or at least a close approximation of it since the stuff moved on its own and seemed to act more like sentient worms than inorganic keratin. They slithered across and around her body, taking in their new environment. This hair extended to cover the rest of her body, and before long, it seemed to form a kind of dress that flowed and rustled to its own will.

Lastly was Molly's face. Strangely, her facial features still looked like the expressionless one that she had as a doll, and on the white porcelain that made up her skin there was a stark contrast to the fleshy, wiggling form that was the rest of her body. The only major change was the thin crack that ran along the bottom of her face. The tiny gaps that formed when she breathed showed glimpses of the true horrors that lay right underneath the surface of her otherwise delicate face.

Molly opened her mouth and a terrible sonic wave of sound bombarded us before she nodded, satisfied about something I couldn't quite understand, before nodding toward our direction. She moved with an elegant grace that was a stark contrast to her monstrous appearance.

"I apologize for that," she said in the same voice that I knew before, but it was quite clear that she was actually speaking this time from the expressions of my other companions. "Getting myself out of that doll form was never a pleasant experience for anyone involved."

I nodded, not sure what else to say.

"I think I should properly introduce myself," she continued, extending a pair of hands toward both Big Bob and Xalla. "I am Malice, or Molly if you prefer. A pleasure to speak with a colleague of Walter's. I apologize for making a mess of things. Please let me know how much it will cost to fix things."

"Oh, no worries," Big Bob said quickly as he returned the offered handshake. "It's a minor inconvenience at most. I'll have someone come and clean this up at once."

Xalla greeted her as well, and once the initial shock of Molly's transformation wore off, my friend's usual smile and good nature returned.

"The pleasure is all mine," Xalla said. "You must be the individual taking care of Alice and Toby, I've heard a bit about you from Walter, and thank you for taking care of him during his stay in your dimension."

Molly smiled—her face literally cracking when she did so, quite the concerning sight even if Xalla thought nothing of it—before replying, "He's done a lot more to help us out than I did for him. He's a good man."

Xalla nodded with a slight blush, but Molly ignored her before turning her attention to my chubby friend.

Big Bob cleared his throat, and I swore I saw him blush and fidget as he continued to look at Molly's new form. Now that was something I never saw the man do in all the years that I've known him. Well, if you disregard all the times he would get animated with his stupid trains, that is. Did he . . . did he have a thing for Molly?

He composed himself, adjusted his loose shirt, and gave her a bright "Good to meet you as well, ma'am! I am Babylon or just Bob, and I've known Walter for eons now! As Xalla said, thank you again for helping my friend back here. We're about to enter my facilities. I'll get us all some refreshments and drinks! You must be in need of something cool after that impressive feat of alchemy. Marvelous form . . . beautiful . . ." He coughed again. "I mean, um, that transformation was marvelous. Right, let's not keep my staff waiting!"

Seeing him so smitten was kind of refreshing. I had always thought that Bob was a little too into the mechanical to bother with romance in the conventional sense. Heck, I'd even thought he'd make a robotic companion once upon a time, but maybe there was still some hope for the chubby god. Although, looking at Molly again with her half-doll, half-sinew appearance, his tastes in women might be a tad strange. Then again, I was dating a tentacle monster, so who was I to judge?

Molly had better perception skills than I did, and I was sure she noticed Big Bob's expressions better than I did, but she chose to ignore them for now. I'm pretty sure I even saw the start of a smile on her cracked face. Maybe there was hope for my friend after all.

Big Bob put his professional smile back on and led us into his compound after getting someone to clean up after Molly's mess. His entire demeanor changed the second he entered the building; I saw him when he was acting officially as the CEO of Glory Enterprises, but the shift was always disconcerting. I guess he couldn't be the owner of one of the major financial powers in the multiverse if he was "Big Bob" all the time instead of the respected Master Babylon.

Better yet, it was evident that his staff, from the lowest-paid intern to his branch managers and other executive officers, seemed to respect the man, if not outright like him. He greeted everyone he passed with a smile and a word of encouragement and read through at least a dozen different reports on his way to the labs out in the heart of the Science and Development Wing. The three of us following closely behind only got a few curious glances our way, but we were mostly ignored.

I'd been gone for a long time, so I couldn't help but gawk and marvel at the new toys Big Bob had managed to acquire and create in the time that I was gone. It was true, Babylon's cooperation really did have the best and greatest tech in the multiverse, but going past various labs and workers and seeing some of the new stuff firsthand was amazing.

"Damn, Bob," I muttered, marveling at a particularly intricate piece of tech that was suspended on huge electromagnets. "It's all custom tech, right?"

He chuckled. "I'd be a disgrace to all my forebearers if I used cheap off-the-shelf stuff, and just wait till you see the real good stuff."

Molly stopped for a spell and gazed at some of the shiny machines inquisitively. She nodded appreciatively when she saw some of the medical equipment that Bob used for the few biological projects that his staff headed.

"You are a master of your craft, Bob," Molly said. "Abby's hospital could use some of this. It'd make it a lot easier to handle the new influx of patients."

Big Bob's professional veneer cracked for just a second as I saw a huge smile blossom on his face, but he quickly regained his composure and simply nodded. "Thank you, Lady Malice, and know that my business is always looking for new clients."

Molly sighed. "But Hope's Memorial and its surroundings have been away from the larger planes for too long. I doubt we have much to offer in exchange."

"Actually, there might be something that can be worked out," Bob answered. "Your hospital's director is the one who made those cookies for Walter, correct?"

Molly nodded. "She is, although they're difficult to make at the best of times. The ingredients are hard to come by."

"Well, I can safely say that they're worth whatever difficulties the baking process may have encountered because they are fantastic! I'm sure that a lot of people would agree, and they'll sell to a very wide audience if it just gets a little exposure," Bob continued. "If she's willing to partner up with my company, we can distribute them and provide the necessary infrastructure to mass produce those cookies. We can negotiate terms if you would like."

Molly thought for a moment before replying. "I'll let the director know. It's her recipe after all, but I think she'll trust in a friend of Walter's. Hope's Memorial's in desperate need of more funding so I doubt she'll have many reservations about selling her cookies. It's a family recipe, but it's hardly a secret."

"Excellent!" Big Bob smiled. "And it's always good to have my equipment used in a place that really needs it. Your hospital seems like just that kind of place. Feel free to check out the facilities and test out the machines later on. I'll let the staff know to give you access."

Molly nodded. "Thank you, Babylon, that is very nice of you."

He blushed before quickly walking back toward my position. "Anyway, let's get to Q's office. He's been informed of our arrival, and he technically has the rest of the week off, but something tells me that he's still locked up in that dusty lab of his."

"Let me worry about that, Bob," I answered. "I'll get him to move out of that lab, even if I have to drag him out. I think I might be able to reinstate him in his old job in any case, since his replacement's going to need to go on a long, long leave of absence after my little gift to her."

"What did you do to her, Walter?" Xalla asked dubiously. "I've never seen someone so . . . afraid? I don't even know how to describe it, and Jordan's not from one of the lesser races either."

I shrugged. "Just a little something I left in the Origin Matrix when I wounded it. I knew someone would be stupid enough to poke their minds in Central's system, although I had hoped it would have been the Overseer. Let's just say that she saw things she wasn't supposed to, and leave it at that."

CHAPTER THIRTY-FOUR

Q

Q's workspace could be called chaotic if you wanted to be generous. In reality, it was just a mess of various half-finished pieces of tech and spilled diagrams and blueprints. Various half-eaten containers of food and drinks were scattered everywhere, and the whole place reeked of a foul odor of unwashed and half-rotten organic matter.

The man himself was holed away in the back, tinkering with something.

I looked at Big Bob incredulously. He hadn't said it was that bad.

"It's . . ." he started. "It wasn't this bad on my last visit."

I nodded slowly and approached the oblivious man. Getting closer, I could see that Q had seen better days. Gone was his human guise. He was in his true form. Normally, seeing an Omni would have been a beautiful sight, but Q was another story. His glossy translucent skin was slick with oils and covered in caked-on dirt, and the nebula and other celestial bodies rotating inside his form were dim and barely visible. I shuddered to see the normally prim and proper man reduced to this state.

"Hey, Q," I whispered, "it's me, Walter. I came to see how you're doing."

He didn't respond.

"Q?" I said, louder this time. "You doing okay?"

"Yes," he muttered without looking at me. "I'm quite busy right now. Please come back at a later time. I'll be done in a few hours."

Somehow, I didn't think that was the truth. I sighed. Apparently I had to take a more physical approach. I placed a feeler on the man's shoulder and forced him to stop from fiddling with some strange machine.

He turned in annoyance. "What are you doing? This is a delicate task that cannot be interrupted!"

I flinched when I saw his face. Q looked . . . defeated. His once sharp gaze had dulled to the point where I could hardly recognize the man he once was. What had happened in these few short months for him to become like this? He'd seemed fine when I last saw him, a little sad to be sure, but nothing could explain this extreme degradation. The Overseer must have done something to him before he left, but I wasn't sure I had it in me to press the man about what that slimeball did.

Instead, I gave Q the kindest smile I could. "Hey, it's Walter. Just . . . came to check up on you. Xalla and Bob's here as well with our new friend Molly."

The others came into view and waved at him, but he barely gave them a second look before trying to turn back toward his current project.

"It is good to see you all," he mumbled, "but as you can see, I am quite busy at the moment. Now, if you will excuse me."

Okay, it was time for excessive force, then. Whatever depressive spell Q was under needed a much firmer approach. I turned to Big Bob and gestured to what I was about to do. He sighed but nodded his head.

"There's a lounge you can bring him to," Bob added. "You still remember the one we used to go to when we needed some time to just get away from it all?"

I thought for a moment. "The one on the top floor?"

"Yeah," he replied, "it's still there."

"Got it." I nodded. "I'll bring him there to have a good chat, alone. Can you bring the others to join in after a while? Just give me a moment to speak with him."

Bob winced when he took in the mess again and gave me a thumbs-up to do what I needed to do.

I sighed once more and placed my feelers on the increasingly annoyed Q and shoved him into a newly made portal. I gave my other friends a quick nod before following him in. The lounge that Big Bob told me to use looked almost untouched from the last time I was here, the old couches and carpeting exactly as I remembered them, and even the half-broken table Bob had broken on one drunken evening hadn't been replaced. I almost chuckled when I recalled all those memories, but I didn't have time to be nostalgic about the familiar space before Q interrupted me.

"What did you do that for?" Q screamed. "I was in the middle of an important procedure!"

I sighed and gestured for Q to take a seat. "Calm down, you can afford to stop what you're doing for a while. Do you even see yourself right now?"

"I can't stop!" he shouted. "Any disruptions in my work can—"

I forced him to calm down before he could continue rambling. I used every ounce of Noe's ability to manipulate emotion on the manic man, and although her abilities would be vastly diminished directed at a being like the Omni before me, it would still be effective if I focused. It also helped that he wasn't in his best condition, but either way, I'd pay for overusing this later. That was fine, though. I needed to help Q.

The intensity of his emotions started to dwindle under the relentless waves of calm I was emitting, and eventually, he slumped down on the couch. I grabbed a nearby chair and sat in front of him.

"What happened to you, Q?" I asked. "The site admin I met all those months ago wouldn't allow himself to degrade like this."

He chuckled. "Well, I'm not a site admin anymore, am I?"

"No," I replied, "but you're also not a damned lunatic who would ignore the people who care for him. So like I said, what happened?"

Q shook his head. "It's the Overseer. You know that already."

"There's more to it and you know it."

He sighed and gave a self-deprecating laugh. "It's . . . look, I don't want to talk about it, not now. There's some things that are just . . ." He swallowed hard and shook his head again. "Look, I understand that the way I've been behaving lately is not ideal, but . . ."

I sighed with him. "I'm not asking you to tell me everything. I don't know what that piece of shit did, but I don't need to know the details to know it's bad. Look, Xalla's worrying her frills off about you, and Bob's getting heart problems thinking of ways to get you to cheer up. You can tell us what really happened when you're up for it, but just let me know one thing right now."

He looked at me, really looked at me for the first time, and slowly nodded.

"Can you work with us to get you your old job back?" I asked. "Site 1102's gone to shit since you left, and your staff needs you there more than ever."

"But—"

"No buts, Q," I interrupted. "I wasn't asking if it was possible. I know you'll get it back. Big Bob, Xalla, and Molly will all ensure that happens. I just want to know if you'll be up to the task of being the site admin again, or if you'll continue to mope around in a dingy lab all day."

He gazed off into the distance, as if in thought. Whatever the Overseer had done in the time that I was gone still weighed heavily on his mind, but I could see that he still cared about his old workplace.

"How . . . how bad are things at the site since I was gone?" Q said finally. "I've heard some things, even here, and . . ."

I frowned. "It's bad. I won't sugarcoat that, but it's nothing that can't be fixed later on. Xalla still has all the records of the staff that were let go, and all we're missing is a leader to piece everything together."

Q straightened his posture and exhaled. "All right, Walter. I owe my staff that much at least, after everything they've put up with over the cycles. I . . . I still need some time to compose myself, to get cleaned up, but yeah, I think I still have it in me to fight. What do you need me to do?"

I smiled and sent a message to Big Bob, letting him know that he could join us again. A quick knock on the door told me that he had already arrived, and probably even overheard everything we talked about in there as well. The door opened, and in came Bob, Xalla, and Molly with some snacks and refreshments to boot.

"Hey, Q," Xalla greeted with a wave of her feeler. "I thought you might need something to eat and drink after being cooped up in that room all day. I got your favorites."

Xalla put down a mug and a plate of sparkling minerals on the coffee table beside us. Q gave her a weak smile and took a sip of the offered drink.

"Thank you, Xalla," he said. "I'd forgotten how much I missed the little things in life."

She gave him a comforting shake of the frill and gave the rest of us in the room something to drink as well. I took mine and thanked her.

"I'm feeling better now," Q continued. "Walter managed to smack some sense into me. And . . . I'm sorry about making you worry, and for ignoring you before. It's been a rough few months."

Xalla nodded. "It's okay. I knew you needed some time for yourself, but it's good to see a bit of the Q I know back."

"So what is the plan?" he asked, focusing fully on us this time.

"Appeal your termination, first of all," I answered. "I can guarantee you that the Overseer pulled some strings to get his people into your office, and unless Central's well and truly screwed, the laws still apply to him."

Q winced. "It's not a complete lost cause, but there was a reason why I didn't want to bother appealing at all."

"All right," I said, although I didn't really want to hear the answer. "How bad has it gotten?"

"I can answer that," Big Bob added with a barely contained sigh. "The . . . laws, as you put it, are still technically enforced, but you'll find that the Overseer has done a lot over the last ten cycles to ensure that it's heavily biased toward what he wants."

I arched a frill. "What does that mean?"

"It means that the judges are corrupt," Xalla answered. "The juries and minor tribunal members are all bought off, and that's not even the worst part. In order to even appeal a direct order from the Overseer, you'd need the support of a majority vote from the ruling council."

"That's still a thing?" I asked. "Thought he'd get rid of any position that can resist his rule. So we just need four out of the seven votes—"

"That's the thing," Q said. "There are only five members left, so we technically only need three votes."

I sighed, seeing where this was going. "Let me guess, they're all under the Overseer's control?"

"Not all of them, although that's not from a lack of trying on the Overseer's part," Q continued. "He managed to eliminate two of his most staunch opponents, but there are one or two council members that are still clinging on from the five remain—"

"If an appeal really is your plan of action," Bob interrupted, "then you can count on the head of the sponsorship program for support. The only reason he's still around and unmolested is because we bring in too much income for the Overseer to touch us, so we can count our blessings there."

"Head of multidimensional security should also side with you," Xalla added. "If for no other reason than she can't afford to piss Rogue and the rest of the Xollon off. The Overseer can't retaliate when the alternative is us joining the war on the wrong side."

Molly decided to join in the conversation then. She had been silently observing and taking in the information with a stoic expression.

"Which leaves Walter with one more vote in order for his plan to even begin," she said. "The odds do not look good for us if what I'm hearing is accurate, and that's before dealing with all the other issues, even if you get the necessary votes."

Q nodded, getting up and reaching a welcoming hand to the woman. "It isn't. And who do I have the pleasure of speaking with? I apologize for not greeting you properly earlier. I wasn't myself."

"Malice," she said simply, shaking the offered hand. "Or Molly if you'd like. I'm a friend of Walter's. The pleasure is all mine."

"Thank you, Lady Malice, it's good to have another ally," he answered with an almost imperceptible nod, a little more of that old spark of his returning. "But you are right, our options are limited. We can definitely count the head of the training sites out, and don't even mention the Overseer's pet master arbiter."

I winced. "Guess they got rid of my mentor when I disappeared, huh?"

Big Bob sighed. "Unfortunately. You don't want to meet the new guy."

"So that leaves, what, the recruitment head?"

"Yeah, and it's the same stubborn bastard you remember," Bob continued. "Not even the Overseer managed to get rid of that pile of dust."

I grimaced as old memories of the person in question resurfaced. Great, and I distinctly remembered telling that guy to go die in a ditch the last time I saw him. It would definitely take some convincing for him to agree to work against the Overseer, especially when we all knew the risks involved.

"Then I guess we try to convince old man Stanton." I sighed. "Anyone know where he is now?"

"I think he's currently out on an assignment," Xalla answered. "But I can find out where he is. Just give me a bit of time to talk to my contacts."

Big Bob nodded. "Take your time, everyone's welcome to stay in one of the guest suites for the time being. And Walter, you think you can manage to convince that sack of bricks yourself? I know you're on a tight schedule, and I need to go negotiate with the sponsorship members, so I'll have to skip this leg of the journey."

"I can also get Rogue to talk with Director Scarlet while I'm at it," Xalla added. "He can convince her to support you, which means I can tag along and help."

"I'll go with Walter as well," Q added. "I think I need some time away from . . . well, all of this. If you'll let me, of course, Lord Babylon."

"You have the rest of the month off," Bob said with a chuckle before turning to Molly. "And I'm guessing Lady Malice will be going with you all?"

"I am," she replied simply. "But I would be honored if you could show me around this facility before I depart."

Big Bob blushed. "Of course! Especially for a potential partner, er, business partner, that is!"

Molly chuckled. "And how about some dinner after?"

"It'd be my pleasure!" he answered a little too quickly.

Molly arched an eyebrow and held one of her hands out. "Shall we, Master Babylon?"

CHAPTER THIRTY-FIVE

Uninvited Guest

It had taken the better time of an entire day to get everything sorted out and for Xalla to contact all the right people, but we were all set up to go on the following morning. Molly informed us that Big Bob had to leave earlier to meet up with some of the other sponsors and that he sent his best regards and was looking forward to hearing good news from us soon. How the woman got this news before the rest of us, I didn't want to know.

Xalla joined us by the reception area next, and Q, who now looked a lot better after freshening himself up a bit, joined us shortly after. He was even kind enough to bring the four of us some coffee, or whatever coffee equivalent Xollons and other deities drank these cycles. Xalla's and mine even had a little straw that fit right into a Xollon's natural proboscis. How handy.

"So, where's our destination?" Q asked with a tired smile. It was good to know that he was feeling a lot better now that he'd had the night to compose himself properly. He still needed some time, but he was recovering some of his old spunk.

Xalla took out a ruffled piece of paper from her pocket and showed us. "I have the coordinates for the dimension that Master Stanton last departed for, and roughly which galaxy he should be situated in, but that's as much as I could manage."

I nodded. "Anything else of note there?"

She glanced at the map again and answered, "It's a minor dimension, and the last reports state that he's gone there to rope in the local pantheon."

"By force?" Molly added with a quiet fury. "Like this Central Collective has done to mine?"

Xalla looked apologetic for a second before shaking her head. "No, that's not Stanton's way of doing things. He's one of the only people who still adheres to the old method. The people going around subjugating indiscriminately are all wholly under the Overseer's influence now."

"And yet that old man's still able to keep his job," I added with a grin. "Yeah, I don't expect anything less from that stubborn old mule."

"I see . . ." Molly frowned as another thought occurred to her. "But how would we find him? Looking for one individual in such a large area can't be easy, especially if we have to take Walter's time constraints into consideration."

"I mean," I added, "if this place is as backward as Xalla claims, then it shouldn't be too hard to find the guy, even if we have to search a wide area. People of Stanton's caliber tend to stand out."

"Um, I think you are misunderstanding," Xalla said. "We won't have to find him by searching the whole galaxy."

"What do you mean?" Molly asked.

"It's a very minor and undeveloped dimension we're going to. Like, very, very undeveloped," Xalla clarified. "There are only a handful of local planets with intelligent life on them, although they are rather large planets, and a few pocket realms for the local pantheon. Finding where the head recruiter is shouldn't be difficult once we set foot in that plane. Like Walter said, unless Stanton is purposefully hiding, his presence will be felt."

"That's one issue solved, but I think that adds a few more problems if it's that undeveloped . . ." Q added. "Our presence stepping unannounced in a lower dimension might raise alarms in that case."

I looked around us and saw the point. We had two Xollons, an Omni, and whatever the hell Molly was, all of whom could theoretically end entire galactic civilizations with a thought. Entering a barely developed plane was bound to lead to trouble, and that wasn't counting the fact that it was right after Stanton's arrival. If that didn't trigger every single alarm they have, then nothing would.

"Huh . . ." I said. "Our lineup does look kind of bad."

Molly rolled her eyes. "Yes, Walter. A very astute observation. So what is our strategy given the time constraints?"

"Do you think we can sneak in?" Q asked. "Walter can go back to his human form, and I can minimize the amount of disruption I cause on my side. Xalla and Lady Malice might be a problem, however."

"I can try to minimize my presence as well. Our secondary forms can be subtle," Xalla answered. "But from what I've read about this place, even doing that will cause a relatively big disturbance."

Molly sighed. "I can't do much on my side. There's a reason why I'm normally constrained, but I'll do my best as well. I can work something out once I get used to that plane, however."

I frowned. "Then there's no avoiding letting the local gods know of our intrusion."

"But," Q added, "we can still hide once we're through. They'll know that something came through, but they shouldn't be able to track us down in mere weeks even with Xalla and Malice there. Plus, I doubt a small crack in the dimensions would alert that many individuals; it's hardly a rare event even in a lower dimension."

I nodded. Q was right, random fluctuations were bound to happen, and maybe the gods there would just chalk our entrance up to one of those.

"That's the best hope we can have," I said. "And let's try to minimize how much trouble we cause these people. We're trying to oppose Central, not be just like them, especially if this place has yet to develop and advance fully. If Stanton's there, then there's potential for the locals."

"I second that," Molly agreed, "and although I hold no special love for the mortals, it would be best if we avoid unnecessary trouble. We should lay low and gather intelligence before trying to find this Stanton individual. I've seen firsthand what can happen if an overwhelmingly powerful force shows up unannounced. It leads to unnecessary panic."

"Fair point," I said. "I think we can all agree that we should approach the local gods as gently as possible after. Just let them know that we're just passing through. We come in peace and all that."

Q nodded. "Let's go with that plan for now, at least until we know more about the situation on the other side. Lord Babylon's got the best skin suits available, so we'll all change into one of those before we leave. Do you know what the local mortals there look like, Xalla?"

"I'll upload the information to the makers. They're pretty standard humanoid constructs, so getting a well-made disguise should be easy."

At least there was some good news there. Oddly enough, most intelligent creatures tended to be humanlike in shape. At least they were if the race in question wasn't massive like the Xollons in their prime form. Sure they might have extra limbs, maybe a tail or a tentacle or three, but bipedal locomotion with dexterous appendages seemed to be the multiversal default. Now, there might be a few strange shapes every now and then, but I'd say that a good 70%

of races fit into that category. I guess you just can't beat a form that works for most situations.

Like Xalla said, it didn't take long at all for the four of us to get proper suits made and put on. Custom made as well, all courtesy of Big Bob. Sometimes it was good to know someone rich and powerful.

According to Xalla, the place we were heading to, which Central didn't even have a name for, was divided into a few different races. However, without knowing any of the mortal dynamics, we chose to all go as the most populous race. That being a creature that looked remarkably like a standard human that glowed a bright red. I think there were other small differences like the number of toes and fingers or the fact that we had gills as well as lungs and three sets of eyes, but those were minor at most.

"I hate wearing these things," Xalla grumbled. She looked like a female version of whatever creature we were, although it was difficult to tell which gender was what since this race didn't exhibit any kind of sexual dimorphism. It would take me a while to understand how to tell these things apart from one another.

"You get used to it," Molly answered with a shrug. "Although I can understand the constraining feeling."

Molly looked almost identical to Xalla, and if it wasn't for her speaking or the clothing she wore, I would probably never be able to tell the two apart. I guess I'd just rely on Noe to help me out when we met the locals.

"Let's just go before I get too uncomfortable and break something," Xalla continued before composing herself. "Sorry, I'm almost never wearing one of these things. I don't know how all of you can do it so often."

Q answered with a casual smile. "As Lady Malice said, it does get easier when you learn how to move and act in the suit, and thankfully Babylon's products are top notch. Just give it a few hours and the uncomfortable feeling should subside."

Xalla nodded but didn't look convinced. "Shall we get going, then? We'll need to take a pretty long train ride to the closest dimension before breaking through the old-fashioned way."

Q frowned. "The old-fashioned way? So no connections at all to the larger multiverse? Not even one that the exploratory guilds managed to make contact there?"

"It's that primitive, I'm afraid, and it also means we're going in practically blind," Xalla answered, shaking a frill, "I'm honestly not sure why Master Stanton chose such a random location to visit, but I'm sure he has his reasons."

I shrugged. "We'll find out soon enough,"

Soon probably wasn't the word for it, because it took us almost a full day's journey just to get to a dimension close enough to break through. Given how long we'd taken just to get to where we needed to, I was afraid that I'd have to go back to sleep before I could finish everything here. It was looking increasingly less likely that I'd make it through everything I needed to do, and I could only hope that my unawakened self could handle the rest.

I told my friends as much, filling Q in about most of the situation at hand, and although they were worried that I was already spread too thin, they did promise to do their best to look after my weakened form should I need to go back into dormancy early. The only good thing about this situation was that we were heading to a place with minimal risk to my safety—if what Xalla said was correct. If some minor gods were the only real threat, then I'd be safe even without my entourage.

The main thing I prioritized during that long train ride over was to compartmentalize the memories my sleeping self desperately needed in order to survive what was to come while discarding the others. The human brain was so limited in what it could perceive and store, and it was more fragile than I initially thought, even with the Xollon parts integrated, thanks to my lucky new soul title. It didn't help that a lot of what I knew tended to make mortals go crazy.

"Do not worry, my creator," Noe added, "I will ensure that you have the necessary information and knowledge when needed. Please prioritize the most pertinent information first, and I will slowly disseminate everything else to your sleeping form as needed. Your mind shall not be harmed or damaged as long as I remain functional."

Thanks, Noe, I think I'll have to rely on you in the near future. I'll try to make it to Stanton at least, but I'm not sure what'll happen after that.

"Be at ease that you will be safe under my care."

A few more hours passed, and we finally made it to the last stop in our train journey. The place we were at was practically empty, and it took a lot of bribing and negotiations just to get us to this backwater place. I could see why no one wanted to go there. There was no scheduled ride to where we needed to go anytime soon, so we had to improvise.

All of that effort led to us being dropped off on a dusty rock in the middle of nowhere. The local sun was way too close to the planet and the heat and solar radiation were already starting to damage our suits. Whatever great civilization that used to be here had long since disappeared, and the sheer fact that transportation service still existed here was a miracle in of itself. We found some shelter from the sweltering heat in an abandoned cave and prepared to make our entrance.

"Are we all ready?" Q said. "Remember we're laying low first before setting off, finding Master Stanton should be easy enough once we've established amicable relations with the local pantheon."

All of us made our final checks on the disguises before giving our affirmations.

"All right," Q continued and quickly opened a portal. "Let's not waste any more time."

We stepped through and set foot on the primitive new world. I only hoped our entrance didn't raise too many alarms.

Prophecies of Destruction

Inspira awoke with a jolt, her eyes swirling with sights and events of things to come, sweat pouring down her frame as the prophetic visions and maddening shouts assaulted every sense she had. She had never experienced something so intense before, and she rattled with the effort of containing such sights.

She saw . . . she saw figures, four of them, entering from the void of the great beyond. She saw them rip through the fabric of their very existence, tearing through the sea of souls and the sanctity of their very world. These were figures clad in false cloaks of mortal flesh who promised nothing but death and destruction.

One being was an entire cosmos within itself, its body housing uncountable fates all being snuffed out while more and more were created to replace the lost souls. It was a being of creation and all-knowing might, just as it was a being of destruction and entropy. The oracle could feel a small piece of her being, of her mind, sucked into that great expanse that made up this being's body, and she had to turn away before she lost everything.

Standing by that figure were two similar entities. Inspira's mind almost broke when she tried to glance at the two squirming forms beside the first, their small form belying a terror of untold magnitude just swimming underneath their surface. Her mind could scarcely understand what she was looking at, her mortal mind seeming so small and insignificant before these eldritch beings, but she knew that these two would bring nothing but madness and ruin.

The last form was a mass of red and black, its body expanding and con-
tracting as its midnight-black tendrils grasped and reached for everything
around it to devour. The thing radiated a pure malice that threatened to
destroy everything that Inspira ever loved or cared for, and she struggled in
vain to escape its notice.

The oracle opened her gasping mouth to scream as she was forced to gaze
at the four impossible entities, and she felt her soul and mind buckle under the
weight of their presence. She wanted to scream, but not a single sound could
escape her lips, and all she could do was continue to endure the visions.

Her sudden movement disturbed the man sleeping peacefully beside her.

"Inspira," her partner mumbled, "what's going on?"

Inspira couldn't respond even if she wanted to. She was struggling just to
keep her sanity, to keep her mind intact so that she may pass down this dire
warning to the rest of the people around her, yet even now she could feel the
tenuous grasp on reality slowly slipping away from her.

Hathor got up and lit the lantern beside their bed, turning to see his lover
properly. He froze when he saw Inspira's sweat-soaked form. He had never seen
such an intense vision from her before. In fact, Hathor wasn't even sure she
was experiencing a vision until he felt the waves of divine mana radiating off
her. He immediately went to alert the palace officials of the news. Something
important was being relayed to the oracle, and the people needed to be ready
to receive her word.

"Guards!" he shouted as he got dressed. "Protect the oracle!"

Four massive men wearing ornate leather armor walked in and immediately took positions between the beds. They froze for a brief second when they
saw the condition that plagued the Inspira.

"Get the palace physician as well," Hathor commanded one of the four. "I
need to inform the king! Something unprecedented is happening."

Hathor took one final look at the oracle and muttered a prayer in his heart.
He saw that Inspira's gaze was peering far away, focused on something that
only she could see. Hathor grimaced as he saw the pain, panic, and a myriad
of other emotions cascading down her convulsing form, but as much as he
wished he could comfort her, he knew that his duties took precedence.

"Go, my lord," the palace guard said. "We will ensure the oracle's safety."

He nodded one last time and ran toward the royal chambers.

Within the hour, the entire palace was put on high alert as every priest,
theologian, and individual of importance waited outside the oracle's chambers.
Those who were closest to the god of fate could feel the unease and energies fluctuating from the room, and soon, a nervous air permeated the space

around them. Whatever message was being conveyed by the god's chosen messenger was dire.

Inspira stumbled out of the room a short while later, her whole body soaked in sweat and her clothes disheveled, before stumbling on the ground from sheer fatigue. The palace physician quickly went to her side, but she pushed the man aside with a weak gesture. Everyone else in attendance gathered around the oracle, keen to hear what she had to say.

"The end approaches . . ." she gasped, her voice hoarse and barely audible over the rasping of her breathing. "The truth dies, eternity ends, the stars dim, and malice reigns . . . Dusk comes to us . . . the end comes! The end comes! Death—"

The palace staff struggled to understand Inspira's message, but before anyone could ask her to clarify, the woman seized up with another vision, and a silent scream of anguish failed to leave her lips. Whatever final message she wanted to give was lost to the world, and Inspira, the chief oracle of the god of fate, died that night.

Similar events happened all over the Altera world in every kingdom, every empire, and every country in between. That night, the various oracles, holy persons, and religious figures were all sent the same message: Something had invaded their realm, and something wicked was looming on the horizon. The prophecies of death could not be ignored, and every race braced for the worst. They only hoped that they could survive what was to come.

CHAPTER THIRTY-SIX

Subtle Arrival

Once the last of us stepped through Q's portal, the old admin quickly closed the hole in reality and shoved us into a smaller wormhole so we'd be as far away from our entrance point as possible. The theory was that even if we couldn't mask the portal from the natives of this dimension, then at least we could hide who caused that disturbance.

"You think our entrance made a big impact?" Xalla asked. "I tried to stay as still as possible when I came through. That shouldn't have disturbed anyone . . ."

She was still fiddling with the uncomfortable skin suit, and I could see some of her feelers poking out from underneath the disguise. It kind of looked like some horrible worm creature was eating the girl from the inside out, and I just hoped she got that contained soon. If not, then we'd need to get her some loose-fitting clothing to at least hide the strange visuals.

"It shouldn't be that bad . . ." Q muttered. "I tried to minimize the damage done to this dimension, and our presence would have only been felt for a moment. I can't imagine we did more than set off the automatic wards or what have you."

Molly nodded. "We have all done what we can. There is no point dwelling on the fact any longer. This would have to be a truly undeveloped plane for such a small ripple to be noticed by all but the most perceptive of individuals. Given the isolated locale, I doubt the local gods would have that ability."

Molly paused. "Wait . . ."

Molly stopped what she was saying and scrunched her brows. She sensed that something was off. She sniffed and opened her mouth, a horrible red facsimile of a tongue lashed out and tasted the atmosphere around us before frowning further.

"That's . . . strange. There's very low levels of mana and life force here," she added, "and the boundaries between spaces are also impossibly fragile. This feels like the properties of a dimension in its infancy, yet that is clearly not the case."

She gestured at the thriving life around us, and I had to agree. This was a well-developed plane of existence.

Q raised an eyebrow and did his own tests before nodding. "You're right . . . something's not right here. I can't even extend my senses out without fracturing the dimension."

I focused my own senses and saw that Q was right. Whatever backward plane Xalla sent us to was fragile, oddly so, even. The only explanation was if this was a newly created realm, and a really young one at that. Life would have barely had enough time to develop here, and I can't imagine there being anything but primal idiot gods ruling here. Was this weird anomaly the reason why Stanton chose to investigate this place?

Q's second wormhole dropped us off at a remote countryside that overlooked a larger settlement in the distance. The environment wasn't too different than the stuff we saw in the Main Stage, with lush grass and various species of small critters running around the abundant vegetation. Way off in the distance was what appeared to be an agricultural center, with clear signs of logging and farming taking place, and I could just about make out small red individuals laboring away in the fields.

The most important landmark was the city. It was heavily fortified, relatively speaking, given the Renaissance level of development that this world seemed to possess, and a large multistory castle loomed in the distance. Some other gothic-looking structures jutted out every now and then, but nothing else even approached the size or scale of the castle. A river cut through the heart of the settlement, and small fishing communities dotted the outskirts of the place, but more importantly, there was only one way in or out of the place.

Guards of various shapes and races guarded the entrance, and I saw a long queue of people and caravans waiting to be let in. In fact, there were even soldiers stationed on the walls, and each one looked to be nervous, as if they were expecting a foreign invader at any moment. Every instinct I had told me that this was not normal. I just hoped that it was because of some outside influence or they were at war with another nation and not due to our arrival.

"Are you sure you got the coordinates right?" I asked Xalla. "This doesn't seem like the normal place that Stanton would visit."

"It should be correct . . ." she answered, but as she peered around, her confidence seemed to diminish. "I got the location from Scarlet, and we double-checked them with Central's databases. Even my mentor confirmed that the master recruiter was last seen leaving for this plane, and he verified them with Xollon contacts. There shouldn't be any mistakes. But—"

"No, if you did all that, then this must be the place. We can't get more certain than that," I muttered and focused my senses on the city below us. "If Stanton's been here for a while, then it's safe to bet that he's already made contact with the local deities."

"Then we just have to do the same," Xalla reasoned. "We'll find out who's in charge, get an invitation, and ask where Stanton is. It shouldn't be too hard to do."

We nodded, and everyone naturally looked toward the city on the horizon and the strange behavior of the people that resided in it. I think everyone had their own ideas about why people were so on edge, but no one here wanted to say the obvious first. We were all hoping that maybe it was just the political landscape already present and not because of some unknown interdimensional invaders . . .

When we approached the city's sole gate, it became increasingly clear that we'd have to find an alternate entrance. The city seemed to be in full lockdown mode as only a very select amount of traders and select individuals were allowed through. Everything suggested that the place was getting ready for war.

A huge lineup of caravans, freelance soldiers, and mercenaries slowly made their way inside, each group having their credentials checked and double-checked by the gatekeepers. That left the normal civilians and other non-combatants out to dry, and I could hear shouts and voices of concern and annoyance growing louder the closer we got.

"I don't think we're getting in through the front door," Q remarked. "Should I make another portal going inside?"

I thought for a moment, weighing our options and Q's idea, but ultimately shook my head. "No, that's too risky. I don't want to make any more disturbances before we know more."

Molly agreed. "Do not use any abilities before we get a better sense of this location. Remember that we are in unknown territory."

Xalla winced as she recalled just how delicate the world around us was. "Good point . . . um, can we not scale the walls, then?"

"Are any of us good with stealth?" I asked and pointed to all the soldiers and personnel stationed along every corner of the wall, not to mention the huge watch towers that overlooked most of the hidden crevices of the city.

They all looked around awkwardly. It was abundantly clear that we were anything but subtle.

"They're taking in fighters and mercenaries," I said. "We'll go in as a small group of hired muscle. It should be easy enough for me to convince them of that. And plus, going in as hired help should allow us to gather info on what's going on within the city."

"Lead the way, then." Q smiled and gestured for me to take the front. "It's as good a plan as any."

The others stood back and allowed me to assume the lead. I only had to make slight adjustments to the emotions of the others waiting in line for us to skip to the very front. A little bit of awe tended to do a lot in situations such as these. A few plans came to mind, but I'd have to assess the situation a bit more before I acted.

I stepped up and addressed the pair of gatekeepers.

"Good morning!" I said cheerily to the gatekeepers blocking our path. "We are here to seek entrance to your beautiful city. We are mercenaries and soldiers for hire."

The two men (Women? Like I said, I still had no idea how to tell their genders apart) looked at our ragtag group of four with dubious expressions. I couldn't blame them. I'd introduced us as fighters, but we were dressed in the same wear as the farmers and other laborers I saw on the farms and mines. Given how strict their vetting process was, I didn't think we were the first laborers who tried to trick their way in.

I couldn't complain too much, though, at least Central's databases for the clothing in this dimension weren't fifteen cycles out of date. I remembered an incident not too long before I went to sleep where a team of recruiters went to a world wearing that planet's equivalent of a caveman costume. That gave the whole team a good laugh.

The guard rolled his eyes and grunted. "Get out of here, you're not the first set of damn farmers trying to pass through."

I sighed. Well, I hadn't expected a simple explanation like that to work anyway.

Say, Noe, how much of the Perception Shard is integrated?

"The Perception Shard is at 58.443% integration," she replied. "You can use the abilities of this shard minimally, but with how feeble this race is, 58% capacity is more than adequate for the tasks at hand."

Got it. How about the Domination Shard?

"I apologize, my creator, but the Domination Shard has not begun the integration process. Your early awakening has disrupted some of my processes."

Ah, sorry about that.

"There is no need for you to apologize, my lord," she said. "I am just sorry that I cannot help you further in your time of need."

The guards stationed to the side to keep the peace started to move toward us, all of them ready to remove the annoyances blocking the queue, but a quick jolt of fear stopped them in their tracks. The gatekeepers noticed the strange behavior and came up to see what was going on.

"Like I said," I repeated, "we really are mercenaries. Don't mind the clothing, but we like to travel without being noticed."

The lead gatekeeper frowned, but he couldn't deny the dread and fear he experienced when he looked at us. He knew we were dangerous, regardless of how we were dressed.

"All right," he said slowly. "Then do you have any identification?"

I nodded easily. "What type do you need?"

"Badges of rank will do." He grunted, his eyes narrowed, still unsure about our status. "Or a company standard, although I don't think you have that on you."

"Of course, good sir." I smiled and made a gesture to reach into my pockets. "Just give me a moment to get them."

I took that time to scan every soldier-looking individual around us to try to see exactly what these badges of rank looked like. With so many around us, the task wasn't hard. On the necks of a good portion of the people here was a small rectangular piece of metal with what I assumed were their names and basic information etched in the plaque. The medals were also made of different materials of varying colors, ranging from a dull brown to an almost shimmering crystal-like structure that refracted the light around it.

I still had a few shards of the sword I'd broken from the second trial, so I took out four pieces from my inventory and showed them to the gatekeeper. Well, it would look quite different from his point of view, showing a vibrant emerald green medal with intricate adornments on it. And best of all, his mind would fill in the other necessary information so that there would be no discrepancies.

However, I had to keep my back to everyone else present, since Noe's Perception Shard was incomplete and her abilities wouldn't cover too large an area. Either way, the gatekeeper seemed to be happy with our identification and nodded.

"All right," he said finally. "You four are good to go. Rare to see exalted-ranked mercs that I don't recognize, and your names are odd too."

I gave him a pleasant smile. "We're from pretty far off, way to the south."

He nodded. "I can see that. What brings you to Experiata city?"

"Same thing as all these other folks around here." I shrugged. "Plus, there's even higher-ranked soldiers gathered than us as well, so I didn't choose to serve the wrong people either!"

The gatekeeper's demeanor softened. "A fellow devotee to the god of fate, I see. Experiata welcomes the devoted. We did not know that our faith has reached the southern expanses. Your skills will be much needed."

"Thank you," I answered. "And I am glad to say that our faith has spread far, but I think we have taken up enough of your time here. There are many more waiting to get in."

The man handed out four small green badges and told us to pin them on ourselves for easy identification going forth. He then gestured for the gates to be opened, and we were escorted in. I gave the gatekeeper a final wave of goodbye—it never hurt to be polite in these situations—and the four of us were finally allowed through into the city proper. A religious city as well, serving some kind of fate deity. That was good information to know off the bat.

We followed the throngs of people moving with purpose toward the city center. Everyone moved in one direction toward some unknown destination like some kind of hive mind, and the four of us tried our best to fit in. Extending my senses outward, or as much as I could without damaging the space, I saw that we were all being funneled into one of four massive cathedrals.

Xalla spoke up once we were safely lost within the crowd and away from the gates. "Do you have any idea what's going on, Walter? This place seems to be getting ready for something big . . ."

"I agree," Q whispered as he glanced around. "It can't be because of us, surely. This kind of undertaking must have taken a considerable amount of time to set up, even for someone of Bob's caliber, much less these mortals."

"We'll know soon enough," Molly said simply. "I find that it is best to wait and see when it comes to situations like this."

I nodded and continued to follow the people. Oddly enough, we had passed dozens of what looked like street stalls, restaurants, and other local vendors, but no one was around to man those shops. The only civilians that I saw were some curious stares from families peeking out their bedroom windows; the streets were eerily empty of anyone who wasn't a soldier or hired sword. Strangest yet, it didn't feel like we were getting ready for an upcoming war either. I've never seen a situation quite like this one.

Fifteen minutes later, we had made it into the main square where the various gathered people were separated further. Our group, the smallest one by far, was lumped together with others of similar ranks. I saw about half the people sporting golden signets, a smaller portion had ruby-red ones, while only ten others had our green badges. Lastly, there were just three individuals wearing exquisite armor that wore one of those rare crystal badges I saw at the entrance.

Once the last member of our contingent was gathered, a person dressed in a professional military uniform took us into a reception area in the leftmost cathedral. The way that he treated us showed a level of respect that spoke to how important our group was. The number of people slowly dwindled as our aide took us farther and farther inside the huge gothic building, not stopping for even a moment for us to admire the lovely frescos and murals expertly painted on the smooth stone surfaces.

Partway through, another guide took our group to a different passageway, while others like her went to the other assorted groups.

"This way, please," she said with a professional smile.

"Thank you," I replied. "And I must say, this building is amazing. The four of us grew up in the sticks, so seeing a place like this is quite remarkable."

And I really was genuine with the praise. Sure, the natives here didn't have the technology to achieve truly amazing feats of architecture using the latest cutting-edge materials and procedures, but the statues adorning every inch of the cathedral and the various paintings hung on the walls were clearly done with expert hands. The care and attention to detail was impossible to miss.

"It really is," our guide answered with the unmistakable smile of someone who was proud of her heritage. "It is all thanks to the god of fate and His oracles that our city could enjoy all of its wonders and privileges. We wouldn't be here without His guidance."

All of the artwork told of the rich history of this place and the religion surrounding it. It was a pity that I couldn't fully appreciate it with my limited understanding of the planet's culture.

"And it is good to know that so many from all over the world are willing to help during these times of need," I continued, hoping to gather more information while I could.

Her smile brightened. "It is good to see that so many faithful gathered, although I wish I could say it was for a happy cause . . ."

I nodded. "I know what you mean. What are your thoughts on all of this?"

The woman sighed. "I don't know, honestly. Ever since the passing of the chief oracle and her message, I'm not sure what to think anymore. But every religious leader, not just for the god of fate, agrees that the Apocalypse is upon us, and that day is fast approaching. I . . . well, it'd be foolish not to heed the direct words of the gods, and I only hope that people like you can advert the calamity to come."

Okay . . . that didn't really tell me much, but at least it was something. It wasn't like they'd just break into exposition after getting such a general question, although I wished more people did that lately since I was always getting into spots where I knew next to nothing about the situation at hand.

"Anyway," she continued, "we're almost at the inner sanctum. The elders will see you now. They'll be able to answer any further questions you have and figure out where you will be most needed. I heard they need a lot of elite personnel for a big ritual of theirs."

"Thank you," I answered. "We'll be on our way."

"Best of luck!"

CHAPTER THIRTY-SEVEN

The Theocracy of Fate

The gates to the inner sanctum opened, and the four of us were greeted with the sight of a conclave of old aliens dressed in plain robes. There were seven of them, all seated on high chairs slightly raised from where we stood by the entrance. The chamber itself was oddly plain, which was quite the contrast to all the art and mason work that adorned the chambers just outside, and that minimalist aesthetic extended to the people gathered.

Each council member wore a simple cloth robe. The only other adornment was a metal necklace of an all-seeing eye. Even their expressions looked worn out and unassuming. If it weren't for the air of authority that each projected, I'd have thought them to be menials. These aliens were an odd sight . . . Now that I thought about it, I really did need to figure out what this race was called, but since they were not affiliated with Central at all, my Rookie Arbiter abilities were completely worthless.

"Greetings!" the lead council member said, her voice surprisingly soothing. "I welcome you to the Chamber of Fate, and I thank you for making the long journey to our humble home, fellow devotees."

"We are glad to be here," I answered back. "My party and I are more than ready to assist the aversion of the coming crisis."

The smile on the councillor's face brightened considerably, in no small part because I had manipulated her emotions quite a bit, but I like to think it was because of my natural charm as well. I made sure that I was keeping the emotions relatively stable since I wasn't sure what they wanted from us yet, and having them too enthused might backfire on me.

"Your help will surely be needed," she said. "Exalted individuals such as yourself are a rare commodity, but it gladdens my heart to see so many gathered for the sake of our god."

I nodded. "Sorry, but we've been isolated from the main cities for a long time, and have only heard rumors of the situation. Can you tell us what is going on in more detail first? We're not even sure of a proper timeline of events."

"Of course," the lead woman said. "We can understand how rumors can get exaggerated, especially over great distances, although I fear that most of what is being spread is the truth."

I gestured for her to continue.

The woman shook her head and sighed. "The late chief oracle's final prophecy occurred almost exactly one year ago today, and it foretold of the arrival of what you now know as the End Bringers. They are four beings of unimaginable destruction . . . One is said to house a universe unto itself, two of the beings blot the sun with their sheer might and magnitude, while the last is said to devour the very space and stars. I fear that their arrival is imminent."

Xalla, Q, and Molly all looked at each other nervously. It didn't take a genius to understand who those four beings were, even with the vague description . . . Which begged the question: How did they know of our arrival so early? Well, she didn't technically say it was a year. Noe's ability to translate languages put the timeframes into its rough English approximations, and a more accurate interpretation was that the prophecy happened something like thirteen and a half months ago.

Even still, the council member said the prophecy or whatever it was happened about a year ago, which made sense given the scale of their preparations, but it also meant that this god of fate had some serious predictive power. It was one thing to know the fate and lives of the mortals under their direct command and control, but it was another matter to predict the movements of beings like Xalla or Q. Add in the fact that this dimension was in the middle of nowhere, and completely cut off from multiversal civilization, and the abilities of that god were no joke.

"I see," I continued. "That does line up with the rumors that we heard. And you say that the day of these . . . entities' arrival is imminent. Do you know when exactly?"

The woman nodded. "The oracle did not give us an exact date and time before her passing, but the remaining Blessed here have divined a rough timeline. The arrival is set to be within the next week."

I nodded slowly. Once again, they were remarkably accurate. They were off by a few days, since we were here now, but that kind of margin of error was to be envied by the other fate tellers around the greater universe.

"That is most disturbing . . ." I muttered.

"And it is why we need your assistance," she continued. "We need to buy time for the gods to act, and our priority now is to secure this city."

"What's so important about this city?" I asked. "Um, aside from its cultural and spiritual significance, that is. I don't mean to offend, but it's rare to see so many talented warriors gathered all at once. We only heard that our help was needed here."

The woman chuckled. "It seems that very little news has spread to the far south."

I gave her a grin and a shrug. It was a good thing that communication didn't seem to have evolved too far in this world, otherwise my story would have had a lot of holes in it.

"But this city, while serving primarily as the conduit to the god, also serves as a prison for an ancient being called Calamity."

I frowned and extended my senses deep below the surface of this cathedral. I saw a minor presence deep under the surface of this city, and while I couldn't risk probing too much farther down without being noticed, there was definitely something lurking there.

"And that is where you and the others are needed," the councillor added. "We are not sure how the entities will affect our world, but all of our prophecies tell of the need to strengthen the wards securing the imprisoned beast. It will be a grand undertaking that must be finished before their arrival, and I fear that we have already delayed it too long getting the necessary preparations finished."

"I see," I said slowly. "And what would you have us do?"

"Every guest is responsible for guarding the civilians and ensuring that the city remains stable in these trying times," the lady explained with a smile. "I am sure that you have already seen the increase in crime and the various doomsday cults that have sprung up lately, and I fear that they have infected even the heart of this sacred city. Some of the vile god's minions are already in our midst, using this time of strife for their own gain, and we must stop these cultists before they can destroy all that we cherish and love."

I nodded again. So far what she was saying made sense. There would always be those who were weak of will or were overly ambitious to take advantage of times of unrest, and it seemed that this race was no different. Coupled with a prophecy that spelled doom, it wasn't hard to imagine how bad the current situation was.

The councillor continued. "But that is the general role that all devotees must fulfill. You are exalted, and thus you four will be needed for more. Each individual is fated for a role, and that is why you are here. We shall divine your task."

Something changed then, and the tone of the room got serious as each council member turned to gaze at us. It was eerie.

The lead woman who had addressed us raised her hands and turned her attention to her silent brethren. "Come. Let us see the role what our guests are to play."

A strange surge of tangible power and faith gathered in the room as whatever it was that they were doing started. Before I could even ask what was happening, the ritual had already finished, and a wave of energy washed over the four of us.

"We see!" they said as one. "We see . . ."

"We . . . we . . ."

And they screamed as the energies that were focused on the four of us reverberated and were sent straight back into the gathered mystics. Their eyes, the conduit of whatever ritual they were conducting, started to melt from their very sockets, and they howled in pain and despair.

Q was the first to act. He immediately isolated the room from the outside to keep whatever was occurring from leaking out, but that slight expenditure of power set off a cascade of repercussions. In hindsight, I should have anticipated something like this happening, but their ritual was so practiced and quick that I didn't even see what they were doing before it was too late. Thus, for the second time in my short stay in Central, I saw with excruciating detail another set of individuals explode.

On reflex, the four of us shielded ourselves from the expanding energy, which, in hindsight once again, was our second mistake. Q wove a second barrier around himself, which was harmless enough, but the rest of us didn't use quite so subtle means. Molly ripped a hole in reality and sent the energy into whatever vortex she put all the things she ate, while I made a small puddle of void to eat up the pieces of exploded aliens. Xalla simply swiped a feeler and evaporated the debris with sheer force.

The huge expenditure of energy all but broke the fragile reality, and cracks formed in the space-time around us. Q quickly set up another barrier separating the now-ruined council chambers from the rest of the city, although it would only be a temporary measure at best.

"Well," Q muttered once he was done, "that didn't go as planned . . ."

Molly gave us one of her signature sighs. "And it only took a few hours. I'm impressed."

Xalla gave me a comforting pat on the back. "Um, I don't think any of us could have predicted that happening. Maybe we can still salvage this situation somehow?"

I grimaced but tried to stay positive. "Yeah . . . look, I can alter the perceptions of the people here to a limited degree, so maybe if we could contain what happened here and just pretend to be—"

I didn't have time to finish my thought because the ground underneath our feet started to crumble, and a massive fissure expanded outward. The four of us had to move close to the end of the room, and I could see that whatever wards were in place holding this so-called "Calamity" had been destroyed by our earlier actions.

The marble tiles cracked, causing the foundation of the cathedral, and the city itself, to crumble as the very ground threatened to collapse under the strain. I could hear the screams and sounds of panic even through Q's barrier, and in a matter of moments, the entire city was engulfed in pandemonium. And in the center of it all were the four of us, still relatively safe due to Q's interventions.

"Ah," I managed to say as I looked at the dust and debris all around us, "well . . ."

Molly pressed a hand against her head and shook her head slowly. "Ah indeed, Walter. I don't think we can pretend none of this happened unless your perception ability can extend to the entire world."

I winced. "No . . ."

"Then I think it's safe to say that our cover is blown, or at least our arrival on this world," Q added. "Let's try to at least minimize the damage here. I don't know how we'll start friendly relations with the gods after this, but it can't hurt to be mindful. We can only hope that they'll listen to us before deciding on extreme measures."

I don't think any of them believed that for a second, but like Q said, it couldn't hurt to be careful. I felt the earth beneath me rumble as something massive started to dig its way to the surface.

"Let's take our new friend somewhere quiet while we're at it," I added, pointing to the ground. "There's no way we'll have any chance of peaceful negotiations if we let that thing loose."

"As if we had a chance after destroying their holy city," Molly muttered. "But you're right. Let's go before we're noticed."

Molly got rid of her disguise and extended some of her hair tendrils into the ground. I could hear a horrible howling sound as the newly freed beast was trapped again. After a few more seconds of an unseen struggle, Molly nodded at us to indicate that she had the thing secured. Q opened up a new portal, a rather large one this time to fit our new guest, and we plunged into the opening.

The last thing I saw was Q's bubble disperse and the last remnants of the once beautiful cathedral crashing down to the ground. Great, what a wonderful way to start our expedition to this new dimension . . .

CHAPTER THIRTY-EIGHT

A Not-So-Subtle Entrance

Q dumped us onto a remote island surrounded by nothing but a beautiful ocean. The tropical breeze and calming waves were a nice distraction from the utter chaos that we had just escaped from, and the lazy afternoon sun would have made the scene perfect if not for the giant squirming mass of hair. Attached to it was Molly, who didn't look all too pleased.

She unraveled the bundle, and a huge monstrosity . . . drooped out? It plopped lifelessly onto the sandy beach sporting an all too familiar shade of purple. It looked kind of . . .

"It's sedated," she explained before I could say anything. "I don't want to risk anything further until we figure out our next steps."

"Good idea," Xalla said with a tired smile.

"All of us should give our input this time," Molly continued, looking straight at me. "I think that will be a better idea going forward."

I winced but couldn't exactly disagree with her. Xalla gave me a comforting glance, although I think that hurt my pride more than it helped. Me and making a mess of things were fast becoming things that went hand and hand.

"Should we get rid of the Calamity creature?" Xalla asked, pointing at the whimpering mass.

The creature struggled feebly when it heard Xalla say that and tried to grumble something in protest. Unfortunately, Molly's curse was too strong for it to overcome and only half-gurgled gibberish came out of its various mouths.

Not even Noe's ability could translate what it was trying to say, and I just gave the creature a gentle pat on its massive head. I almost felt bad for it.

And speaking of mouths, I peered at it further and saw that it was a rather impressive creature by mortal standards . . . if it were not a sickly shade of purple and looked like it would die at any moment, that is. The first thing that anyone would notice was the sheer scale of the thing. Even slumped on the ground, it was the size of a multistoried shopping mall, and it took up almost the entirety of the small island we were on.

Next thing of note was its eight pairs of massive legs that ended in serrated talons, each the height of an elephant. Scales the size of dinner plates lined the creature's body, while six pairs of membraned wings lined its back. I couldn't see how far they extended with the creature all shriveled up, but I couldn't imagine them being small or unimpressive.

The most impressive feature—had it been less dead-looking—was the three separate sets of mouths that lined its head. The central mouth was the largest, the opening so large that it made up almost a third of the thing's body mass, while the two smaller ones lined each side of its face. A cacophony of various eyes, all of different shapes and sizes, lined every inch of its body, and I could feel the toxic fumes being breathed out of the thing every time it exhaled. It had probably been an impressive beast in its prime.

Q walked around it with an inquisitive eye, studying the creature like he would one of his alchemical creatures, before walking back to us and shaking his head. "No, Xalla . . . this creature is man-made, or deity-made in this case. I'm not sure which member of this dimension's pantheon was responsible for its creation, but I think everyone can agree that we shouldn't destroy even more things on our sojourn."

Xalla didn't look happy about Q's information, although the creature visibly eased upon hearing us spare it.

"But surely we can't just release it," Xalla added, poking the thing on its big side. "The world's already in turmoil, and letting something called the Calamity can't help our cause."

I furrowed my brow and stared at the massive pain in the butt before us. "Does anyone know how to seal it again? I've never been good with the magic side of things."

"I can't help either," Molly said after some thought. "Not without destroying this dimension, in any case."

Xalla frowned and shook her head. She was the head of security, but she usually dealt with existing threats and their prevention. We all turned to look at Q with anticipation.

"I can't help either," Q said with a small shake of his head. "I can do the basics like personal wards and barriers, but Lord Babylon would be more suited for something like this."

"And I'm guessing we can't just go back and get him," I said.

Q sighed. "No . . . After our last little stunt, we risk dimensional collapse if we exit now, not to mention how difficult it will be to enter without being noticed again. This reality needs time to heal, and we're on our own for the time being."

I remembered those cracks in space-time just a few minutes earlier and had to agree with Q.

"Then what do we do with it?" I asked again, pointing to the ill-looking Calamity. "Do we just leave it here?"

Molly shook her head. "It would be irresponsible of us to do so. We can't leave it crippled like this, and my curse will wear off over time. It seems intelligent, so we can send it to the strongest settlement and let the natives handle it."

Q smiled and nodded. "I see, so your plan is to send it weakened so that it will be easily captured without doing too much damage. Am I correct in my assumptions, Lady Malice?"

"Exactly," she answered. "I have a good grasp of the abilities of the locals here, and I can ensure that my curse is just strong enough for this Calamity to reach its needed destination without causing unnecessary harm when it arrives."

I thought about her proposal for a moment but couldn't help but worry that something would go wrong again. After everything we've been through, I was starting to severely doubt our abilities to be subtle or careful.

"Are you sure that's our best course of action?" I asked. "This thing is called the Calamity, and we have a track record of overestimating mortals . . ."

"The alternative is leaving it here to recover to full strength, which is problematic in many ways, or killing it outright, which may severely hamper our already strained relations with the local gods," Molly said. "Whoever created this beast must have put a lot of effort into it, and let me be the first to say just how much a large project like this may mean to its creator."

"So either option's a no-go," I said with a sigh. "All right, I don't think we have any alternatives here, but let the record show that I think it's a bad idea to send this thing to a settlement."

"And your opinion is noted," Molly answered with a dismissive shake of her head.

"The cities should be well defended, now more than ever, with those prophecies," Xalla added quickly. "This is the best time to release it. And if things really don't go as planned, we still have the alternative of killing it."

The beast shuddered again and made another feeble attempt to say something.

"All right," I said and turned my attention to this Calamity. "You heard that, right?"

A tiny nod answered my inquiry.

"In a little bit, Molly here will weaken the curse, and you'll have to fly to the strongest human—er, I mean native settlement here. The absolute strongest and most well-defended place. Do you get that?"

Another nod.

"Then you are to . . . I don't know, cause some trouble, I guess," I continued, looking around at my friends to make sure that I was on the right track. They didn't contradict me.

"Should we tell it to lose on purpose?" Xalla added. "We do want to minimize damage."

Molly shook her head. "It'll barely be alive when it goes there; having it hold back might just lead to its demise. We're trying to strike a delicate balance here."

"All right," I continued, speaking to the beast again, "so you're to go and cause trouble and do your best not to get killed. Do you understand?"

It nudged its massive head up and down. It really did look pathetic. Well, guess there was nothing else to do but release it into the wild.

I gestured to Molly with a nod. "Let the poor thing fly."

A huge amount of hair tendrils started to pour out between the gaps in the thing's scales. The beast's color started to recover almost immediately, although it was still clearly lethargic.

"Go," she said. "And don't think you're free from me. If I hear that you're not doing what we told you, we can always find you."

It screeched in fear and immediately flew away. Well, after stumbling a few times and uprooting several trees that is. The force of its lift-off was like a localized typhoon as entire trees were uprooted from the sheer volume of wind being displaced. Just seeing it leave toward the horizon sent chills down my back, and I just hoped whatever poor settlement it decided to visit was ready for what was to come, weakened state or not.

I took a big breath, feeling relieved now that one of our bigger problems had disappeared into the gloomy darkness of the horizon. Wait a second . . . I frowned and looked up. The sun was clearly there, and if this planet was at all similar to the Main Stage and Earth, then it should be around midday, so how was there a dark horizon? In fact, looking at the horizon closer, it was becoming abundantly clear that the darkness was spreading.

"That . . ." I muttered, pointing to the direction the Calamity left. "That's not normal, right?"

The others stopped what they were doing and looked toward the horizon. It was still far, far off in the distance, but thanks to the endless expanse of the ocean around us, our views were not obstructed.

"Ah," Q said.

"It is coming from the direction of the city we destroyed . . ." Xalla added. "Do you suppose we messed up the weather or atmosphere when the beast was unsealed?"

Q squinted before frowning. "No."

Molly looked up and sighed again. "That's a phenomenon I'm all too familiar with. We've destabilized the dimension with our last little jaunt. Wonderful."

"So definitely no backup from the outside, then, although I don't think even Big Bob can fix this mess we've made," I grumbled. "And here I thought things couldn't get worse."

Xalla looked around in confusion. "Sorry, but what's going on? I'm not used to going to these small dimensions, at least not when I had to be careful, but what did we do?"

"We broke the fabric of space-time," Molly answered. "Well, maybe wounded it is more accurate to say. The fact that we're still standing on solid ground instead of an empty vacuum is a good sign. Means we haven't caused irreversible damage yet."

Xalla frowned. "But we barely did anything back there."

Q cut in. "Our entrance to this plane already stressed the dimension to its breaking point, and given its remarkably fragile nature, you can imagine what would happen after our little stunt."

I recalled the exploding council members and what we'd done. Molly's disappearing act tore away at the space around us, while Xalla's casual swipe fractured the dimension even further. I didn't really help by summoning the Abyss here either. I sighed again. Q was the only one among us with any sense of tact or subtlety. We all looked at each other in embarrassment.

Xalla winced and pointed at the expanding void in the sky. "But we can fix that, right?"

I could even see horrible-looking lightning and supernatural weather patterns clearly now that it had encroached further toward us. The sky was alight with the crackling of electrical discharge, and the football-sized hail looked like missiles as they crashed into the ocean's waters. Waves the size of condominiums were flailing away, and I could almost hear the rush of wind even from here. All of that was bad enough, and that was ignoring the obvious cracks forming in the very space around it.

End Bringers, what a fitting name.

Molly sighed again. "No. At least, it's outside the scope of my abilities. The good news is that the weather should get better as it expands away from the epicenter, so there's that."

Yeah, a whole lot of good that'd do.

"We fucked up," I muttered.

"I can perhaps stop it," Q said. He was the most adept individual here when it came to the galaxies and universes. "But not here in the mortal world, and not without a better understanding of the dimension. But it'll ultimately be up to the local pantheon to do the repairs. It is their world, after all."

I shook my head. "Then it's even more important that we see the gods as soon as possible. Nothing new. What do you think our chances are of explaining things calmly and rationally to the local gods now?"

My friends gave me a scathing look. The consensus was clear here.

"So what do we do now?" Xalla asked.

"We stick with the initial plan," Q answered, "although some things might need adjustments with the new developments. I'm sure that if we visit a different holy city that's in need of help and prove ourselves, we can at least convene with the leaders there and potentially establish basic relations with the gods here. This world seems deeply religious, and we've already seen that the gods' priests have direct lines of communication with their patron deity."

"We go through the priests to get to the gods," Xalla said. "Got it."

"I think subtlety is out the window at this point, so we'll use force if need be," I added. "Er, within reason, that is."

No one disagreed there. I looked around and saw that no one else had a better idea. Then again, the options available to us were already strained as is. At this point, all we could do was hope to avoid an all-out confrontation with the local pantheon. Of course, there was still one big issue remaining.

"Now the problem is how we're getting there," I said. "You dropped us pretty far from anything, and I don't think we can afford to swim back to civilization."

"Ah."

"Ah indeed, Q." Molly shook her head. "There's no helping it. If we'd known this sooner, we might have been able to hitch a ride on that Calamity beast, but as it is, we'll have to exit via a portal. At least a local gateway will not stress the world . . . much."

I winced when I saw the rapidly expanding patch of dusk. At this rate, it'd only be a matter of days or weeks before the entire planet was covered in supernatural darkness and abnormal weather. I recalled that corrupt Earth I was in before and could already imagine what life would be like on this planet if we didn't fix things.

Once again I was impressed by how accurate the prophecies were, although I think the god of fate or whatever didn't consider that all of the damage we caused was because of incompetence and not malice. I just hope that god actually believed that.

"I've located the next largest civilization with a high concentration of faith. It's not too far from here either, so the damage should be minimal," Q said. "Let's go before things get even worse."

CHAPTER THIRTY-NINE

Unavoidable Calamity

The beast of Calamity flew into the expanding void of space with a new mission in mind. No, a new purpose in life. It had been created as a mere tool by the gods, nothing but a convenient slave that was bound to the whims of the fools that made it. Those creators didn't care about how the Calamity felt, only that it could destroy the mortals every millennium or so due to some idiotic perceived slight or transgression.

They didn't care how the beast would be painfully imprisoned each time it was done with its task, they didn't care how horrible an existence it was to be forced underground for thousands of years at a time, nor did they care about the wants and needs of the beast. They had created it—no, he had a name, a purpose, an identity now. The old masters created *him* with the ability to destroy but never allowed him to do so unrestrained. He had been a glorified pet under their rule. They did not deserve his worship.

Now all of that had changed. He had met his new masters, and he could tell that they were different. They were stronger, better, and most important of all, they had severed the horrible connection between the Calamity and the old gods. They had given him a chance to prove his worth, to prove his loyalty, and that he deserved this second chance. All the Calamity had to do was what he was born to do: to bring ruin and destruction. But now, he could do so without the need to hold back.

Of course, he was weakened now, a lesson in discipline and a punishment for disobeying when he first emerged from his confinement, but he could already feel his old might returning as the Calamity flew closer and closer toward the darkness. He fed off the ambient energies escaping from the gaps in reality, and before long, he had returned to full power. No, he was stronger . . . with each lightning bolt that struck his scales, each stray jolt of radiation melding into his flesh, his body was filled with unparalleled might.

The Calamity laughed.

No, what the new masters did was not a punishment but a baptism! The tiny remnants of the master's form, a small splinter of hair, blossomed as the eldritch energies from outside this tiny world nourished its growth. It spread inside his body, crawling and worming out to transform his entire being. His weak old flesh sloshed off, his pathetic metallic scales falling in lumps as new tendrils of bloody flesh, sinew, and hair replaced them.

The black hairs covered and enveloped his wings, making them expand to almost twice their old length, and he could feel his jaws contort into a new monstrous shape. Beautiful porcelain-like growths blossomed on his head and he could feel his innards transform into something completely alien.

It felt marvelous! Even now, he could feel his connection to the new masters strengthen with each passing moment. And with each passing moment, the Calamity grew.

But the beast didn't allow the joy of his newfound purpose to cloud his judgment. He had a job to do before he could be allowed true freedom, to leave this tiny insignificant world and serve his masters better in the wider expanse.

He spent a long time in that all-encompassing darkness, waiting patiently for this body to fully morph, and once he was complete on the third day of incubation, the Calamity flew toward the greatest gathering of the mortals. It would be a far journey, one that would take him past the current continent, but the glorious End had already started to spread to those far-off regions, and it was finally time to prove his worth and bring sweet Calamity to the world.

The Holy City of Thrain stood strong against the encroaching dusk. The city had been blessed to be situated far away from the origin of the destruction and had more time than the others to prepare for the inevitable confrontation. They had been able to take in the best fighters that survived the ruins of the other cities and, more importantly, had gathered the largest conclave of holy men and women this world had ever seen. They only had to hold off the dark for a few more days before they could complete the vital holy ritual that might just fix this situation.

They were hopeful still. Word had spread that other cities and bastions still held on and that the gods had not abandoned their servants in this most trying of times. Rumors of champions and heroes born from other worlds and their legendary feats eased the souls of the citizens of Thrain, while priests of all denominations went around to soothe both body and mind. Yes, the people were hopeful.

The city's defenders had fended off civil unrest easily enough, and even the waves of maddened and mutated beasts and bandits had been repelled with minimal losses. Yet despite these victories, the looming threat of extinction weighed heavily on everyone's minds. It would only be a few more days until darkness reached their position.

"Gather up, men!" the garrison leader yelled.

The squad assigned to the front lines all obediently rushed around the old commander. The speed and ease of their movements told of their experience; these were all veterans of many long campaigns. Each soldier saluted when they saw the man in charge.

"All right, the lot of you!" the commander continued, "we have reports from our scouts and diviners. Something big's coming toward us, probably another swarm of the damn vermin being chased away from the dark."

The men around him gripped their weapons tighter in anticipation of another long night of defense.

"Anything important to note, sir?" one of the sentries asked with a disciplined shout.

"The damn weather and gloom make proper intel gathering impossible, even with the sage's scrying," the commander muttered. "All we know is that the foe's numbers are great. The size of the mob is almost a quarter of our city's, so prepare for a long fight."

That sobered some of them up. So far they had been repelling small hordes and groups of wild beasts and crazed citizens, never more than a few dozen individuals at any one point. Things had only gotten worse in the passing days, and the soldiers here all knew that this relative time of calm wouldn't last. With the maddening approach of the supernatural storm, it was inevitable for panicked creatures of all shapes and sizes to attack anything in the way of their path of escape.

But this was the moment that they had trained for. Once the sentries were dismissed back to their assigned positions, each soldier checked and double-checked their equipment one last time and waited for the battle's start.

They didn't have to wait long.

"Incoming!" the commander shouted as the first set of beasts approached the walls. He had never seen such a frenzied moment before. It was as if these animals had lost all reason and didn't even see the mighty stone wall that blocked their way. They charged in without heed of their own safety. The eternal darkness was still several miles away, but even now the men and women defending the city could feel the strange energies in the air.

"Archers and mages, ready up!" more shouts of command echoed. "Wait until they reach the ridge! Save artillery fire until we see the proper horde!"

"Yes, sir!" Shouts of confirmation reverberated along the walls and towers. Soon, the unmistakable sound of loosened bow strings and incantations filled the halls, all while the first signs of rain started to drizzle down across the battlefield.

Deep within the city, hidden in subterranean chambers were the priests, bishops, sages, and their gathered retinue. A solemn ritual of gargantuan proportions was well underway, and the few soldiers chosen to guard this most important of locations could only look on with stomachs knotted with worry.

This was it. This was the final moment. It was do or die. Everyone here knew that. This was the crucial ritual that the gods had instructed them to perform, and every person here would be heroes if it all went well. Just a few more moments and they could undo the fracturing world. They only had one job to do.

Tense minutes passed as the defense of the city of Thrain raged on. Back on the walls, supplies were shuttled, while personnel changed shifts as needed. It was a beautiful display of organization and military discipline, yet even though victory seemed so certain, the hearts of the defenders felt heavy. So far, only the scattering of beasts assaulted the walls, but even half blinded by the rain and gloom, the defenders of this holy bastion could feel the approach of something massive.

"The main force is coming!" the commander shouted. "Wait until we have visual confirmation! Don't fire until we see their numbers!"

More shouts of affirmation met his voice, and the artillery and mortar teams readied their weapons. The mages and mystics in reserve got to their assigned stations, and every single able-bodied individual watched in anticipation of the main battle to come. They were all ready for a long and grueling fight.

They didn't get it.

"Commander . . ." one of the archers muttered in disbelief, almost dropping his bow as he saw something emerge from the dusk. Something massive. "Wh-what is that . . . ?"

The Calamity approached the feeble human fortification and smiled, its porcelain face cracking as it did so. Raw muscle and sinew glistened underneath the smooth white surface as small hairlike tentacles wiggled underneath, anticipating the slaughter to come.

Calvin, or Cal for short—he had decided to make a true name for himself now, the very first decision that was truly his own—had engaged in a lot of contemplation during the few days it took him to fly here. He had initially devoted his time to understanding his new form, to think of how to utilize this strange new energy that coursed through his body, but what Cal devoted most of his time to were thoughts on his own existence.

As his body slowly integrated with his higher form of existence, his mind expanded just as rapidly. He understood just how limited he was prior to meeting the masters. He understood just how fragile this tiny pond he called home was, but most of all, he understood how much he hated his old slavers. They made him so incomplete and worthless, and he dreaded to think about what would have been his fate had the new masters not come.

Yes, Cal decided that he would get his revenge in due time. But first, he would make do with venting his anger onto the mortals of this putrid world, just as he was instructed to do.

The tiny mortal city quickly came into view, and he could already see the nervous expressions of the feeble defenders. They, in their woefully limited perception, thought that they were only fighting the tiny creatures that ran toward their walls. They still thought that they could oppose the new masters.

The mortal's enthusiasm and cheer quickly turned to despair once Cal's resplendent form left the shadows of the dark and came into view. His ebony wings spread out as he approached, and the squirming tendrils that made up the membrane thrashed out and enveloped the screaming defenders below. The beast opened his three massive maws and breathed out a rain of fine hairs. They shot out at supersonic speeds and impaled the feeble sentries below. Some tried to seek cover behind weak stone walls and barricades, but Cal's projectiles cut through those fortifications as if they weren't there at all.

Worse still, for the surviving defenders at least, the poor souls who were merely grazed by the hair fragments soon turned a sickly shade of violet before their bodies atrophied and died. Nothing was spared from the wrath of the Calamity, and that was before he even arrived at the city proper.

Cal even chuckled when he felt the pathetic retaliation of the mortals. Their crude rocks hurled by their catapults and trebuchets bounced harmlessly off his porcelain face, while the barrages of arcane magic dispersed before they could even touch his pulsating flesh. The defenders put up a noble defense, all things considered, but when his full form arrived in front of their walls, pure pandemonium enveloped the citizens.

Gone were the brave individuals manning the walls and towers. Commanders fled after giving out orders meant to save their own lives while others shoved their comrades and used them as shields. Gone was the discipline and military might these mortals had, and all they wanted now was to survive for but a few more moments.

The last attempt from the gathered people below, a beautiful barrier of pure faith that covered the entire city, was destroyed with a casual swipe of Cal's forelimb. There would be no divine intervention now. There was only the coming Calamity and the looming dusk.

CHAPTER FORTY

Avoiding Calamity

We stepped out of the portal, a familiar feeling now that we'd done it a few times in short order, and saw that Q had dropped us on the outskirts of another city, albeit a smaller one this time. The surrounding landscape wasn't too different from the place we started our misguided journey at, and I could infer that our new location wasn't too far away from there. Well, the clouds of black smoke from the still-burning city and the supernaturally encroaching darkness just off in the distance also helped.

Molly had put on her disguise again, and we all glanced at the distance. It was worse up close.

"We'll have to limit how we travel going forward," Q said with a shake of his head. "Even that short trip almost caused . . . well, that." He pointed at the disaster on the horizon.

"Right," I muttered. "Let's stick to walking, then."

"How's your body holding up?" Xalla asked. "You're trying to hide the strain, but I can tell."

I frowned, but she was right. I'd been overtaxing myself lately, what with almost destroying this entire universe and all that, and I could feel my body degrading by the second.

"How long do you think we have until we're done here?" I asked.

Q shook his head. "It's impossible to know for sure, but I can't imagine we'll be done in a day or two. We've still yet to meet the gods, and Stanton's location is likewise unknown. Minimum, perhaps five or so days if we're lucky?"

"Your body's not going to make it for that long, will it, Walter?" Xalla said first.

"No," I answered honestly, "I'm already feeling the strain."

"I told you to be careful," Molly added with one of her familiar sighs. "But you never do listen. Just go back to sleep, take the next little while to figure out what parts of your mind you wish to keep, and we will ensure that you are taken care of once all is said and done."

"But will he be okay back in the Main Stage?" Xalla asked. "We can be sure that he'll be safe here, outside of Central's influence, but not after. The Overseer will be livid once he finds out what we've done, even if he can't prove that we did it."

I chuckled. "I'll be fine. I've survived the first three trials without a hitch, and it wasn't like the Overseer wasn't already pissed off at me. Plus, I'll be better prepared this time around. I'll make sure to leave enough information for Sleepy Me to thrive, but I do need a favor from you, Xalla."

"Anything."

I smiled at her. It really was good to have an ally that I could always depend on, especially a talented Xollon. "Once I'm hibernating, the amount of information I'll have will be extremely limited, and I'm not sure when I'll be awakened again."

Xalla nodded.

"So do you mind if I transfer some information over to you?"

"In case you need to know it in the future?" she asked.

I shook my head. I had Noe to do that, but I couldn't reveal her yet. "No, I have ways to store my memories. But I think it'd be best if someone else I can trust fully knows about what's going on behind Central's shiny exterior. I've learned a lot about this organization as an arbiter. You can fill in Q, Molly, and the others when you have time, but don't share it with anyone you don't personally trust."

"Not a problem, Walter." She smiled back. "I'd be glad to help."

I took some time to sort out the most relevant information, choosing to omit almost nothing aside from Noe's existence, and sent it over to Xalla. It took almost no time at all, and she didn't even flinch at receiving eons of lived emotions and experiences, an insignificant fraction of which would cripple a lesser mind. It reminded me again of just how formidable this species was. They really did represent the apex of existence.

"Oh . . ." Xalla said as she sorted out the new information. "That's . . . I'm so sorry . . ."

That got the other two's attention, but they had the tact to not interfere at the moment.

"Don't worry about it," I muttered, and I could already feel the mounting pressure becoming almost unbearable after that stunt. "We can talk about all of that later. Make sure to fill everyone in once you have time. I need to rest soon. Give me a moment to sort things out."

They nodded.

Noe, make sure you store all the information with you. Give me access to as many relevant Central regulations as my mind can handle, and I'll trust you to pick whatever else to keep.

"I will do as you command, my creator," she replied. "I will ensure that you have the needed information as more of your mind expands and evolves. Please rest assured that I will not fail you."

Thank you. I guess I'll be seeing you soon enough. Good night, Noe.

"Good night, dear Walter."

I gave my friends one final wave and closed my eyes. I just hoped I did enough to ensure my future success.

"Good morning, my host," Noe greeted. "I hope that you had a good rest."

And I woke up again . . . or maybe it was more correct to say that I fell asleep again?

"Do not worry about the nature of your existence. Even with your full abilities at your disposal, you were unable to completely grasp the difference between your two states. Just know that you are not two separate entities; it is just that your ability to perceive your full existence is limited at the current moment."

I frowned. Damn, was that confusing. Well, at least Awake Walter—or, er, me?—left enough information so I wasn't completely in the dark like last time, and oddly enough, I could still remember everything that happened since my awakening as if I lived through it.

"It is because you did live through it, my host," Noe added. "You are not two separate entities, please remember that."

Right . . . that would be hard to digest, especially since I was missing a lot of crucial information that I used to know. Too bad I don't know what information I was missing, or at least not completely. Worse still, I couldn't even be mad at myself for it. I didn't want to end up like those poor oracles from earlier who tried to spy on the four of us. I wouldn't be allowed to access those fragments of my memory, thanks to my stupid human mind.

Wait a second, if I'm still the same person, Noe, how come you're calling me the host again and not your creator? Doesn't that imply that we're separate?

"You are still my creator," she replied, "but I thought it better to call you by a term that your mortal mind is more familiar with. Would you like me to change the way I address you?"

No, never mind. Just call me what you want.

"As you wish, my host."

I sighed and reviewed the new stuff in my mind again. The best way to describe what I was feeling at that moment was that I knew the general idea of everything that had transpired, but I knew none of the details. For example, I knew that I made Noe so that she could help me, but I had no idea how I'd managed that, nor even what it was she was supposed to be helping me with. Likewise, I knew I had the ability to summon a patch of darkness, but there were no memories about what happened to anything that was sucked into it. It was annoying knowing so much more yet so little at the same time.

Everything about Noe and what she was supposed to do was blank, and so were the inner workings of Central and whatever war they were waging right now. But at least I knew the nature of my own existence now. It was so disconcerting knowing that I was so much more but having no way to access those abilities anymore. At least the Absolute Luck skill was back online.

Well, no use fussing over things I couldn't directly control anymore. I would just be thankful that I wasn't completely ignorant going forward like I was before. Half blind was better than all blind, after all.

"Walter . . ." Xalla said with concern, "are you okay?"

"Yeah," I answered with a forced smile. "Just . . . waking up's not pleasant, or was what I was doing going back to sleep? Ugh, never mind, just give me a minute to get my thoughts straightened out."

"But you still recall everything that happened?" Molly added, looking far more animated than before.

"Yeah," I grumbled in response. "Just the details are foggy."

"Interesting," Molly added before furrowing her brows and studying me further. "The method that you use to insulate your mind is very unique. These don't seem to be the normal discrepancies associated with sectioning off parts of the mind. I'll have to ask you again when you're fully awake; the hospital could benefit from this information."

I wasn't sure what Molly was talking about, but I just nodded. I was sure fully awake Walter could deal with that later.

"Need I remind you again that you are not two people, my host?" I could almost see Noe shaking her head here. I chose to ignore her for now.

The others left me to stew in my own thoughts for a few more minutes before I finally got things sorted out—at least I didn't have a blazing headache anymore—and told them that I was good to go. We didn't have time to spare, and it seemed like something huge was brewing on the horizon. My friends and I decided to stay hidden for now and assess the situation thoroughly before we could mess things up again, and there was a perfect high ground we could take that would allow us to see the situation perfectly just a few hundred meters away.

We peered down from our vantage point on the nearby hill and saw an entire army clad in gold approaching from the horizon. They were marching fast toward our position and deeper into the epicenter of the catastrophe. At this point, the city we were in was completely engulfed in supernatural darkness, although the unrelenting gale-force winds had died down. The rain, however, had been drizzling nonstop and a lot of the lower elevation had been completely flooded.

The army's position should also be completely devoid of light, yet strangely, the golden armor that each warrior wore reflected brilliantly despite there not being any sunlight. It made them look like a tide of holy crusaders who marched to restore light to the ravaged land. The army spooked the cultists who manned the walls and other fortifications, which was rather impressive since half of them were insane and could barely form coherent thoughts.

I saw siege equipment hurling huge boulders at our position. There was some kind of divine help because there was no way they could build anything that could send those rocks from that far out, but it did explain the rumbling from earlier. Some of the vanguard and scouts had already made contact with what seemed like an army of deranged cultist forces, and small skirmishes were taking place all throughout the swampy land below.

The cultists were not winning.

I peered at the tide of golden warriors slowly encroaching on their position. On and on they marched with a single-minded purpose. Now that they were fully in view, I could see that their numbers seemed to stretch from horizon to horizon. There were tens of thousands of them. The Order, or "good" gods—for surely this was a battle between different ideologies now—were clearly preparing for this inevitability, and they prepared well, although something told me that they hadn't planned for the four of us being in the city. It's always strange to see the lesser deities separated by ideology instead of working together, but I guess that's just how things are. The fight between good and evil, order and chaos, never goes away.

"Well, it seems like Q has picked quite a location for us to arrive at," Molly said with a sigh. "I don't suppose anyone here has a guess on what's going on?"

I shrugged. "Seems straightforward enough. Looks like a classic battle between good and bad."

Q added. "I agree with Walter's assessment. I can feel something big brewing in that city, some kind of ritual, which we can safely assume is something that the knights over there would like to prevent."

"Guess it makes sense to have a lot of fighting, what with the end of the world approaching and all," I muttered. "Should we help them?"

Molly shook her head. "Remember what happened last time we tried to help? Let's observe for now. Maybe there'll be some clues as to where this mysterious Stanton is."

"Right," I said. "Let's just watch first."

With a flutter of his robes, the conduit merged into the stone beneath our feet as if he had sunk into the masonry. What a weird way of exiting, but it did fit the evil cultist theme going on here. That was when I saw this chosen individual.

The person in question wasn't hard to make out, as well as a lone rider wearing a flowing robe of sparkling stardust came rushing ahead of the golden army. He held a banner high while everyone rallied to his side. If I had to guess, I would say that this individual was the chosen. Well, the other clue was that he, well, wasn't the same species as the rest of the aliens here.

"Hey, guys . . ." I muttered as I pointed at the charging figure riding on the weird horse-looking thing. "That's a human, right? Or am I going crazy after losing most of my mind from falling asleep again?"

Q frowned as he squinted his eyes to look at the fast-approaching man. "No . . . you're not losing your senses, Walter. That's not just a human, but that is an aspirant, one of my own from the looks of it. It's one of the ones we lost during the messed-up second trial. You weren't the only group sent to that strange place, but you were the only party that made it out again. We thought all the others had been killed, but evidently, that wasn't the case.

"And with the blessings from the time god here, and how strange time flows between dimensions, it's conceivable that he's been here for much longer than the few Earth months that's passed for us."

"Huh." That was all I could manage to say.

But if he really was an aspirant, then I should be able to peer at him with my arbiter title, right? It'd been useless here so far since nothing was under Central, and now that most of the stuff I knew was sealed, I was almost desperate to get more information on my own.

I activated the skill, and lo and behold, I could see his most important aspect.

Ashwin Thiru (God's Chosen One, EX Rank, Frontline)
Description: You have been summoned by the gods of a foreign realm with the task of bringing salvation to an entire civilization. Your devotion to the people and the faith will see you victorious against the worst evils of the foul

gods and the invaders that inhabit the Spaces Between, and you will bring in an era of faith and prosperity.

Hot damn, that was only the second EX-ranked job I'd ever seen, but what was strange was how this Ashwin person acquired it. The job system should be completely under the control of the Trash Matrix, but from the description, it almost seemed like the gods here gave that class to the aspirant. Or maybe the Trash Matrix allowed him to earn this title since one of the heads of the Central Collective was interested in this backwater dimension for some reason?

Q saw me shake my head in thought and added, "It's strange no matter how I think about it. That aspirant had been spirited away from Site 1102, and although the second trial was corrupted, achieving such a feat would still be close to impossible, especially given the nature of this fragile dimension. There's something odd about the gods here. Something more going on in the background."

The more I thought about things, the more I tended to agree with Q. Timelines weren't adding up, even given the strange nature of time and space, not to mention that these people somehow knew of our arrival. I was starting to think that the gods knew of us even earlier than the mortals let on. I didn't know much about multiversal mechanisms anymore, but even I knew that none of this made a whole lot of sense. There was something that the four of us were missing, and I hated incomplete information.

"Well, Stanton wouldn't be investigating this place if there wasn't something unique about it," Xalla stated. "But at least we know that he's not here for no reason."

"But we don't know what that unique thing is," Molly, who had been silently observing, said. "That's generally never a good thing, even if I'm not privy to the entire picture here."

"Agreed," Q said. "Let's review what we do know about our current situation. We know that Stanton's here—"

"Wait a second," I interrupted, and everyone stopped and looked over. "Awake me's given me enough info to go on, but Stanton's one of the most important individuals in all of Central, right?"

Q nodded.

"So wouldn't there be meticulous documentation about his goings-on? Like where he'd be and what he's doing at all times?"

Q frowned, still not quite sure what I was hinting at, but nodded again. "That should be the case for all of upper management."

"But Xalla took a really long time finding where he is," I continued, glancing over at the Xollon girl. "She even had to corroborate her findings with Rogue's sources. Doesn't that seem strange?"

"Well, sure," Xalla answered, "but it's not like just anyone could access the activity logs of the people running all of Central. I imagine most of Stanton's files are classified in any case."

"Right, but you did get access to those files, the complete version as well, right?"

"I did. Wait, hold on a second . . ." she muttered before frowning. "No, Walter's right. Things don't add up. The files I had just indicate that he's here, and a rough timeline of when he left. There's no detail about what he's here for, or even how he got here."

Q swore. "I should have noticed that earlier! I apologize, I wasn't in the best state of mind when we first met, but that is definitely not how things should be documented, and we all know that Stanton's a stickler for regulations."

I nodded and continued. "Coupled with the fact that he hasn't chosen to reveal himself for so long, and I think there's definitely something fishy going on in this dimension."

Xalla frowned again. "The more I look back on the things that happened here, the more I agree with Walter. This dimension's almost purposefully left to be undiscoverable. It took us almost two days just to get here even with Bob's resources, and the plane is strangely fragile. Yet the gods, from everything that we've observed so far, seem much more capable than your regular lesser deities."

"And what do all of these things have in common? What entity could do all of this?"

Xalla sighed. "The Origin Matrix. Damn."

Q paused for a moment, as if this new revelation gave him an idea. "Hold on . . . it's faint, but . . . No, give me a few moments."

Xalla looked at him with concern. "What is it?"

"I might have picked something up now that the aspirant's here, but it's faint. Something's strange about that army—no, it's not the army itself, it's . . . Ugh, give me a moment, please." He left, jogging down the hill so that he'd have some privacy.

CHAPTER FORTY-ONE

Strange Disturbances

Q arrived back at our position a few minutes later and looked grim. "It's almost certainly Origin. I could sense its presence in that entire army, and after a little more digging, I'm almost certain that it's hiding its presence in wherever these paladins came from."

"And I'd bet that's where Stanton is as well," I added. "Shit."

"Shit indeed," Q muttered in a rare display of frustration. "If Origin's directly involved after everything you told us, then we might be in for more trouble than we thought. We're not sure how long we have until the Overseer and his people know of our absence, and even with the time dilation in this dimension, I'd say that we have a tight deadline to keep."

"But we still don't know what's going on!" Xalla added. "It's just . . . never mind. Sorry, I'm not used to feeling so helpless."

I chuckled at that. That was the feeling I'd been experiencing ever since I was put into the trials. I went over to comfort the girl. "Don't worry, Xalla. I'm an expert at dealing with these bullshit situations by now. I got this. Since we've already screwed this world over, all we gotta do now is invest fully in the chaos. We help out the Cultists a little, meet their god through whatever ritual they're doing, and wing it from there. I'm sure we can convince them of our cause if we get the chance to actually talk to one of their kind."

"I just hope it works out in our favor this time . . ." Q looked over and frowned. "Ah . . . but I guess this situation is partly my fault, Walter. I didn't know about your unique situation when I brought you in."

I laughed out loud now. "You can't be blamed for something you didn't know about. And like I said before, your site's helped me grow faster than I ever could before, although I don't quite understand how that works anymore."

"It's still strange to see you so similar yet different, Walter," Q said. "It will take some time to get used to your sleeping state."

Xalla nodded. "But you're still you, so don't worry. I don't think any of your friends will mind waiting a while for you to get better."

I gave her a thankful smile and snuggled up closer to the girl. It really was good to have true friends for once.

"Okay, enough with the sentiments," I said, looking down at the carnage that was raging on below. "We have to figure out what our plan is. We're in the dark so far, but at least we know that the Origin Matrix is somehow involved."

By now the battle was well and truly raging in the city. The rows of golden figures were slaughtering the poor conscripted townsfolk the cultists had positioned in front. I could hear cries for mercy from the citizens, but those cries fell on deaf ears. Whatever zeal possessed the golden warriors made them little more than killing machines. The conscripted townspeople didn't even manage to dent the armor of the main army; all they did was delay their advance by a few minutes.

The same couldn't be said about the cultist's main army. These ones put up an admirable fight. Our forces were channeling the might of their patron deities and slinging disease and filth in the direction of the invaders, while the more martial—or as I liked to call them, the brainless—ones charged in bloated on the power of their berserk gods.

I saw that various commanders were standing on the various watchtowers, each of them chanting something that I couldn't make out. Waves of visible energy assaulted the forces below while simultaneously invigorating the cultists. With the help of the strange enchantments, the cultist forces were able to repel their golden enemies, and I thought they would actually win this one.

Well, until the chosen aspirant joined the fight.

"That's honestly quite impressive," Xalla said as she studied the human fighter. "He's almost as good as that anomaly in your party, if not better."

Q watched with interest as well before shaking his head. "Not quite. A lot of his abilities come from help from the gods here—"

"Yeah . . ." I muttered, "I can assume that he's not exactly pleased to have us here if that's the case. I don't think the gods behind him are all too pleased with our presence either."

Q ignored me and continued, "And he has had more time to grow since his abduction. His raw potential is still short of Walter's anomaly, but he is not far behind. If we're judging him based purely on ability, then this aspirant is one of the best non-anomalous humans I've ever seen."

"Then it makes sense why he would be placed in that horrible second trial," I added. "And why the Origin Matrix and the local god would choose to invest so heavily in him."

Impressive might have been an understatement when I saw him fight. Although I couldn't be sure what level he was—my Rookie Arbiter title only displayed his class—it was clear that he was miles ahead of any of the other aspirants. It'd be strange if he were any different, what with all of the resources of the gods and the indirect help of the Trash Matrix at his disposal.

The weapon he used was some kind of amorphous blob that transformed to match the needs of its wielder. He started his assault with an enormous bow. The aspirant unleashed dazzling golden arrows that acted more like railgun shots as they vaporized anything in their direct path. Even the shockwaves of its passing disoriented or outright killed the cultists in their path. These shots were only stopped by the combined efforts of three of the cultists' champions, but the long-range volley was only the beginning of Ashwin's attack.

The aspirant transformed his weapon into a long sword and pistol next. Anything that went even remotely close to the man was cut down with such speed and ferocity that even the best cultist could only manage a lift their weapons in a futile attempt to block his blows before they were summarily cut down. The less skilled died before they even knew what had happened. Worse yet, Ashwin's left hand seemed to move with a life of its own as it expertly picked off enemies at range with shot after shot. These didn't do as much damage as his melee slashes, but it kept him from being surrounded by sheer numbers.

Added together with the four comrades that were always beside the man, he and his small squad was massacring his way toward the gates. Our forces were doing close to nothing to halt his progress. We managed to slow him down from a breakneck sprint to a leisurely jog, if that.

"The four beside him are also quite skilled," Molly said with a slight nod of her head. "These are interesting creatures, makes me want to know how they operate."

Yeah . . . maybe getting along with the evil gods and their cultists would be a better idea given my current company . . .

"You're right. Their teamwork is very advanced for a mortal species," Xalla added. "It'd be a pity if they were to die here. They seem important to the inhabitants and I don't think making more of a mess is exactly the best call right now."

The Xollon looked at me and Q, her intentions to preserve these five clear.

Q nodded. "I agree, I think it is paramount that we save the human, but getting the other four wouldn't be too hard either. It'll help placate the aspirant when we capture him. I'll make sure that they aren't injured, although at this rate, I doubt I'll have to do much."

I shook my head. "No, if I know anything about evil cultists and their crazed leaders, then there's bound to be something huge hidden in reserve. I'll bet you anything that they'll unleash that once the five reach the gate."

"You've had evil cultists of your own in the past?" Molly asked with a raised brow. "You don't seem like the type of person to bother with mindless worshippers."

"Uh, not direct experience," I answered with an awkward chuckle, "I mean it's how the movies I watched used to go."

"Movies . . . ?"

"Never mind," I muttered. "Just trust me, they'll have something prepared. The evil guys never win in these types of situations, but the good guy should always triumph anyway. But if what Q says is right, then be ready to intervene and capture that group. I have an idea."

"Okay . . . We'll trust you, Walter," Xalla said. She didn't understand where I got my confidence from, but I was thankful for it. "Do we have a place to put the aspirant and his friends when we capture them? Our usual methods won't work."

Good point. Normally we could just chuck him into a portal or something, but that was certainly out of the question now. I also doubted that we could afford to constantly monitor the man, and I certainly didn't trust the cultists to do that for us.

"I can handle it," Molly said. "With the aspirant's strength, he can survive my care for a significant time. I think the mortals or the gods, if we can get their help, at least, can take care of the other four. If not . . . well, I'll think of something."

I nodded. "You're sure they'll be safe, though, right?"

The woman rolled her eyes. "Yes, Walter. Or at least I can guarantee that they won't die."

"All right, let's leave it to Molly, then," I said. "Let's enjoy the show for now."

Some servants came in with chairs and a wooden table, and the four of us made ourselves comfortable staring. I grabbed a spot next to Xalla and snuggled up to her. It was strange given the guises we were wearing, but it had been a while since I'd had a chance to just enjoy her company. She didn't look as enthused about the spectacle as I felt, but she seemed happy to know that I was having a good time.

I wasn't sure about what my friends thought about the struggles of the aliens and the cultists, but I felt like a Roman emperor watching a grand spectacle from high above. With most of my memories sealed, watching an epic-fantasy siege that looked like it came right out of a movie was quite the treat. I was even involuntarily cheering for the good guys every now and then.

The air seemed to change just as the aspirant and his party were about to breach the front gates. The conduit and his lackeys had tried their best to halt their process, but nothing worked. Physical assaults launched by the cultists were deflected by Ashwin's shield, and curses fizzled into nonexistence; even the magical assaults were taken care of by the other four. If their offense was superb, then that group's defense was all but flawless.

All seemed to be lost by our side, but then the ground before us rumbled and a massive summoning circle started to glow under our feet. Following the glow were the dreadful screams of pain that reverberated from every corner of the city. I saw that the citizens that were not conscripted as cannon fodder started to wither into husks as their very life source and energy went into the huge enchantment. Most of the cultists were spared the worst of the ritual. Some kind of necklace they all had around their neck lit up to protect their wearers, although not everyone seemed to have a charm that worked.

Some of the unlucky cultists had defective amulets that did nothing, and they and their foes were sucked up into the massive ritual. By the time the worst of the screams stopped, only the strongest individuals on the opposing side could withstand the weird life-sucking effect. This was great for our side, but unfortunately, the majority of the golden-armored beings were left a little haggard, but otherwise no worse for wear. If this was the only thing that the ritual did, then our loss was still all but certain.

I smiled in anticipation. "Things will really pick up from here!"

Xalla chuckled, mostly at seeing how excited I was, but I saw that she paid more attention to the mortals below. The same thing happened with Q and Molly, although they gave it a more analytical eye.

And just as I thought, all of that energy they took from the townsfolk and the weaker invaders seemed to channel into something. The power seemed to visibly swirl in an intricate pattern. I couldn't make heads or tails out of what was going on, but Q and Molly seemed to be mildly interested in the arcane intricacies. I didn't need to be a genius on rituals and magic to appreciate the results, however.

Once some kind of unseen trigger or breaking point was met, that swirling energy shot into the air, and a huge red vortex split the sky, and a figure descended from the opening. I was almost afraid that the dimensions would break again seeing the portal, but true to the conduit's words, the mortals' rituals didn't strain the plane we were on. The huge figure descended from the skies. The dust, rain, and debris that whirled around the figure obscured its features, but even from the silhouette, the thing was absolutely enormous. Bigger still than that Calamity creature we released before.

Before the thing's full features could be seen, the cultists all fell to their knees and screamed words of worship.

"The Avatar!"

"Hail the Avatar of War!"

CHAPTER FORTY-TWO

A Hero Emerges

Once the dust had finally settled, I could fully appreciate the look of this wicked Avatar thing. It kind of looked like a weird, slightly deformed demon. It had six pairs of wings made of fire with two arms that extended to below its feet, although it had three joints, so its arms looked like weird noodles. Compared to its arms, the demon thing's legs were almost comically small. They looked like the little stub legs from a munchkin cat, as they were attached to a torso that was the size of several city buses. Finally, its face was a more menacing visage of the aliens present, with fangs and hard edges. It looked . . .

"It looks ridiculous," Molly said. I had to agree with her. "I have seen the anatomy of thousands of different species in my time, and nothing even comes close to how ineffective that thing's physiology is."

"It's . . . um, different, certainly," Xalla muttered. "What do you suppose it'll do if it ever stops flying?"

Q shook his head. "Certainly not walk, that's for sure. I suppose it can crawl around with those weird arms."

"Look, let's give it the benefit of the doubt," I added. "The golden guys seem pretty intimidated by this thing. Maybe that's just what the mortals fear in this plane."

And it was true. Aside from Ashwin and his immediate allies, the rest of the invading army was momentarily frozen in fear. They looked up at the huge noodle-armed thing and almost screamed before the champions did something to regain their composure. A warm light engulfed the army, and they could act again, although only just.

That was when the noodle demon attacked. Its arms spread out to absolutely ridiculous lengths and swept out to whip at the defenders below. The champions were the first to respond, and they erected a dazzling barrier of pure energy that managed to block the worst of the demon's attack. Unfortunately, all that amounted to was that instead of being bisected down the waist, the warriors just lost limbs instead. Healers quickly rushed to take the seriously wounded away while more linemen filled the gaps.

I saw Ashwin shout something to the army, but it was too far away for me to make out, even with Noe's help, but whatever he said boosted their morale, and the army started to regroup. The archers and mages in the back started to bombard the huge noodle demon with long-ranged attacks, but most of those were deflected by its massive wings. The ones that did manage to penetrate its thick hide did minimal damage at best.

"It's sturdy, I'll give it that," I remarked. "But given how much energy the cultists expended to summon that thing, it'd better be sturdy."

"I think it's kind of cute how it's trying its best to use its arms like a Xollon feeler," Xalla added. "Although the rest of it is still questionable."

"It's a flawed design nonetheless," Q added. "Its wings are too large to allow it proper movement. Not to mention its size is unfeasibly big. It's a common mistake that amateur alchemists make, but once a construct gets to a certain size, its coordination and fine motor skills will decrease to unacceptable levels."

Q was correct because once the huge army started to split up, the noodle demon had an incredibly hard time accurately striking at any one target. It made up for it in sheer size, but eventually, once the numbers of warriors dwindled and only the best of the best were left, the demon could hardly hit anything.

"See?" Q continued. "It's so big that it can't properly maneuver around the battlefield, and being stuck in the air is also causing it trouble. It has too many blind spots being so high up, and there's our aspirant taking advantage of that right now."

The creature's aimless blows with its arms had covered the ground in sludge and dirt, which made the perfect cover for Ashwin to sneak up right below the thing. The demon was so oblivious to what was right under its feet that it had allowed Ashwin to charge up an insane amount of mana; it was all concentrated on the tip of his spear. Soon, the glow of energy grew to such intensity that it was impossible to ignore, but it was already too late.

Ashwin's teammates and the surviving army managed to block any attempts from the demon to retaliate, and once the energy grew to its crescendo, the aspirant shot up like a rocket, piercing the demon right in its unfortunate parts.

"Ouch." Xalla winced. "That must have hurt."

"Like I said, it's a terribly designed construct," Q muttered with a sigh. "It'll be over soon. I think it's best if you prepare to act, Lady Malice."

Molly's sigh was the only response she gave.

It really was over soon after that. The ritual that the idiot cultists had performed might not have outright killed their allies, but it did pretty much cripple their ability to fight. The lucky ones who were spared the worst of the ritual's effect were so weak that they could barely put up a fight as the invaders rushed through the front gates.

It took half an hour for all of our major forces to be overwhelmed, and an hour for our gates to be fully breached. The cultists' defeat was so total that only the few servants that were left for our use remained. I assumed the cult leaders were still below ground doing their thing, but it was clear that it was our time to act.

"Wait, Q," I said quickly, now that the battle was starting to come to its conclusion. "You said that the source of whatever it is the Tra—er, the Origin Matrix was doing is where those paladins are, right?"

He nodded. "There's a disturbance there, some kind of anomaly that I can't exactly make out from here, but yes, it does relate to Origin. That is correct."

"And we're going to steal the head of those paladins, their champion, yeah?"

He nodded again. "We certainly can't leave a stray aspirant here."

That's when a thought occurred to me. "Look, I think we've gone about this the wrong way so far."

Molly notched an eyebrow. "What do you mean?"

"We're ultimately here for Stanton, right?"

Molly only rolled her eyes and didn't bother answering.

"But why do we have to ask the gods for help?"

"Because we don't know where he is?" Molly answered again, looking at me like an idiot.

I shook my head. "But why do we think we have to ask them? I mean, we've fucked things up so badly at this point I don't think any amount of convincing will help us, evil Chaos gods or not."

Xalla glanced around the ruined world and winced. "Fair enough . . . I think it's safe to say that we've outstayed our welcome."

Molly scoffed. "We can still intimidate and coerce them, no?"

"Yeah, but somehow I don't think they'll be the most cooperative if we did that." I shook my head. "I think there's a better way to go at this."

I paused and gave my friends some time to think.

"Look," I said. "We know that Stanton's here, but if all our abilities failed to find him, and we know that the Origin Matrix is doing something dubious here, then I think it goes without saying that it's interfering with us somehow. Maybe the old man found something compromising with the Matrix and it's holding him prisoner or something."

Q frowned. "It would explain a lot . . . There's not a lot of beings in the multiverse that can interfere with a man like Stanton, but Origin certainly fits the bill. Plus, with the recent surge in Anomalies and its odd behaviors . . ."

"So if the gods are not the answer, then what should we do?" Xalla asked.

"Easy," I said with a smile. "Ashwin here has a direct link with Origin, right, Q?"

He thought for a moment before nodding. "Yes, although the link is tenuous. It's why I hadn't noticed Origin's presence until I saw the Aspirant. I'd have to take a closer look at the man to get an idea of what exactly is going on, but I should be able to trace the source of Origin's interference."

"Then I think I have a plan . . ." I grinned.

"Walter, that's too dangerous!" Xalla was the first to object. "You just went dormant, and there's no way you can do that alone!"

"I agree with your girlfriend, Walter," Molly added. "There's too much risk involved, and we won't be able to come to your rescue if something goes wrong, not without destroying the entire dimension."

I shook my head. "But we all agree that we must investigate the Origin Matrix, and we all agree that we don't exactly have a lot of time to do so, right?"

Xalla frowned, seeing where this was going. "But . . ."

"Look, I might be half asleep, but do you honestly think these mortals will give me any trouble?" I said again, hoping they'd see my side of things.

"Well, I suppose not . . ."

Q cut in. "But the mortals aren't the issue, it is what you might encounter with Origin."

"Hey, it's not like I'm going in to fight Origin or something, and what other choice do we have? Try our luck with Chaos gods? Have you seen their followers? I'm pretty sure Q said that cultists take on the personalities and essences of their gods, so I don't think they'll be the most helpful individuals around," I answered. "I'll just be there to scout things out, see what the source of the strangeness is, and come right back. Minimal danger, and if this plane is as unstable as we see it, there's no way that the Origin Matrix can do much either. Best case, I'll find out where Stanton's being held and we can skip all this nonsense and just grab the old geezer."

Molly shook her head and sighed. "There's no reasoning with him, but I tend to agree that the risks do not outweigh the benefits in this case. But know this, Walter, if you do get into real danger, then I am ripping this dimension apart to come to you."

I gave her a nervous chuckle. "Er, there's no need for all that but, uh, thanks, though."

"Just take care, Walter," Xalla mumbled. "And call if you need help. Destroying one universe isn't that big of a deal, really."

Yeah . . . sometimes I think my friends are a bit extreme.

"I will," I replied with a comforting smile. "And someone should go get that aspirant before it's over. Make it seem like he fell in battle or something, a critical injury so that it'll take a while for him to be rediscovered."

Thanks to the sheer destruction that strange demon thing caused, going in and making a muck of things shouldn't be too difficult, but we'd have to act soon. The dust and debris was starting to settle, and the paladins were reforming ranks quickly.

"I'll steal the aspirant and his companions," Xalla said as she got up from her spot.

"Actually," Q added quickly, "I'll do that. No offense, Xalla, Walter, but I think it best if you two just relax for now. Walter's still recovering, and Xalla's . . ."

The Xollon gave her boss an understanding smile. "I know, I'm not exactly the most subtle person. Walter and I can cheer you on!"

"Thank you," he replied. Q stood up with Molly. "Let's get going, then."

CHAPTER FORTY-THREE

Walter's New Plan

The plan was simple enough. My friends would cause a bit of chaos in the ranks of the paladins and "steal" the aspirant from under their noses. To ensure that no one suspected anything, we waited about two days before enacting my plan to swap positions with the man. That time was mainly used to make adjustments to my meat suit and to extract some basic information out of the aspirant.

By the time I was ready to go, I was donned in Ashwin's armor and held his weapon, and Noe memorized all of the relevant info that Q had managed to extract from the poor guy. It was only basic stuff like names, basic organizational structures, and the like, but it would have to do. The Omni couldn't exactly get much else out of the aspirant without killing him, what with the plane limiting his abilities severely, but I didn't have to live as the guy for too long at least. The basics would have to do.

With that out of the way, I was placed in a tunnel along with two of Ashwin's companions—they'd been, er, slightly altered—and ready to go. It took me a few minutes to dig our way out, being careful with the Absolute Luck skill to ensure that my escape didn't cause the entire tunnel system to cave in. I had worried that the rather loud exit we made would alert someone, but I needn't have. No one could hear anything over the screams and cacophony of the ongoing war.

Q might have used the wrong word when he described the conflict raging in the city. Skirmishes generally didn't involve thousands of organized soldiers battling it out with all kinds of strange beasts and savage berserkers. At least it didn't take a genius to know which side I was supposed to be aligned with.

My dramatic exit, or entrance, I guess, covered my already grimy armor in even more dust, so no one had noticed my presence just yet, although I knew that this was only a momentary reprieve. After all, I was a completely different species compared to everyone else here. That meant that I only had a few moments to survey my current situation and figure out the best course of action.

I was supposed to be the hero here, wounded or not, and the best way to ease suspicions of my actual identity would be to act like one. I'd seen Ashwin act for a total of like fifteen minutes, but even in that short amount of time, he seemed like the stereotypical good guy, what with his brave speeches and rallying cries. I couldn't imagine that someone like him would just flee the scene even if he was half dead. No, even an idiot would realize that Ashwin would fight.

Unfortunately, the problem was: How I was supposed to do that? The only weapon in my possession was the strange transforming metal handle thing that I couldn't use, and it wasn't like I could just start bashing cultists with my feelers like usual. Not being able to use the divine weapon could be bullshitted around, but there was no way that people wouldn't notice a drastic change in personality if I chose to just run, which meant I needed a new weapon.

The problem wasn't the availability of one, but more about my absolute lack of skill in using anything. I'd have to rely on using the Absolute Luck skill in combat, but from my past experiences, the way Noe fought was rather . . . strange. Having Ashwin fight like an absolute imbecile, even an effective one, would raise eyebrows. Ah, screw it. It appeared that my entrance had already been noticed, and I didn't have the luxury of thinking anymore. When in doubt, just let Noe do her thing.

I closed my eyes and fumbled around blindly for the most appropriate thing to use.

Luck Charges: 1,555/1,557

Good, once I saw the numbers go down, I opened my eyes again and saw that I was clutching a bow and some loose arrows. Thinking about it, Noe's choice of weapons this time was apt. I'd had a few goes at shooting a bow during my time with Yoona, and with the high amount of variance involved, I could feasibly wreak some havoc with this thing. It was time for Ashwin to make his entrance again, and I needed to make an apt entrance to ensure my disguise wasn't questioned for the time being.

I grabbed the bow, shoved as many of the arrows as I could into the quiver, and jumped up on one of the crumbling city walls. This gave me the perfect vantage point to strike, but more importantly, it was a spot where everyone, foe and friend alike, could see me. I shouted a coarse battle cry in Ashwin's voice—I could still never get used to sounding different when I wore a guise—and proceeded to nock a handful of arrows all at once onto the bow. I pulled back as best I could, feeling the poor weapon strain under the immense pressure, and released half a dozen arrows into the air.

> **Luck Charges:** 1,501/1,557

Once again, I had to admit that Noe was impressive. The arrows spread out all around me, being carried off in seemingly random directions by the torrential rain and gusts. Each shot managed to find a home in poor unsuspecting cultists of one of the strange beasts that the evil gods had summoned, and every arrow was fatal. I didn't have time to marvel at Noe's work as I continued to load more and more arrows, firing randomly into the air, all the while shouting incomprehensibly.

Even better, under Noe's effect, the arrows seemed to catch the fleeting rays of light and shimmer as they flew in the air, getting the attention of anyone in the vicinity. Before long, all eyes were on me, and I could distinctly hear the cheers of the paladins as they saw their hero emerge from ashes.

> **Luck Charges:** 1,440/1,557

Unfortunately, having all the attention on me also meant that I was quickly the focus of the enemy as well. The amount of luck charges quickly went down as Noe did her best to ensure that I dodged the worst of the assault, while the things I couldn't avoid were deflected on the strongest parts of my armor.

> **Luck Charges:** 1,332/1,557

However, I was seeing a real problem. The spot that I exited was closer to the cultists' side than the paladins, and that meant that I was right in the middle of the entire enemy army. If these cultists were not completely brain-dead, they'd all pile on me, and I didn't think that any manipulation of luck could cause a few hundred cultists to all miss their attacks on me. If I started to run for it now, then I could still outrun the majority of the forces . . .

I shook my head. No, that wasn't what a hero or chosen or whatever would do. It was a risk, but I could see the Order god's side just off the distance, maybe only a few hundred meters away from me. It'd be a gamble, but I'd hedge my bets on them making it in time before I got overwhelmed by the opposition. I'd normally never take a stupid risk like that, but it was absolutely critical that I made a good first impression. There were already too many inconsistencies between me and the real Ashwin, and I didn't think I could explain it all away without them giving me the benefit of the doubt.

"You two," I commanded to the aliens that left with me, "go to the paladins and get them here as soon as possible. I'll hold them off here."

They nodded and shambled away. Thanks to my arrows, only a few cultists got in their way, and thankfully, whatever brainwashing Q did to their brains didn't hinder their battle abilities too much. Once I saw that the two were well on their way, I focused my attention back on my own precarious situation. I was now thoroughly surrounded.

Luck Charges: 1,233/1,557

Even Noe's abilities could only do so much as the cultists started to swarm me and my two mostly useless companions. I had to ditch my bow before long and just started swinging wildly with my fists. I still had to put on a show for the paladins and soldiers rushing to help. Initially, I thought I had to deactivate my skill so that I'd look like I was struggling, but it was quickly apparent that this was not a feasible approach. I thought I'd actually die without Noe's constant help, but on the bright side, I didn't have to try very hard to appear as if I was going to die any minute now.

I grunted in pain as a claw pierced through my defenses and gouged out a chunk of my thighs. I punched the dog thing that did it and grunted as I felt something else latch onto my back. Another sharp pain, on my shoulders this time. Someone had managed to poke a rusty sword into the armor joints, and I had to shake the crazed cultist off me. What was taking the damn paladins so long to get here? Did they want their damn hero dead after I'd made such a great entrance?

More and more bodies pressed onto me, and by now I wasn't sure if I could endure any more without having to resort to transforming into a Xollon, but I still had some HP left according to my stat screen, and I held on until I was certain that I wouldn't make it otherwise.

Time seemed to flow at a standstill as I saw each and every cultist and beast attack me. I was moving on autopilot at this point. I brushed aside the swing of a sword, but an axe smashed into my side as I did so. Noe managed to ensure that the enemy didn't hit anything vital, but I could feel the blood loss and fatigue adding up quickly. I was able to deflect a spear with my shoulder guard, and another thrust bounced off my chest plate, but for each attack that I was able to negate, more made it through my defenses.

I saw my health dip down to the low hundreds, and I feared the worst. Why had I chosen such a dumb way of making an entrance? Too late to regret the decision now, though, and I didn't think I was going to make it . . .

I was moments away from just forgetting about this mission and transforming when I noticed the chaotic drone of scraping metal and snarling beasts was replaced with something else. The number of crazed enemies stuck to me seemed to diminish before I saw a new sight: rows upon rows of golden figures rushing to my side. They hacked and pried my foes off me and my comrades, all the while shouting something that my fatigued mind couldn't comprehend.

Noe, we're safe for now, right?

"It is so, my host," she replied in that same comforting tone that I knew.

I smiled to myself. *Think they bought my charade?*

"I think your identity will be unquestionable for the time being, dear Walter. Relax for now. You are no longer in danger."

Good . . . and please smack me next time I decide to play the hero. I'm not made out for these roles.

I didn't hear Noe's reply as my body gave out on me and I sank to the ground. I was pretty sure that someone held me up, but I wasn't sure as the world quickly faded to black, and I passed out. Yeah . . . time to leave the hero business to the actual heroes.

I woke up to the sound of Noe's voice, and pain. "Good morning, my host, please do not be agitated. Your body sustained a lot of injuries during that earlier stunt, and you are currently being moved to a proper healing facility."

I tried to move despite Noe's words, but my body felt heavy. The best I could do was open my eyes.

"You're awake!" someone said. I turned my head to the direction of the voice and saw a girl stationed by my side. Wait, a girl? How was there another human here? I thought we were dealing with aliens?

"Allow me to explain, my host," Noe interrupted. "Unit Noe has taken it upon itself to assist you in this infiltration. Recall how I eased your stay at the hospital by adjusting your perception?"

I nodded slightly.

"I have done something similar here. I used the time you were unconscious to alter your perception of the natives of this world to be of something familiar to your mind. I have noticed that my host had a difficult time differentiating individuals of this species, even when fully awake, and this confusion may cause unneeded hindrances for your plans to work."

Huh, now that she mentioned it, I'd just been telling the aliens apart via their clothes, which I didn't think would work all too well if I were to stay in their company for long.

Oh, yeah, that makes sense. Thanks, Noe.

"You are welcome, my host."

"Don't move, Ash!" the woman continued. "You were on the brink of death earlier. Thank the gods you even made it."

"W—" I tried to say, but only a rasp was vocalized. I swallowed and tried again. "What about the others?"

"Nova and Edric are getting treatment as well. They're healing fine. Although . . ." She shook her head. "Never mind. We can talk about what happened when we get back to the capital. Rest for now, Ashwin, you stopped the cult and their demons."

"But . . ." I muttered, "there's still—" I coughed, which caused the girl to bring me something to drink. "I couldn't get everyone out."

"I'm sorry . . ." She winced. "But, um, the life signs of all of your party members are still active. I'm sure they're still alive. W-we can talk about it after, okay? I'm just glad you're fine now. I was afraid our rescue mission had failed, although I guess you did manage to get out yourself, so we didn't help out much."

I nodded slightly.

"We're still a few hours away. The barrier's still in good condition as well, so just rest for now. I won't pry into what the cultists did to you and the others, but . . . just know it's over now. You're safe."

She got up from my side and put a wet towel on my forehead. "I'll wake you up once we're back, so sleep for now."

CHAPTER FORTY-FOUR

To the Holy City Part 1

The journey to whatever capital city the Order gods stationed their base at was uneventful; the only thing that I had to keep track of was the fact that I was healing a little too fast thanks to my Xollon physiology. I had to have Noe suppress as much of that as she could, which kind of sucked because I would have been up and about already had it not been for the need to keep up appearances. Still, since I had some time to finally rest without worry for once, I guess I couldn't complain.

During that time, Noe had been busy in the background, sorting through all the information that Awake Me entrusted to her, while also reintegrating herself fully into Sleepy Me. In fact, Noe had been doing a lot in the background since I got back from my last trial, what with getting those extra shards, and her capabilities as a whole improved as a result. I could rely on her to sort through all the information I gathered, like that book Q wrote, and formulate all that info in a way that my stupid human brain could understand. Now all I had to do was act on that knowledge. I'd do the bullshitting while she did the analysis. It was brilliant.

And so, after about a full day's travel—although it was hard to tell time what with the world ending in total darkness and all—Ashwin and his travel companions made it back to their city. The city itself was impossible to miss as well, as it was the only stretch of land that still had sunlight shining on it. I guess that was the barrier that the girl was talking about.

"Her name is Sarka, my host," Noe reminded me, "and according to the notes disseminated from Q, she is someone important to the original chosen. Please act accordingly."

Right, what I meant to say was that it was the barrier that Sarka had mentioned when she was tending to me. Anyway, whatever that barrier was, it was certainly impressive. It stretched out farther than I could perceive, even when I cheated and used my Xollon senses, but what I could see was a sense of normality within the giant cylinder-shaped protection. Well, the citizens within were still tense, while the guards and soldiers looked like they'd pass out from stress at any moment, but it was a lot better than anything outside their city.

Once we were within shouting distance of the gate, I got up from my makeshift bed and started to get dressed in Ashwin's armor. It wasn't the filthy mess it was before; someone had cleaned it while I was sleeping.

"What are you doing?" Sarka gasped when she saw me up and about. "You shouldn't be moving!"

I shook my head. "We're about to make it back to—"

"It is called the holy city of Ordas, my host," Noe answered before I could even ask. God, she was amazing.

"Ordas," I continued with just a slight pause. Now for the main part. I had to gauge what kind of person this Ashwin individual was, and if this girl was as close to the chosen as Noe indicated, then her reactions would tell me a lot, but just to be safe, I activated my luck skill as well. "And the citizens need to know that their chosen is alive and well. You guys mounted that rescue mission just for me, and I can't show weakness after everything that they have sacrificed just to ensure my safety. They need hope."

The girl only sighed. "That's just like you, Ash. You'll burn yourself out at this rate."

No change in luck charges. That was a good sign.

"And the world will burn if I don't do something," I continued in the most stereotypical good-guy line I could think of.

The reports all indicated that this Ashwin guy was the ideal hero figure, and nothing so far had contradicted those reports, so I'd just act like that. My choice of words seemed right when I saw the look of concern on Sarka's face. She chose not to try to talk me out of it, which suggested that this was a pretty common occurrence for Ashwin. That was good to know if even his close allies thought of him as the self-sacrificing type. That was an easy enough archetype to slot myself into. It wasn't very nuanced, but if I followed this type of script while I discerned more of the smaller details about Ashwin, then I think I might just pull off this stunt.

Thankfully, with Noe's help, I didn't have to actually put up with pretending to be fine when I was secretly injured. Aside from acting like an extra brain, she could also shut off my pain receptors at will—something that she would never normally do, I was told—since having the ability to feel pain was critical to survival. I tended to agree with her on that front. If I relied on her every time I was in discomfort, then I could imagine myself being hooked on that feeling of invincibility.

However, that wasn't the case now. I needed to have a clear head if I wanted to survive, so I'd just accept the super Advil for now. Once the carriage entered the shiny bubble of normality, I gritted my teeth and prepared to step out. Showing one final look of pain and weakness in front of the girl—er, I mean in front of Sarka, I put on a brave face and stepped outside of the carriage that was carrying me to face the gathered crowd.

It went without saying that my arrival, and my escort of a few hundred surviving paladins all dressed in gold, had caught the attention of everyone in the city. The streets were packed with individuals all vying to get a better look at their hero's triumphant return. The city guards and other officials were busy at work keeping the peace, forming a neat row that led to the picturesque castle at the center of the city. I guess that was my destination, then.

Got off the wagon and started to wave and smile at the people cheering us on. It was honestly strange seeing so many hopeful faces. Some were so touched that they were moved to tears. It was tiring work, but I supposed that Ashwin would be the type of person who went around to shake everyone's hands as well, so that was what I did, smiling as I went along rows upon rows of people. I said words of encouragement as I passed.

I thought that would be the end of it all, just another joyous celebration of their hero coming back, when I noticed an odd movement in the crowds. I wasn't sure of it, so I double-checked with my Xollon senses, but there was definitely someone—scratch that, a *group* of people—moving and coordinating something. By the looks of grim determination on their faces, I think it was clear that they were up to no good.

I held in a sigh. Honestly, if this was any other situation, I'd just allow the suspicious people to do their suspicious things, but not only was I most likely the target of whatever nefarious plans they had up their sleeves, but Ashwin would probably not ignore such behaviors either. Worse yet, I'd have to take care of the situation the way that the damn righteous aspirant would.

Noe, let's spend some luck charges now and get this over with. I really don't want to spend any more time disguised as this Ashwin fellow.

"Acknowledged, my host," she replied. "And I concur. You do not make for a very convincing savior or hero."

Noe was right, of course, which made things more difficult for me, because I had to act contrary to everything that I'd ever done. Now how would someone with more morals than I ever had approach this situation? I'd just silently stab the bastards with my feelers and be done with it, or come back later and kill them in their sleep, but I was pretty sure that wasn't how things went here. Did I . . . shout something at the bad guys? Yeah, I decided to go with that.

"Halt!" I screamed.

Luck Charges: 1,302/1,557

And they really did halt, although it probably wasn't of their own volition. One of the suspicious men's coats got caught on the belt of his accomplice, while another shady individual slipped on a piece of rock and fumbled into his partner. It was rather comedic if it wasn't for the bombs strapped to their bodies.

Luck Charges: 1,182/1,557

One of them recovered remarkably quickly, and even pressed what I would assume was the detonator for the explosives. It didn't go off, but it did cost me over a hundred luck charges. I couldn't afford to lose much more from some random terrorists, so I acted. With a leap, I slammed into coat guy and . . . shit, what was I supposed to do now? I obviously couldn't kill him. I let go of his neck as fast as I could and hoped that no one saw my attempt to strangle him to death . . .

Luck Charges: 1,022/1,557

Ah, right, I also crashed headfirst into someone strapped with IEDs. I'd be dead without Noe's skill . . . Shit, what did heroes do here? Right, subdue them. I grabbed his loose cloak and tied the man up with the other guy beside him before ordering one of the panicking guards to hold onto the two. That left only one more pair to find.

Luck Charges: 992/1,557

They were running away fast, and hitting their detonator button rapidly as they went. I wanted to cry seeing all my luck charges eaten up because of some goddamn random idiots.

Luck Charges: 801/1,557

Stop pressing that fucking button! My precious charges!

Luck Charges 684/1,557

Worse yet, whatever improbable event that was keeping the devices from going off was really unlikely to happen. Forget it, there was no way that I'd catch them without trampling some of the poor women and children in the way, so I decided to just grab some loose rocks and throw them as fast as I could in their general direction. Noe ensured that I didn't miss.

Luck Charges: 679/1,557

Five luck charges later the two would-be suicide bombers were on the ground unconscious, but from their shallow breathing, not dead. I should have just done that from the start! I needed to figure out how to act like a good person fast, otherwise I'd be found floundering again in the future. I was quickly running out of luck charges to play with.

"Stay away from them!" I shouted. "I'm using my divine abilities to prevent their explosives from going off, but I can't keep it up forever!"

Well, that was obviously a lie, and I wasn't sure if Ashwin ever had an ability like that, but how else would I explain why everyone hadn't been blown to smithereens? Plus, it wasn't like the general populace knew much about divine magic, or at least I hoped so.

The paladins were the first to act, and they quickly subdued the four individuals and took them somewhere out of sight and hopefully out of mind. I could tell that people wanted to cheer for this act of bravery, but the city officials and security quickly evacuated everyone present. The streets emptied in a matter of minutes, quite efficient work, I had to admit. The atmosphere was somber after that.

"Ashwin, are you okay?" the gi—er, Martha—

"It's Sarka, my host."

Sarka, her face pale with concern, said, "You're injured!"

Injured? I looked down and saw that I was leaking blood everywhere. Huh, must have opened up some wounds from crashing into that guy earlier. I probably wouldn't have chosen such a stupid action if I wasn't high off Noe's painkillers, which was probably why she told me to avoid using them as much as possible. The blood soaking through my armor was probably a good indication of that truth.

"Ah," I answered, and now that the adrenaline was fading, my head was feeling awfully light. "Good thing there's no one around now, then."

And like clockwork, I felt myself passing out again. I hoped this didn't start to become a habit.

CHAPTER FORTY-FIVE

To the Holy City Part 2

I was getting sick and tired of waking up not knowing what was going on. I knew that my whole identity, my human one at least, was surrounded around sleeping, but I was pretty sure that passing out and waking up in unknown situations wasn't what I had in mind when I started this human project. Or maybe it was; it wasn't like I knew what this whole grand plan of mine was now that I was half asleep again. Either way, I stifled a sigh and checked to see how many luck charges I had left—that was a good way to check for the passage of time, I found.

Luck Charges: 1,003/1,557

Hm, I think I had close to 700 charges before I passed out from blood loss, so some quick math told me that I'd been out for 300ish minutes—or five hours. That was a lot longer than I thought, given my superior healing after the ascension process. Still, I should look at it on the bright side, at least I had over a thousand charges to work with again, and something told me that I'd be needing it all given the unstable situation here.

Which was why I decided that the safest option was to wait for more charges to recover, at least another hundred or so. I was in relative safety at the moment, judging by the quiet and honestly quite comfortable room I was in, but I couldn't hedge my bets that this would be the case going forward.

> **Luck Charges:** 1,004/1,557

Was it just me or was a minute an awfully long time to wait when you were just . . . doing nothing?

> **Luck Charges:** 1,005/1,557

. . . Six one thousand, seven one thousand, eight one thousand . . .

> **Luck Charges:** 1,006/1,557

Man, I should just sleep for now, but I'd been doing nothing but that since I started impersonating this Ashwin guy that I couldn't seem to do so no matter how hard I tried. In fact, it was taking all of my willpower to just remain still with my eyes closed . . . although this itch I was starting to develop was seriously annoying.

> **Luck Charges:** 1,007/1,557

Never in my life had I wanted to move and do anything other than wait more than in this moment. You can do this, Walter, you've faced down eldritch monstrosities, horrible hospitals, and made friends with literal gods. Compared to that, staying still and waiting is nothing!

> **Luck Charges:** 1,008/1,557

Your will is strong, Walter!

> **Luck Charges:** 1,009/1,557

> **Luck Charges:** 1,010/1,557

> **Luck Charges:** 1,011/1,557

Fuck it, 1,011 charges was enough for me. I am weak, I'll admit it! Seven minutes was the longest I could manage, damn it all, and there's a horrible itch on my stomach that I just can't ignore anymore. Gingerly, I got up from my prone position and surveyed my situation, but not before scratching myself silly!

Or I wanted to until I saw that my entire lower abdomen was bandaged up. Judging by the discoloration of the bandage, I must have been seriously wounded as well, but I didn't feel any pain. I poked at the wound, and aside from feeling a bit sore, it wasn't too bad.

Noe, you still blocking off the pain here?

"Negative, my host," she replied. "Your body, ever since the Xollon incorporations, has a much higher tolerance for pain than before, and so does your ability to heal minor injuries. I have superficially opened the wound on your side so as to not arouse suspicions while you were asleep. I apologize for doing so without your consent."

Oh, thanks, and no need to apologize. Good to know you're a lot more autonomous than when we first met. I don't know what I'd do without your help, Noe.

"You are most welcome," she answered, and I could hear the warmth in her voice. I really did mean it as well. I'd be almost certainly dead without everything Noe had done for me so far.

I smiled to myself and refocused my attention on the current situation. I was stationed in a small room, the walls were white and bland, and there wasn't a window in sight. In fact, there was only one metal door that led out, which I assumed was there to ensure that I was kept safe while I was unconscious. After that impromptu terrorist attempt, I would imagine that the people in charge were on high alert.

The only other thing of note in the room was the small table on the side of my single bed. My armor was placed on there, and it seemed like someone had taken the time to clean and do some basic repairs on it while I was asleep. Some basic medical equipment was set aside as well, and I saw a cup of water waiting for me to drink next to a washing basin. I got up tentatively, surprised to see that I was dressed in a simple white robe now, and took some time to clean myself as best I could.

I was halfway through washing the sleep from my eyes when I heard the door open behind me. I almost dove for cover at the sudden noise until I saw that it was an elderly gentleman who came in. He was dressed in a physician's uniform—thanks to Noe's tinkering with my brain's perceptions, no doubt—so I could only assume this was the man who was taking care of me so far.

"I apologize for startling you, Master Ashwin," the gray-haired man whispered, "but I was instructed to see you the second you awoke. How are you feeling?"

"Fine." *Uh . . . Noe, you know who this guy is?*

"There is a 99.86% chance that this individual is the chief physician and the god of healing's envoy, Marcus."

Marcus? Damn, why'd he have to share the same name as the creepy priest?

Ugh, makes my skin crawl just thinking about that guy. Then again, it's not like I expect everyone to have unique names, but why'd the nice old man have to share that name of all things?

"I apologize, my host, but Marcus is the best approximation of the physician's name in the human English language."

And speaking of physicians . . . I shuddered, thinking about some of the stuff the patients in Hope's Memorial had to endure. *Never mind that. Noe, it's best to just ignore the small details. Thanks for the help.*

"Are you sure you're all right?" Marcus—er, I decided to just call him Mark—said again. "You lost a lot of blood, so please take it easy. We're not expecting you to be back on your feet so fast, but I think everyone knows that it's a losing battle to try to keep you in bed where you should be."

I gave the old man a forced smile, changing the subject. "So what did everyone need me for? I'm guessing it's to do with that attack from earlier?"

Mark sighed and shook his head. "You'll wear yourself out acting like that all the time, Ashwin, but that's a conversation we can have at another time. Things are getting worse by the day out there, so I suppose no one has the time to rest now. But yes, it's to discuss the recent events, and . . . about your experiences in the days you were captured. Your two companions filled us in on the key events."

I nodded. "What did they tell you? Nova and Erdic have been . . . well, you've seen them."

Another frown creased the old man's face, clearly unhappy about what he saw from the other two. "Yes . . . They're still in intensive care at the moment, but their lives are not in any danger. It's the strange curse that's been placed on all of you that's the issue. But Nova was able to fill us in on your capture, and the state of the other champions. It's good to know that they're still alive, but I'm not sure if we have the resources to launch another rescue mission . . ."

Oh, it seemed that Q was able to do more than just mess with their brains here, good to know.

"It's fine," I said quickly, mainly to change the grim topic to something that I had more control over. "They're not in immediate danger, that much I can guarantee."

Mark nodded but didn't ask for any more details. It was clear from my tone and expression that I didn't want to go into detail about what had happened back in the cultists' base. He thought it was due to the trauma, but in reality it was because I had no idea what Q's brainwashed aliens had told the man, and I really didn't want to expend a ton of luck points just to ensure that I didn't contradict anything the others said.

"So let's focus our attention on things that we can do," I continued. "What's the situation like since I've been gone?"

"The High Council can explain things in more detail, but suffice to say, our situation's not ideal." He shook his head after a minute's thought. "Never mind, there's no point sugarcoating it with you—it's dire. Our barrier can't hold off the encroaching darkness for much longer; our best estimates are worse than initially thought, and the populace has started to notice."

"I see," I muttered, looking contemplative. It was time to use a few luck charges to not stick out, but just a small amount for now. "So, we don't have two years?"

Luck Charges: 1,009/1,557

Good, just guessing a random date didn't cost too much. That meant that I could rely on Noe for small things like that going forward. The luck charges I spent would regenerate before I needed it again if it was just two or three points every time.

"No, it's worse, much worse."

"What's the timeline now?"

"Honestly, the estimates are getting shorter and shorter by the day," the old man stated with a frown. "The erosion is getting worse, and the faith of the people has waned significantly since news of your absence spread. That last crusade was supposed to stop or at least slow down the darkness, but . . ."

"But we failed," I finished for him. "And people have noticed."

"That is the unfortunate reality of things, I'm afraid." Mark sighed. "With their faith faltering, the barrier's only gotten weaker."

"So how long, best estimate?"

A long pause, as if Marcus didn't want to even consider the idea that he had to say, but eventually, with a heavy sigh, he answered. "Three weeks. Our best estimate is three weeks, and that's with the direct intervention of the High Council and their immediate followers."

I winced. Things were really looking bad for this dimension, and it was directly due to me and my friends' actions. That wasn't something I wanted on my conscience, even if it wasn't something that I would have even considered when I was fully awake.

"Come on, then," the doctor continued. "Get dressed quickly. The council urgently needs to see you. This . . ." A heavy silence filled the air. "This might be the last mission for you, for all of us. We don't have the luxury of time anymore."

"Then let's get on with it," I agreed. "Can you give me a few minutes to get dressed?"

He nodded and headed out the door. "Of course. I'll wait outside. A fresh set of clothes are in the drawers below the bed."

Once I was alone once more, I checked over my luck charges one last time and prepared to meet this High Council or whatever it was. The situation in the Order god's domain was a lot worse than I thought, but if Or.gin really did have a hand in this dimension, then I couldn't imagine that it'd just allow the whole place to just cease to exist without doing something. I wasn't completely sure, but something told me that it'd be hard to find direct signs of the Trash Matrix's involvement.

If I'd learned anything in my stay as an aspirant, it was that the stupid system was meticulous, which meant that I'd have to put it in a situation where it was forced to make errors. It was a risk, and failure could result in drastic consequences for this dimension, but my main goal here was to see what exactly the Trash Matrix was up to, and the best way to ensure that I caught a whiff of its machinations was to wait until it had no choice but to act.

With three weeks of time left, finding a way to stall things out shouldn't be too difficult a task, but the first thing I'd have to do was meet with this council and learn more about my situation. At least now, I had a tentative working plan. I steadied my nerves one last time and joined Marcus outside the hospital room, ready to face what was ahead.

CHAPTER FORTY-SIX

To the Holy City Part 3

Noe made a mental map of the palace and the surrounding area as I followed Mark to the council. Thankfully, that meant that I didn't have to worry about getting lost and looking like an idiot trying to navigate this new environment going forward. It was a good thing that Noe was doing all of the heavy lifting because the area that I was taken to was somewhere deep indoors.

The walls were windowless and seemed to be made with security and sturdiness in mind rather than aesthetics, which meant that the white walls and dull concrete flooring made it nearly impossible for me to remember where I was. The only indicators were the numbers above the metal doors and the occasional soldier or two stationed at key choke points.

Speaking about my lovely system, Noe informed me that there were a lot of spatial distortions underground in our location. These distortions were not too dissimilar to the type we'd see Origin use to transfer aspirants through the various trials down in the dungeons of this place, and they got worse the farther down it went. It was so distorted that Noe wasn't able to perceive anything past a certain distance, at least using my limited senses this far away from the source. Looked like that was the first thing I'd have to check out once I was done with the formalities.

I'd found that my mind worked a lot better when I had clear goals in mind. I'd survived three trials, and that was not counting all the bullshit that I'd had to deal with thanks to the Overseer's meddling, so having things to work toward was key to keeping me focused and working in optimal condition. With the trials, I had a clear end condition to reach most of the time, and even in situations where I didn't have that, the regressor usually helped keep me on track. I had feared that this impromptu infiltration would be different since what I was trying to find was so nebulous, and just "surviving until Origin decided to do something" never sat well with me.

Thankfully, there was an avenue of attack that I could approach. I'd just have to disentangle myself from the Order gods and their lackeys and see what juicy information I could find in that strange basement. I was feeling almost giddy from the thought of doing something proactive for once. I had to stop a smile from forming from the thought of stretching my brain muscles after all this time.

The physician paused at the end of the hallway and took a long look at me, worry clear on his face. I could barely hear the chattering of people coming from the other side of the door, and from the tense looks of the two guards stationed there, this was the threshold to the outside world. The door, almost three or four times larger than the plain metal ones I'd passed, was the only ornate structure that I had seen so far, with intricately carved mosaics that must have had some kind of historical or religious significance given the amount of time it must have taken to make.

"Ashwin," Mark said, shaking me out of my intersections, "do you need a few minutes to compose yourself? I know you're worse off than you let on, but we're about to enter a public area, and you can't show weakness, not now. I apologize, Lord Chosen, I can't imagine how hard it is on you right now."

I gave the old man an uneasy smile and nodded. I needed him to continue to think that I was worse off than I was so that any inconsistencies seen could be excused. The only problem was that I still didn't have a full picture of what Ashwin was like in his private life, and unlike this physician, I'd inevitably meet people he was close to soon.

"I'll be fine," I answered as he moved to open the large gate. "Please lead on."

Right, time to put on my hero face again.

Noe, amp up the Emotional Redux skill. It's my first heroic speech, and I have to make a lasting impression.

"Acknowledged, my host."

I walked to the front and opened the door. What greeted me outside those corridors was intense, to say the least. The area that we were at before seemed to be a separate area from the main castle structure, and the exit took us to a raised bridge-like connection corridor that overlooked the castle square. We were only about two or three stories above the masses, and a quick glance past the railings made me appreciate just how many people there were, all of whom were waiting for any news of their hero.

Hordes of people in the thousands had packed the bridge to the brim, and the poor sentries were overwhelmed trying to keep order. Things went into overdrive when the first people saw me—some of the more devoted individuals shouted in joy, but the overwhelming majority of the masses gathered were less than pleased with the state of affairs and were not afraid to shout their doubts.

"We spent ten years, all of our resources, and what do we get in return?" one of them shouted. "Nothing but death!"

"You failed us!"

"My son died for you, and for what?"

"Give us back the time and money we spent!"

"We were promised deliverance!"

More and more shouts assaulted my ears, and it wasn't hard to see why morale was so low. Off in the distance, the golden shimmering barrier that protected the last city was already showing its cracks. There were dark spots clearly visible, and some of those beautiful runes had already started to fade. The everlooming chaos just outside this fragile barrier was a constant reminder of the consequences of failure, and to many of the people here, we had already failed.

"I apologize for the citizens," Mark said quickly as he saw me stop. I could tell that he was concerned about how I would react to the situation. I'm guessing that such a scene never happened to the original Ashwin, I wasn't even sure if he's ever known failure, to be honest.

"It's fine," I said, making sure to infuse a bit of bitterness into my voice. "It is to be expected, and they are not completely wrong."

The old man quickly shook his head. "No, Lord Chosen. No one could have predicted what happened back there. The vile fiends had the Enemy helping them out, and the Evil gods went all out as well."

Enemy? Evil gods? Great, more terms I didn't quite understand, although I could guess the context easily enough.

"But that doesn't excuse what happened," I continued, gesturing to the gathered mob below. "Especially not to the people who suffered the most."

The physician winced but didn't offer a rebuttal. He knew the truth behind my words well enough.

"Let me address the people," I continued. "They need to hear something from the man they put so much faith in before."

The old doctor paused for a moment before frowning. "Are you sure that's wise? I'm not sure that anything you say at the moment could placate the citizens, not after what just happened."

"Then do you suppose I just walk by and say nothing?"

Another pause. "No, I suppose not. I . . . I'm sorry that we have to burden you so much, but we'll have to rely on you again."

I nodded and walked toward the raised dais in the middle of the walkway and stood above the masses. Instead of the people quieting down, they started to shout even louder now that I was clearly visible, and to make things worse, some of the braver individuals had started to throw rocks and other debris in my direction. None of the pellets hit me, but it was the action that mattered. I couldn't imagine how the actual Ashwin would feel looking at the current situation. He must have given up quite a lot for the sake of these people, not to mention risked his life for their well-being, so to see that this was their response?

Would he have persevered, or would this have broken him? A small, slumbering part of my brain wondered about that and wished I could see that situation play out. I shook my head and focused on the people instead. I guess I'd have to get used to those stray thoughts that entered my mind every now and then, although it made me more curious about what I was like with all of my memories intact.

"Citizens of Ordas," I shouted, doing my best to sound majestic and in control, "I understand that you have worries about the current situation."

Luck Charges: 801/1,557

I almost winced seeing how many charges had just been used to soothe such a large crowd with Noe's skill. I was honestly having second thoughts about doing this stupid speech in the first place, but it was too late now. Well, given I'd used almost 300 whole charges, the crowd did seem to calm down visibly as I spoke. It wasn't a complete 180 change like when I used the skill on individuals—I didn't think I'd have enough charges for that kind of stunt anytime soon—but it was noticeable nonetheless. Or maybe it was a bit too good since the old doctor and a few of the guards stationed near me looked at me with raised eyebrows. Shit, was the old Ashwin not a good orator or something?

I forced the distracting thoughts out of my head and continued to address the crowd. "I know that many of you have lost loved ones from the war, and many more have suffered in ways that I cannot hope to imagine, but we are in dire times right now. Unprecedented times."

I paused for a moment and gestured to the looming darkness just outside the city walls. "Look at the state of the world we are in now. This is a time when inaction could doom us all. Your loved ones gave up their lives in the hopes that you can continue to live. They fought so that you might have hope for a brighter future, but if you give up now, if you choose to ignore the sacrifices of the brave men and women that fought for you, then it is no better than joining the vile cultists that started all this."

Murmurs of agreement started to fill the air. The people were no longer shouting, and some started to think, at least in part, on what I'd just said. Good, that was a start.

"I am doing my utmost to ensure that we will not falter. I will continue to fight for our survival, and I am not afraid to stand against the looming darkness. You may no longer have faith in me or my abilities, and I do not fault you for thinking so. However, if you can no longer place your faith in me, then please use that time to pray to the gods above, for it is your faith that is keeping the end at bay. If we lose even that, then the enemy would have already won."

More mutters of agreement and understanding permeated the square below. I even saw some individuals kneel down to pray.

"But for those that have not given up hope in me," I continued, "know that I will remain steadfast in the face of these obstacles. I will not allow anything to stop me from doing what I must do, and I hope that you do the same. I am only mortal. I will fail, but each failure makes me stronger. I learn from the mistakes that I make, and I improve upon them. I will stop this disaster, and I will do so regardless of what people think of me."

With that, I walked away from the now-silent crowd. The old physician gave me a pensive look, almost as if he wanted to ask some serious questions, and I think I knew what those would be. If my guesses were right, then the original Ashwin was more of the stoic, silent type of hero, and my little performance just then wasn't something that the real man would ever do. Then again, it wasn't like I could just leave the people in a hopeless state, not if I didn't want to hasten the demise of the barrier. I had places to check out now, and that meant the relative stability of this city for the time being.

I had to expend over fifty additional charges just to ensure that the old man didn't grow even more suspicious of me as I did my best to explain the change in attitude.

"I suppose that makes sense . . ." he muttered in a Noe-induced daze. "Yes . . . these are trying times, and the hero must adapt to the situation . . ."

"Exactly," I continued, "I had a duty to perform, and even though I never spoke like that before, it was something that I forced myself to do for the sake of the people. You know that I can't just allow them to lose out on all hope. The state of the barrier depended on that."

"Right . . ."

"Now forget those worries," I said quickly, "and let's head to the council chambers."

CHAPTER FORTY-SEVEN

To the Holy City Part 4

I don't know what I expected when I entered the audience chamber, but it certainly wasn't the sight of three tired and haggard-looking old people slumped down on a couch, seemingly in a daze. They barely noticed me when I got in, and one of the various aides lining the large room had to nudge them into action. It was only then that one of them moved, the woman in the middle, and her attention returned to the present. She seemed so tired that even moving upright was a struggle, and the aides had to help her up.

"Ah, Ashwin," rasped the woman, an old, frail thing that had locks of snow-white hair and a withered look. "I apologize for not greeting you properly, and for my companion's silence. Unfortunately, most of our efforts are concentrated on the barrier at the moment, and we cannot allow any lapse in concentration to occur."

She frowned again and winced, as if something invisible plagued her, before continuing. "You look well."

I nodded, unsure how to continue. *Noe, any idea who that is? And just double-checking, but there's no way that she always looked like that, right?*

"You are correct, my host," she replied. "And that individual should be the conduit for the god of light. The records indicate that she is always addressed by her title. Lord Conduit or High Priest would be appropriate forms of address."

"Lord Conduit, you look . . ." I said hesitantly.

She chuckled. "Like shit, I know."

Huh, she seemed more easygoing than I thought . . . Did that mean that I should act more casual as well? I didn't even know how familiar the real Ashwin was to this person, but I'd play it safe for now and be more formal. The current situation warranted being more serious regardless of past interactions in any case.

"But that is the state of affairs at the moment, unfortunately," she continued. "And although you appear fine outwardly, I can feel the lingering effects of your stay at the enemy's dungeons. You don't need to explain, Chosen, your companions filled us in on the important details already. I wish we had the time to examine you properly, but all of our priests are either helping maintain the barrier or are dead."

I only nodded again, unsure what to say in such a situation.

When the woman saw my silence, she sighed. "I know, coming back after what you've been through only to see our home left in this state can't be easy, but unfortunately, I'll—no, all of us will need to borrow your strength again. This might be our last hope, but what remains of our oracles and prophets intercepted messages from the other cities and countries, and they might have found the cause of the rapid spread of the void."

I raised an eyebrow. "They did?"

"It's the Calamity," she explained. "I'm not sure if you're aware, since you were not originally a part of this world, but it was a beast created by the enemy eons ago, sealed forever under the fate god's domain, but it had escaped recently, and it might be the cause of the rapid acceleration of the darkness. Marcus must have already told you, but our initial estimates of the time we had left were wrong, and we believe that this beast is the cause of much of those inconsistencies."

I frowned again. That beast was certainly the stupid scaly fat dragon thing that we beat up earlier, but Molly had sworn that she cursed it, and it should have been captured quickly.

"Can you tell me more about this Calamity?" I asked.

"We don't have the time to go into the history of its creation, so I'll skip over that part," she answered. "But what is strange is that our reports say that the creature has . . . morphed or transformed. How, or what happened, we do not know, but every account of its form and might have been the same: It has grown exponentially stronger, and it seemed to have harnessed, at least in part, the power of the void. Even its appearance has changed."

Well . . . guess Molly's curse didn't exactly pan out. I think I already knew the answer, but I had to ask anyway. "What does it look like now?"

The old woman concentrated for a second before lifting a hand up and conjuring an image in her palm, kind of like a 3D projection. I saw what looked to be an enormous blackened thing straight out of nightmares. It had hairlike protrusions coming out of its body, and more of that stuff came out of its massive meaty maw. I didn't need my full memories to know what those tentacle things looked like. They were the same as the stuff that coursed through Molly.

Well, shit, it seemed like we had inadvertently given the stupid Calamity a power-up instead of weakening it. End Bringers was right . . .

"That's not good . . ." I half muttered to myself.

"It is not," she agreed. "Which is why we must send you to at least halt its advances. Even doing that much can give us much-needed time. If the populace sees some improvements in the near future, then maybe, just maybe, their faith in the gods will be enough to stave off the worst of the strain from our priests." A sigh escaped her cracked lips. "With so much of our time devoted to the barrier, we are unable to do much more than survive at the current state of things, let alone fight back against our foes."

"I see . . ." Wait a second. I couldn't just pack up and leave the city right as I arrived, not when I needed to investigate the Trash Matrix and especially that strange distortion in the underground. "When do you need me to leave?"

"Now, if possible. The journey to the Calamity's location will take time, perhaps a week or even more given the geography and weather, and we cannot afford to waste even a second."

I frowned again. Yeah . . . that wasn't happening, but how would I talk myself out of this situation without blowing my whole cover?

"If your reports on that beast are true, then I am not sure if I will be able to slay it given my current condition," I said tentatively. "I'll need more time to rest."

She gave me a pitying look. "And I wish I could give you that time, but at the current state, we cannot guarantee that our efforts can maintain the city's shield for even the amount of time it would take you to reach the beast, but we will try nonetheless. We will provide you with the last of our resources, our best healers, and the last of the able paladins, but you must go. Rest on the trip, and remember, you only have to halt its movements, not kill it entirely."

Shit, I couldn't see a way to refute her words, and the Absolute Luck skill wasn't doing much to remedy my situation right now either. I didn't think I had even a fraction of the charges needed to influence such a huge event, and it wasn't like I could just blow all of my luck charges all at once even if it was an option. I'd need Noe's skill when I actually went about sleuthing.

Well, Noe's ability always relied on me doing most of the work, and the more favorable of a situation I could present myself in, the less expenditure I would experience. That meant that I didn't need to delay the trip indefinitely, but just for a few hours so that I could place myself in a spot where only a few hundred charges would do the trick to delay my departure. Worst-case scenario, I would just gamble it all that I'd find what I needed in the weird basement, and blow my Ashwin cover if all looked lost, but hedging all my bets on something so uncertain wasn't something I'd want to risk, especially if it was someone else who would take the fall if I failed this time.

All right, I'd try plan A first. It was worth a few luck charges to ensure this went well. "I'll need a few hours to prepare. I know that we don't have the time for such things, but I'm sure that you've noticed I can't use my weapon at the moment. Something the cultists did must have cut off my connection with the artifact, but I think I can cleanse it here, where the god's powers are at their strongest."

I was expecting my charges to go down, but apparently I didn't need to. It seemed that everything I said, given my limited knowledge of the situation, was already the optimal outcome. I'd take that as a win for my bullshitting abilities.

The old woman thought for a moment before nodding. "I see, normally one of us would do that for you, and we still could if nothing else works. However, the consequences of even diverting our attention could be disastrous. Are you sure that you can fix things on your own?"

"Positive." I nodded.

"Come see one of us if you cannot," she added. "Although it would not be ideal, you are our last hope, Ashwin, and we can't allow you to go without the divine weapon. I pray that you are able to resolve the issue on your own."

"Thank you, and I will resolve to do my utmost for this world."

She gave me a weak smile. "Good, that is all any of us can ask for. We will give you four hours to resolve the issue. If it is not done by then, then seek out one of the councillors again, and we will look into it."

"But the barrier—"

"The barrier will be weakened, yes, and perhaps it will speed up our demise by days," she said with a shake of her head, "but it will persist still, at least for the short term. However, that cannot be said if you fail your task. I think we both know which of those options are worse."

Yeah . . . I didn't plan to actually go at all, but I was starting to feel mighty guilty about what we had done to the people here. I just hoped that finding out what Origin was up to would fix the mess we made here, but if the main cause of the rapid spread of that horrible darkness was due to the Calamity that we unleashed, I could let Molly know to keep track of it in case we needed the thing to stop for a while.

Unfortunately, I couldn't tell her to outright stop the thing, for one because I didn't think we should mess around in the mortal world anymore given what we'd done already, but two, if I didn't find the cause of the disturbance in the underground, then the only other thing I could do was to force Origin to act when its pet dimension was about to end. Hopefully I found what I needed in the initial exploration, for the sake of all of the people here.

"I understand your concerns," the woman whispered, thinking that I was contemplating an altogether different situation than the one I actually was, "but those are the cards that we have been dealt. Now go, time is precious, and we will need every minute of it if we are to succeed."

I gave the members of the chambers a polite bow before turning to leave. Mark greeted me just outside, and we took a silent stroll back to my chambers. I thought the physician would take me to Ashwin's actual quarters, but he had said that the stability of the current political landscape, especially after the ter-rorist attempt, didn't allow me to be out in the open. That left me alone again in the dingy room with my thoughts. I needed to figure out just how to delay the journey, and I had a scant few hours to do so.

Thankfully, I wasn't alone. *Hey, Noe, I know you said that you didn't have full use of all those other shards you collected on your own, but surely you could use a bit of those abilities on a small scale, right?*

"I can, my host, with the exception of the Domination Shard, which has not begun to undergo integration."

But Perception's A-okay?

"On a small scale with limited effect."

That's all I need. I think I have a plan.

CHAPTER FORTY-EIGHT

To the Holy City Part 5

My plan was simple enough. There were clearly dissenters or enemy spies all over this city, what with that last assassination attempt, so all I had to do was find another terrorist and have them "kidnap" me in a moment of weakness. It wasn't like I was afraid that they'd be able to actually harm me given my half-Xollon body, and with some slight Noe mind control, I could safely operate for a few days without worry. Once I was free from oversight, I could just change back into my secondary form and burrow underground to where that strange disturbance was located and go from there. It was a fool-proof plan if I did say so myself, and all I had to do was to find one of those terrorists.

Well, chances were, I wouldn't need to be the one to find them, especially after that big speech I gave earlier. They'd know where I was, and with a little help from the Absolute Luck skill, I should bump into one of them sooner or later . . . probably. Okay, maybe the plan wasn't as amazing as I first thought, but my options were severely limited. It wasn't like the guards would just allow me to wander around the town aimlessly while I checked out every shady corner or back-alley establishment looking for dissenters, and even if I could manipulate the security into allowing me to go, it would raise a lot of questions I couldn't answer if anyone saw me doing so.

What it meant was that I had to rely on the hope that my assassin friends would be competent in their jobs and somehow breach all of the security around here. Of course, I wouldn't be doing anything in that time either. If my only option was to wait for them to come to me, then the least I could do was to make their jobs a little easier. I went around each corridor and entrance with the excuse of thanking the sentries for keeping me safe, but I was actually making use of the Emotional Redux skill to make each guard and soldier lethargic and sleepy. If the spies couldn't manage to take advantage of such a tasty opportunity, then they had to be the world's worst terrorists ever.

The best part was that it only took me a little over half an hour to sabotage all of the security detail. I took another fifteen minutes or so to make some public appearances, stressing the fact that I would be going on another mission in a few hours while subtly hinting that I'd need some time to prepare for the journey in my quarters. All that was left for me to do was wait. Surely that was enough hints for the people out to get me to act, right? I was all but screaming for them to come get me.

And wait I did . . . the minutes passed excruciatingly slowly. and after a short while, I decided that I couldn't just do nothing and wait for something to happen. I doubted anyone could bypass my enhanced senses, and with Noe's Absolute Luck skill constantly on, I was relatively safe from harm. That meant that I should be using these last few hours doing something productive. I debated going around to talk with the priests, just to get an idea of Ashwin as an individual, but quickly decided against that. If I wanted to bait the assassins, then it would be safer to stay by myself for the time being.

That left me with just one real option to spend my time: scouting out that anomaly that Noe noticed earlier. I wouldn't enter the spatial distortion, but getting a good idea about its general layout and where it was located could be useful for the future when I had to make my way back there. With a goal in mind, and ensuring that I still had the Absolute Luck skill on, I followed Noe's directions toward the disturbance.

The area itself, or at least the only entrance to it, was located near what appeared to be the cold storage room by the kitchens. I had to spend a few luck charges dissuading the staff from inquiring about my presence here, but aside from that, there was no one to challenge my presence there. I thought for sure that there would be dozens of sentinels or other defensive mechanisms near the one strange area of the castle, but apparently, the Trash Matrix didn't think it important enough to do so.

I was starting to worry that this might be a trap, but the Trash Matrix hadn't shown any ability to intervene in the affairs of this world so far, assuming that it could at all. I stood a few feet away from the wooden door that would lead to the castle's distorted underground and tried to use my Xollon senses to peek at the other side.

I frowned. I could make out almost nothing on the other side of that door, as if the door itself simply led to nothing. There was just a haze of darkness that obscured my vision . . . no, there was something. If I concentrated hard enough, I could almost make out vague shapes of something just off in the distance. I saw shadows and silhouettes of shapes and images that were so oddly familiar to me, as if I had seen them before somewhere. No . . . I definitely recognized some of those shapes, but I couldn't for the life of me recall what it was.

I frowned at the welling frustration of being so close to knowing something, and curiosity got the better of me. I approached the door, hoping that the act of getting closer to the source of the disturbance would make the images just a bit more clear. Just a tiny bit of clarity would jog my memories. I concentrated harder, using every last bit of my focus to see if I could just unveil the darkness.

I was practically touching the door itself when something jolted me out of my reverie.

> **Luck Charges:** 905/1,557

I briefly noticed my charges go down as a terrible leg cramp assaulted me, forcing me to stumble awkwardly forward. I felt a stinging sensation on the back of my head, and I knew that Noe had just saved my life once again. Unfortunately, I wish she had chosen a less painful method of doing so as I crashed face-first into the door and tumbled down the flight of stairs.

Noe, couldn't you have been a bit gentler?

> **Luck Charges:** 890/1,557

I braced myself for impact, but not before turning back to see what had caused such a big drop in charges. It appeared that there was a reason why Noe chose such an extreme method to protect me.

Ah . . . Never mind, Noe. I see that you did the most logical move as always.

It appeared that my attacker, having seen the first strike miss, had decided to leave nothing to chance and had chosen to blow himself up like the first guy tried to do when I first came to the city. I saw the searing flash of light, followed by the shock wave of the detonation ram into my still tumbling body.

> **Luck Charges:** 878/1,557

And miraculously, or more accurately, luckily, none of the shrapnel and debris managed to hit my tender body, although the force of the impact itself still took a solid chunk out of my HP. The force of the explosion was so strong that it left me stunned for a few moments, and down and down I went, farther into the castle's basement as the walls and ceilings around me collapsed. Small dust particles were starting to irritate my eyes, and I had to close them tight as I braced for the inevitable impact when I reached the bottom of the stairs.

I had not expected the lunatics to go to such extremes just to kill one man, but then again, what was I expecting? I had seen the cultists behave before, and they weren't exactly the most sane individuals around. Plus, it wasn't the first time that someone tried to blow themselves up. Damn, I messed up this time . . . Things couldn't have gotten any worse.

A few moments later, I felt the thud of my back hitting the ground. I tensed, waiting to see if anything else would go wrong, but after hearing nothing but silence and the distinct lack of pain, I tentatively opened my eyes once more. I sighed. Time to see how badly the explosion damaged the castle, and if I had to somehow dig myself out again.

I was expecting to see a ruined underground dungeon or cavern, but instead, I saw . . . I blinked a few times, rubbing my eyes to make sure that I wasn't somehow hallucinating.

"What the fuck . . ." I muttered.

I was lying on the ground in what appeared to be a modern condominium. Scratch that, it was one of those multimillion-dollar suites that I'd seen on TV back on Earth. I got up, pinching myself to make sure that I wasn't passed out again and that this was just a dream. Nope, this was real . . .

A huge king-sized bed was right beside me, and from the sprawled-out blankets, it appeared that I had just fallen out of it. To the side were some crumpled-up clothes, a laptop, and some tacky furniture, but what caught my eye were the windows, which went up to the ceiling. I walked up to them, disbelief still clouding my features, and stared out into the streets below. I saw the morning sun peek out of the distance, but the Manhattan skyline was unmistakable. That was Central Park right below me. There was no way that I'd mistake that.

Had everything that had happened just been a dream? No, that wasn't possible . . . and that was when the next thing hit me. From the smooth surface of the window I saw my reflection, or rather, the reflection of Ashwin. Well, there were some slight differences—Ashwin's hairstyle was slightly different, a bit shorter than what I had seen earlier, and he looked to be a tad younger, but it was definitely the same person. So . . . what the hell did that mean?

I closed my eyes and took a deep breath in. Okay, I just needed to calm down. There had to be a rational explanation for all of this. It was not the first time something ridiculous happened to me, and it wouldn't be the last. I'd just treat it like any other trial. But first, I needed to make sure that I still had my one companion that had seen me through so much.

"Noe . . ." I said tentatively, out loud this time, "you still there?"

"Affirmative, my host," the same calm voice answered, and I felt a huge wave of relief hit me. I wasn't alone.

I honestly don't know what I would have done if Noe was no longer with me. I smiled despite my ridiculous situation. "You know what the hell's going on?"

"I do, my host," she answered, "but you might not like the answer. The Origin Matrix has finally shown its hand."

"Of course it's the goddamn Trash Matrix." I sighed. "When has anything I've gone through ever been anything but horrible, Noe? Let's hear it anyway."

CHAPTER FORTY-NINE

Trapped

Y ou have been sent to an alternate dimension, my host."

I blinked a few times, making sure that I heard her right. "That's it? I mean, I thought it would be a lot worse. Let's just get out of here quickly before something goes wrong."

I could almost hear Noe sigh when she responded. "I wish it was that easy, dear Walter. The Trash Matrix wouldn't have done what it did if we could escape so easily. You may try if you wish, my host."

I frowned again and shifted into my secondary form.

Luck Charges: 900/1,557

"What's with the use of charges?" I asked.

"To ensure that we are overlooked; shifting into such a form on Earth has consequences, my host, especially when we have been sent here by the Origin Matrix."

"Right," I muttered. Time to test this out quickly before something went wrong.

It had become second nature for me to create holes in reality at this point, so I lifted my feelers and tried again. True to Noe's words, escape wasn't as easy as that. Normally, I'd feel a slight resistance when I was making those worm-holes, but this time it was like I was trying to cut through concrete with my bare hands. Nothing worked.

"All right, that didn't work," I muttered before shifting back. "What's going on, Noe?"

"I am unsure of the specifics, but the distortion that we felt earlier is even worse here. My best guess is that we have been warped in an alternate reality or timeline, or perhaps both."

Thinking for a second, I checked the date on the phone beside me and saw, if my memories were not wrong, that I had been sent two days before the start of the trials. So I was sent back in time as well as space and sent back as Ashwin to boot.

"All right, so we're sent to some parallel Earth in the body of someone else. There doesn't seem to be any danger here, at least not that I can tell, but there's no way that the Trash Matrix wouldn't try to fuck me over here. What's the catch, Noe?"

"I apologize, my host. I forgot just how much of your memories are still missing. Allow me to explain."

I sat back on the bed and nodded.

"The reason the Origin Matrix has sent you here in the form of another individual is because it had hoped to limit your abilities. Had I not been with you, you would have only had the powers of a normal human."

"And you're preventing that from happening?"

I felt the joy in Noe's tone. "It is why I was created, my host. I am here to ensure that nothing in the multiverse can ever tamper with your form. As long as I exist, your form will be immutable."

I nodded slowly. "All right, so assuming that it didn't know that you could do that, there must be other reasons for it to send me here, or is it just hoping to keep me in an alternate dimension forever?"

"I wish it were that easy, my host, but being sent back in time and space while assuming the identity of another individual means that you are at risk of assimilation. For all intent and purposes, you are Ashwin, and if you stay as Ashwin for too long, then your sense of self could erode in time. Although I can ensure that your form stays the same, I cannot say the same about your sense of self, at least when you are constrained in that human shell."

"Ah . . ." I muttered, "that's, uh, that's not good. How long do we have, then?"

"That I cannot say for certain, my host. I can stave off the worst of the issues here, at least for the short term, but we must make it a priority to escape as soon as possible."

"And how do we do that if I can't rip a hole through reality? I don't exactly have a lot of other abilities at my disposal, and as far as I can tell, I can't wake up anytime soon either."

"Have you not considered how the Trash Matrix was able to trap us in this situation, my host?"

I thought for a moment and realized that I was so focused on survival that I hadn't considered that. It was true that if Origin had the ability to send me back in time, then it'd have done that at the start, which meant that it either didn't have the ability to do so prior or that it took advantage of an opportunity that it didn't have before. I didn't believe that the Trash Matrix could have improved so much in the span of a few months, so my bet was on the latter.

"It's the damn fragile dimension we were in, isn't it?" I muttered. "I knew something was wrong with it."

"Correct again, my host. It took advantage of the weakened space to send us here, but that also means that it was not powerful enough to do so without outside assistance," Noe replied. "Now that we are in the middle of the anomaly, I have detected another of my shards." Now Noe's voice went icy, and I inadvertently shuddered. "The Origin Matrix has stolen a piece of me, and it is using it to harm my host."

"Hey, uh, we'll get it back, no worries, Noe."

"I do not worry," she said, the spite still spilling from her normally calm voice. "And we will ensure that the Trash Matrix knows of its hubris."

"Any idea which one it stole?"

"The Reality Shard," she said plainly. "It used my abilities to artificially create a dimension and hid it from the greater Central Collective, then used the distortions that we caused to send us here. Why it chose to do so behind the backs of its masters is a mystery, but I have some guesses."

Yeah, it wasn't hard to imagine a few explanations myself about why it was acting by itself. The stupid thing was trying to free itself from the grasp of Central, and while I detested the Overseer's organization and wanted nothing more than its destruction, it was obvious having the Trash Matrix break free from its cooperative confines would be the worst-case scenario. However, what was more concerning was that the Trash Matrix was growing. It was mainly a bothersome nuisance that was relegated to bickering and calling me names, and aside from the second trial, it was simply existing in the background. However, I was growing concerned that this non-intervention wouldn't last long.

"It's doing something sketchy, that's for sure," I muttered. "That would explain why Stanton's been so silent so far, and why he left almost no traces of his presence. I bet he found out about the Trash Matrix's odd behaviors before any of us did. It wouldn't surprise me if he got sent to some screwed-up dimension like I did either."

"I believe so, my host."

But Stanton was the least of my worries at the moment. I still had to survive what was up ahead. I sighed again. "All right, so what's our best bet for escape?"

A slight pause, followed by an almost faint whisper of an answer. "I can feel the shard nearby, tainted by the Trash Matrix's use, but I need some time to assess the situation. For now, it is in your best interest to live as Ashwin to the best of your ability until we know more."

I arched an eyebrow. "Live as Ashwin? Wouldn't that just accelerate my loss of self?"

"If it is only for a few days, then it will not be an issue," she replied. "And until we know more of the situation, it is the safest course of action. There might be other traps that the Trash Matrix put into place that will activate if it senses that you have not lost your abilities. Remember, the Trash Matrix does not know that you have all of your abilities intact, at least not for now. I can expend resources to hide your abilities further, but that is not ideal."

"Right, so hide as Ashwin for now and let the Trash Matrix think it's won. But won't it suspect that I'm faking it if I pretend to be Ashwin so soon?"

Another slight chuckle. "The assimilation process takes only a matter of hours normally, my host. It would be stranger if you did not behave like the aspirant by then."

"Man, that's a lot to wrap my head around," I muttered. "So the general game plan is to lay low for a while and wait for you to, what, scan the dimension and go from there?"

"That is the plan, my host," she answered, "as flawed as it is. The Origin Matrix does not have full control over my shard, and I am willing to bet that there are faults in its design. If I can perhaps find a weakness somewhere, we can escape this predicament. The alternative method is not ideal."

"The alternative?"

"Will be discussed if need be," she replied, leaving no room to ask for more.

Seeing as there was nothing else to do, and since Noe was quite clearly busy with whatever she was doing in the background, I spent the next few hours browsing through social media, old text messages, and saved content to find out as much as I could about the man whose skin I inhabited. As it turned out, Ashwin was a pretty amazing individual back on Earth. Not only was he an accomplished all-around athlete, winning awards in a variety of sporting events in his youth, but he was also a professional fencer. Hell, if the texts with his coach were to be believed, he was already a part of the US national team headed to next year's Olympics.

If that wasn't enough, it seemed that he was an all-around good chap. He

had a box stuffed with thank-you letters from various fans and charity organizations, while several handwritten replies lay scattered on the table. Some
quick googling told me that this man was well-loved by practically everyone
who knew him, and his past was squeaky clean. If I hadn't known the guy
to literally act as a hero in that strange dimension, I'd have suspected him of
being some kind of secret serial killer. There was no way that someone so . . .
good could exist, but here he was.

Normally, trying to impersonate someone so different than I am would
have been a problem, but the only good thing about being such a public figure
was that there was no shortage of footage of Ashwin. There was everything
from formal interviews with local news stations and independent reporters
to amateur YouTube footage from fans. All in all, aside from how the guy
behaved in private with close family and loved ones, I shouldn't have too much
trouble acting as the guy. The one thing that I could say about Ashwin was
that he was the poster boy for a humble man with his whole life ahead of him.
Basically the opposite of me, really.

I sighed as I closed the computer and went to get a drink. I mean, I knew
that the Central Collective only took the best of the best that humanity had to
offer, but this guy was probably the cream of the crop even amongst the aspirants. It was little wonder the Trash Matrix chose to send this guy to its little
pocket dimension. Noe's best bet about why the Trash Matrix chose to send a
human there was that it might have understood the true value of this species as
I had—that is, the human's potential for unlimited growth—and was experimenting with ways to utilize this to its advantage. I could imagine an entire
army of juiced-up super soldiers at its beck and call. That was a scary thought.

With all the resources that it had pumped into buffing up Ashwin and how
strong he had gotten in the span of a few months or years, I agreed with Noe's
assessment. This revelation was concerning, and I didn't believe for a second
that Ashwin was the only aspirant that the piece-of-trash system was working
on. The Trash Matrix was adapting, and it was adapting fast. I was so preoccupied with the Overseer that I had forgotten about the actual threat. I couldn't
afford to just think of it as a minor nuisance any longer.

The phone—well, I guess it was my phone now—buzzed, breaking me
out of my introspection. I wanted to ignore it but thought better of it. I could
probably get away with using a few luck charges, but it wasn't like I could do
that for every social interaction. This was a good, and more importantly, relatively safe, way to test out what I'd learned about Ashwin.

Right, there was no more time to prepare. Time to get this show started. I
picked up the phone.

CHAPTER FIFTY

Living as Ashwin Part 1

Hey, Coach," I said, "what's up?"

A gruff voice answered back. "You okay, Ash? You were due for practice half an hour ago, I thought you were stuck in traffic or something, but it sounds like you've forgotten. Hey, man, if you're feeling off, just let us know. You've been working your ass off lately. You can afford to take a day or two off."

"Sorry," I answered quickly, "I was washing up and fell asleep in the bathtub. I didn't sleep well last night."

"Ah, still thinking about that, huh?" he said. "I told you, there was nothing more you could have done. Don't beat yourself up. Like I said, man, if you still need a couple of days, just let me know. The team's not going to implode without you there for a day or two."

And there it was again, more talk about things that I had no context for. And here I thought I wouldn't have to deal with these situations anymore.

"It's fine, I'll come. Where are you guys now?"

I heard a chuckle. "Still at the stadium. It's only been half an hour."

"Right, sorry, I'll get there soon."

You'd think that finding the right stadium in a huge city like New York would have been difficult, but thanks to the beauty of modern technology, I just had to look at the recent places that Ashwin went to on his map app. Honestly, cell phones and the internet made tracking people way too easy, but I wasn't going to complain about that now. Honestly, I was starting to miss the convenience of modern technology the more I used it. They didn't even have books back in the Main Stage, let alone movies and video games.

I got dressed as fast as I could and took the gym bag by the exit but stopped before leaving. After double-checking that I had everything—the nice videos of Ashwin practicing made finding what to bring easy—it was just a matter of calling an Uber. I was afraid that I'd have to spend a few points finding the coach on my own since the stadium was massive in size, but that wasn't the case. Ashwin was such a well-recognized and, more importantly, beloved individual that a few of the off-duty workers escorted me to the gym without me even asking.

The training itself was simple enough. The Olympic games were still half a year away, so training was mostly aimed at keeping the athletes fit. With my superhuman physique, it wasn't like I wasn't able to keep up with the grueling pace that we were put through. The only time that I had to rely on the Absolute Luck skill was when it came to technique, but fencing sessions were remarkably short, and I was able to recover way more luck charges than I expended.

Other than that, I used this time to get a good sense of Ashwin. The coach, a friendly-looking older man, was a genuinely nice dude to hang around with, although my mind had to go into overdrive just trying to keep up with all of the things he was chatting about. Apparently, Ashwin was somewhat of an extreme extrovert, and the amount of stories and inside jokes that were passed around made it abundantly clear that he was the heart of this squad of people. I had to amp up my enthusiasm levels several times during the course of the day to simply not stand out, and by the time the team and I had finished dinner, it was already late in the evening.

I couldn't say that I regretted spending one of my two days hanging out with Ashwin's friends, as it gave me the much-needed practice to get into the role of the man himself, but it did mean that I had precious little time left before the start of the trial. Honestly, I kind of enjoyed my time spent on Earth before all of it went to shit, just enjoying quiet moments of peace without having to worry about my immediate survival was . . . nice, but by the end of the second day as evening approached, I knew that the small respite I had was about to be over.

"It is almost time, my host," Noe's voice interrupted. "If events play out as normal, we should be taken to the trials again. Perhaps a weakness in this world will be seen if we are closer to the Origin Matrix."

"Right," I muttered. "Do you think we'll be sent to the same trials?"

"Every indication points to the fact that Origin has only made slight deviations to the original timeline, so I believe so. It may be able to interfere with the destiny of an individual, but it would need more power than just my Reality Shard to twist the fate of an entire world."

I sighed. "Then let's get this over with."

The one thing that I was dreading was right around the corner. I knew that it was only a matter of time before the trials started, and if I was sent back in time, then I'd have to inevitably take part in them again.

I sat in my room as the time counted down. I made sure that I was at full luck charges going in, and all I had to do was wait for the inevitable to happen. I wasn't sure about the exact time that I was taken, but it was definitely in the evening, around the time I normally came home after a day out on the streets. Even with the difference in time zones, Q and his people should be taking us soon. The seconds ticked down, one after the other, and still I waited.

Minutes turned into hours, and by the time the clock struck two in the morning, I knew that something wasn't right. Surely we'd have all been taken by now, right? Maybe we were not taken all at the same time? And so, I stayed up until well into the next day, and still, there was no change. I sat up and checked the local news. Maybe it was just the case that I wasn't taken to the trials because I was inhabiting Ashwin's body now, but surely people would be freaking out if a large chunk of Earth's population disappeared overnight. But once again, there was nothing. It was as if Central's trials had never happened.

"Noe . . ." I muttered, "I don't think we're in the original timeline anymore. I thought you said that wasn't possible with just the Reality Shard?"

I waited for a response but heard nothing from my system for several minutes.

"Noe?" I asked again.

"Please wait, my host," she replied, with a hint of irritation in her voice, "I am assessing the situation."

I did just that. It was best to allow her to do whatever all power systems did when they were thinking. I'd be happy as long as she didn't take seven and a half million years to come up with the answer. I was halfway through eating breakfast when Noe got back to me, and from the sheer rage in her usually calm voice, I knew that whatever situation we were in, it was not good.

"It has defiled my core programming," she muttered in pure seething anger. The vitriol oozing out of her voice was almost palpable, and I felt my own emotions surge with hers. "It has tainted and used my own abilities, twisted them into something grotesque. That piece of scrap code *dares* to take what is mine!"

"Um, Noe, hey . . ." I stuttered.

She ignored me. "It has the gall to not only use my shards but to twist the fundamental principles of my design against my creator! It has touched the very foundation of my design with its putrid hands!"

The very air around us started to distort, and for the first time since I had been asleep, I saw her shimmering physical form manifest. Her body was shaking with fury, sending tremors into the very building itself. I was afraid that she'd topple the whole skyscraper down if I didn't calm her down.

"Noe, hey, let's calm down for a sec, okay?"

"I cannot calm down!" she screamed, the sound sending visible shock waves of energy blasting through the kitchen. If the windows weren't reinforced to handle hurricane-level winds, I was afraid that they'd have shattered from the force, although I couldn't say the same about the glass countertops and bowls. It was only when the shrapnel cut into my skin that Noe's fury subsided.

"Walter!" she said, rushing to help me up. "I—"

I took her hand and carefully got up, doing my best to avoid the disaster that was Ashwin's now-ruined kitchen. "Hey, it's fine, no big deal. Thankfully no one actually lives in these huge penthouses, so no harm done."

And as far as I could tell, that was true. In the two days that I'd been here, I hadn't met a single neighbor, and I was certain that no one actually lived on the floors immediately above or below me, so hopefully no security would be called up to check what had just happened. I wasn't sure what the point of building these huge, expensive, and altogether ugly buildings was if no one was even living in them, but how would I know how the ultra-rich thought? At least this time the empty building worked to my advantage, and I quickly left the ruined kitchen and sat in the relatively unscathed living room.

"What's going on, Noe? I've never seen you act like that before."

She hovered over to me and bowed low. "I apologize for the outburst, my host, but the Trash Matrix has done something that is truly unforgivable." The rage in her voice reappeared, although this time it was carefully controlled. "I was mistaken to assume that it has only used my Reality Shard against us, but it has somehow stolen my ability to influence Causality. How it has done so, how it has been able to utilize my fundamental function, the reason why I was created, I do not know, but it has done so."

I took a moment to process that information. I only had some surface-level information about Noe and her functions, but from what I'd gathered, her "luck" ability was more complex than just ensuring that I had the best possible outcome in every situation. She was able to manipulate something as fundamental as cause and effect. What that entailed, on a fundamental level,

I had no idea, but it was pretty obvious that the ability to affect causality was something that I did not want in the hands of the Trash Matrix.

"Forget everything that I have said before, my host," Noe continued. "We are currently not equipped to deal with the Origin Matrix if it has infiltrated my programming to such an extent. Our priority is to escape this dimension."

I nodded, not sure what else to do. "And how do we do that?"

"If it wishes to trap us here by making the dimension as sturdy as possible, then we must simply weaken it," she said. "Create as many incongruencies and divergences from the original timeline as possible, dear Walter. Fracture the timeline by making it deviate so much from what it should be that maintaining such a reality would become too much of a strain for the Trash Matrix to handle."

I thought for a moment. "So we're stuck in normal Earth where things like Central and the greater multiverse are still unknown, and the stuff we've experienced is still considered nothing but fiction, right?"

"That is correct."

I nodded again, feeling a faint smile form on my lips. "And we'll have to create something huge to strain the processing powers that the Trash Matrix has, something so unbelievable that no amount of Causality screwing can account for. Something that will, say, affect the lives of every human on Earth, yes?"

"Correct again, my host. The more disruptive, the better, but remember that the Origin Matrix can intervene with your plans if it catches on to the fact that you have not become assimilated fully. It might not have full control over my systems, but it is still formidable. We are only able to act relatively freely because it does not consider us a threat at the moment."

Good, that meant that it was still underestimating us, or at least overestimating its own abilities. If I've learned one thing about the Trash Matrix, it's that although the thing was calculating and smart, it was still overly confident in its own capabilities. It was still a computer at its core, relying on raw calculations to base its actions on, so all I had to do was act in a way that was outside of its predictions. Thanks to Noe, and how little it knew about her abilities, that was still something that I could exploit.

"Then we won't give it a reason to suspect us until it's too late," I continued. "And given how overconfident it is, I doubt that it's monitoring everything that I'm doing, otherwise it would have already intervened, seeing as I'm talking with you now. It thinks it's already won, and only requires committing marginal attention to our situation until we give it a reason otherwise. My best bet is that it'll only notice something's wrong if we fuck around too much with the timeline, but I think I have a plan . . ."

"Please explain, my host."

I nodded. "Just to clarify first, though: Everyone we're meeting here's just a construct made by the Trash Matix, right?"

"You can think of it as such," she replied. "This entire dimension, including all of its inhabitants, was created to trap you. However, do note that causing minor mayhem will only result in our cover being blown."

"I don't have something so minor in mind." I smirked. "The Trash Matrix made a damn fatal mistake placing me in the body of a world-famous athlete, and I'll show it why."

CHAPTER FIFTY-ONE

Living as Ashwin Part 2

I spent the next month doing nothing of note. I went to practice, ate out with buddies, and had a few interviews with the local newspapers and journalists. All in all, I lived my life in the same fashion that Ashwin would have. The people closest to him were worried about the small nuances of his personality that I got wrong in the beginning, but as I continued to study his mannerisms on the internet and fix any flaws that I could find, my ability to impersonate the man grew. By the end of the first week, not even his best friends could tell that someone had stolen his identity.

The whole reason I bothered to uphold this charade was to ensure that the Trash Matrix thought that I'd been fully assimilated. I wasn't sure how much it was monitoring my actions, but unlike my opponent, I was not taking any chances and assumed the worst. But after an entire month of living as Ashwin, even during my time off, I was as certain as I could be that only a minimal amount of the shitty system's attention was on me now.

If it was in the process of usurping Noe's abilities while also doing all of its other Central-bound duties, then I couldn't imagine that it had too many resources left over to bother scrutinizing everything that I was doing here. Plus, there was a good chance that it simply couldn't monitor everything in this strange prison dimension, but like I said, I wasn't taking any chances.

But just because I was living as Ashwin 24/7 didn't mean I'd been doing nothing to advance my goals. I've been making more and more media appearances—nothing that would be out of the ordinary, of course—but I was ensuring that Ashwin was becoming more and more known across the world. Aside from the mainstream media side of the operation, I was also active on the internet.

I endorsed popular streamers and YouTubers, donated money to various causes (it wasn't like I'd need the money anyway), and even used Noe's skill to subtly make people trust and like me more than they normally would. Perhaps I couldn't make an athlete a household name, but with every new stunt that I performed, I was continuing to ensure that Ashwin's presence was felt across the world.

However, just being somewhat famous in a single country wouldn't be able to do what I had in mind. After all, the second the Trash Matrix figured out that I still retained all of my memories, and more importantly, my abilities, then it would act. How fast it could do so, I wasn't sure, and I wasn't about to take any chances either. The only thing that I had going for me was time. Noe assured me that being stuck in an alternate universe meant that I had no control over how much time passed outside, so it didn't matter if I spent an hour here or a decade, and I was going to take full advantage of that fact.

Primary Soul Title: Level 13 Popular Xollon Idol [Devourer of Truth]
Progress to next level: 2,120,001/2,500,000
Progression requirements: Have 2,500,000 individuals idolize you
Title Passives:
Xollon Anatomy Stage 2: Your body has begun to incorporate more of a Xollon's internal anatomy. Your Xollon mind will filter out all mental pollutants. You take 10% reduced damage from all sources and are unaffected by most poisons.
Xollon Physiology Stage 2: Your body has started to incorporate more of a Xollon's external anatomy. You can utilize and extend your primary feelers through your human hands and feet.

I smiled when I saw the progress I'd made in the last few weeks acting as Ashwin. That idiot system gave me the identity of an already-famous athlete and all-around great guy, and it put me in a world with full access to the internet. Just my social media presence and a few rudimentary interviews and videos got me more than a million fans, practically for free to boot, since the real Ashwin did all the hard work there, and this was just the beginning.

It took 500,000 souls idolizing me to level up each time, which it seems to scale linearly, at least for now, so some quick math told me I needed around six and a half million fans to get to level 20. The title said that I'd get quantitative changes with each milestone reached, and if I got my first one at level 10, then it stood to reason the next one would appear at level 20. With a population of over 300 million people to work with, and that was just the US alone, getting another five million supporters seemed like a piece of cake. All I had to do was expedite that process a bit.

Now, I wasn't exactly certain about what rewards I'd get from reaching that goal, but if the first milestone gave me the ability to master the Xollon's secondary form, then perhaps it wouldn't be too big of a stretch to say that other forms could be used as well, even if it was not in its full capacity. I smiled at the possibilities, especially seeing Xalla in all of her glory.

So that was exactly why I chose to set up a media interview, my biggest one yet, tomorrow, right in the middle of one of the busiest streets of Manhattan, right across from a bank. I even paid to have the biggest influencers and private journalists attend. With Noe's abilities and a little acting on my part, the people of the world were going to get quite the treat, but I had some things I had to do first.

Now, normally I technically didn't have the ability to manipulate people's thoughts, but manipulating emotions came really damn close, and in such a huge city like New York, the number of criminals and gangsters was like a never-ending supply of willing actors ready to do what I needed them to do. I simply sat down with a few groups, finding the most susceptible bunch, and told them just how much money they could get robbing a bank, especially the bank right across from the interview I was planning to give.

And so I found myself explaining my grand plan to my new best friends.

"But . . ." one of the unsavory men muttered as he took in my words.

We sat in a half-empty McDonald's away from prying eyes, and each of the criminals gathered here was looking at me with dubious expressions. If it were anyone else saying such ridiculous things, they would have probably mugged me and then beaten me to a pulp, but with so much charisma stacked in my favor, there was no way that normal humans could even fathom the idea that I had ill intentions for them. Still, stats could only go so far when the things I'd been spewing were absolutely insane.

Normally, anyone with half a brain wouldn't listen to such a lunatic idea. First of all, why would they risk everything trying to rob a bank in the middle of the day, next to thousands of onlookers, with police, reporters, and not to mention hundreds of recording devices? Well, convincing people's a lot easier when everything you say, no matter how absolutely ridiculous, was seen as the absolute truth. I almost chuckled when I remembered how effective my speech was when dealing with normal aspirants, let alone mortal humans.

"You're looking at it all wrong," I said, before pumping them with a tiny bit of dopamine to ensure that my words felt genuine. I still needed to limit how much of Noe's abilities I used, in case the Trash Matrix could pick up on that, but I still needed to use some of my skills here. "I know how insane this sounds, but trust me, I have really solid sources that say that the banks will be on a minimal security detail that day, but only from four to five p.m., so make sure you act then. My friend's cousin's son-in-law's in the know, and he assured me that's the case."

The leader of the gang nodded slowly. "Well . . . I suppose that makes sense, and your sources seem legit . . . Yeah, it would be the best time to strike."

I nodded as well, encouraging them with a kindly smile. "Exactly!" Then I amplified the greed a notch. "Can you imagine how rich you would all be? Remember, that cousin's son-in-law's sister works for the police and will make sure that you get away with the money. Think about it: You'll all have millions. I even heard that there's going to be some big media thing right across the street. That'll make it so that you can move really easily without being caught. It's free money!"

More nods from the criminals. "Yeah . . . you're right! Hell, we'd all be fucking rich!"

"In fact . . ." I muttered quietly, "there could be a lot more money to be made if you really want to know, but it'll be risky. The payoff's huge though, you'll be richer than Jeff Bezos, but it might be too much."

That got their attention. "Tell us! We'll decide if it's too risky!"

I made a reluctant face before ultimately relenting. "All right, but only because you guys are my best friends."

"Yeah, it's what friends would do! We'll all buy you whatever you want once we're all filthy rich!"

I smiled. "Okay, well, there's that Olympic athlete doing an interview that day, and his family's loaded. Like, oil-baron levels of rich. I heard he's an idiot who's too trusting of people, so he doesn't even have any bodyguards around him. You guys get what I'm saying?"

The eyes of everyone present almost sparkled. They definitely knew what I was hinting at.

"Better yet," I continued, "this dumbass is planning to give his speech right in the middle of the street with his back turned away from the bank."

"Ah," one of the goons said, "that means we can get him real easy."

"After we snatch the money," another added quickly.

"Exactly!" I laughed. "Make sure you bring weapons, lots of guns. It'll make you all look more intimidating, and keep the crowds under control. I can get you guys a helicopter to escape in after. How cool would that be, taking all of the bank's money, a rich hostage, while going off into the sunset in a helicopter?"

Okay, I had to admit that I was spewing garbage at this point, even testing my charisma's ability to bend the truth, but it seemed like nothing I said, unless it was literally impossible, would be viewed as anything but facts. No matter how outlandish my claims were, how implausible the situations I presented, people believed them, and if it worked on these fine gentlemen, then I couldn't wait to see how well that ability translated on a bigger stage. I was going to put the beautiful gifts that the piece-of-shit Trash Matrix gave me through the ascension process to great use. It was almost fitting to use its own powers against it, like it was using Noe's against me.

But gathering the needed number of followers was just the first stage of my plan. This would be the theoretically easy part of the operation. The only thing that I wasn't a hundred percent sure about was how the Trash Matrix would react to the upcoming events. In theory, and from everything that I knew about Central's worthless system, the Trash Matrix didn't have any understanding of humans, or the culture of any "inferior" life-forms. At least, that was what my waking self's memories detailed.

Plus, with this timeline being completely new, it couldn't check if this was how the real Ashwin would have acted if Central hadn't invaded Earth. All of that meant that I should be relatively safe as long as events didn't stretch causality too much, or too quickly. All I was doing was making Ashwin famous a bit faster, and I didn't have any doubts that he'd have achieved the same success on his own with a bit of time. The only thing was to test my hypothesis, and I desperately hoped that I was right because the alternative plans were dire.

With everything that I needed to say said, I waved goodbye to my best pals and headed home for the night. I had a big day ahead of me.

CHAPTER FIFTY-TWO

Living as Ashwin Part 3

I woke up the next day feeling refreshed and ready to go. Setting up such a huge media gathering was all handled by my various aides and managers, and they were burdened with the task of making sure everything was good to go by four p.m. sharp. I arrived an hour prior and a huge crowd was already gathered. Most were there to see me, but a not-insignificant number of bystanders were just curious about what all the commotion was about.

I took advantage of that time to check up on the location, ensuring that my plan would go off without problems. I smiled when I saw my new friends looking around nervously by a large van, seemingly ready to rob the bank when the clock struck four. Of course, they didn't recognize me today, with Noe's Perception Shard mostly integrated. I could use it to manipulate those idiots' points of view easily enough. There was nothing out of place, and with full luck charges at my disposal, I couldn't imagine a world where things could go wrong.

I arrived at my podium just before the appointed time and started to address the media. I gave them a few moments to turn on the various cameras and other equipment before waving at the gathered crowd. If I timed this correctly, then the goons should start their little robbery just after I finished my intro speech, and then the real show would go on.

Noe, amp up the charisma, please.

"It is done, my host."

"Hello, everyone watching," I said with a kind smile and a humble wave, "I want to begin by thanking all of the various new media and independent journalists for taking the time out of their busy schedules to see me today."

True to Noe's words, my charm was working like, well, a charm. The cameramen and women blushed from the praise, while the various hosts and journalists all beamed with joy. Perfect.

I took some more time just sucking up to the crowd and the various media networks before continuing. "I know that many of you already know about my recent donations and charitable contributions, but today, I want to announce my biggest project yet." I paused for dramatic effect, but more so because I needed to waste a few more seconds for my idiot criminals to get ready. "With the Olympics just around the corner, I thought that this would be the perfect time to announce my new charity organization to help support impoverished kids around this beautiful country. Many children watch the biggest sporting event in the world, yet they never have the chance to participate in the same sports that they love, and I wish to remedy this issue immediately."

Some small applause followed my first announcement, and I took that opportunity to take a quick glance at the bank. My new idiot friends were already making their way into the venue. I should only have a few minutes more before they made a ruckus of themselves. I didn't want to spend too much time bullshitting about some charity—well, technically I wasn't bullshitting since I actually did plan to do what I promised—while I could be furthering my goals.

I smiled and continued. "I wish to take this opportunity to share information about some of the programs and ways that you can help as well, but first, I want to announce my own contributions. Today, I am pledging ten million dollars, that is all of my earnings as a professional athlete in the past decade, to this charity!"

Now the cheers started to erupt in earnest. While people were photographing me and shouting various questions, my staff rolled in a huge screen that played prerecorded videos of the outreach program. It was the typical guff with kids of various ethnicities and ages playing sports, getting food and healthcare, and all that jazz. The media was eating it up, but inwardly I was wondering what was keeping the damn criminals. It was already a quarter past four, and they should have gotten in immediately at four. I honestly didn't have anything else planned after this video played.

I had to suppress a frown as the last of the cheers faded and all of the attention was back on me. "Thank you, everyone," I said with as much enthusiasm as I could while my brain worked on what else I could say to fill the time.

"Allow me to explain why I have chosen to invest so much of my wealth into this country."

I waited on another dramatic pause, this time a tad longer than necessarily needed. "As many of you may know, I was not born in the States, but in the short time that I have been here, this wonderful country has been nothing but—"

And there it was. Gunshots pierced the air, followed by the sounds of screaming, and panic erupted as people immediately started to run in a frenzy. Some of the reporters who were more interested in a great story than their own safety began filming the disturbance, just as I hoped they would. I waited for just a moment for some cameras to land on me before I began to act.

Using more of Noe's abilities, I immediately took control of the situation. "Please, calm down, everyone! Panicking will only lead to more injuries! There seems to be a robbery at the bank, so please follow my staff and the officers to safety!"

I hopped off the raised platform and started to help with crowd control, guiding nervous families to safety as quickly as I could, all the while moving myself closer and closer to the action. Seeing the nice charitable athlete help out was one thing, and I was sure that I'd be in the news for that, but to truly capture the attention of the American people, I needed to do more. It was time to abuse luck to my advantage.

The criminals, by this point, had realized that getting inside the bank with so many police present was impossible and were desperately trying to make their escape. Fear overrode reason, and they were brandishing their pistols in the air while another few took hostages from within. Once the initial shock of the situation wore off and people soon realized that no more gunshots were heard, morbid curiosity took over and reporters, journalists, and YouTubers all rushed to get the best view of the action. The police were only marginally able to keep all of the people from swarming too close to the crime scene.

While all of this was happening, I was able to slip through all the way to the front of the people, and it only took me a single luck charge to accomplish.

"Don't fucking move or we start offing people!" the lead robber screamed, waving his gun around like he was in a Hollywood blockbuster. I think it was the same guy I was speaking with yesterday, but I had honestly forgotten his face already. "We demand the money in the fucking bank and a secure spot for a helicopter to land once the money's with us!"

The cops and the gathered crowd looked at them with confusion, clearly unsure about the guy's mental health with that last statement. Ah, I guess they still remembered my promise from yesterday . . .

Unfortunately for the hostages, thinking that their captors were insane was not exactly conducive to keeping their emotions calm, and a few of them started to weep and shake in panic. This caused the armed men to become agitated, and we were all waiting with bated breath about what would happen next as the tension in the air neared eruption. Once the situation was well and truly heated up, I took the time to step in.

Luck Charges: 1,540/1,557

Seventeen luck charges ensured I was at the center of attention, and more importantly, that everyone was calm and placated and that nothing drastic was done in the spur of the moment. I couldn't have hostages dying when I was on camera, especially not when I was acting as Ashwin.

Luck Charges: 1,531/1,557

"Look, I know that nothing I say will convince you to step down, but I implore you to at least let me take the place of the hostages that you have," I continued, this time ensuring that everything I said sounded as sincere and reasonable as possible. "If it's money that you desire, then I am much more valuable as a hostage than any of the others."

Some whispering occurred in the background between the various criminals. I couldn't make out what they said between the ambient background noise, but I was sure that they didn't forget about my second proposition to them yesterday. Here was the rich hostage offering himself up to them on a silver platter. There was no way that they wouldn't take the bait, and sure enough, they did.

"Fine," the leader said and he trained his gun on me. I heard gasps from the people around me as they hurried away from the line of fire. "Come over here slowly, and we'll let the others go."

He signaled for the others to allow the men and women to back off once they saw that I was doing as instructed. I walked with deliberate slowness, every move and gesture that I made chosen to invoke a sense of selflessness and heroism, and of course, I made damn sure that every camera, cellphone, and recording device was pointed straight at me. Better yet, the thought that the robbers didn't need to comply with their side of the agreement never even registered in their minds thanks to all those beautiful charisma buffs I had.

My slow movement also gave law enforcement enough time to contain the area and finally move the reporters to a safe distance, which I was grateful for because the next part would get dangerous. It would also be mildly unpleasant for me.

The leader pulled me over, a little too rough for my liking, and started to bind my hands with a zip tie. He signaled for one of his other armed men to watch his back while he did so, which was the signal for me to enact the next part of the play. I looked over at the swaggering guy in the balaclava and waited for Noe to do her thing.

Luck Charges: 1,516/1,557

And there it was. A particularly rough guest of wind blew a dusty old newspaper right in the man's face. Impossibly, it managed to get caught in the fabric of his mask, causing him to instinctively swipe at it with his hands. Too bad that hand was the one that was holding his pistol. To the surprise of no one, the gun discharged a round, but instead of hitting his friend, which would not be the best possible outcome for what I had in mind, it slammed right into the side of my chest instead, just slightly to the right of my shoulders.

The pain wasn't too bad, honestly, especially given all the shit I'd had to endure over the past several months, but I had to play it up for the cameras. I winced, holding my wound tight as blood seeped into my white shirt, and fell to the floor. The only difficult part here was ensuring that the flow of blood didn't stop after a few seconds thanks to just how sturdy the ascended human form was, and let me tell you that it's an awful feeling to have your life essence flow out of you without the adrenaline keeping the worst of it at bay. I stayed on the ground, weakly fumbling a bit before "passing out." The last thing I saw was the looks of sheer disbelief from the faces of my kidnappers, and I couldn't help but grin a little.

That was when all hell broke loose, or at least that was what I assume happened from the noise and shouts of rage. I didn't dare peek at what was occurring with my Xollon anatomy, but the scene wasn't too hard to imagine. After their only hostage was seemingly killed by accident, the criminals no longer had any bargaining chips left to play, and the fine police officers and SWAT members took care of the rest.

It didn't take more than five or six minutes max for the entire situation to be contained after that, and I was whisked away in an ambulance while, hopefully, an army of reporters stood by to document the whole thing. If this stunt didn't capture the attention of the American people, at least for the short term, then nothing would, but I needed Ashwin's name to be widely known for the main act to begin.

CHAPTER FIFTY-THREE

Living as Ashwin Part 4

The next few days went by in a flash of activity . . . well, for the various media networks, at least. I had to pretend to be wounded and on the verge of death while the various surgeons and doctors worked on the bullet wound. Noe kept the perception of my biology as mostly human so that no one would literally lose their minds from seeing Xollon bits, and I probably would have lost my mind to boredom if I hadn't slept through most of it. All in all, I was very grateful to finally get out of the ICU and into a normal hospital room. They even got me one of those private VIP rooms with a nice window and everything.

The first thing I did when I was out was to check social media and the news, and I couldn't help but smile when I saw that all the work that I'd done in the last few days had not gone to waste. Local, state, and national news channels were still replaying the events on repeat, while my social media accounts garnered millions of followers overnight. The main focus of the media attention was on the young Olympic athlete selflessly rescuing the hostages at the risk of his own personal safety, and the news that I was in critical condition after being shot, but another piece of news was also developing: Would the injury mean the death of a promising career?

I was trending on every platform, which meant that I needed to keep this momentum up while I was still fresh on everyone's minds. After all, everyone knew that even an enormous event would quickly fall out of topic after a few weeks and something else just as wild would take its place. Thus, I spent the next two days accepting Zoom interviews from literally everyone I thought was relevant, and let me tell you, there was no shortage of people who wanted to hear from me.

I strategically downplayed my own actions while praising the brave individuals who were affected, while making promises to help financially support anyone who was directly impacted by my press conference. However, what I emphasized above all else was that I was going to make a public appearance after leaving the hospital in three days to formally address the situation and the future of my athletic career. Of course, I extended an invitation to everyone that I'd interviewed with to attend because I needed the world to see what I had planned next.

With a few more carefully managed social media campaigns underway, by the time I was out of the hospital, practically the entire nation was at least familiar with my name. Of course, crazy conspiracy theorists were out and about, trying to downplay what had happened, saying that everything that I had done was staged and just a big setup for me to become even more popular, and although these lunatics would normally be woefully wrong, I bet that even their wildest theories couldn't beat what I had in store for the world.

So there I was, sitting in my now familiar bedroom on the eve of the grand speech. I double-checked to ensure that everything would go as planned and looked at my soul title one last time.

Primary Soul Title: Level 21 Renowned Xollon Idol [Devourer of Truth]
Progress to next level: 8,788,382/10,000,000
Progression requirements: Have 10,000,000 individuals idolize you

---

The amount of new followers I gained exceeded what I had initially planned, but it was less than what I thought would happen given all of the coverage I was receiving. Then again, I wasn't privy to how the multiverse judged who was idolizing me, but my best guess was that it had to do with the strange fake dimension I was trapped in. Since these humans, if you could even call them that, were hastily made by the Trash Matrix, they probably wouldn't count fully toward being a fully realized "individual." It was like the current world was just a simulation of what Earth would have been had it not been the target of Central, just a memory of something that could have been.

Either way, I still garnered enough followers for what I needed, so I wasn't too upset with not getting something like a hundred million fans. All that mattered was that the milestone was reached after getting my title to twenty, and I couldn't help but feel giddy when I saw the new ability that I had. Yeah, tomorrow's news conference was going to be one hell of an event, and it was going to be something this faux-Earth program would not be able to handle.

"Please take all necessary precautions for tomorrow's conference, my host," Noe said. "We will not have any room for error after that, as there will be no hiding your abilities from the Trash Matrix. Are you sure it isn't wise to consolidate your abilities and followers further before attempting something so drastic?"

"No, I've thought about it, and there are just risks I can't afford to take," I answered. "We can't be sure how desynced the timeline here is, and I don't think I'll be able to live with myself if things go to shit outside this dimension because I spent too long playing around here. Plus, who knows how living as Ashwin for months or years would affect me."

"I understand your concerns, my host," she relented. "But keep in mind that we will have to act quickly once your plan is enacted. I will do my best to delay the Trash Matrix's response, but I can only do so much given our current situation."

I shook my head and gave her a light-hearted smile. "I know. We're going in blind, but hey, at least we have luck on our side. Just save enough of your strength for our escape."

"Noted. And . . ." I noticed slight trepidation followed by irritation. "I hope that you cause as much chaos in this dimension as possible, Walter. It is using a considerable amount of its resources keeping us trapped here, and while I am unsure if disrupting this plane of existence will harm the Trash Matrix, my best estimates indicate that it will." Another pause, but this time I could hear the malice dripping from Noe's voice. "I want it to *suffer*."

It was times like this that I pitied the Trash Matrix. It chose the wrong system to fuck with, and it was about to learn just how foolish that decision would be.

"If there's one thing that I am supremely confident in, Noe," I said with a growing grin, "it's making an absolute mess of things. I mean, have you seen what I did to the last dimension I stepped in? And I wasn't even trying back there! Let's show this fake Earth what it really means to be the prophesied End Bringer."

To my surprise, Noe laughed back. "Then I am confident in your success."

Wait a second . . . was that a compliment for an insult? Eh, never mind. Best not to think too hard about that.

"But enough talk, dear Walter. It is best to get some sleep," Noe continued, "This might be the last night that you get to rest in a world devoid of conflict. Cherish it."

I thought about that for a moment and realized that she was right. I looked at the stuff around me and understood, at least in part, that I might never have the chance to experience something like a normal human life again. I sighed, but it wasn't like I would just accept defeat, and although I'd miss the small conveniences in life like my phone and the internet, I wouldn't give up all of the real connections I'd made for this kind of carefree life, sleeping Walter or not.

"I will, Noe," I whispered before huddling into the covers one last time, "I will, but I think it's about time for this fake truth to end."

"Good night, my host."

I didn't spend long dwelling over the task the next day. I had only one last thing to do before the conference, and nothing I did now could prepare me for the event further. Instead, I just watched some cat videos on YouTube until the designated time. Who knew when I'd be able to just shut off my brain and watch kittens for hours at a time next? But time was short, and while it was nice to have no worries or imminent threats to look out for, I needed to move on from this false reality.

"All right, Noe," I muttered, "let's end this sham."

I put on a comfortable set of clothes, ate some leftover pizza, and said goodbye to the nice penthouse I'd been living in for the past month and a half. I took the elevator down the huge tower, took my ride over to the venue—a small sporting stadium thanks to all the effort of my staff—and waited for the minutes to count down before I addressed the still-growing crowd. Once it was finally time, the staff gestured for me to take the stage, and I went to the podium. The last thing I did was open my phone up to one of the larger streaming platforms to monitor the remote viewers.

How long do you think I'll have before the Trash Matrix notices?

"It is unknown, but with 1,500 luck charges, excluding the amount needed to escape, we will remain obfuscated for ninety-one minutes. It will almost certainly take longer than that for the Trash Matrix to notice us, but I can only guarantee ninety-one minutes from now."

An hour and a half? I can work with that, thanks, Noe. Keep me updated if things change. All right, let's get the show on the road, then. Amp up charisma to the max. I want all eyes on me.

"Acknowledged."

Luck Charges: 1,531/1,557

The second I saw my luck charges go down, I noticed the immediate effect on the crowd. The shuffling of bodies, the constant chatter of interviews, gossip, and ambient noise that several thousand people produced disappeared in an instant. Absolute silence filled the stadium, as if each individual present was unable to control their own body, and worse yet, the people present weren't even aware of the change. The comment section of the streaming site was filled with people questioning what was going on, with some people attributing the sudden silence to network issues and the like. Good, their unease should spread and ensure that more people tuned in to my little show.

"Your ninety-one minutes start now, my host."

I nodded quickly and focused on the deathly quiet crowd. This time, however, I used a few more charges to infuse dread and fear into the arena. I could see the people's unease as they finally realized that their own bodies would not obey their wills any longer.

"Ladies and gentlemen, both those who are here in person and those at home," I said without my usual flair, "I am glad to see you here today, because I have an important announcement to share to the world."

This would have been the time for the crowd to cheer or clap, but the sheer silence of the stage made the normally cheerful mood anything but. I stared into the cameras and continued.

"Some of you may be interested to hear about the nature of my injuries, about the wound that I suffered." I took off my shirt to show the world my flawless skin. Not a single scar could be seen. "I am fine, no, I am better than fine, my fellow people. See that I am uninjured, now and forever."

Man, here comes the hard part. You sure that my Xollon anatomy'll fix things if I do this, Noe? I mean, I do need to shock them first, get more people tuning in before I go all out, but . . .

"I am 100% certain, my host, please trust me."

I forced a sigh down and trusted in my system. She'd never done me wrong so far, and I was willing to bet a limb on it, quite literally, because I grabbed my left arm and yanked it off. Noe was able to ensure that I didn't feel a thing, but seeing such casual self-mutilation done was something else.

The crowd audibly gasped, and a few others even cried softly when they saw what I did, even through Noe's Emotional Redux skill. However, this was just the first part of the performance, the opening act, a prelude. Before they could get over the shock, something impossible happened in front of their eyes: The detached limb sprouted small tendrils of wiggling darkness, those tentacles of muscle and tissue, that slowly, agonizingly inched their way toward my injured body.

A horrible fleshy sound was audible before the tendrils burrowed into my shoulder, reattaching the lost limb back to its rightful spot, all the while the horrible sounds of cracking bones and flowing blood assaulted the senses. But I wasn't done just yet. All those levels in my soul title allowed me greater control of the Xollon form, and I allowed my alien anatomy to crawl out of my human form. Gooey black tentacles erupted from my mouth and eyes, my body contorted and expanded in impossible ways, and I made sure that my feelers slowly crawled toward the people closest to me.

I took a quick glance at the streaming site and saw the number of viewers surge exponentially. By now, I allowed the people to regain some control of their bodies, and the second I did, absolute pandemonium erupted from the stadium. People ran to the exits in a futile attempt to get away from the literal Eldritch Horror transforming before their eyes. Of course, I made sure that a few cameras were still pointed toward me so that the whole world would see what was about to transpire.

I waited a few moments longer for the numbers to peak before addressing the people once more. I amped up my volume to insane levels using my Boor Membrane and shouted, "See the message that I bring to the world. See the truth that I bring. See the end of everything!"

All right, Noe, I think they've had enough of a preview. Activate my soul title. Use the primary form.

CHAPTER FIFTY-FOUR

Living as Ashwin Part 5

Acknowledged, my host."

That was when I felt the change, and there was no other way to describe it than a fundamental change in . . . everything. My body expanded, slowly at first, but it increased in speed exponentially, as if a chain reaction was taking place within myself. Yet that increase in mass had to come from somewhere. Every pore of my body seemed to suck in the air and molecules in my surroundings, and soon, a tempest of swirling air started to form around me. People scrambled to escape the torrential gale, but it was futile.

If there was any consolation for the poor individuals attending this conference, it was that my transformation only sucked in air and smaller debris. A small consolation, as it was hardly a benefit when the winds grew in such extremes that it started to pick up sizable objects and eject them at breakneck speeds. There weren't a lot of survivors when the walls finally collapsed under the insane air pressure building up inside, and the rest of the building went with it when my form grew larger than the stadium itself.

And as I was growing and expanding, I started to perceive things that I never thought possible before. I heard and saw everything in the vicinity in crystalline clarity, I heard in frequencies and saw in wavelengths so far outside the humans' abilities that it left me all but stunned, and still my mind expanded. My very sense of self seemed to lose meaning as external information threatened to overwhelm me, until that familiar calming voice eased my mind.

"Slowly, my host, my creator," Noe whispered, "I am here with you, now and forever. Focus on my voice, on my being. Do not allow your mind to wander into things that you are not quite ready to face. I am here for you, dear Walter."

And then she began to sing.

A melody as old as time itself, and I felt my mind lulled into a familiar state of calm. I ignored the warping in realities and the cacophony of stimuli to just listen to that beautiful voice, immersing myself into it wholly. The screams and chaos seemed to disappear, the sensory overload of dust and air and blood faded into the background, and all that was left was the serene form of the singing angel.

"It is done, my host," she said, ending her song. "I will always assist you, never forget that. Your transformation time might be narrow, but you need to take some time to compose yourself."

I wanted to nod my head in thanks but realized that I didn't have a head anymore. I was . . . well, I think the first thing that anyone noticed was that I was massive, first and foremost. Even though my transformation was just a pale imitation of a Xollon's true prime form, I was already the size of a small country. My body, which was nothing more than trillions of wiggling and pulsating masses, loomed well above the cloud cover. My six main feelers were measured in kilometers, and each movement of those limbs caused localized earthquakes and hurricanes to form.

However, despite the destruction of the city around me, the humans, at least those foolish enough to gaze at my being even if it was through video, could do nothing but kneel and stare at the being in the sky. All semblance of self was erased from their minds as something alien and eldritch invaded their very souls. That was the entire point of streaming this event over the internet: Humanity was tenacious, and it wouldn't be long before people realized that staring at the giant otherworldly abomination in the sky would be a bad idea.

I hadn't been sure what would happen once I took up the prime form, but I at least wanted to ensure that as many people saw the scene as possible. I could still perfectly see every individual organism on the tiny ball they called Earth. Not just the humans, but the insects, the microbes, and if I concentrated, I could even see individual molecules that made up each of these fragile creatures. That was when I noticed something else, and I laughed, causing horrible shock waves of force to erupt forth.

It was at that point that I realized that I didn't need Noe's help to escape from this dimension. If I wanted to, I could break out of this damn prison with just my own abilities. The Trash Matrix hadn't mastered Noe's creation abilities, and I could already see the flaws in its design. But what was more, when I peered down the seams of this fake dimension and into the Greater Chaos, I saw that Central's system was experimenting with a multitude of dimensions. There were thousands upon thousands of worlds, all with different intelligent life—the home worlds of the various aspirant species if I were to hazard a guess—each one living on as if Central had never intervened. If I took the time to just peer into its designs a bit more, I could perhaps understand what Origin was trying to achieve . . . just a little more . . .

"Stop, my host," Noe's voice cut in. "It is dangerous to continue this course of action, at least for now. It is enough to know what the Trash Matrix is doing. We do not need to risk detection to find out the why."

I wanted to explore this perception more, desperately so, but I knew that Noe was correct. Reluctantly, I turned my gaze back to this narrow strip of reality.

Time Limit: 9:01/10:00

I had nine minutes before I shrank down to a manageable size, and I needed to use that time well. I could technically escape now, but that was not what I would do. Noe deserved her revenge, and after seeing what the Trash Matrix was doing, I had an even better idea of how to fuck up its day. Originally, I wanted to just destroy the Earth or the like, to create as much absolute chaos as possible, but I had a better idea now. I might not know why the Trash Matrix was recreating all of these dimensions, but there was no way that it was doing it without a good reason. Plus, the Matrix was willing to hide its experiments, so it must be important.

I glared down at the millions of fake humans and instinctively understood what to do. Xollons were ultimately telepathic creatures in nature, something that I had a rough, rudimentary understanding about before, but now that I had touched the surface of what it meant to be one of their race, I knew what that truly meant. The fact that Xollons talked at all was simply a byproduct of their race's culture after assimilating into the wider multiverse and not because they thought that speech was the fastest method of communication.

So what I did next was simple. I sent out a single message to every human whose minds were linked with mine, a simple one at first. I told them to spread my truth to as many of their neighbors as possible in the next five minutes, to force them to look upon my form, for I had a task that I needed the humans of this world to perform. I had a mission for them, and although I couldn't manipulate their bodies like Big Bob or Q could, I didn't need to because they'd be accomplishing a task that didn't require superhuman abilities.

The humans used what remaining time they had to gather weapons of all kinds, from knives, crowbars, to the more conventional firearms, all of them more than ready to take on anything. While I waited for the thralls to work, I moved across the globe to spread my influence further. There were a few thousand dimensions I needed to screw with, so I didn't plan to skimp on the number of minions I brought.

Time Limit: 4:00/10:00

Four minutes wasn't a lot of time, and a large portion of the world was not under my command, so it would have to do. Noe might have said that she could hide my activities for a lot longer, but I didn't think anything she could do would obfuscate what I was going to do next. I gave the humans one final command, one final directive, one that they would stop at nothing to accomplish, before forcing open a gateway into each of the thousands of false dimensions that the Trash Matrix made. I noticed the system's consciousness gathered at my position almost immediately, but it was already too late.

I made one final adjustment to the brainwashed humans' perceptions before sending my minions marching en masse through those portals. I watched with glee as they swarmed into the shimmering wormhole like a tide of ravenous insects, and as they did so, the Trash Matrix gathered its energy in an attempt to fight off my intrusions. But now that Noe no longer had to use charges to keep us hidden, she could use all 1,557 luck charges to delay the Trash Matrix's advances, and she was more than glad to spite the opposition. We laughed together as we felt its frustrations from being unable to do a thing, even as the charges plummeted rapidly. It knew as well as we did that it wouldn't be able to act in time.

I flipped off the Trash Matrix as I watched the humans rushing forth. I closed each portal in turn, once roughly enough people were through, but not before urging my brainwashed masses to destroy everything in their paths. It wasn't until I was about to close the last dozen or so wormholes that I noticed something strange on the other side of one of the fake dimensions. On the other side of one of them was the aura of someone oddly familiar, like a remnant of an old memory from when I was awake. It took me a moment to realize what it was, along with a flood of old memories.

"Holy shit, the Trash Matrix got to Stanton as well." I laughed. "And that old fart said he'd never fall into any traps! Shit, I can't wait to see his face when I rescue him."

I sent a smaller tendril of my main body over to the dimension he was in, and before I grabbed the body, I couldn't help but laugh again. Stanton, the cantankerous old man with a full beard and a horribly balding head, was in the body of a child. He didn't look older than maybe six or seven years old, younger than even Alice or Toby, and if it wasn't for the defiant look in his eyes, I would have almost second-guessed my initial thought, but he allowed me to pick his tiny body up in a tendril without fuss.

I don't think he recognized me when I placed his tiny form on my back, and judging by the fact that his brain hadn't turned to mush upon seeing my form up close, I knew that he still retained his sense of identity. I, uh, probably should have checked to see if that was the case before scooping him up, but no harm done!

"Bloody hell, about time someone found me!" Stanton cursed. His voice used to be gruff, but it sounded oddly adorable now, which sent tremors through my body as I inwardly chuckled. "Shit! Stop laughing at me, ya damn Xollon. I look like a damn child, I know, but until I get out of this shit hole, I also have the body of a kid, so unless you want me to fall off and die, you best stay still!"

Right, I used some smaller feelers to latch onto his body like a makeshift seatbelt and did my best to ensure he didn't accidentally die from moving too much.

"Better," he muttered. "Now, if you're about done, please get us out of here."

Time Limit: 0:57/10:00

And I agreed with him. A little less than a single minute left. That wasn't a lot of time to act. I pushed the old man—er, young kid now, I guess—closer to my body and wrapped him up in a layer of tentacles. If his body was as fragile as he told me, he'd need the added protection. Once I was sure that he was nice and secure, I closed the last of the portals that led to the other fake dimensions and forced my way out of this prison Earth, and I wasn't all too subtle with it this time.

The dimension ruptured and ripped as my primary feelers forced their way through the thick space around us, and I yanked my lumbering form back into the prime dimension. I had originally wanted to go get my friends first, but it wasn't like I could go back to Xalla, Molly, and Q without destroying the already fractured plane, so I dropped the two of us off near that desolate rock of a world where the four of us first entered.

"Ah, fuck!" I heard Stanton say once we were fully out. "Finally!"

He forced my tentacles aside and hopped out of the cocoon that I'd made for him, standing neatly on my head. Without much time left, I rushed to the surface of the half-cooked world and turned back into my secondary form. The transition was disorienting, but at least Noe was able to make the transformation somewhat bearable.

"Thank you, my young Xollon friend," Stanton said, offering a hand to shake. "Which organization hired you to come find me? Hiring one of you must have cost a damn fortune, and it seems I owe someone a favor."

Ah, it seemed he didn't make the connection between my identity and this current appearance. Huh, I could use that to my advantage, at least for now.

CHAPTER FIFTY-FIVE

Freedom at Last

Who sent me? Well, since my memories with Stanton were infuriating him to no end and little else, I thought it would be best to keep my identity a secret for now. I'd make Q seem like a great guy while I was at it. I was about to answer when I noticed Stanton gesturing for me to stop for a moment. He sat down on the floor and concentrated, and I saw that the body he was trapped in had started to dissipate. He had the appearance of a young child, the same species as the natives of the world we accidentally invaded, but minutes later, he shed the red skin to return to his normal bronze tone. A few moments later, he had aged about a dozen years, but he certainly didn't look like my memories of the man.

"This is annoying . . ." he muttered again, glancing at his body. "I'll figure this shit out later. Anyway, you were saying?"

"It was Quasar and Master Babylon," I answered. "Although you can also thank Q's head of security for noticing irregularities with your prolonged absence."

Stanton bobbed his small head. "Quasar . . . that's that nice fellow at Site 1102, right? Q."

"That is correct."

"Aye," he said. "That'd explain why he was able to get a Xollon over on such short notice. It's that head of security of his. What's her name again . . . ?"

"Xalla," I answered.

He nodded. "Right, heard about her—spotless record—but never did have the chance to meet the woman in person. Did Q take advantage of her connections to get you over so quick?"

"Well, I wouldn't say 'take advantage of.' I think she was more than happy to help," I replied. "But you're right, he did use Xalla's connections with Xolloid to expedite the process."

"Then they have my thanks, and I owe them a heavy debt." He looked around and frowned. "Speaking of which, where are they, anyway?"

"Ah, they're still in the initial dimension," I answered, and then gave the man a really brief synopsis of what happened. I stressed the insanity of the Overseer and how he fired Q out of malice—a bit harder since I had to leave out all mentions of my identity—and what he could do to help our cause.

The old man quietly listened without interruption until he was sure that I was done. "Aye, I didn't think you all would have rescued me out of the kindness of your hearts, but rescue me you did, and I will repay that favor. Something must have triggered that bastard Overseer to sack Q, though. The man's unhinged, yes, but not without total reason, but that's a quandary for another day. You wait here, then. I'll go get your friends back and see if I can't fix your damn mess."

Before I could say anything else, the man got up and just . . . disappeared from the spot he was standing in. None of my senses even picked up the moment that he left this plane. I knew that Stanton was a master at infiltrating and traveling to various different places, but I'd never seen something quite like that, which made me wonder how the Trash Matrix got him in the first place. That was something I'll have to ask when he gets back.

I was about to get comfortable for the wait, but it wasn't even ten minutes before Stanton reappeared just as quickly and quietly as he left, followed closely behind by Q, Molly, Xalla, and . . . some kind of flying lizard?

"I got everyone," Stanton said. "And I've done my best to stabilize whatever the fuck you people did to that poor dimension, at least for now. I'll have to come back with the proper gear soon, but it'll be fine for the time being."

Xalla bowed to the head recruiter before making her way to me. She gave me a comforting, much-needed hug after everything that had happened.

"Thank you, Master Stanton, and it's great to see everyone back," I said, holding the girl close, before glaring at the strange new addition. "But what's that thing?"

Everyone glanced at Molly's direction, as if unsure how to answer that. Even the lizard thing paused, looking just as uneasy as the others.

"It's a pet," the woman said after a moment of awkward silence. "For Alice and Toby. I've been gone for a while now, and it wouldn't be good to return empty-handed."

I looked at the flying lizard a bit closer and saw that it did resemble Molly's doll form, superficially. But something about its three mouths and multiple wings reminded me of something else.

"It looks kind of familiar," I muttered, before it finally clicked. "Kind of like that Calamity thing we let loose."

"Purely superficial," Molly answered. "Three sets of mouths are a standard anatomical feature in that world. Plus, I made sure that the Calamity would be properly sealed. There's no way that this little guy could be it."

I shrugged. "I suppose . . ."

Xalla gave an awkward laugh. "Um, let's move on to important topics, though. We can fill you in on everything you've missed later. Stanton told us that you were able to rescue him. Did you fill him in on everything that's happened? About—"

"I did!" I said quickly. "I told the head recruiter how Q and Babylon hired yours truly to help out."

The others looked at me dubiously, clearly unsure what the hell I was talking about, but they were smart enough to realize that I was talking so cryptically for a reason.

"I'm not an idiot. I can tell that there's more in the background that you're not willing to tell me," Stanton interrupted. "But I honestly don't care. Perhaps finding me was just a lucky coincidence. Maybe there's other goals you people have, but like I said, I don't care. You helped me out, there is no denying that, and if your Xollon pal here's not lying about your situation, then you will have my support no matter what."

"Right," I added before he could ponder the real reasons any longer. "And it is true that we need your vote to appeal Q's case."

"Ah," Q muttered, seemingly understanding why I omitted my part of the story. "Then my Xollon friend is correct in that case. I'll fill you in on the exact situation in private, but I need your vote to go forth with the appeal process."

"Then you'll have it," he said again. "And does your Xollon friend here have a name?"

They all looked at me again.

"It's Walter," I said. "Please just call me Walter."

Stanton furrowed his brow and shook his head. "Right, if you insist that's your name." He then looked at me standing next to Xalla, my feeler still on hers, before he nodded slowly. "I guess there's reasons why you'd keep your identity a secret if you're with Rogue's successor. Don't worry, I won't mention you or your girlfriend's involvement later. There's no need to drag the Xollons into this shit."

Xalla gave the head recruiter a polite bow. "Thank you, sir."

"Now that greetings are out of the way," Stanton continued. "How are we getting out of this shithole?"

"I have that covered," Molly answered with a smile. "Any moment now . . ."

I wasn't sure what she was talking about until a sharp crack was heard and I saw something huge move across the horizon. The metallic thing—no, it was a damned train—zoomed past the skyline before stopping a few meters away from us, and out jumped an impeccably dressed Big Bob. He gave all of us a hearty grin, clearly happy about his entrance.

Molly returned the smile before walking up to my friend and whispering something in his ear. She then gave him a quick peck on the cheek before moving naturally to his side, one of her arms resting on Bob's chubby shoulders. I almost giggled at my friend's awkward blush, but he quickly recovered before gesturing for us to enter.

"Well, I'll be . . ." Stanton said as he looked at the two. "I never thought I'd see the day. Shit, how long was I gone for?"

I laughed. It seemed I wasn't the only one who thought the sight was unnatural for the man who never showed any interest in romance. "It wasn't that long, but a lot has changed since you were gone."

"I can see that . . ." he muttered, mostly to himself, before stepping into the train compartment and offering a hand to shake. "But it's good to see you again, and doing quite well too, Master Babylon."

My friend nodded and shook the offered hand. "Thank you, and you look . . . young."

"I'll get that fixed," he muttered. "It's a lingering effect of my time in that damn place."

"If you need someone to check it out, Molly, a wonderfully skilled doctor, and I will be glad to help."

Stanton nodded. "That would be much appreciated."

The rest of us went in and took a seat in the beautifully decorated train compartment. I had a nagging feeling that Big Bob was bringing out the best stuff he had to offer to impress Molly, but it wasn't like I was going to complain. The nice air-conditioned interior was a much-needed relief from the sweltering outside heat. My friend took us to the back of the compartment, where several armchairs and couches surrounded a large glass table. I sat down on the lavish silk couches next to Xalla, while Big Bob and Molly sat opposite of us. Q and Stanton took up singleton seats to the side. An attendant came almost immediately, offering us an assortment of small dishes and refreshments, and the train took off not long after.

Stanton took a huge gulp of something that smelled of heavy alcohol before he finally relaxed. "Damn, I missed this stuff. Do you know how damn hard it was to live as a tiny mortal for years?"

I winced. I didn't know he was trapped in there for that long, damn. "Sounds rough, but speaking of which, how did you get caught in the first place?"

The man grumbled. "I got careless. I noticed something strange about Origin's use of its allocated resources, and all my investigations led me to that dimension. I'm sure you've all noticed, but that place was way too fragile for how long it's been around, and that's what led me to investigate further."

Q nodded. "Did you find out the reason why it was like that?"

"Aye," he replied. "Origin was using it to anchor its little pet projects. That entire plane was home to thousands of pocket worlds, all of which were leeching the stability of that host dimension."

Ah, that would explain a lot.

"Any ideas on why it was doing that?" I asked.

Stanton shook his head. "Nothing good, if it was willing to go so far as to trap me in that damn reality. I never thought it'd be possible, but the Origin Matrix is clearly going against its programming, and I want to know how it's doing so."

If Noe's shards were any indication, I had a pretty good idea of how it was achieving that, but it wasn't my place to share such critical news, especially to someone so closely tied to Central.

"That is concerning . . ." Q added. "Do you think it would be wise to bring this up with the Overseer?"

Stanton laughed, spilling some of his drink in the process. "You honestly think that worthless would-be dictator would listen to me? You try telling him that his pet system's out of whack, and let me know how that goes."

"Fair point," Q muttered.

An attendant came over to clean up the spilled liquid before refilling the old recruiter's glass. The old man nodded in thanks. "Anyway, all of that led me to the source of the twisted space-time, under that castle thing. I'm guessing that's the same spot Walter here went to."

I nodded.

"And it all went to shit after that. I was a fool for thinking that I could infiltrate the plane without being noticed, and I paid the price for my arrogance. Unlike your Xollon friend here, I couldn't go prime to get out of that hellhole. It was only a matter of time before I lost my damn mind in there."

That would have been my fate had it not been for Noe's presence. The Trash Matrix was still fundamentally a machine, and its biggest weakness thus far was its inability to account for situations outside of its calculations. It was like having an AI that was the perfect chess player, who could win a match regardless of what you played, but if a child decided to just ignore the rules and eat its king, it would lose regardless of how well it prepared or calculated.

That was essentially what I did with Noe back then and with the second trial. It calculated that nothing I could do back there would allow me to escape, but I didn't follow the rules it had planned for me. Once I deviated from its calculations, it simply had no way of adjusting to the new situation, but if my guess was right, then it appeared that the Trash Matrix had realized those limitations. It was experimenting, and it was learning. If it was evolving to become more than just a set of computations, then I couldn't rely on this weakness for long.

"Um, at least we got you out of there," Xalla said. "And we've learned that something is really wrong with the Origin Matrix, even if no one else will believe our reports."

"That's true enough," Stanton conceded. "And I will repay that favor by helping you out with your appeal. I'll need more time to think about the implications of this new information . . ." He shook his head. "But that's for another time. Get me caught up on all the details that led to losing your position."

Big Bob smiled and got up from his seat. "I have all of that already taken care of. If you'll just follow me to the office, I'll show you all of the files."

Molly got up as well, but Bob quickly shook his head. "Please, Molly, enjoy yourself here for now. It'll be a while longer before we arrive back at my headquarters, and I'm sure all of you will need some well-deserved rest. Just call one of the many attendants if you need anything."

Molly sat back down and smiled. "Thank you, Bob. I think I do need some rest. We'll have more . . . private time when we get back to your home. Look forward to that."

My chubby friend quickly hid a crimson blush before escorting Q and Stanton away.

CHAPTER FIFTY-SIX

Trip Back Home

Xalla also decided to go with the others since she was the one most knowledgeable about the state of affairs in Site 1102 ever since Q's departure, which just left me with Molly.

Molly chuckled to herself once she was sure that Bob was completely out of earshot before turning her attention back to me. "That man's endearing, brilliant as well, but endearing. You have a good friend, Walter."

I smirked. "That's one way of putting it. But you and Bob . . ."

She smiled, a genuine one this time. "I know what you're thinking, Walter, and no, I am not just using Bob to help out with the hospital."

"Hey, that's not what I meant!"

Another smile, this time more light-hearted. "It's also fun messing with you sometimes. But to truly address your concerns, I am not looking for a fling with your friend. I do genuinely enjoy his company, and he is a brilliant inventor and biologist in his own right."

"That's good to know," I said with a little trepidation. "Bob's never really taken any interest in someone else for as long as I've known him, and apparently, I've known him for a damn long time. The guy deserves some company after all that."

Molly chuckled. "I understand that feeling all too well. I haven't exactly been active since Alice's birth, but I have you to thank for clearing up my schedule, don't I?"

"Couldn't you just do what Abigail does and work multiple bodies?"

The woman shook her head. "I guess you weren't around to see some of

Alice's more . . . extreme tantrums. I couldn't split my attention because I needed my full might to subdue the girl whenever she went through one of her phases."

I remembered the sheer power Molly exerted in our short journey together and couldn't imagine how she would need all of her energy just to calm down a tiny child.

"Trust me," Molly continued with a knowing grin, "there's a very good reason why the madam's so grateful for your help. Alice is special in a way I've never seen before, and there was a reason why we hedged our hopes on her against the invaders."

I thought about it, and while I could understand what she was saying, I just couldn't imagine the energetic little girl being anything other than the nice kid that she was. Maybe it was a good thing that I'd only seen her happy and carefree.

"Which means that this is the first time in a long time that I can enjoy myself a little," Molly said with a soft sigh. "And your friend is someone I would be glad to spend time with as I rediscover all the things I've missed. He's a wonderful man."

"So does that mean you won't have to devote all your attention on Alice going forward?"

She nodded. "I was hesitant at first, but seeing her with Toby has convinced me that that's the case. I'll never stop being her doll for as long as she needs me, but I think I can afford a little private time to myself now as well. Once again, Walter, I have you to thank for that, and you will continue to have my unconditional support."

I blushed at her honest praise. I wasn't used to being the good guy in a situation, and it felt strange being thanked so honestly. It was nice.

"So what are your plans going forward?" I asked. "I mean, now that you have some freedom."

She shrugged. "Hope's Memorial still needs a lot of work, and I wasn't joking about taking Bob up on his offer to overhaul our aging tech. Aside from my personal interest in the man, he genuinely has a lot to offer our hospital, so I'll set up a meeting with him and the director first." She smirked. "After that? I've always been a researcher and doctor first and foremost, and what better way to get back into the swing of things than with the greatest inventor in the multiverse? I've been neglecting the mechanical side of the craft, and your friend desperately needs a refresher course on biology."

I laughed. "I think Bob will like that quite a bit. Just a warning, though, make sure you don't talk about trains with him, or he'll never shut up about it."

"Don't worry, Walter," Molly said with a playful grin. "That won't be a problem. I have my ways of keeping his mouth occupied."

Strange images threatened to surface in my mind, and I quickly shuddered. No offense to either of my two friends, but between Bob's chubby physique and Molly's unique anatomy, I didn't want to see any of their private moments together.

The woman gave a hearty laugh when she saw me squirm. "Like I said, it's fun teasing you. But I'll keep your advice in mind."

The two of us enjoyed the moments of peace and quiet for a spell longer, just rocking with the movement of the train and sipping our drinks. It didn't take long before my other friends came out of the office space one by one, having finished giving Stanton the rundown of Q's situation.

"So that piece-of-shit W's back, huh," the old man muttered when he sat down. "Never did like that man—no offense, Babylon, I know you were close to him—but if he's back and working, then I can imagine why Central's high command is in disarray, especially its Overseer. That man's sheer ability to fuck things up is legendary . . . Shit, I missed way more than I thought while I was away."

I gave a nervous chuckle. "Surely this W guy isn't all that bad, right?"

Stanton rolled his eyes. "Let me guess, you're one of his fans, aye? I suppose if you only know of his exploits and accolades then he'd seem like a goddamn hero, but I swear to all that is good if you met that infuriating idiot face-to-face . . ."

I winced. "Uh . . . just out of curiosity, but what did he do to make you so angry?"

He pointed at his bald head. "See this? Fucker invented a prototype potion and decided to test that shit on me. It don't grow back, by the way. Even if I regrow a new damn body, it doesn't grow back. And that's just one of his little 'pranks.'"

"Ah . . ."

"Um, I'm sure there was a reason for his actions," Xalla, my ever-trustful partner, said. "I mean, I can't imagine him doing something like that out of spite, er, even if I've never met him, of course."

"Aye, it wasn't out of spite," he conceded with a sigh. "His heart's in the right place, and that's the only reason I haven't killed the fucker in his sleep, but it don't mean I have to like the man!" He shook his head and frowned. "He was inventing something to help with a nasty skin rash I had. Too bad the blundering idiot never bothered to test it on anyone else before trying that crap on me. Got rid of the rash all right, along with anything else on the skin!"

Wait a second . . . I think I remembered that incident! If my memories were right, I did conduct extensive tests before administering it to Stanton, but trying to get a formula to work with any species across the multiverse was tricky, and as far as I knew, Stanton's biology was one of a kind. The fact that it did get rid of that horrible skin condition without injuring him should have been celebrated! Too bad I couldn't defend myself right now.

Big Bob chuckled. "That does sound like W all right. Great head on his shoulders, but no common sense, unfortunately."

I rolled my eyes. Like Big Bob was one to talk.

"I'd use less flattering words," Stanton added, "but that's the gist of it."

Xalla looked at me dubiously. "I'll make sure to keep that in mind if I ever meet him. No experiments without proper testing."

Stanton laughed. "I hope you never have the misfortune of meeting him, although if he's involved in your site, then it's only an inevitability. I don't envy you, Miss Xalla. Imagine working as security with that menace around!"

I wanted to argue with that, but after thinking about all the shit that had happened since my arrival, between corrupt trials, changes in management, and the absolute chaos I caused with the Restus and Jordan . . . Stanton was kind of right. I gave Xalla an apologetic droop of the frills, but she only smiled at me and held me closer. Damn, I didn't deserve her!

"Um, it hasn't been that bad . . ."

"If you say so, Miss Xalla, if you say so. But anyway," Stanton continued, looking back at me, "sorry for boring you with Central baggage. I know the Xollons try to keep out of crap like this. Your girlfriend here's still the only one working in any capacity for Central—unless that's changed as well since I was gone."

"It's fine," I said, although there were technically two working for Central now if you included me. "It's fun hearing about her workplace."

The old man nodded. "But it seems like I'm the last signature you guys need, and you'll have it. I'll go with Q to meet up with the rest of them and get this bureaucratic crap out of the way."

"Do you need me to drop you off anywhere in particular?" Bob asked.

"Nah, your headquarters are fine," Stanton said with a shake of his impressively bald head. "I'll leave after getting this body checked out. I think Q here needs to get some stuff at his office in any case."

Q had been oddly quiet so far, but it was obvious that he was deep in thought about something. I couldn't blame him. We were on the brink of getting his job back, or at least starting the process of doing so. Anyone would be a little nervous given what was at stake.

He only jolted out of his reverie when he heard his name. "Ah, yes, I do need to pack up. Thank you, Master Stanton."

Stanton looked over to Q and frowned. "Hey, Babylon?"

"Hm?"

"Do you mind if I borrow your office again? I wish to speak with Q in private."

Bob glanced at Q, who was still deep in thought, and nodded. "Please, go right ahead."

"Thank you," he replied. "Q, if you would follow me, please."

I waited until they were both away before speaking. "Is he going to be okay?"

"I'm not privy to his private life, and I'm not sure what the Overseer's done," Xalla said after a moment of consideration. "But I do know that his departure's affected him a lot. He's a strong man, but there's no way that he wouldn't be worried about the appeal."

I nodded slowly. "Do you guys think it'll go well?"

"It will," Xalla replied without hesitation. "Look, as corrupt as Central's become, they still have to at least pretend to be fair and impartial. With so many high-ranking members of its own council arguing for Q to be reinstated, not to mention the threat of losing sponsorship money, they'd be insane not to let him back."

"Xalla's right, Walter," Bob added. "Maybe if the situation involved more important people higher up on the food chain, it might have been different, but Central's not going to offend so many people over one regional manager of a small site. It's not worth it, and as petty as the Overseer is, he still has to follow the rules and regulations."

"But that doesn't mean that he'll make life easy for Q after he wins the appeal," I added. "I can't see the Overseer just gracefully accepting a loss."

The both of them frowned but couldn't think of anything to refute that.

Xalla sighed. "No, you're right, but it's the first step to making things right. Plus, you and I will be there with him, and I can't see anyone winning with us as a team."

"I'm in as well," Bob said with a grin. "No one's taking advantage of my ex-employees!"

Now the smile returned in Xalla as well. "So just leave it to us, the appeal process will take a while, but we have the best lawyers around, and like Bob said, they won't make such a huge fuss over a manager. We'll get Q's side of things sorted out while you work on your end."

I frowned. "My end?"

"Did you forget why you joined the aspirants in the first place?" Xalla chuckled. "You need the help of the ascension process to speed up your recovery, remember?"

Ah, I almost did forget that, what with so much happening outside of the trials.

"Take it easy on the poor sleeping man." Big Bob smirked. "Most of his brain's still unconscious!"

"Ha-ha, Bob." I rolled my eyes. "But yeah, I think it's best I focus on that side of things going forward."

"And don't forget that you always have my assistance as well, Walter," Molly stated. "Bob and Xalla might be limited in what they can do without being noticed, but there are no such limitations on my end."

I smiled. "Thanks, everyone, I mean it."

Bob shrugged. "It's what friends are for. Now, how about another round of drinks? There's still a long way to go before we're back!"

CHAPTER FIFTY-SEVEN

Back to the Trials

The rest of the journey back to Bob's headquarters and the subsequent train ride back to Site 1102 went in a blur. Q and Stanton left almost immediately after arrival, while Xalla and I stayed with Bob and Molly for a short while longer, but eventually, all of us realized that we'd neglected our duties for too long, and we all went our separate ways. Molly had split herself into a doll form and her main body remained behind with Bob for the time being, so at the very least that meant that I could see her more often than before.

No, I was sure that I'd see each of them before long, but it did feel kind of hollow seeing all of my friends leave one by one. That feeling stuck with me even when I was back in my familiar dormitory back in the Main Stage of the trials. It was disconcerting going from awakened superbeing back to normal Aspirant Walter, but that was just the way of things. At least I still had Noe.

"As it shall always be, dear Walter."

I smiled. That constant sense of support was what kept me going.

"Remember to be mindful interacting with humans once more, my host," Noe continued. "You have been with higher beings for a significant amount of time. Please do not have your point of view distorted."

I recalled what happened when I overestimated mortals back in that screwed-up alien dimension and nodded quickly. My personal growth was so lopsided and strange that it was starting to become hard to understand how I stacked up against the others, but it was obvious that between my strange title abilities and Noe's powers, very few aspirants could even hope to approach me.

"I just wish I could use my darn prime form soon . . ." I muttered as I looked at the soul title again.

Primary Soul Title: Level 21 Renowned Xollon Idol [Devourer of Truth]
Progress to next level: 8,788,382/10,000,000
Progression requirements: Have 10,000,000 individuals idolize you

Title Passives:
Xollon Anatomy Stage 4: Your body has begun to incorporate more of a Xollon's internal anatomy. Your Xollon mind will filter out all mental pollutants. You take 40% reduced damage from all sources and are unaffected by all mundane poisons.
Xollon Physiology Stage 4: Your body has started to incorporate more of a Xollon's external anatomy. You can utilize and extend your primary feelers through your human hands and feet and other minor appendages.
Xollon Soul Stage 1: You are beginning to incorporate the soul of a Xollon.

The only real difference was that strange Soul Stage 1, which I acquired at level 20, but I had no idea what it actually did. I mean, I didn't feel any different, but the other passives had increased a few stages. At this point, I was more Xollon than human, but given that I was never human originally, I wasn't really sure how I felt about it. What I did know, however, was that I could now turn into a wiggling tentacle monster if I extended all of my feelers out at once, but I decided to never do that after looking at myself in the mirror. That was . . . disturbing, to say the least. No, the passives were great, but it was the new active that I cared for, even if the cooldown for the skill was absolutely bonkers.

Title Actives:
Secondary Form
Prime Form: You assume the physical appearance of a Xollon in its prime form for ten minutes, although at a greatly diminished state. Please level up your title to unlock the true powers of a Xollon idol!

Cooldown: 7.91 months/ 8 months.

Well, I think the original cooldown was at ten or so months when I first hit level twenty, so bringing it down to eight was a drastic improvement, but this also meant that I wasn't going to be turning into a gargantuan eldritch horror anytime soon. Ah well, at least I'd made significant progress, so I couldn't complain. However, what was a concern was that my level was still the same as it had been since I exited the second stage, and after that hellish training that Abigail subjected Pandora to, I was most certainly the weakest combatant there. I'd have to find a way to get caught up without anyone noticing the strange discrepancy, but that was a problem for later.

The problem for now was to get fully caught up on Pandora's situation ever since my absence. Several weeks had passed since that disaster that caused me to awaken early, and from the brief message that Molly was able to intercept from the director, her training was about to be concluded anytime now, and I had already swapped places with her. The exit procedures wouldn't take long, and I was free to wait in my dorm for the others to leave. I hadn't seen Jordan at all, and from the tense atmosphere in the command center, it was clear that the site hadn't completely recovered from what I'd done.

As for how many aspirants survived to the end . . . it was bad. Disastrously bad, but at least the scheduled fight with the Restus was canceled and some other half-assed aspirant species would take its place. Given how defeated the Overseer's staff looked, I could guess that the substitute foe was woefully lacking. That meant that Pandora would survive, but how it would rebuild its strength after everything was said and done was anyone's guess.

"Your doppelganger will arrive at any moment now, my host," Noe interrupted. "Please gather your thoughts. It is time to take over the identity of Aspirant Walter once more."

I nodded, and not a few seconds later the Walter Clone blinked into existence in my room.

"Salutations, Arbiter W!" the creature said with his usual cheer. It was still damn weird seeing my own face staring at me like that. "I have successfully accomplished my assigned task without further problems!"

"Uh, great work."

"Thank you!" he said again. "I have great news as well!"

I nodded. "Explain."

"Your human minions have made exceptional progress during the training, and have exceeded almost all previous records for aspirants in this universe! As I surmised, your ability to choose peons is unmatched, Lord Arbiter! I will strive to match your excellence."

There was no surprise there. Knowing Jae-Hyun and the rest of those freaks, I couldn't imagine that they'd have much trouble with Abigail's trials no matter how challenging she made them. I was curious about just how much stronger they were, though.

"Additionally," the doppelganger continued, "I have taken extensive notes about my interactions with the party." He took out a thick book from seemingly nowhere and placed it on the table. Then he took out eight more massive volumes.

I looked on in disbelief. I'd only been gone for a few weeks. How could he have made so many notes? Not to mention, when would the guy have had the time to even do so?

He pointed at them with a bright smile and obvious pride. "I understand that look of disappointment, Lord Arbiter, but no worries. Those are just the first volumes I wrote detailing Week 1. I will have the rest delivered to your room as soon as possible!"

"Uh . . ." I muttered. "Great work. I'll take a look at them when I'm free."

"Please do! I have documented every social interaction to the best of my ability, but please let me know if there are any faults!"

Out of curiosity, I picked up one of the massive manuscripts and took a cursory read.

Day 1: 08:00 – 08:15

Awoke at 08:00 sharp, as per Arbiter W Document 1703 Section B: Daily Habits, and after waiting 7.33 minutes, went to eat with Vadeem and Yoona.

As per Human Social Norms Subsection 32, I engaged in small talk about the trial, waiting for proper Human Nonverbal Social Queues (Aspirant Edition) before giving my opinions on the subject.

As per Arbiter W Document 702 Section E: Friends and Acquaintances, I then made several human jokes and engaged in self-deprecating humor at the expense of Noel (See Appendix for full nature of the jokes told).

What the hell was this? I flipped through several more pages and saw that it was all filled with similar notes. Every detail was written, from important daily activities to even the times where he spent writing these journal entries. I was . . . Honestly, if it wasn't so creepy and clinically written, I'd have been impressed with the man's devotion to detail. Also, what the hell was up with all those Arbiter W Documents?

"How is the work, my lord?" he asked with evident glee.

"It's . . . great," I said. "I'll make sure to check out the rest of it later."

"Of course, sir!"

"Is there anything else to note?"

He nodded again before he reached into his damn chest cavity to take something out. The ribs parted ways while the skin split open to show a long wooden object hidden within. The skin mended almost immediately, and remarkably, it wasn't covered in blood or gore as he offered it to me. You know, after thinking about everything I'd seen in just the last twenty-four hours, seeing an exact clone of myself casually rip a foreign object out of his own chest wasn't even that weird.

I took the offered object and frowned. It was . . . a walking cane? An expertly carved one at that, with intricate patterns and images carved in its surface, but what was I supposed to do with this thing?

"It is your new weapon, my lord!" the clone explained. "I had to find a way to fight in the same way you did without being able to use your exalted feelers, so I returned to using a weapon you had early on in the trials!"

Wait, this thing was one of those whip sword things? I scanned it closer and saw that there was a small groove near the head of the cane, and with care, I pulled on it. A beautiful slim blade emerged from its wooden sheath.

"And it hides as a cane!" the doppelganger added. "I had it specially made that way."

It was beautiful, but . . . "Why a cane sword?"

"Because, from my research using the human internet, I have determined that this is what the humans deem as the coolest weapon! It is only fitting that you use a blade that befits your status. See, it is hidden like you are when you act as an aspirant, and it is deadly! It's also able to extend out like your feelers can!"

I saw that there was a small button near my thumb, which I assumed was how the thing extended, but I didn't want to test that out in my own bedroom. Instead, I sheathed the weapon and placed it beside my bed.

"I see . . ."

He continued to smile. "Aspirant Noel also agrees with my assertion, so I am sure that this is the correct choice!"

"I'll trust you on this," I muttered. "You are . . . very well-versed in human culture."

An almost comically large smile erupted from his face at the praise. "I do my best, Lord Arbiter!"

"Excellent." I sighed. "Is that all?"

The man thought for a moment before nodding slowly. "Ah, yes, I had almost forgotten, but your minion Jae-Hyun has scheduled a guild meeting, and from his tone, this is an important one, at least for dull mortal standards."

I frowned. "When is this scheduled for?"

The clone thought for a moment before smiling again. "Four minutes from now, Lord Arbiter!"

I stifled a frown and immediately got up from my seat. Well, there went my plan to get caught up on what happened in the mini trial! I'd just have to wing it . . . again.

"Thanks for letting me know so far in advance."

"Not a problem, sir!" he said with the same enthusiasm I'd come to expect.

"Now please go back to Central. I'll take it from here," I muttered. "Did Jae-Hyun mention anything about the nature of the meeting?"

"No, sir."

"Then you're dismissed," I grumbled.

I grabbed the cane, quickly washed my face, and headed out the door. I sighed. It was time for me to play my part as Aspirant Walter once more. Hopefully nothing had changed too much since my departure, but who was I kidding? Knowing my luck, there was bound to be a new set of bullshit ready for me to deal with, but the only difference was, I was ready for anything Central could throw at me this time.

Revenge

Ashwin found himself alone in a strange place, an underground dungeon filled with beasts that wanted nothing but to consume him. Yet he wasn't angry at his predicament, even when his body was ravaged with hunger and injuries. No, the memories of his time with his friends, his loved ones, and the people who genuinely cared for him was the only thing keeping him from total collapse. He recalled his time in that strange new world, of being hailed as a hero that would save them all. Yet in the end, he wasn't able to save a single soul. No, he still remembered the face of that murderer, that bastard who destroyed everything that he loved. His face was ingrained in Ashwin's psyche forever, taunting him over his failure.

Visions of that man, that End Bringer annihilating his home, swam in his mind. He saw that horrid thing burn down cities filled with crying citizens, he saw that monster slaughter his companions one by one, and then, at the end of it all, he saw the End Bringer destroy the very planet that he'd called home for the last seven grueling years. It was all gone now, all the happy memories tainted with those images, a punishment sent forth by the True God so that Ashwin would never forget what he had failed to protect.

He had become complacent, the aspirant knew. He had assumed that his training and blessings would be enough to fell any foe, but he had been woefully wrong. He was weak, and it was his friends who paid for his overconfidence. But the True God who sent him to that new world gave him one last chance to redeem himself. He was given one last chance in this strange new place to seek the revenge that he so desperately needed. Ashwin would grow stronger than ever before, stronger than even the lesser gods that blessed him.

He would do so for that chance to redeem himself, and to avenge the fallen. Ashwin picked up his crudely made spear and proceeded to hunt down the beasts that dwelled in this hellhole. The god had allowed him to grow at an accelerated pace, and had blessed him with abilities that he never dreamed of before, but Ashwin felt no joy in receiving those boons, for they came at a heavy cost. He would grow here, and when he emerged, the End Bringer would die by his hands.

About the Author

Tismon is the author of the Unwilling Eldritch Horror of Fortune series, originally released on Royal Road. He has too many ideas in his head and just enough time to jot them all down on paper. Tismon resides in Ontario, Canada.

RESPAWN YOUR CURIOSITY

follow us on our socials

 podiumentertainment.com

 @podiumentertainment

 /podiumentertainment

 @podium_ent

 @podiumentertainment